THE CITY: THE JANE HARVEST

A. NICKY HJORT

Lavish
Publishing LLC

First Edition

The City book 1

2017 Lavish Publishing, LLC

All Rights Reserved

Published in the United States by Lavish Publishing, LLC, Midland, Texas

Paperback edition

ISBN: 9781944985332

Cover Design by: Wycked Ink

Cover Images: Adobe Stock

www.LavishPublishing.com

Contents

Acknowledgments   vii

Prologue   1
Section I: The City   5
Chapter 1   7
Chapter 2   15
Chapter 3   25
Chapter 4   35
Chapter 5   41
Chapter 6   51
Chapter 7   61
Chapter 8   67
Chapter 9   77
Chapter 10   87
Chapter 11   91
Chapter 12   99
Chapter 13   105
Chapter 14   117
Chapter 15   125
Section II: The Heats   127
Chapter 16   129
Chapter 17   139
Chapter 18   147
Chapter 19   157
Chapter 20   163
Chapter 21   171
Chapter 22   179
Chapter 23   187
Chapter 24   193
Section III: The Rising Sun   203
Chapter 25   205
Chapter 26   213
Chapter 27   221
Chapter 28   227
Chapter 29   231
Chapter 30   237
Chapter 31   241
Chapter 32   247

About the Author   257
Also by A. NICKY HJORT   259
Also from the Lavish family   261

For Cristin and our invisible wire

Acknowledgments

This list of people who deserve my gratitude for the completion of this narrative is long, and let's face it–my attempt to somehow honor that can only fall short and seem most inadequate. But for them, I shall try. For them, *as Isla would say,* I would do anything.

First, I would like to thank the members of my tribe who support me...no matter what. You forgive my absence while I write and edit and rewrite and then bring me back into your fold without question or doubt. Thank you. I love you. I always have, and I always will. Why? We are forever connected by a wire that cannot ever be cut–even if we wanted to. I shall not bother to list all of your individual names. You know exactly who you are. You are my tribe. You are my people. You are my heart.

Secondly, I would like to thank again the incredible and oh-so-talented Kathy Moczerniak who does so much more than edit my books. She takes my story and molds it into an epic creation that even I hardly recognize as something I am worthy to create. She gets me. She understands my stories better than I do. She is a match made in heaven for me and this work.

Thirdly, I would like to thank Lavish Publishing for bringing me and this must-be-told story into an amazing family of friends, collaborators, and peers who support each other unconditionally. This is no small thing in this challenging industry. Thank you, Lavish. I adore you.

But as usual with my books, there are several people without whom this series of books simply could not have existed. My brother Jeremy Hjort who was the first to read the original version of Book One and I expect will be the first to read every book that follows. He keeps telling me this is my 30-book series. My answer...how cool will that be, brother? Also, Michael Neff who runs a fabulous conference where he is the sci-fi guru. I watched him, of all people, fall instantly in love with Isla's story and knew beyond a shadow of a doubt that this book would be in print one day. As for my purple-eyed King, without experiencing the sacred space in the Unum that you have gifted me, never could I have taken Isla to such a holy place of divine love and connection. A place where all the answers are for those who seek to find them. Thank you, dearest one. And last but never least, I thank the brilliant Suzanne Collins who taught me that some stories must be told. Not should be told…but MUST be told. The City is one of these stories. This is Isla's story. The next evolution of the only story and thus the only way to move from a *story* to *truth*. My readers' story. My children's story. My own story. The every story.

And now that it has been started, it simply must be finished. Let's do that together then. You, me, and all the others. Why? Because how else will we call forth the Rising Sun and find our way back Home. Now, my beautiful Isla, they are all yours. Thank you for giving me the chance to introduce your story. You amazing inspiration of insane awesomeness–I love you. Did you know? Of course you did. Go on then. Steal their hearts just like you stole mine. Go on. They are waiting for you. They always have been.

Prologue

A WOMAN with platinum blond hair sits in her chair, tapping her right foot while the screen on the table in front of her emits a green light.

"Begin final log entry of Dr. Jane Dawn, Chief Officer of War Medicine, NASA. The date is December twenty-fourth, year two thousand fifty-five."

She clears her throat and motions her hand in quick waves toward her as if that will speed up the process of uploading the program—one she herself wrote for her own personal uses.

The green light flashes three times while it scans her retina for confirmation, and a sphere appears that types these words as she says them:

"They have come to harvest me.

"Surely I don't have long now—minutes, at most—to counter my inoculation. The three-pronged needle hurt, and the anti-strain burned more than I expected."

She looks up, willing her eyes not to release a single tear; there is no time for such nonsense. She flattens her face into a mask and prepares for what comes next. In the screen's reflection, she witnesses her hair change colors right in front of her from pale blond to a grayish-blond and gasps, but there's no time to pause, so she continues.

"An invisible fighter drone, carrying the demise of everything that has ever been worth anything, just blasted through the sky above our billion-dollar facility, and all I can do is shake my head. Such madness! I may not hear or see it, but I'll be damned if I cannot feel the vibration of evil paint the sky red to welcome the coming death.

"And so…the very last war on this planet ends before it even begins because of our team's brilliant success. Or is it failure? I just can't be sure yet.

"Yes, I can.

"If I could still speak to you, Gaige, I'd ask you why you left me here all alone like this. I know. I know. I can hear you. *'Get over it. I'm already dead.'*

"You asshole. I hate you for dying first. I really do.

"No, I don't. That's a total lie, and shitty moments make for shitty lies."

Scanning the office, she tries not to think about all the swirling lies, but the plaque on her desk draws her attention. *"Why, sometimes I've believed as many as six impossible things before breakfast." - Alice in Wonderland.*

"Me too, Alice. Well, used to."

She slams her fist on the desk to stop her shaking hand, and the screen flickers. Her last project titled "Biome Modification" flashes in the margins, demanding she approve the final protocol, but she refuses to hit okay.

"Damn it. They are here. I can smell their eggy breath. God they smell terrible. I stare at our designs, lost in what I know are my final thoughts. No, probably not. That's impossible, even for Alice and me."

She snaps her fingers, and the sphere disappears.

Looking up at the ceiling, she places two fingers over her heart. And even though no one can hear her, she says, "You're the only one who ever knew we discovered the truth, Gaige. Fuck. The only one. Don't you know that? I never told anyone that we found our way into the tenth dimension."

The record light was dark; her words would never be heard again.

Two soldiers blast down the door of the room where the prominent war expert, known as Jane Dawn, sits at her computer, both hands over her lower abdomen. As her computer powers down, she mutters, "Even though it may have just killed us both, us all actually."

As one soldier stands in the broken doorway, the other approaches her, a large gun in hand. "This is your last amicable offer from the Chancellor known as Lither. Join the Mozek ranks or die."

The woman replies, "By rank, do you mean level or stink or both?" She clicks her tongue and adds, "How about never? That asshole will have to kill me."

"That's exactly what he hoped you would say." The soldier aims.

"Hope? Funny word choice."

The soldier disengages the gun's safety. "Last chance."

"I wash my hands of this genocide, but tell that tit I said that if I could undo this, I would do whatever it took, whatever that meant, even unravel time be–"

The bang of the soldier's gun echoes throughout the room, but the rows and rows of books hardly seem to notice. Except one, that is. *Alice in Wonderland* falls off the highest shelf and skitters across the white marble floor until it rests just out of reach of the woman's lifeless hand.

After quickly clipping off the woman's hair, the soldiers drag the limp body away and dump it in the Liebhorr cryo-chamber next door. As per assignment, the body is to burn like the rest of the biome bacterial experts, the ashes ordered to be collected for examination before the first seeding of the first harvests. However, that hardly seems necessary under the circumstances. Laziness gets the better of the pair, and they dump her in the freezing chamber instead.

But then again, the soldiers do not notice the three puncture marks over her heart. Or the subtle change in her hair color. And the only person who knows about her developing fetus has already been murdered.

Section I: The City

So take these eyes,
And give them sight.
That search for you,
On the hope you might…

One hundred and fifty years later in the City…

Chapter One

GLANCING UP BRIEFLY, I am distracted by a miniscule yet mesmerizing reflection of light bouncing off the metal contraption and two layers of thick glass that surround me. The sliver of bright white flashes back and forth like a little winged creature in flight, and unable to resist, I loosen my death-grip on my Velcro leg straps and smile, probably for the first time today. Thinking about my movements being the source of something so illuminating and gorgeous, my grin spreads and replaces my entire face with a rare beak of genuine delight.

I place my arms in their cold titanium lateral port sites like the dead and gone robotic surgeons who first invented and perfected this device. Only this time, I guess, I am both subject and investigator. *Impossible.*

Envisioning the thin wire coming out of my machine, I shudder. Sensing but not actually feeling the cyber-monster penetrate my body might be worse than the alternative. The fine, hot wire, a constantly adapting bio-modulating Ethernet cable invisible to the naked eye, materializes out of thin air before it dives down the circular port in the back of my neck, giving it access to my central nervous system. Instantly, the malicious device paralyzes my arms while it invades my body just like a malignant computer virus, overriding my internal code. My lips quickly drag down again, and my face resumes its foul, blank expression of artificial idiocy. A look I have mastered so well it scares me.

"I am no computer," I might scream if I could be bothered, but what's the point? Neither the chief robot nor the monitors, the empty-eyed guards who constantly boss me around, can possibly care what this penguin has to say. *Stinking Mozek soldiers and those creepy eyes.*

After all, I am just a 53–a human, an endangered and virtually worthless species. I'll never take flight even if I grow wings. And I know better than to think I'll ever survive this so-called life or that I actually matter to the Mozek race–to anyone for a matter of fact.

In her disgustingly monotone and soothing voice, the chief robot, who controls all of the machines in this part of the City and therefore now my nervous system, speaks to me from inside my own mind. "Good morning, beta, Isla Jane, today's operator of FDA testing site 32."

Not good. I grunt but decide not to speak.

"We see as the most highly ranked living member of your family, you bravely assume today's Levana kith red-card assignment. Lucky us."

"Lucky?" I cough.

"It is Monday, April twenty-ninth," she claims.

"Chief robot, what does 'lucky us' mean from a computer's perspective?"

Nothing. She goes silent for a few moments when she can't properly answer me with pinpoint accuracy.

"Monday, April twenty-ninth," she eventually repeats with pinpoint accuracy.

I squint and grunt. "Guess I'll have to take your word for that," I reply, matching the nauseating lack of inflection in her voice like a pro.

"We hope today you find your bacterial balance good and your neurons firing clearly."

"You hope? Odd word choice, chief robot, don't you think? Can robots think like I do? What year is it anyway?"

More silence. One day, she's going to surprise me with an answer.

My turn. "Robot, how did I get here?" One day, I am going to surprise her without a question.

"Isla Jane, we hope today finds you thinking clearly."

Can a computer hope? Probably not. I give up the cat and mouse game before she does something like necrotize me. "Yes," I say, faking a frown-smile, another of my other specialties, hoping I'm not about to be a clump of smoldering pus.

"Good. Here in the City, it takes lives to saves lives. You know that."

Do I? I'm not so sure. "Yes, it does," I confirm anyway. Lucky me, now she recites her daily blurb-a-la-bullshit. At least she's predictable and reliable. I *hope.*

Immediately, I zone out and pretend I'm anywhere other than here trapped in this red-card assignment in the Foundry, the scientific compound where I get to play gladiator of the bacterial biome. I prefer to play gladiator of the Heat in the Orb where we battle for sport, I think.

Imagining myself playing the champion fighter for my kith in a Heat battle for Ink rewards, pegged against an army of tattoo-covered alpha males all foaming at the mouth, I suppress a grin. My daydream plays on, and I don my shield and sword before I mount a four-winged dragon-sized insect slathered in poisonous scales and spikes. I toy with the image of my beast ripping them to shreds one by freaking one, but then I command my mutant minion to burn them all to a crisp instead. As teems of the cruel tits crumble to ash in my imagination, I snicker. Besides, this chick named Isla Jane can kick any guy's ass in the Orb, so why not kill them all at once? Seems simpler that way.

Quickly, I suck my brief moment of joy in, hoping the chief robot was too busy with her blah, blah speech to dissect my mass murderous plans. Well, not really. A Heat battle is just a projected mind game, after all. For a moment, I consider feeling guilty about my vicious daydream. Then I decide against it. After all, most of the leading males, commonly referred to as alphas, that I know are hardly better than the war-mongering assholes that landed me here in the City.

Once I reorient, the chief robot continues her calm and boring mantra. I sigh, and since I can't actually move my arms trapped in this fucking contraption, I click my tongue in boredom.

"Some years ago, an evil intelligence in concert with Home's superpowers incited global chaos with biome-directed warfare."

Sigh.

"At a pinnacle moment, the Russians…"

More clicking.

"There was no turning back. The planet…"

I'm totally gone now thinking about sharp blades and new battle moves.

"Billions died instantly after being inoculated, unable to withstand the destructive powers of the mutated bacteria living on their skin."

Sigh. Gag.

"The salvageable humans were transported twenty-two light-years away…"

Will she ever shut up?

"Into the Gliese System, while the advanced and benevolent Mozek from the Andromeda Galaxy…"

Kill me. Kill me now.

"To repair the collective biome, we must…"

Oops, I miss a few monotonous sentences here because I'm day dreaming about flying through the air on the back of this massive insect while it melts a pack of monitors instead of 53s for a change. Crap, I better stop that before she reads my mind and condemns me as a traitor. I bet being necrotized as a punishment for my evil thoughts will hurt. I'll slaughter some Enlil's instead, I think. No one cares if I murder them.

Where is that robot in her speech? Oh yes, the part about tilting the axis of Home when the counterattack altered the nature of gravity, even momentarily. What a bummer. Who knew a degree or two mattered so much?

"We are almost finished stabilizing Home's core and rotational axis, but until then…"

I'm so yawning now.

"The City is the only place the Mozek can safely maintain the balance between the good and bad bacteria on your skin."

Sigh. Shrug. Sigh again. Back to my daydream please.

"Ink feeds the good and thus maintains the odds…"

Ah, I'm back and imagining again. I've jumped off my winged beast and am poised to slaughter my opponent, an Enlil tramp who keeps sticking out her tongue at me.

"Without enough Ink, you will all…"

That muscular tongue sure will make a nice trophy.

"…die. You have seen many of your family members die, Isla Jane. Have you not?"

Grunt. Grunt. I suck my air in hard and hold on to it because that chief robot just hanged me with a noose made just for me.

"Have you not?"

Bitch robot. I'm choking on her rope now, and she knows it. Maybe robots can think. I drop the Enlil's tongue on accident while falling down in a hurricane force wind. But that lousy question makes it hard, too hard, to stay present in my imaginary Heat fight. "Yes, chief robot. Too many dead to name."

I gag. She now has me struggling to breath with such a painful onslaught of memories. "Too many dead to name," I say again.

"If we do not find a way to permanently balance the bacteria by creating the perfect biome elixir, and therefore wipe out all resultant human disease before you return Home, no one will."

Shit. Where did that Enlil's tongue go? I'm trying so hard to hold on to my dream. What is wrong with that computer? Let me be!

"There will be no humans left. Do you understand the importance of our work, of your work?"

Dream over. "Yep. Got it. More dead for the dead." I sigh and click my tongue to prove I still have mine so graciously attached to the back of my mouth since I can't give her a high five or toss her a sign with these useless arms of mine.

"Wonderful. We thank you for your sacrifice. We will reward you with Ink honors. Your only option is to undo the war's biological effects and stay alive."

Not wonderful. What sacrifice? And fuck my Ink and the war, I would like to add. But again, why bother? As my anger sputters uselessly, I sigh a final time and surrender to another day of the same crap. If I could use my arms, I would rub my scratchy throat, but I can only cough. I cough three times.

During one of our sessions, Elder Khaan, my greatest mentor, told me it is a scientific fact that if you hear the same phrase, true or not, more than seventy times, your subconscious mind accepts it despite all glaring evidence to the contrary. I wonder how many times I have heard the robot's speech and cringe.

I also can't help but wonder if I tell myself I am still living back Home with Elder Khaan seventy-one times, will I stop waking up screaming his name?

No, probably not.

Back to work.

Most days on the Ink stage, our family draws a red card within our set for the day, and out of pity, I take one for the team by playing the red assignment out and doling the less dangerous cards to those I know can manage to finish without getting killed. Today is a red-card day. Lucky them. Or am I the lucky one? I just can't be sure yet. Yes, I can since it's certainly not me.

Sometimes the worst of the cards I pull is blue, and I might take that one or pass it over to a lower ranked sib so I can rest before the next red-card day. Rarely do I pull yellow or orange, but sometimes I get extra, extra lucky. Our kith has never drawn a white or black card, so to be honest, I don't even know what those colors mean.

Seems like the odds of life, just like this red card, are always stacked against me. *Against me.*

The thought lingers for a moment before I drop it and go back to better feeling thoughts.

My serum bottles line up twenty meters away for my supposed protection inside a dual glass-enclosed chamber next to the robot who's ruining perfectly good daydreams with her stupid questions about the dead. Labeled FDA-32, my shelf moves into loading position, and my infallible ears hear the dangerous little bottles clang and click into place.

One, slightly different than the rest, catches my eye. From here, it looks pink, which is odd. Shrugging it off, I begin today's assignment here in the Biome Repair Elixir department of this section of the Foundry, trying not to blow up, not to die, not to disappear into nothingness, not to think, not to do anything other than survive. Not, not, not, so much not.

My tongue clicks again, and since I kind of like the slimy little thing, I hope none of my enemies in the arena plan to cut it out and keep it for a trophy. If I could, I would flip myself off for such a stupid train of thought, but in my machine like this, my paralyzed hands can't make such a complicated gesture. I just roll my eyes and flick my tongue around instead.

But my thoughts, determined as usual to swing me back and forth from my own hanging noose, keep diving into more misery. *So how did you get here, Isla? How did the human experience disintegrate into something so far from life? And if the freaking Mozek are so advanced, why do I need to do this bullshit work at all? Shouldn't they have the cure for all that supposedly ails us?*

Briefly, I wonder if the chief robot can actually hear all my thoughts, but then I decide I couldn't care less, either. What can it possibly do to me that the war hasn't already done?

Careful, my nervous inner voice adds. *Things can always be worse.*

Worse? How exactly, I wonder. How?

Now we live, but mostly just die, in a two-paned glass world on another planet. Well, I assume it's a planet because I have to face the fact that I've never been outside the glass walls.

Heck, I don't even remember getting here. Here, I am trapped inside this city without a clue if I will make it another year, month, or even day. Here, anything can happen at any moment. Nothing is guaranteed, and nothing lasts. Thus, nothing matters, and nothing changes.

As the terrible and horribly logical conclusion reaches the depths of my boiling gut, a sinking, shockingly familiar premonition overwhelms me–the holder of this red card. *Red...*

Trying to calm myself down, or perhaps, if I am being honest with myself, just in case the unthinkable happens, I envision this building from the outside, my mind expanding to consider all options. *Red equals...*

The outermost globe of the Foundry, the size and shape of an old space station, turns clockwise and is built from gun-gray metal and reflective glass materials. Next, the inner globes house ten sections, each with two levels and perhaps two thousand square meters of area or so, encased in clear, double-paned glass and stainless steel, which rotate counterclockwise.

My ears perk up because I think I just heard the vibration in the room shift. But that's not possible. I'm not actually in the Orb, the place where we battle our Heats. I was just pretending. I'm in the Foundry. Safe and sound.

"Could it be?" I mutter. "No, it's okay. I'm okay." I tell myself.

Yet there my gut goes again. *Red equals...*

My eyes, darting side to side quickly, follow my ears and start noticing everything they can as quickly as my ocular muscles will move...just in case.

All the windows are barred, so even if I could reach them in a crisis before the internal ceiling fell, I would be trapped, so not safe and sound, inside.

"Thank Gods things are just fine," I whisper and try to smile. But it's no use. My gut is onto something. And my gut is always right. Shit.

I remember the color of my card. Red. *Red equals...*

My ears tingle, the vibrational shift clearer to me now. I am not fine.

The pressure in the back of my neck builds as a wave of heat courses down my spine. I might look up, but honestly, I'm too afraid to because I am certain something has just gone terribly wrong with one of my bottles. *I'm dead.*

Immediately, I grasp that my previous conclusion was wrong. Things do change, and they can get worse. Much. In fact, they just have.

Before I hear or even see the first spark, I sense the vibration of the chemical reaction–hot, way too freaking hot–pulsing through the circuitry of the machine integrating with my brain. Heating up exponentially, my central nervous system clamps down, syncing completely with all available points of data from the chief robot. *Bloody hell, what have I just done?*

My thoughts, trapped like specks of dust suspended in mid-air, too heavy to fly away, too light to fall to the ground, are enveloped in this vortex of one tiny moment, analyzing what's left of my existence as they twirl in front of me for what seems like an eternity. I keep dropping them on accident, just like that Enlil's tongue, to save myself from falling down.

One burning moment of dwindling possibilities imprisons me just like in every Heat battle: life vs. death, me vs. this red card, me vs. the impossible, me vs. this fire.

Needing more information, my melting brain begs, "Am I going to die?"

The robot's peaceful reply sounds so foreign to my floundering mind. "Isla Jane, the probability..."

Impossible.

Something peppery in the pit of my stomach tells me I don't have time to wait for her precise response, so I intuitively back down my connection. My priority is life, not statistical accuracy from a droid of doom no matter how soothing her voice. Even a total idiot can see I am in mortal danger. We all are, actually.

My liquefied neurons, not in a pleasant and calm voice, shout. *This is no ordinary fire you've just started, Isla. It's bad–very bad.*

Minutes, I have minutes at most to escape, and I tremble as a wave of fear courses through my body. My teeth chatter, and I clench my jaw to stop them. That's when the first boom echoes through the entire chamber–a massive blowout.

About one hundred meters away, the entire inner testing center ignites, and the chief robot explodes. I'm tempted to laugh but can't afford the luxury of joy when I'm surely next.

Maybe life here in the City wasn't so bad after all?

All of a sudden, the forty-four habitation structures lining the outskirts of our city, basking in sunlight from two overlapping globes of orange delight, seem like an ideal place to live. The hot, grainy sand that coats everything here sounds fun to play in.

Even the high wind of the dunes, the sand piles just outside the thick glass wall surrounding our makeshift residence, whistle like a beautiful bird. The Mozek and their sulfur-laden breath smell minty fresh and delicious to me. The trumpets at my next Heat battle seem like they are calling me Home, declaring me the victorious verus.

"Get out of the machine now, you idiot!" I scream. The words, hollow and empty, keep echoing in my head. In shock, I glance around my device, trying to figure out who said them. Then I remember–me.

My arms, effectively incapacitated by their deep connection into my machine, do not respond. Normally, it takes at least five minutes to recover, but I have ten minutes to get out of here…maybe. Maybe not even that.

Panting, I yank my balmy head up hard, ripping the port in the back of my skull free from the invisible cable of my machine. To say this hurts is less than adequate to describe the searing pain coursing down my spine. I suppress sickness and try to move my arms once more. Nothing.

Once, twice, three times, I slam my skull against the wall of glass behind me. My vision doubles, yet I refuse to allow it to distract me from my task–survival.

A thin crack spreads in the see-through wall around me like a sliver of hope in a sea of despair, giving me the strength to stand up despite the thick black straps that hold my legs in place. Watching the abraded skin on my thighs instantly swell and blister, I almost smile. Almost.

"Get out, you dumbass!" I yell instead. I don't want to die. Not like this. I am only twenty-one. I want to go Home even though I have been here so long now I can't even remember the place.

And I refuse to believe the Mozek's claim that my memories remain altered by the transport that brought us here. Let's add that to their long list of crap that runs out the door and down the hall.

Sure wish I could run out the door and down the hall. I check again–nope. I still do not want to die.

I concentrate on moving my arms again–nothing.

Tongue's fine though, so I stick it out again. Then I decide to live and get ready to do whatever it takes to make that one thing–life–amongst so many other possible deaths, happen. *Impossible.*

Life! I choose possible life.

Lifting my right foot, I glare at the fine, smooth curve of my favorite Ink– the rising sun. Willing it to life too, I pound the innermost wall of glass with that ball of gorgeous fire. For sure, it's some of my Ink dealer's finest tattoo work, yet I can't recall the day I got it, to tell the truth. Sometimes, I think it's a sign or special message meant just for me, delivered up by the artistic hands of some unseen but merciful Gods.

Of course, I realize that's utterly ridiculous.

Or is it? I just can't be sure yet.

Thoroughly motivated by imminent death at this point, I kick hard, harder, harder still. The inner layer of my machine showers me with countless little glass knives while the outer sheet comes down in one piece like a guillotine. Thankfully, since I like that glorious globe so much, I pull my right foot back just in time to save it.

Or is it about to save me? I just can't be sure yet. Or can I?

I press my muscular tongue to the back of my teeth and consider that for a fraction of a second while I gather the courage to live this life a little bit longer. Then I step over the glass spikes and run for all the morsels that are obviously still worth licking. *Impossible.*

Chapter Two

GASPING, I round the curved hallway, still trying to dismiss the absurd idea that somehow my foot Ink, the single rising sun, so blood-thirsty and awe-inspiring, is a secret message and keep pumping my legs, trying to escape the blowout. My blowout. My red card. My fire. My fault. My screw-up lighting up this joint.

Quickly, I inspect the units flashing past me. Two of the eighteen remote testing stations form an outer ring of units around the sixteen in the inner ring. Each work area is comprised of a metallic and glass sphere inside another sphere–the design everywhere here in the City. The work buildings, the battle arena where we fight our Heats–aptly named the Orb–and even the living quarters all look similar. Even the other 53s who live and work alongside me all look the same under their Ink, now that I think about it.

Crap. There I go thinking again…

Could we each be just a person inside another person? This a planet inside another planet? A dimension inside another dimension? This a fire inside another fire? This red card assignment inside another assignment? Our city inside another city?

Thinking briefly about my foot, I push the observation too far…even for me. Is the sun on my foot rising inside another sun?

"Get a grip, Isla. You are running from a blowout." I squeal, trying to move my fingers. They twitch slightly, sort of. But maybe I have only imagined it?

My mind goes back four minutes in time to when I crossed the serum components like always, hoping to make the perfect combination for the robot to analyze. But instead of bubbling and fizzing out, the liquefied tissue laced with billions of various bacteria, pink this time to start…so odd, immediately burst into a raging flame. Some virulent chain reaction, perhaps?

Within a nanosecond, I telepathically initiated the emergency alarm activator. But it spread so fast. Too fast for that serene bitch–the chief robot in pieces all over the ground–to contain it.

Now, here I am trying to survive without your help, robot.

Short of breath, I stop, trying to find my next move, and shake my head again, harder this time to punish myself for making such a deadly error. Then I glare at my foot once more, rage flushing my face from my insides. I stare down my personal machine, FDA-32, from the protection of the intersecting walkway that connects the two rings of machines. Oblivious to my disgust, it hardly notices my frank disapproval in between snaps and crackles of the melting metal bars that used to surround it. If I could, I would kick thirty-two shards of glass at it for effect. Instead, I swallow hard and clench my jaw tightly.

My throat feels parched. The back of my neck gritty and gray like the bottom of a dirty ashtray from the old days when humans were still stupid enough to pay ten dollars a pack to induce avoidable mutations by smoking.

Now we get them for free. Thank you, evil bacteria living on my skin and in my gut. I love you. *Not.*

Trying to reach down into my waist-strap, my fingers fumble while I scramble to locate a box of gel-encapsulated water to soothe my sore throat. Maybe if I drink one, I can gather enough saliva to desecrate this disintegrating deathtrap where red-card assignments force us to remotely operate the serum testing stations.

Stations inside stations, perhaps?

"Shut up, Isla. Move your ass!"

I giggle softly at my split personality while glancing over my shoulder to make sure no one can hear me over the crackling flames. Unfortunately, my clumsy fingers find only damaged goods. I cough and curse the dried up boxes. Spitting will have to wait.

My machine collapses, the edges ablaze and liquefied like an ocean from the underworld. For a moment, I experience true bliss. Then I remember the fire. My fire. My card. *My fault.*

The blaze is now spreading beyond the boundaries of the confinement chamber and heading for the general meeting area. That's bad news for the entire building. Maybe even the entire compound, the entire city. *My fault. The loss of all remaining humanity. No pressure there, Isla!*

The fire's so hot that the little hairs on my arms stand up. They salute the sky like brainwashed soldiers determined to rid my arms of some faith they find deplorable. But then they shrivel back down like the clueless minions they always were, trying to retreat underneath my prickly skin for protection against their own prejudice.

"Genocide never serves anyone, you idiots," I remind my arm hairs while I attempt to escape out the exit scanner of this section of the Foundry–the scientific compound where the other 53s and I occasionally flail trying to save what's left of humanity so we can return Home.

If we don't re-create the perfect bacterial biome to heal us–the F Serum–we will all die a terrible mutant death no matter how effectively the Mozek save our decimated planet with their heroic rescue.

I try to remember what it used to feel like to breathe the fresh air back Home without glass walls and filtration devices. So easy, simple, clean, and light without the sulfur of this place, but I can't anymore.

How long have I been here? Why can't I remember the transport? And why did the Mozek bring us to this of all possible places? I guess because the atmosphere is otherwise so similar to Home. Must be, but who knows?

Scanning my Inks, I search for an answer that isn't written there to find. *So many Inks, Isla, but so few answers.* Given the chance, I'd trade all my Ink for answers, even a few answers. If I had dollars, I'd hand those over, too.

I roll my eyes at the outdated concept of paying money for anything, especially cancer rolled up like a cruel gift in a stick that I light on fire and inhale intentionally. *Fools.* That's like giving myself a daily red-card assignment. *Wait a minute; I do that all the time. Ugh. Red equals dead.* The thought pulls me back to my reality–inevitable death.

Glancing at the destruction erupting all around me, I can't help but imagine all humanity gone like the dinosaurs, and I shudder. The biome poisoning from the Global War that landed us here has literally unraveled our DNA from the ends, although no one knows why exactly. Without a cure, who knows how long we have left. Weeks? Months? Years? No one knows for sure. Not even that calm twat who speaks to me inside my mind. Well, used to speak to me. Now the chief robot is nothing but melted titanium wires and shattered glass.

Serves her right in my humble opinion. I'd laugh, but there is no time for such luxury.

Drops of sweat sting my swirling eyes, which ache from all the fumes. I want to close them, rest them, but I can't. There's not enough time for that either.

I wonder, if my eyes weren't so dry, would I cry? Probably not.

I can hear at least twenty of the other 53s safely outside the building, encouraging me with whoops and hollers. Sighing, the pressure in the back of my neck lessens slightly. *Thank Gods.* I don't think I could handle the guilt of killing so many innocents. That leaves, at most, only a few of us in danger on this side. The hellhole. My hellhole. My red card. *My fault.*

I think I can reach the exit until I see the flames spread along the ground and breach the metal tubes that bring forth the volatile serum components for me to cross and react. I barely cover my eyes in time to avoid seeing more explosions.

Nice. My arms must be starting to respond.

Large glass panels launch past me, shattering into pieces on the floor. *Damn it. Not nice.*

Plan A: exit scanner. No good, I decide.

I'm totally screwed. Actually, I'm fucked. So I quickly head back to the central area, the inner most circle of this structure, to come up with plan B.

Knowing the steel support beams that encase this chamber are burning and getting hotter by the second, I fight the urge to lean on them and rest while I look up at the ceiling. Imagining blisters erupting on my thick, calloused hands to match my thighs, I clasp them together, still hoping for that backup plan to present itself. *Well, B, where are you?*

My brain reels looking for an escape. Is there one?

Envisioning this building from the outside, my mind expands to consider all options once more: the outermost globe, the inner globe, the barred windows of this department.

Yep, not screwed–utterly and completely fucked. *Yoo-hoo, plan B?*

Everything grinds to a terrifying halt, and the room stops rotating. Time stands still, and I am frozen again, unable to react to something so unbelievable. A quiver travels the length of the curved beams holding the ceiling up. It's coming down... any moment. Damn. Am I the only one left behind? Did all the others make it out alive?

My teeth chatter again. How can I feel so cold and so hot at the same time?

Please, Gods, help them. Help me, but help them first; I'm already dead.

Wow, I really need another option. A new spin on my problem, perhaps?

I clap for my missing blisters and brilliant word play. Then I cough again. A mucus ball comes up, and I choke on it, still laughing at my pun. I guess if I'm about to die, I might as well get a few last laughs in.

"Shut up, Isla," my other half, the one who actually cares about surviving, hollers at my inner comedian.

Okay, back to pragmatic Isla, the one who always finds a way out.

There are only two doors for each area here, entry and exit, through the scanners that the Mozek use to probe us. As if life here isn't punishment enough. Not to mention the blowouts. My blowout. My red card. *My fault.*

"Their fault," my reasonable twin says. *Shouldn't the benevolent Mozek who are saving us not want to torture us?* I should ponder that thought for a while, but honestly, I don't have time right now.

I wipe the disgusting slime from my mouth and keep thinking about things that actually matter and might determine whether or not I get to do more thinking in the future.

The entry scanner still exists, at least as far as I can tell. Maybe I can go back out through it? Plan B. Lovely. *Thank you. About time, Mister Answer to All My Problems.*

The smell of fire pulls me from my gratitude. *Red death.* The sweltering heat crawling up my neck reorients me to my current surroundings. I am no longer so gracious with my thank yous.

I holler, "Screw red, pink, blowouts, cancer, all of it."

No one responds. Maybe they are safe far, far away from here.

Now, can I get out safely, too? *Hmmm...*

Do the entry doors even swing the other direction if, by some miracle, I reach them on time?

"Probably not," I mutter. Plan B sucks. But it's all I've got, so I go with it.

Shaking my arms, I desperately try to work them even if they are covered in little elitist devil-hairs that want to annihilate me for no logical reason, but they are still partially numb from the damn machine. Honestly, it still shocks me how the Mozek could take something as brilliant and helpful as remote viewing robotic surgery and turn it against me. This same machine that was intended to save thousands of human lives in the operating room, now offers me the chance to work with compounds way too deadly to touch…or even be near.

"Thanks for that, by the way, you assholes."

I take a deep breath of smoky gray toxin. The biting, sharp smell of sulfur burns my nostrils, warning that the internal barriers have been breached. There's not much time left now.

Wake up arms; wake the hell up. Move, move, move, I command. My limbs obey best they can.

Gods, please. Get everyone else far enough away before this entire place blows. If not, time's up.

The entry scanner is still fifty meters away, and my hands are about as useful as Play-Doh. But then I take another deep breath and choke on charred flesh. *Shit. I'm not alone after all. Shit, shit, shit.*

I would love to claim I have no idea what that smell means exactly, but that would make me a liar, liar, ass on fire. Wait a minute; my ass is on fire. Surely under the circumstances, a little Ms. Hot Pants like me can move faster than this. Yep, just checked. Still not ready to die. Not yet.

By some miracle, the feeling completely returns to my fingertips. *Hell yah!*

In honor of my champion kith family, I make the Levana sign: two fingers pressed down on my chest twice. Then I stomp my feet, yell out a few curses, and flip off my melted machine to remind it I am a fighter who intends to escape.

Bowing quickly, I accept the challenge as warring gladiator, opponent assigned against this fire, and decide to prove my valor.

"Levana kith will remain undefeated!"

I veer to the right and then the left to avoid the falling beams. A wave of nausea slows me down a little, but not much. If I let it, the second floor scaffolding will trap me along with at least one other 53-worker who was just too slow for his or her own good. The same worker who won't report in kith alpha quarters tonight, nor make morning ration tabulation at the Ink stage tomorrow. They'll never cheer on his or her favorite fighter at the next Heat battle, nor ever pull another red card.

Trembling, I furrow my brow and slap my own face to help me get my act together. I refuse to die like this, trapped in a building. Seriously, a fire is a joke compared to what I have survived in Heats and on other assignments. How is this for real? Could I have it all backward, all inside out?

Even though I hear the monitor alarms sounding for complete evacuation of the Foundry, I can't help but pause one last time in thought. *My fault. My red card. My blowout.*

This blowout looks so different from the usual explosions here in the Biome Repair Elixir section we call the BRÉ, where we supposedly save lives while we waste our own. And I want to forget it, really I do, but I can't help but remember the color of the bottle this disaster comes from. Pink. Carotene even, unlike the usual ones that are just see-through glass. The raging flames are a little pinkish, too. Not really red but spicy pink, which makes no sense to me.

Thanks to my exhausting disposition, I yearn to understand more, always asking, searching, and begging for an answer that might adequately satisfy my mind. So naturally, I am dying to know what is so different about this pink serum that makes it cause a blowout this bad. The worst I have seen in a really long time, actually. Yet I can't figure it out even though I need to…so badly to survive here, where no one ever explains anything. But there's no more time left to think it through. All I can do now is get out the entry scanner or die.

"Get the hell out of here, Isla!" I yell to motivate my slow-burning ass.

Unfortunately, another 53's pleas for help distract me just as my gloriously functional hands smash the entry scanner with part of a fallen beam.

Plan B keeps looking better and better after all. I'm almost out now.

But the other 53 is not. She never will be. Her leg is trapped under a burning machine weighing thousands of kilos. The fire is on top of her now. I can still smell her hair burning. *Oh my Gods, I hate that smell.*

She can't get out because there is no way out. Game over.

That doomed diva will never again walk the ten-kilometer perimeter of the fitness track that encircles the Gridiron, a modernized version of the Coliseum on the north side of the City, trying to prepare for her next Heat. She's gone, her days of playing gladiator in mock battle officially over. No more cards, no more Ink honors. She will never make it back to Home.

I cringe. The bad news for me is that I recognize her right away.

The creep cries out my name like we are best friends or something. But we are not. She belongs to Irmin, my sworn enemy, so I should be celebrating her imminent demise along with my brilliant plan B. After all, who knows how many times she has tried to slice me apart in the entertainment Orb, the central globe inside the Gridiron where we fight our Heats.

Remembering her weapon of choice, I clench my chattering teeth. The trident–a fork of horror, always trying to spear me like a fish–was always what she swung at me. *Evil bitch.*

I affirm that I am no fish, yet honestly, I feel no inclination to celebrate her downfall despite my certainty that she would clap for mine. I try like a bunkmate with a snoring subordinate sibling below to ignore her mortal predicament that manages to climb up the ladder and destroy my precious hours…or perhaps moments…of rest. Her face, the smell, her screams, I can block out. But those freaking snores keep drawing me in, and I climb down below in my mind to shake her awake so she will fucking stop making that terrible sound.

It's not my fault she ends up trapped like this. Not my fault.

Well maybe it is…a little. The fire, perhaps. But the machine? No way.

Maybe more than a little, like a lot. Damn!

My cheeks flash red, and unable to stop them, my clenched fingers dig into my temples as my shoulders involuntarily rise up and dig equally painfully into my neck.

The beta's cries–they are too much for me to bear. I'm almost out for fuck's sake. She is not my problem. And besides, I've seen way too much suffering for one lifetime. So why should I look back and watch more? I am no fish!

Powerless to stop myself, I have already turned around, telling myself I am just trying desperately to lower my shoulders back to a normal, more tolerable position. Even now, I know better; that's a lie.

I spin back and forth, but all I see is her. All I smell is her. Those screams, those snores. Damn it. My legs shake so hard I can hardly stand erect without reaching out for something to hold on to. The room spins like a carnival ride from hell, and I feel like a rat trapped in a maze minus any cheese at all…because there is only punishment for me to find in this place.

Before I lose my composure completely, I refocus and start climbing out the small hole I have made in the entry scanner, trying to pretend I never looked. Trying but failing because I don't turn around fast enough. There is no fast enough. It doesn't exist. It never has.

My nemesis registers me witness her last moment swallowed up in fear–the only emotion intolerable to her cruel clan.

Well, crap. I might as well see this through.

When I look back at her, I flatten my face, hoping to look both brave and unaffected, but watching her ignite is like seeing myself die in a mirror. I try to even out my expression again but fail miserably. Because we are both beta Janes, we look so similar under our Ink that it makes me vomit. I wipe the stink from my mouth and spit to clear the terrible taste of acid.

Her singed gray-blond hair used to be the same as mine: silky smooth, plaited in fine patterns, some hanging to her shoulders. Even contorted by her screams, her sharp nose, angular jaw, and piercing expression command respect. And those liquid coolant blue eyes of hers, so familiar, look right through me.

Instantly, she calculates that I am not coming back to save her. Plan B never included her. I am a worthless fish even if I want to help. I have no option to show her missio, or mercy on the battlefield, from the fire. The flames name her the defeated one in this fight. No valuable bead can save her now like it might have in battle as a token to exchange for her life.

She goes silent like a chief robot without any answers to satisfy me.

The only sound that remains is popping and sizzling flesh. *Fuck that! Silence was so much better.*

In the last agonizing second before her eyes close, I witness fear, hope, disappointment, and finally disgust wash through her expression, her final glare, while the pink flames extinguish her short, little life. So wasted, so useless.

I hate to admit that I want to look behind the image in the mirror to know her better even if she belongs to the meanest of all the other groupings. Do I know her name like she knows mine? And if I do, does it make observing her downfall better or worse? Despite my disgust for her kind, I can't escape the notion that even those vicious deviants deserve more than this pathetic life. Perhaps I have no choice but to walk back into the blaze and try to rescue what's left of her even if it will surely kill me?

But I already know there is no choice here. There never was.

She is dead. I can't save her. I never could have. The machine is just too massive. The fire has already consumed her. So I keep crawling out the jagged hole in the door instead. My thigh catches on a sharp edge, and blood runs down it like a tear pumped straight from my heart. That filmy sac-covered muscle of pathetic uselessness which is as determined to mourn my fallen enemy as my mind is determined to *not* think about her snoring gasps on this, her final night.

My mind, superior to my heart, obviously must find a way to save me from what I have just witnessed, so I hand it control and deny my weak heart its voice.

Slipping on my own life force trying to get out and away from her corpse, my mind belts out, "I am free. I am out of that hell hole," while I parade around like an idiot survivor. In some ways, it dawns on me–so is the other Jane. Out, that is. Maybe even more out than me?

Awesome. I just have to make it a little farther, and I will be free and clear and alive as I run out the front sliding glass of the main entrance to the Foundry. So why do I feel huge but small, thrilled but empty, happy but devastated, burning hot but so damn cold?

Must be that stupid heart again. Ugh.

Another beam crashes to the ground, and the rest of the ceiling falls as the finale ensues. I see the flames spread along the mechanical walkways to another portion of the building. Holy crap, this fire plans to take the whole compound out. Hesitate another second and I will be incinerated in the aftermath too, so I scramble to my feet. If I don't survive, no one will be there to rock Cale back to sleep tonight from his night terrors since Elder Khaan, our once adored alpha male from my kith, is dead. I can't afford to waste another moment contemplating my situation, this flawed heart, or my fallen enemy.

The hot dripping down my leg increases, hoping to get my attention once more.

"Piss off, and leave me alone," I tell it and take a deep preparatory breath.

Despite my bleeding thigh, I tear off as fast as my wicked feet and that perfect rising sun will take me. Furiously, I race down the walkways–away from this disaster, away from erupting serums, but mostly away from that empty feeling in my stomach that no amount of nutrients will ever satisfy, no amount of winning Heats will ever distract me from, and no amount of Ink will ever cover.

If I thought crying would release the crippling pressure in my pinched face, I might try it. But by now, I know better, so I don't waste any priceless drops from my eyes even if my whole leg is red now. *Red is dead. Like her...*

Thinking momentarily of all the useless squares in the dead beta's braids, I frown. Since she is a leading female like me, there will be at least ten aching bellies as the sun descends in the flat, empty sky without them. And probably some of the other 53s will waste their tears over her death. Not me, though.

This really is not your fault, not your problem, Isla Jane.

My calves cramp from sprinting so hard, and I scream, "I am no fish!"

For a moment I stop, huddled over with hands on my bloodied knees to catch my breath. But I never can. No one ever does here where it takes lives to save lives, here in the City...of Red Death.

I look at my stained skin and gag because I am acutely aware that my blood might as well be her blood. Still heaving, I step out the front door. One hundred meters away, I drop safely to my stained knees and gasp for air. It's so good, so clean compared to the smoke that I want to laugh and smile and scream. But I can't. Not yet. *Let it go. Drop it. Get over it.*

"Shut up!" I yell before I realize the terrible sound driving me crazy is coming from the city sirens outside, not me. *Or her.*

Obviously, I am free now to go home to building Forty-Three B because this riot just finished my assignment for me. Not for long, though. Somehow, I will have to face another tomorrow; I always do. Why should this tragedy be any different than the rest? In a life filled with nothing but tragedy layered with tragedy, how could anything be different?

Yet even as I ask this question, I sense that something is already different. It's pink, so close to red, and I'm the rotten fish cooking in it from the other side of the melted girl's eyes. *My fault.*

Plan B–also no good, I decide and walk toward the other survivors still whooping and hollering as the whole outer globe of the Foundry explodes.

When the other 53s see me alive, minus any popping or sizzling, they go silent. Whether it's from shock or gratitude, I cannot honestly say, already knowing all too well that nothing matters right now but finding a way Home and away from this terrible place.

Unable to resist, I look up at the two suns so high and permanent in this temporary existence. Are they even real? Is any of this really happening? The globes certainly look real enough. I compare them to the single sun on my ankle and decide beyond a shadow of doubt that I miss Home even though I don't really remember the place. I also decide that I am going back there one day no matter what it costs me.

In my memory, I recall Elder Khaan say, "Isla, the heart always finds the way Home despite all the odds against it. You, my dear, are that way." I cough to clear my raspy throat.

Chapter Three

I WAKE before the rooster crows today, as usual. Then I laugh at my inside joke since I've never even heard a rooster do such an absurd thing. That just happens to be one of my favorite sayings from before we came to the City. Once though, I saw a picture of a rooster in a book about a place called a farm. He looked horrible, and his neck reminded me of the scraggly skin around Elder Khaan's purple and green finishing sac, swirling around the neck of a dragon tattoo at the head of his finishing stick, that useless piece of flesh between his legs.

Disgusting, ugly things, those sticks and roosters.

My fragmented memory flashes back to what I remember of Elder Khaan's departure ceremony when the monitors shrouded the few pieces left of him with his drone cover, placed him in the salvage processor–the machine that embalms our remains–and shot what was left of him out into space.

Space–whatever that means.

A tear threatens to slide down my furious little face, so I stall it with a veneer of indifference. Besides, what's done is done, right? So what's the use in crying over spilled milk? Whatever milk is.

"Don't think about it, Isla," I grumble uselessly. As if I ever actually follow my own advice. Then I sit down and take deep breaths to remind myself that crying is not an option. One breath, two, three.

Do I feel better or worse now? I just can't be sure yet, so I try the opposite approach and take a deep breath and hold on to it. That seems to help. *Thank Gods.*

I am almost through the worst of this crippling wave of pain. Inhaling deeply once more, I tighten my abdominal muscles to keep the spasms in where no one, me included, can find them.

If I hold out another twenty seconds, I've got it made.

I start counting as quietly as possible. I make it to ten. That's good, really good. I pace my breathing back to normal, but then another gut-wrenching wave crests, so I start counting again.

"Ten, eleven, twelve," I mutter under my breath as a distraction. *There. That's better.* "Thirteen, fourteen." *Better still.*

The worst is over now. I can do this. I know I can. I make it to twenty.

"Will the hurt ever let up?" I want to ask Elder Khaan, my greatest teacher, but I can't. I never got the chance. One minute he stood here, the next he just disappeared.

Sometimes I can still feel the gritty sand that stained my knees when I collapsed on the ground after witnessing it. They say it took three monitors and multiple injections of skag to stop my flailing. But to be fair, I can't be sure since I woke up two days later in confinement. Bits and pieces of that day are all I have left. The drug stole the rest from me. Screw that thief!

Skag. Even the word sounds jagged and cruel to me just like the coveted poison it describes. As far as I am concerned, anything that numbs my lips and blurs my mind cannot possibly be in my best interest.

Some days, I wonder if I am still strapped in a white jacket, drooling in my padded cell and if every day since Elder Khaan left me has just been a skag-induced hallucination. I check my knees to be sure. *Good. No sand marks.* Then I pinch myself. Thankfully, it hurts.

Underneath the memory of my mentor's beastly mug, I know he was a beautiful person, and I was his favorite. So even if his face, much like the rooster, looked too ugly for words, maybe I should allow him one drop of salt for old time's sake. But I won't; I can't. With me, one tear always leads to a second, and then where would I be? Bawling like one of the little 53 bairns, probably. Certainly I don't have time for playing overgrown child, even for Elder Khaan.

Inevitably, when I think of how unforgettable he was, I try to figure out what exactly makes me Isla. I say my name, "Isla." Like an eye (minus the ball) and a la (minus a song). Eye-la. What is an Isla? I think it once was the name of a river in Scotland, whatever the hell that means.

"Damn, Isla, how did I really get here? Why can't I float down a river back Home? Where is Home?"

Surely I must be more than a flowing body of water in Scotland with blue eyes and gray-blond hair who's all drenched in Ink, so determined to drown my rising sun. Gods, I must be. Someday this will all make sense. It just has to.

Back to the Ink stage. I force my attention. I must arrive on time. Earlier is even better. Unless, of course, I want to die, that is.

Shaking my head, I start walking.

It's been two days, yet I still can't catch my breath from losing that Irmin tramp in my red-card fire. Her haunting stare and her hair, the same rare color as mine, swirl like poison in my brain.

So much loss here for me. For us all, actually. So much suffering in this terrible joke of a useless life after some evil creeps infested our Home planet with bio-engineered bacterial warfare.

I can't really care about that Irmin of all people, I keep reassuring myself. After all,

I am no fish. Yet I keep seeing her drowning in pink serum everywhere. She follows me, laughs at me. Pink blisters erupt all over my face despite my refusal to acknowledge them. And even though it's totally absurd, I feel like part of me burned up with her. Ridiculous, I know.

The image of her trident spikes dripping with blood from my blubbering heart pops into my mind, and I reach for them as if somehow they might save me instead of slicing me further. Recoiling from the pain of the vision, I accept that maybe in death the other beta Jane has finally speared me properly...unlike all her failed attempts during Heat battles as my opponent.

Needless to say, I try to appear happy but just can't.

My wounds are just too fresh, I guess.

Reaching down my front side, I press into my skin, searching for the holes resulting from all three blades. They are not there, yet they are. I am sure of it. So, for the tenth time today, I remind myself that even accomplished 53s with colored sleeves are required to fake pleasure at receiving our squares and our boxes. Making my best frown-smile, I almost fool myself. Almost.

I must get my act together and fast. Without a doubt, I should cherish the nutrients that supposedly quiet our hungry bellies and quench the thirst no one ever really escapes here in the hot, dry air of the City even though I do not.

"Lucky me. I am so freaking happy," I snarl.

I plaster a bigger fake grin across my face. After all, against all the deadly odds, I have completed both of my sleeves before the age of twenty-five. So about my basic needs, I don't really worry anymore. As the highest possible ranking female in our grouping, or beta, I always receive more than my share of nutrients, leaving more than enough to hand out to the ones who depend on me. And that's a good thing. Otherwise, what would little, old, frail Kinley Beth and her wimpy eleven Inks do? Seriously, what idiot thought she was worth bringing into our kith?

"Other than being an annoying thorn in the side, Kinley is not really my problem," I want to yell. Instead, I bite down on my lower lip, wishing I could kick her out of Levana so I wouldn't have to look at her ugly face anymore. The image of her disgusts me so much that I clamp down hard enough for a faint taste of metal to flood my mouth. It tastes like one of my precious squares.

To be perfectly honest, I already know I'm lying to myself about Kinley and the burden she brings. Actually, I am distracting myself from it. *Half-ass* distracting myself, at least.

I bite down harder. More metal.

Sighing, I acknowledge the truth that Kinley will always be my problem because part of me is such a sucker for the weaker ones. Jokingly, I think of her as bacterially challenged, which makes me laugh...sort of...right before I clench my fists and scream. A little drop of blood from my overzealous heart drips down my lip, and I let it linger a moment before I *half-ass* wipe it away.

So if not today, Kinley will be my biggest freaking problem by next week. I've seen it a dozen times before and therefore recognize the telltale signs of her spiraling illnesses. Giving myself logical commands about it, I thump my forehead to engage my brain. *Look the other way. Let it go. Finally let the monster die this time.*

But I suspect I won't. Somehow, I just can't. I'm too weak. Totally pathetic, actually. Maybe I am a fish after all? Or worse yet, an Alice? Just like that little girl in the book from the old days which Elder Khaan read to me secretly at night as I hid in his quarters after the final bell rang. Not the standard Alice picture book, supposedly simplified for the benefit of our overtaxed spirits so far away from Home, but the original forbidden version, the unnecessary one.

Swallowing hard, I taste more blood gathering in the back of my throat, still choking on my lower lip like that foolish girl Alice, who drinks elixirs which make her gigantic and then small again while she insists on chasing a funny white rabbit around. *Idiot.*

And between chatting it up with disappearing cats and mad tea party guests, Alice apparently gives herself very good advice…which, of course, she very seldom follows. Just like me.

A chill runs down my neck, and I wrap my arms around my chest as I pause rocking back and forth. For a second, I wonder…could I be Alice? Is hers just another fish story inside my fish story? Am I still Home but trapped in a rabbit hole of some sort?

If I had eyelids, I would blink back such a stupid question. Instead, I just stare straight ahead and flap my gills.

It kills me that I am powerless against my self-defeating nature no matter how much I want it to be different. I realize in my brain that helping others like Kinley only hurts me, yet for some stupid reason, I struggle to do the smart thing like look the other way and march on.

Needing a more tolerable train of thought, I try to focus my flapping tail fin on chasing a rabbit…since I've never even seen one in the City. Are they as fast as Elder Khaan said? I wonder. Would I dive in after one like Alice did?

Probably. No, certainly.

For fun, I decide to nickname myself Isla-Alice Jane, the sucker, since I've never had a nickname that has stuck. Hopefully, though, I never meet a queen who wants to chop off my head for painting roses red.

Unable to stop myself, I put my hands around my neck and swallow. Still, I taste metal. *Back to what matters, Isla.* "Move…much faster," I spew.

I suspect most of the others don't wonder about things like I do. Like how we got here, twenty-two light-years away from Home, in the first place. Like why the Mozek guards, who are supposedly saving us, need guns. Like why almost all of us have the same birthday in any given year. Like why we are never shown pictures of the progress back Home. Like why the Mozek ever came in the first place? Like how they knew we were about to have a Global War? Like how…

Honestly, I could go on for ages. Ugh.

The other 53s don't even question the colored cards they pull which dictate the mandatory tasks they complete as work here, commonly called As for assignments. What exactly is the source of the bacterial strains I am forced to cross at my workstation? Well…before I blew the place up anyway. And what reaction am I looking for? Why am I strapped in a machine while the monitors guard me instead of the other way around?

And speaking of the monitors, what are they probing me for every day?

Like I said, I could go on for ages…

Why does the chief robot ask me and not the others which combination to try next when I get a red Foundry card? Why does she say, "lucky us," on those days and claim that I have done it before and I must do it again? *Ugh, still going…*

As usual, my mind always searches for the answers to endless questions, most of them dumber than dumb. Yet they just keep popping in, swishing, swirling, and robbing me of peace and, during most nights, precious sleep.

Instead of thinking, the other 53s must put their empty heads down and keep looking for more Ink to color them and skag to numb them. In fact, everything here revolves around earning Ink honors: by risking life and limb to complete the assignment cards or battling in the Heats against the other kiths. It's fair to admit that Ink honors determine how much I have to eat, where I live, where I work, and ultimately, how I will die. Same for the rest of the other 53s, too.

Unless, of course, we get back to Home before we die.

"Ink this. Ink that. It's like a wicked obsession," I say.

My face gets hot, and I bite down once more, drawing out more metallic nastiness while I growl, "I don't even like my precious Ink, except for my rising sun," aware that such blasphemy merits a trip to the kill fields. But why do we even need kill fields in the city erected to save us?"

"Shut up, Isla, or I am going to kill you myself," I say.

The idea of swinging dead from a hanging rope enters my troubled mind, and I gasp for air like a fish out of water. I wonder—would I be afraid to die? Nope, probably not. That thought makes me laugh.

More than likely, I would just stand there motionless, all pissed off that I had not escaped. Maybe I would even put the noose around my own neck.

Yes, that sounds like something I would do.

I laugh again and bend over to catch my breath. Then I stand up tall and plaster another blank mask across my face and keep walking anyway.

Steadily I advance, staring out into the dunes through the glass wall of separation like I will walk right through it as easily as my sharp gladius blade slices through my enemy's gut in battle. The urge to touch the thick glass consumes me. I simply have to know what is on the other side. Does the ground feel like roasted sandpaper, all scratchy and gritty out there, too? Where does all that sand come from anyway? And why do we have two suns here?

But then I remember lingering aimlessly is punishable by indefinite imprisonment and rub my jaw to relax it some and keep going.

Arriving late to the Ink stage is not an option. It's just not, so I move my legs faster while I pull my hand back from the bizarre glass and shove it in my waist strap holding my Levana cloth in place. When alone, I do not wear the covering even though it declares my allegiance to my kith. I much prefer to see the perfect smoothness of my flawless skin. Soon I will be Inked everywhere, so I cherish the marble-smooth surface for as long as I can, still so clean and gorgeous.

As I run, my thoughts travel to the smoking Frightening Zone, the unexplored territory beyond the dunes, under never ending acid rainfall. Countless mutated things roam there under the deadly cloud cover. Even though the electric fences and double-paned glass protects us, I worry, *What if the alien monsters ever get through?*

My heart pounds. *Lub dub. Lub dub. Lub dub.* The rate high and getting higher.

The high laser fences scattered throughout the dunes, and their "Danger" signs remind me of the day I first learned about the Global War and how badly it ended. Apparently, I am one of the last living organisms from Home. Only some of us humans made it safely to the City before the transport system went down. The Mozek could only rescue so many of us after the initial waves of mutant bacteria had already poisoned our bodies.

Fingers to my neck, I count the quick beats. One hundred and ninety, at least. Even though I am running, I take deeper breaths to slow it down.

During our Foundry assignments, we are still trying to find the perfect bacterial combination in our erupting biome elixirs, commonly known as BEs, to recolonize those of us still alive. In fact, each day we either advance one step closer to salvation or humanity's end.

Smugly, I imagine the monitors chant, *"Produce or you all will die like those dinosaurs did,"* while they wave their shiny weapons in my face. But I still want to know who decides who needs a gun? Why am I such a nothing to them if they are saving me? Why do they treat me like a threat? I'm just not sure.

Shut up, Isla. Stop thinking and just run. Now!

So to keep myself from withering to absolute nothingness while *not* thinking about that, I daydream about overgrown meadows. And for the chance to smell a real rose again, I just might tell the Mozek to piss off and sacrifice my head to the queen for the fun of it. The thought feels amazing, and immediately, my heart slows way down. I am close to my destination now.

Maybe one day I will walk right out the entry scanner of the Foundry and see if the monitors know how to shoot their shiny, precious guns.

"Sure you will, Isla. Whatever."

As my heart races once more, I remember I can't, or my whole kith, most importantly Cale, the youth I hold dearer to me than all the others, goes down with my resource-providing body. Like a vice, my responsibility as the beta sib crushes me. I have to keep producing more Ink honors for him.

Why? Because Elder Khaan's gone now, and I'm all he has left. Poor thing.

"Gods I miss you, Elder Khaan," I wail, unable to stop the words.

Deep down, I think Elder Khaan's mind searched, too. Maybe he even found some of the answers I seek but couldn't or wouldn't tell me? Who knows?

Secretly, he taught me how to read. But I cannot tell the others. So like always, I stare in the distance when I walk or run by, trying not to betray my observing eyeballs as if I don't know what the signs say. But why do we even need signs if no one can read them but me? What good are they? Who are they directing? And why?

Like all the others, I am only allowed to memorize my three allotted picture books or flip through the images of my animal book. Anything more is considered unnecessary, a waste of limited resources.

And since the City cannot afford to waste anything, the unnecessary is not just frowned upon, but punished by the most extreme of measures. Even my meager food and drink supplies are so perfectly tailored to my body that I do not excrete waste because I make none. Apparently, waste was a major problem on Home. *Well, good for us. Way to go, City of Efficiency.*

And since we can't say for sure how long we will be here...avoiding problems like sewers, piss, and shit seem *so* important to me. *Whatever.* I say let's just pile our waste, extra books, all of it, up in huge heaps on the other side of the glass if we are so close to dying every minute of every freaking day. Let's stop working these absurd assignments and party like this is home of the King-God, gathered by teems of shiny lesser Gods without a care in their all-mighty heavens.

But that makes too much sense for a craphole like the City that claims to function from a place of perfect logic. *Perfect, my ass.* Maybe the mind isn't so superior to the heart after all?

Rumor has it that about a year ago, all of a sudden, some serious scare, this crisis of untold proportions occurred, but we managed through it okay, somehow spared at the very last minute by some miracle worker that no monitor or overseer are willing to identify. I think it was all just a ploy, an excuse to keep us functioning at a level of fear where we agree to anything they demand.

Last week, the monitors moved our danger level back up to severe.

Ugh. *Okay, sure.* Here's the way my perfect logic works. Die if I do. Die if I don't. Tough choice some days when the outcome is always the same–death. I choose party like Gods with shit piles everywhere.

But it's not likely to end so well this time, they say. I hear we are all in major trouble and are definitely going down this time just like poor little in your face Kinley. But I don't believe it. Not for a minute. Even when I remember that Harley Mae is the one who likes to share this absurd rumor. She thinks she knows everything, that Enlil traitor.

The thought of her makes me clamp down on my collarbone and yank my arms down hard even though I am still running. *What an idiot.* Harley belongs to Enlil and constantly brags about how smart she is because she can recite all three of her picture books and can list at least ten animals by name. I mean seriously, she needs to get over herself, that self-inflated brat. I am so *not* convinced she owns such a superior intellect because I've seen her screw up her braid patterns like a thousand times. Most bairns can do better than that. So I'm pretty sure she's just a moron like all the rest of her siblings.

I certainly don't feel like damaged goods. I am just fine. Deep down, I know. Other than my calf, that is. But whatever. That's an old story. One everyone but me has totally forgotten about.

Stopping briefly to rest, I reach down and rub my calf. I thump it three times to remind it to function better, to bury my secret a little deeper. When I look at my reflection, I see only strong, fast legs. What calf injury?

Looking up, I notice a band of twenty or more Irmin skipping toward the stage. I bend over and rub my calf to let them get as far away from me as possible. They are such assholes, always taunting and teasing anyone nearby. They even punch each other in the face for the fun of seeing who can keep standing after the hardest hits. Every once in a while, they hit so hard one of them ends up whisked away, probably going to see one of the medicals. Brainless monkeys, those Irmin. I am so glad I have more in this head of mine than they do. They scream a few curses at me, and I play the dumb fool like I can't hear them. But I am not dumb, and I am pretty sure they know that. Or perhaps I am giving them too much credit. Maybe they know nothing at all.

Besides, my brain moves as quickly as ever, more so than the average 53, at least. So I surely don't need their respect or approval as long as I have my own. I thump my leg once more for good measure and smile, deciding I'll stay away from both Irmin insults and medicals–who do all the healing I have never once witnessed–no matter what.

The word "medical" reminds me of my special book.

My thoughts shoot twelve hours into the future.

Tonight after the sleep bell rings, I will most likely spend a few hours looking through my medical book. Honestly, the only reason I know about the medicals is because of Elder Khaan with his slurred speech who dutifully and respectfully described the robed, ageless Mozek medicals who collect, quantify, and file the serums intended to cure the human body of disease. Scowling, I consider how many times I've almost died for a bunch of volatile bottles, held captive by some creature that claims he cannot die. Again perfect logic, my ass.

Honestly, sometimes I think this big brain of mine is more of a curse than a blessing. Sometimes, even though I hate to admit it, I wish I was slow and stupid like so many of the others.

Stopping briefly to catch my breath once more, I spit on the hot sand and observe my saliva dry immediately. Gone and wasted like Elder Khaan.

Wasting away makes me think of my future plans once more. *Screw that.*

My face heats up, and I start pounding my legs against the sand.

In order to prepare for my next idiotic Alice move, I will spend my only moments of peace during my next red card assignment at the Foundry, searching for just the right cure for Kinley's ailment. Once I figure it out tonight, that is. Then, of course, I will spend some more of my precious time off tricking her into taking another secret concoction that will save her hide. Again.

Spitting a second time, I admit that it's time I got a little tougher. My sweetness is killing me.

Once I get closer to the Ink stage, I pucker up my lips, making a kissing sound for my best sucker face. Then I frown. Without meaning to, I stop and stare at the rising sun on my right foot, just above my wounded calf, as the stage comes into view. There are hordes of 53s already assuming their positions, and I just stare, shocked at how many of us there are–probably two or three thousand.

Although underneath my Ink I look exactly like a few of the others, my legs are even more powerful than the rest. My heart may be a sack of filmy wispiness, but my muscular thighs move quickly, so I always crown verus, or champion, during my Heats against the asshole unlucky enough to be assigned against me. I am just so fast that I inevitably escape whatever daily natural disaster tries to kill me with my rising sun peeking out over my meandering line-covered legs while whoever tries to kill me too. Fools.

A familiar question erupts. *Is my rising sun Ink inside another Ink?*

Flicking my cheek as punishment for such a screwed up thought, I spit a third time.

Truthfully, I hate the rest of my Ink even though I am so good at earning it. Thanks to my unparalleled speed, before I even reached my third year, I earned three bairn level Inks: a kitty with big round eyes which always has the letters H-E-L-L-O next to her, a blue and purple winged butterfly, and a simply drawn bird with wide, circular eyes. Easily, I recall the day, a decade or more ago, that I picked out that black baby bird for my right shoulder. I called her Jane-do-do as an inside joke even though she is the only Ink I have ever bothered to name, and I have a lot of Ink. Too many to count, probably.

And, so my Ink dealer says, having won so many Ink honors is rarer than hen's teeth–whatever that means. And even though I would prefer to smash that ID's nose in, I have to take my Ink dealer's word for it at face value, whatever that's worth. Certainly not much, in my humble opinion.

Amused by the thought of smacking my ID, this morning, I am the very last 53 to climb up the Ink stage, a massive steel platform about four meters high and a hundred meters across. Here I will accept our kith's assignment cards and our rations, the food squares and drink boxes, that I am blessed enough to distribute amongst the lower ranked in my clan.

Instantly, my ornate sleeves push me straight to the front of the crowd in the far right corner where the Levana kith gathers just like always.

"The best pickings for the best Ink-drenched bitch, I guess," Kinley whispers behind me. "Oh, hi Isla Jane," she adds a bit louder.

I try to ignore her, but she puts her hand on my shoulder and traces Jane do-do's outline with her shaky index finger.

"Stop it," I demand, but of course she doesn't. That might suggest she respects my authority as her beta sibling.

"Such a unique combination of tattoos in your Inking anchor, Isla Jane," she says because my Inks are nothing like the others who stand next to me.

I think I'll try my infamous silent treatment.

"Did the ID pierce your tongue?"

Grunt.

"I'm talking to you, beloved beta."

"Whatever."

"Why do you refuse to wear the standard 53 stamp decorating the rest of us?"

Honestly, I can't be sure if it's a rhetorical question or she genuinely expects an answer from me.

"Boring," I say and step farther away from her.

"Why no Levana stamps to declare your allegiance to our fabulous family?" she continues with her stupid questions and gets right behind me again.

Trying to ignore her, I roll my shoulders and rub my neck. "Because I can't let any one thing or image claim me forever," I reply, both because she won't stop tapping her annoying foot, and it's actually true.

"Oh, whatever, beta." She snorts and gives me a little more space.

Thank Gods. Maybe she'll shut up now.

Each Ink I add to my anchor, the particulars of the design I wear on my skin, I pick out personally. That's no small thing since I have so many: decorative lines cresting up my neck like a royal collar, lilies and other flowers in various stages of bloom, draping down my covered arms and spilling onto my flanks and lateral buttocks.

Most of my designs are black and white, of course. I leave the colored Inks to the idiots who find their flavor amusing. Bright colors are as tedious and flagrantly absurd as the concept of green dollar bills and metal coins as far as I am concerned.

The thought of my uniqueness brightens my face momentarily, but a dark grimace quickly replaces it when I realize that Kinley, that fool behind me, totally owes me, as usual.

The jerk moves tightly in once more, and I can smell the rot of her foul breath, the acetone scent of mutant-bastard microorganisms eating her gut and climbing up her innards like thieves in the night to rob her diseased mouth of the rest of her chance at a normal life. *Whatever normal means.*

I pinch my nostrils.

But what stinks the most is that I can't even rub her imminent demise in her sarcastic, shriveled-up little face because, just like my searching mind and this burning calf, I have to keep it a secret.

Why?

Probably because I am going to end up saving her stupid ass from her screwed up bacterial imbalance again. *Loser. Piss off, you.*

I spit a fourth time to warn them all, Kinley and the monitors alike, that they got nothing on my anchor, and they can stick their rancor directly down their neck ports.

I take a deep breath and deny the odor behind me like it never existed.

Why?

Because even if I have to keep it a secret for all eternity, I am searching for something so clean, so righteous, so pure that I have no word for. Some elusive data that is so much more precious than Ink, black or colored, or even ideal bacteria in this City of Stench.

As the corners of my lips turn back up and drag my heavy cheeks with them, I decide that I will find it...that data, that program, that whatever you call it...even if it freaking kills me, because I know it exists. Somehow I just know. I feel it in my bones, taste it in my spit, and smell it oozing out of my very skin.

Chapter Four

QUICKLY, before I get pissed off about Kinley again, I clip my awarded squares in my hair beads. The boxes of hydration I slide under my arm bands and around my waist strap because I certainly can't have any of those unclaimed bairns trying to steal my precious resources before I give them to that crunchy creep behind me. Gods know that Kinley can't make it on her own if her life depends on it, which it doesn't, of course, thanks to me, the buffoon.

You're such a pushover, Isla, my inner voice squeals. Like somehow I could forget in a million years. I flick my own face to make sure I'm listening. *Wake up, Do-Do.* But I never listen. Here comes my Alice routine again followed immediately by thoughts of the queen, whose roses I'm hoping to paint red.

Taking a deep breath and sighing, I imagine the beautiful little sucker in my hand. I rub my fingers back and forth trying to hold on to the image. Will I even recognize the flower if I do get back Home? How does it really smell? Can I eat the tender petals? And what do they taste like?

What I wouldn't give to hold a rose and let its sharp thorns cut my calloused little fingers while I paint it red. It sounds so beautiful to me with its tight bud of suede-soft petals protected by those terrible little spikes, eventually opening up to offer the most wonderful scent. Both clean and elegant, the aroma must inspire newly discovered hope. No, it would probably be more than hope. Something even grander...like faith. *Wonderful.*

Glancing around the perimeter, I think, *Not wonderful.*

The petals between my empty fingers fall to the ground, and I cough while I fumble like a fool trying to catch them. But it's no use; like the holographic petals that descend from the sky before the start of a Heat, they were never really there. *Crap.*

Back to avoiding the unclaimed bairns, I drag my hopeless, helpless thoughts forcing my lips to hurl down further like dead weight, dragging my brow involuntarily down as well. As a desperate countermeasure, I sigh over and over, pushing my air out fast and hard, still trying to lift my battered face off the ground. *Stinking bairns. Also not wonderful. This is not Wonderland.*

The bairns, still as of yet unaffiliated with any particular kith, display their treacherous invitations to feed them, hoping to keep my eye for a second and smother me with the guilt of denying their adorable faces. I can almost hear them crying out my name. But instead of Isla, they call me Alice. *Well screw that.*

"Where did you learn to taunt me like this?" I mutter in between scowls.

Furious, I move as fast as I can, eyes peeled to the ground, away from the Ink stage and all those hungry mouths that I do not want to feed. I have enough responsibility for my collective brothers and sisters who belong to my kith already. Way too much, in fact, for my liking.

Darn those smooth-skinned, pale youths who put on their best looks, hoping for some handouts from the strong ones from the front. At least ten of the miniature morons follow me as quickly as their bare, little feet can take them. I stomp my feet and walk faster. Thinking it's some kind of a challenge, they whoop and holler while speeding up to match my pace. *Fools.*

Spinning on my heels to face them, I scream, "Leave me alone, you stupid bairns! I don't want you!"

They stop, shuffle their pale, bare feet, and look up at me with those terrible eyes of theirs, big and bright and moist around the edges. Awful.

One of them even dares to reach her hand out to me as a drop of salt stains her cheek. Despite the sinking feeling in my gut, which makes no sense to me at all, I spit on the ground and stomp my feet again as I shake my head *no*.

The little one pulls her hand back immediately. For a moment, that feeling in my stomach intensifies, and I feel like sickness will come spewing out of my mouth.

I flash back to the fire, to my melting enemy who had always wanted to spear me with her trident. Unable to stop myself, I yell, "I am no fish!"

Stammering back and forth, the closest young girl looks at her hands and slowly glances up. "I a-a-am A-A-Alexis," she says with a blooming tear dripping down her sour face and then runs away.

I laugh hysterically at her pathetic ability to speak properly as the others, terrified I will laugh at them too, follow suit behind her.

Inexplicably, I frown again. "Piss off. I hate you," I say as they leave my field of vision. In response, my inner voice starts in. *Sure you do, Isla. Who's you anyway? That's probably why you still feel like a fish, right?*

If I had eyelids, I would blink them in disgust while this shiver runs through my cold blood even though I'm sweating. Desperate for warmth in this heat, I rub my arms back and forth searching for comfort here where there is none in the City. The City of Cold Blood.

To be honest, I know that even more than a square or box, the bairns hope for someone, some brine-covered idiot like me to be exact, who is kind enough to take in another sib. They want more than anything to belong to someone who can make sure they won't go another night without a place to sleep or a square to eat. But we are almost out of Elders to manage our clans, so surely none of us will survive another sib.

Less than convincingly, I say it one last time. "I am no fish." But the words cling on to my lips for dear life, and I can hardly get them out before they strangle me like a barbed noose. A single drop of salt stains my face to match the one the bairn named Alexis shed a moment ago, and I wipe it quickly away.

Then I remind myself that Levana is just one of many kiths without a qualified leader to guide it. All they have is this fool, the poor creatures. If I take in more bairns, I won't have enough squares for the ones that already struggle to survive under the ruse of my guardianship. Every new one I take in hurts the others. So I can't. I just can't. *Piss off. I hate you.*

For once, I listen to my own advice and keep walking. Then I break out into a quick jog, which feels much better. *I don't have long now.* I pump my legs hard as I run, aiming to escape any straggling bairns and that heaviness in my heart that keeps leaking into my gut so burdened with all my screwed-up bacteria. I bear down, hoping I can push it out my backside, but it's no use; I am simply stuck with it. The BRÉ red card assignment starts in about thirty minutes, and any idiot can guess who took ours. A fish named Alice. I mean Isla. Hopefully I can hold it together until then. Reaching up to make sure my face is still dry, I think, *Stay tough, Isla. Stay tough.* I bear down again.

It's not my fault if no one wants the bairns and the burden they bring. Nobody helped me. Surely they need to learn to help themselves like I did.

Here in the City, with such limited resources, only the strongest and best suited to battle survive. It would be different if we still arranged our kiths as traditional families from Home: no choice–you got who you got. Like a roll of the dice–an idiot, a cripple, a sucker. But since we get to choose whom we include in our kiths these days, surely we should choose wisely. The smartest, the fastest, the most likely to earn Inks in battle and pay back the debt invested in them via the squares, boxes, and probiotics given to them before they were big enough to earn them. Makes sense, I guess. Much like Ink honors instead of money. Maybe the Mozek aren't so stupid after all?

Thankfully, each year there are fewer bairns than the last, so this problem hardly exists at all anymore. In a few short years, we won't have any at all, I bet. Well thank Gods.

The sappy little wimp inside me starts whining. I can hear her already. *Who takes care of the weak ones, the slow ones, the dumb ones who will never outsmart their assigned opponents? What happens to them, Isla? How is this life fair to them? How can they be blamed and punished for their faults, those weaknesses that are beyond their control?*

Sometimes I'd like to strangle myself. *I hate you, Isla.*

"Eat or be eaten," I grumble like it's brilliant advice. It's not. I have never said such a ridiculous phrase before, but it makes me feel tough even if it's total bullshit. If I think like this often enough, maybe one day I will believe I actually mean it. Then maybe I will be strong enough to stand by my own advice.

My thoughts stray to Baylor John. He will probably roll over dead on his hawk-covered chest for every one of those parasitic children. *Idiot.*

If I punched him in the chest, I wonder, would those wings of charity collapse and finally knock the air out of his chest for good? My face flashes so hot I think it will start sizzling when I imagine his round, happy, little face as I slow back down to a walking pace. Baylor, that gamma ranked fool from the kith Salus, gives half his squares away to the little ones he hasn't already taken under his roof. So thank Gods he owns chest and back Ink honors or his sibs at home might starve before he even returns from his red card assignment at the DED–Distribution and Exportation Department–tonight. *If he gets back, that is.*

My stomach sinks even further, and my pulse quickens. Then I break into a run and hiss like a snake. Hissing feels nice, so I do it again for sheer pleasure.

"Leave me alone!" I yell to no one in particular, my tongue still flickering back and forth like the devil even though I am alone, like usual, in this city where I am always starving inside despite enough squares to eat.

But what exactly am I starving for? Is it the rose? Is it something more? The elusive data or fish food, perhaps? Something I have no name for, maybe?

And if so, how do I find something I don't even have a name for? How will I recognize it if I finally do find it? Could it be right in front of me and I can't or won't see it? Like I can't see Elder Khaan now that he has blown away into total nothingness even though sometimes…sometimes…I swear I can still sense him watching me from somewhere I don't know how to look back at.

My right flank cramps, and I almost have to stop as that same hollow, hungry feeling swells in my upper abdomen when I remember him. Elder Khaan.

Here we go. One drop always leading to the next. *Crap.* Surely a child or Baylor is to blame for this. I try to count to ten, but I just can't. The drops are falling from my eyes too fast now.

Unable to stop the stream of weakness pouring out my body, the memory of him sucks me into the black hole inside my chest. The way Elder Khaan, the closest thing I ever had to a father, always stood when he watched me do my lessons–telling me, teaching me, guiding me. Pushing me to do better, to be more than the nothing I actually am. What an idiot, the way he believed in me.

Trying to find some reprieve, I curse Baylor's sweetness, yet fail and eventually let Elder Khaan's memory consume me in this City of Loss.

In my mind, Elder Khaan props his one good arm on his hip while the other one that looks like brown leather from the burn he suffered in a wild Heat just hangs there. And that limp arm of his, wasted, twitches now and then from the nerve damage. Totally useless for work, his arm manages to get out of any further assignments despite his refusal to go for a medical's help. Why would he have refused help? It makes no sense.

Damn, I remember how he used to look at me almost as if he could see inside me with those big brown eyes with the faintest golden speckles peering through his scarred face, which frightened some of the others but never me. I saw only goodness in the scars constricting the movement of his deformed lips unable to turn up even on the rare occasions when he grinned.

I heard his smile in his words but never saw it on his face, requiring me to feel for it, search for it instead of just finding it. I guess that dragon burned his face into such a mess I could only see the face beneath the face he used to have before that Heat that nearly killed him. I'll never forget it. I wasn't supposed to be watching. But the visor was right there and well…I just couldn't resist. Guess I'm not the resisting type.

I wipe my face again. Sopping wet. If I wasn't so upset, I would be mortified from my embarrassing display of weakness.

But I will join my ugly mentor soon enough.

Hissing like the reptile I am, I wipe my hands on my thighs and pinch myself until it hurts so badly that I can no longer stand it. Even though I can't say for sure, I bet the monitors will kill me if I don't complete my card on time. Unless they get super lucky and I do something even more exciting like blow up the joint. *"Lucky us,"* I remember the robot say.

Life's a bitch, and then you die, they say. If you're lucky, that is. And I'm always lucky like a robot, so that's settled then, I suppose. Maybe one day I will meet this *they* and help them learn a new saying.

Until then, I must keep moving, trying not to die. I'm halfway up a gradually sloping hill now that peaks at the place I am both trying and not trying to get–the Foundry.

The rocks, on either side of the path maybe three meters wide, are stained with a disgusting layer of sulfur that reminds me how far away we are from Home, where the air was once clean and must have smelled like something other than the rot eating our guts from the inside.

If there was a way to escape this Mozek world without dying, I might try it. But I can't. How could I all alone? And with what protective gear or spaceship? And even if I dared, where would I go? Out in the dunes like those four jokers a few years ago? To struggle out in the Frightening Zone with the mutant vermin under acid rainfall that can't wait to cut, slice, and gobble me up?

I don't think so. What's the point?

Almost to the Foundry now, I blink my dry, burning eyes to prove that I still have eyelids to protect them. Then I remember I am booked to play boss of the biome so I can save what remains of the human race. Great. Sounds like fun. I blink again and wish I was anywhere other than the City of Sulfur and Decay.

Chapter Five

THE OUTER GLOBE of the Foundry compound comes into view as I approach from the southern border. Trying to keep me from getting inside on time, the reflective glass with barred windows pulls me back into the glory of the two overlapping suns behind me. Unable to resist the magnificence of not one but two rising suns, I wonder how so much beauty above can coexist with so much pain below. I try to remember Home and see what's left of it here in this mirror that shows me nothing more than red, dry sand between spheres upon spheres of buildings...but everything that might remind me of where we came from is gone.

It's all gone.

Disgusted, I stare at the gunmetal gray, curved beams that encase the Foundry like electrons that surround the neutrons and protons in the nucleus of an oversized diagram of an atom. Is this place no larger than an atom trapped in some odd dimension of spacetime? I consider my bizarre idea and let my head rotate slowly with the beams like the moon once did. Once did...before the effects of the Global War altered gravity and rocked Home slightly off its axis by one degree, sending it spiraling slowly but always moving closer and closer to the sun. Then unable to orbit at the imperfect angle, the moon and its effects on the tide were useless, and the poor thing just sat there orbiting nothing at all.

No moon, no ocean tides killed all the fish because the currents in the water no longer circulated the krill upward. And one by one, everything in the ocean died.

I look back at the suns behind me and pinch my fingers, trying to crush them in retribution for what happened to my Home–a place no one even seems to remember anymore but me. *As if I still remember it either. Who am I kidding? I have forgotten it all too.*

Whispering, "Fuck this shit," I take in the haunting view of the dominating structure in front of me–like an atom times ten to the millionth power. As always, I gasp at the size of it. I would consider the structure all-powerful, like the Gods, if I hadn't just seen a few pink drops destroy the whole building a few days ago. I wonder how something so massive could be so fragile.

Maybe it's all an illusion and it is smaller than an atom times ten to the negative millionth power. Could we have shrunken so small we exist between spacetime?

"Shut up, dumbass," I say and punch one hand into the other.

Blinking to confirm that I am not hallucinating, I wonder how they could have replaced this structure so freaking fast. Another ridiculous thought, which I also quickly dismiss, enters my mind. *A globe within a globe?*

Shaking my head from the pain of my own punch party, I refuse to entertain my pointless philosophy session any longer. Instead, I choose to imagine how I will spend my little free time tonight helping Kinley with her bacteria. Missing just a few of the right strains, which must affect some type of tumor suppressing gene, she has some new, deadly cancer every few months. The details don't really matter since the underlying issue is really all the same.

And the monitors, those jackasses who run this twirling globe of sparkly metal, don't believe in wasting unapproved biome elixir on 53 tongues like hers.

Really, I'm not sure why we keep testing so many strains if it's such a big deal to use them. Why bank on the Ink's effects to balance the good and bad bacteria when we can generate new colonies of the good stuff? Why not give the shit away even if it might be worth nothing more than used up alien promises since we are the only humans left and the alternative is for us to die? Like so many other things here, it makes no sense.

So I keep trawling, trying to stave off Kinley's mutations while she remains totally clueless about it. Lucky for her, I keep sending my stupid ass back to where we make the stuff: this section, Biome Repair Elixir.

You have to be brave in the BRÉ where Biome Repair Elixir shit is always exploding. But if not brave, at least fast and therefore highly ranked on this crap ladder like me. Ironic how the word "rank*"* means level and stink at the same time, I notice.

My rocking fast feet earned me, as just a youth, one of the most highly ranked *(level and stink, ha)* positions after I came in first place, crowning verus champion my year of the Stain Heats, the same obstacle races that will rank *(level, not stink)* this year's bairns soon enough. Too soon, I'm afraid.

Once inside the opening gate, my eyes scan the perimeter. Everything looks identical to the prior building before the whole terrible thing blew. *How is that possible?* We could be in the same building, exactly the same. *Terrifying, still not wonderful.* An emotion, so intolerable, so un-survivable, consumes me. It feels like a *no* wrapped in another *no* coated with countless *nevers* and packed in a beating.

To distract myself from the nightmare of a life where nothing changes even after the place blows up, I start counting 53 workers. This morning, I count twenty-two 53 workers assigned to red cards in the Biome Repair Elixir section. In my mind, I march the hallways of the inner and outer rings of remote testing stations: nine plus nine plus eight plus eight contraptions of doom and two more for the overseers, who are the 53s who serve as minions to the chief robot.

Thirty-six units, only twenty-two workers?

Have the Mozek given up on us finding the biome elixir? Shit, this can't be good. Where are they assigning all the other cards then? Or are there so few of us ranked *(level and stink)* so highly that they are limiting the number of red card distributions?

There were twenty-five of us here, at least last time I counted, before my blowout. *Think, Isla. Remember before that.* And that was down from thirty just a month before. Why is that? Where did the assignments go? Are they coming back?

Here comes that sinking feeling in my gut again. *Hold it, girl. Don't go there. It helps no one.* Clenching my jaw, I stop my teeth from chattering. I breathe in slowly, trying to reel in my heart rate.

I would ask those gray goon monitors for some answers, but I know better than to bother the Mozek. Mimicking the monitors' only response to my questions, I spew, "It takes lives to save lives in the City, Isla Jane. You know that."

I imagine replying as I chop one of those goons in half with a gladius blade, "You know what I don't know? What you are. Why do you all look and sound the same? Are you a machine? A drone? What? Let's look inside. Ha!"

But those ghosts with their empty eyes have nothing more than worthless words of wisdom that can never motivate me to produce their precious serums by saying such stupid things. If there were any sand to spit upon, I would. I step in the front mechanical sliding door instead.

Maybe I should stop speaking to the eyeless idiots since all they spit back at me is crap anyway. And to top it off, the only reward they have to offer me is another Ink honor, which I don't need. I have enough Ink to balance my good and bad bacteria forever. *Let me go Home!*

Since I just barely survived the last fire and glass riot, I earned another Ink and skag for my supposed bravery, quick wits, and exciting moves. *Exciting? What? Who gives a crap about that?*

And an extra one, too, for promising to keep my mouth shut to the others about my pink little drops that caused the inferno. The overseer even acted, I don't know... guilty? As if it was their fault instead of mine. *Imbeciles.*

But why does that matter? Why do I need to keep it secret? Who cares about the color of the flames? Not me, that's for sure. I mean, fire is fire, isn't it?

Another absurd idea interrupts my train of thought. *Fire inside fire? Whatever.*

I can pass the Ink on to a sib who needs it more than I. I already have a scheduled visit to my Ink dealer tomorrow anyway, so I don't need it.

What to choose for my anchor this time? What Ink image will make it even more unique? No one has an anchor like the one on my skin, and I plan on keeping it that way.

Hmmm... Dragon, like Elder Khaan's ugly stick of flesh between his legs?

Moaning softly and smiling, I say, "No, a rose. I want a rose; I'm sure." Maybe a pink one with a trident speared through the middle to make it official.

Before I remember to shrink that smile back down to nothing, I chuckle. *Shit!* Quickly, I slam my hand across my mouth and glance about to make sure no one heard me laugh.

Sizzled-up Jane pops in my mind again. I should be thrilled that menace with a three-pronged knife is dead, but I'm not. I'm frowning now for sure and drop my hands back down. That Ms. Crispy Jane was my sworn enemy, so why do I possibly give a flying crap about what happens to her?

What happened to her–she's fried and gone. Shaking my head, I think of her last moment again. *Fried. Dead. Sizzled-up.* At the same time, I slip through the second sliding door for scanning, and the warning bell rings.

Wow, that was a close one. Almost cooked like the other Jane.

Unable to afford disobedience when I am almost late, I assume a subservient demeanor. Quickly, I strip down for the newly built, identical entry scanners and avoid making eye contact with the no-eyes of the goons. They probe me with their metal rods and then make me stand in the center of the new, large white machine. *Finally some proof this isn't the same building.* I want to smile at the observation but can't. It's just too risky.

After I step in, the doors close behind me. I raise my arms above my head and widen my stance. The machine rotates back and forth until it confirms that I'm clear. *I'm clear? Absurd. I'm anything but clear.*

They constantly search me. Why? What terror might I possibly bring to this place? Aren't they helping us anyway? Do they really think I'm dangerous to them somehow? And if so, why? That's so upside down–them afraid of me while they swing their guns back and forth to save me. It's almost as if they expect me to fight back. *How ridiculous.*

The doors open to let me out. Guess I passed. *Passed what, Isla?*

Then I feel a subtle vibration come from the entry scanner behind me. Eliza Rachel steps out with a panicked look on her face while she trembles and avoids the missing eyes of the monitor next to her. "What do you mean repeat the scan?"

The monitor raises its gun a few inches. "I said repeat the scan."

Its voice spreads through me, and a shiver wracks my body and turns my stomach. Not human, not quite robotic, not quite…anything discernable. Just a sound from an eyeless, soulless being with a big gun meant for saving us.

She quivers. I can feel her fear ten paces away.

"Follow me, 53," the mystery creature replies, marching her back to the front door.

As she marches, I try not to think about this too much. What makes her a 53 and the monitor a monitor? Is 53 a name or a number? None of the others know about numbers, I realize. As far as they are concerned, it is no different than Anne or Beau or Amelia, just choppy and short. Yet I know better. We are numbered as 53. What could that mean? Why don't I already know? Is it 53 pharmaceutical compounds, 53 groups of humans, 53 kiths, 53 suns, 53 cities? That's a lot of cities inside cities. If I had time to imagine something so ridiculous, I would, but a monitor heads my way, so I get moving instead.

The overhead warning bell rings, and Eliza Rachel cries out, "But the bell!"

The thing's gun digs into her forehead. I can almost feel the mark it will leave and know that even though I have no idea what the hell kind of being a monitor really is, this one is about to fucking kill Eliza Rachel if she doesn't comply.

The monitor belts out, "I said repeat the scan, 53. Now!"

I scamper away without looking back, ignoring her whimpers. To settle myself down, I tenderly caress my twelve patterned half-meter-long braids and the victory beads from the Heats. This soothes me, slowing down my mind which yearns to reach back to Eliza and calm her.

Doesn't she know cowering makes her look more suspicious? Whatever she has done wrong, she should just spit on the floor and pretend like it never happened, like those things are crazy and she can't be bothered with their stupidity.

I hear the same subtle vibration alarm from the entry scanner again. *That can't be good, Eliza. Not your problem though, Isla. Keep going. Keep marching, girl. Think about something better like your hair.*

This time, unlike Alice, I listen.

Mercifully, my mind goes back to thinking about my hair. Each time I win a Heat, my opponent is forced to decorate me with their most treasured hair bead–bits of odd shaped glass, metal, or other precious artifact.

And since I'm so good at winning in the Heats, my hair is a walking museum of sorts. Filled with an array of gorgeous colors, it looks just like a miniature rainbow when I twist it back and forth. I love it. The idea of being a rainbow thrills me, even a little fake one, since I've never seen one in real life, only in a book. Without my gorgeous rainbow bead-decorated braids, I am hopeless beyond reprieve, colorless, lifeless, dead even.

So is that stinking Kinley.

Like all the others treasure their Ink, I treasure my hair. It is beautiful and soft and settles me when nothing else can. And if I had hours to waste, I'd squander them unbraiding and re-braiding it, decorating it, rainbow-ing it.

But alas, I don't, so I just daydream about it.

Thank Gods my hair and I make it safely out of range of both the first scanner and Eliza's whimpering.

Now I enter the next device. I guess we have two now?

Fearlessly, I follow the directions of the monitor, opening my legs, palms, and eyelids for this second level of scanning.

Today like always, while coming in, I hide nothing, so I don't bother to worry. But leaving will be different; leaving will be dangerous, big-time. Thanks to Kinley-The-Lame. But I will have to worry about that then.

By some miracle, Eliza makes it to her station just in time. She must have passed both her scans after all. The second bell rings, and she moans like a bairn with a sweet square coated in mind-numbing flavor.

I throw her a wink to celebrate with her.

Then I smile as I enter my new testing station. After all, I have survived another morning of weepy-eyed children with all my squares intact. Perhaps both Eliza and I will survive work as well?

The thought is lovely, almost hopeful. Almost.

Ten hours later, once the Foundry close bell rings, I know my safety is over. *What a joke, right? As if this place is ever safe.* My heart pounds with anticipation and fear for what I am about to attempt. *Idiot.*

Cursing my stupidity, I try to change my mind. But I know myself too well. My self-inflicted profanity is a waste of time. In between foul words in my mind, I hear Elder Khaan's voice. *"Pivotal, Isla."* I roll my eyes and fake a gag.

Elder Khaan liked to remind me over and over again that you can map out your life by a few pivotal moments. Like I'm electricity in a circuit board, my current starts heading down one path, forsaking all the others. Once my energy has passed through, I can't turn around to start over. The possible synaptic connection is lost, leaving only one way forward. Each junction is based on a choice, a pivot of sorts. Momentarily, I wonder if this is one of those critical moments in my life. Then I choke on the silliness of the idea. As if this grand gesture of supreme foolishness matters to anyone but me.

But what if I am like a circuit board? What if we all are? Will this choice to help Kinley lead me where I hope to go? I doubt it.

Maybe I can still call the whole thing off? I tempt my harder half. But again, as usual, I already know better. I'm too far in. My sound advice falls on deaf ears.

I reach up and clumsily trace my soothing braids. One by one, I march out my plaits, each motion a little smoother than the last, and my pulse lowers slightly. But is it enough to quiet the lies screaming from inside my eyes? One look at me and anyone with even half a brain will see I'm up to something. Obviously, something moronic like an Alice move.

"Kiss it," I threaten Kinley who rests safe and sound in her quarters, clueless that I'm about to risk my life to try to save hers. I curse her as if somehow she forces me to do this, which is absurd, of course, because this is all on me, Isla-The-Fool. I have done this. I know I have. And I'm pretty sure that pisses me off the most. If she had asked for my help, at least then I could blame her for my predicament, but nope, all me. *Dumbass. Piss off. I hate you.*

I can't blame anyone but me.

Who's the joker now? I accuse the disgusting little voice inside my foolish heart, which sings so sweetly and purely, making my mind want to gag. Don't I realize that helping her hurts me? Hurts all the others I must feed?

When will I ever learn?

After I count my hair patterns seven times over, my vitals normalize. A specific plan forms in my spinning mind, so I jump on it. Even if it's stupid, real stupid. But stupid is better than nothing, I guess.

I step up to my overseer, furiously tapping my right foot. The harder I tap, the less nervous I feel. "Overseer Steve, I am asking for an allowance."

He just nods, his eyes transfixed on my foot like I have hypnotized him with a pocket watch I saw once in the medical book, which annoys me almost as much as him by this point. I stop the tapping and lock eyes with him. His eyes go slightly out of focus like he's lost his balance and thinks he will find it in the next room. Too much skag, probably.

Attempting to sound harsh, which I am, sort of, but for totally different reasons than I am about to claim, I continue. "Overseer, I am trying to arrange a mock Heat with the Irmin tomorrow." He connects in, and I know I have him back from la-la land. Great.

He clears his throat twice. "Okay. Cool. Sounds exciting. Who's the benefactor planning to sponsor the event? Did you get mass approval?"

Approval? Sponsor? What is he slurring on about? "Benefactor? Me, I guess."

"Oh, I misunderstood. Mock Heat. Got it."

"Cool. Whoop, whoop. Go Levana," I holler and make my family's sign, notably not stomping my feet to the thump, thump, thumping in my chest that is still growing.

This is a bold-faced lie.

My cheeks flush, but the words are out, and I can't drag the deception back in to cool them. So I keep going, getting louder and hoping to look mad, real mad instead of terrified of betraying my true intention. Anything is better than afraid at this point because I am way too far in to undo this now.

I add, "I can't stay late tomorrow since we all freaking know I'll most likely be back here with another red shit assignment. Got it?"

His eyes blur over again, and I lose him for good probably. He's on another planet called skag now, I bet. *Pathetic junkie like the rest of them.*

Slapping his shoulder for effect, I reel him back once more. "And since I don't want any crap from anyone for leaving on time tomorrow, I volunteer to put the biome elixir bottles away tonight."

"Oh. Okay, I-I-Isla J-J-J–" The dumbass stammers over even one syllable words.

"Jane," I finish for him and keep on going. "That way, even if Harley Mae slows me down like she always does, I will be back to the fitness track on time to show Jaxston Steve and his crew of thieving jerks that he's a slow punk loser. I mean, check out this hair. I need another bead, don't you think?"

"Yes. Okay. Um…"

Fucking loser. He's nothing more than a skag junkie. *And he had so much potential. What a shame.*

My cheeks have lost all their redness now.

I make my sign again, and he signs back, sort of anyway, in this lazy, sleepy style with his two fingers in a V shape around his right eye. Actually, more like a V on his tripped out cheek.

Everyone, loaded or not, knows the Enlil kith hate the Irmin kith as much as we in Levana do.

I start to go on and on about how much I can't stand Harley either. Not because she's slow but because she prances about as a know-it-all, bragging about her useless brain.

But it's pointless. This dude is floating in and out of solar systems too far away to be on any map I have ever seen.

Quickly, I decide to act clueless that he's tripping through black holes and resume my ranting and raving about what creeps the Irmin are, forcing him to focus slightly. His haze-eye disappears.

Ordinarily, he is anti-Levana, but he is assuredly more anti-Irmin.

Internally, I swear off all the complicated layers of subtle separation here, trying to remember which allegiances hold priority. Usually, I would get distracted thinking about topics like this one, but I'm still too afraid of getting busted doing what I'm about to do.

My cheeks go red again.

That overseer Steve, when he's not king of la-la, hates his almost identical looking counterpart Jaxston Steve so much that he takes pity on me and agrees, in between slobbers, to my plan to rub my glorious speed in our shared enemy's spiteful face.

When he sits down to gather himself, I quickly slip my favorite blue braid bead in the largest bottle of biome elixir, the general repair probiotics. Certainly, I don't want to forget which bead is coated with Kinley's possible cure while it swings from my dopey scalp so bent on saving fools that are clueless to my outrageous charity, do I? *Imbecile.*

Quickly, with my heart slamming around in my chest like a big band from hundreds of years ago, I twist the bead back into my hair and grump out endless profanities about my situation: having to stay late to show Jaxston who's boss, trying to decide which of his beads I want. Blah, blah, blah. Steve-Lala-Lost just sits there, and I consider screaming to see if he will notice but decide against it.

To be honest, on the inside, I am screaming but not at him, Harley Mae, or Jaxston Steve. *Stupid micro-brained inner voice all coated in sap and suds that bet my whole life on this unbelievably absurd plan.*

Which just worked, by the way, the tiny, little circuit board brilliantly announces while I celebrate making it out of the Foundry coated in one miniature, virtually undetectable drop of life-saving bacterial probiotic on one of my beads in one of my braids.

So many little buggers in a drop—so small yet so big.

Pivotal even. *For Kinley.*

"But also for you, Isla," I hear Elder Khaan say in my mind, and I smile with all my heart.

Right before I slap myself for such a dumb gesture, that is. *Thank Gods. Logic, I missed you so.*

As we step out of the second exit scanner, I break out into a run to get as far away from my temporary, buzzed-up ally as I can. I'm still terrified of what I have just done, but my fear is coated by my wimpy little victory. This makes my heart so happy that I dare to yell more profanities at the glass wall separating me from certain death out there as my mind loses control again.

The fences glow, flashing red lights that watch and warn me. *Against what? What's out there?*

But then I stop in my tracks and chide myself for being so thrilled about something so foolish—helping someone else survive in this world where only miniature victories are possible in the City of Shrink.

I just stand here breathless, looking at the glass for who knows how long, wondering what Elder Khaan meant about mapping out my life on a few pivotal moments. That was the only word he ever used—pivotal.

What change does it imply exactly? Where am I headed? And why?

Knowing time is growing thin, I spin around on my right leg, held up straight and strong over my rising sun, and head the other direction–away from the Foundry, away from all the layers of separation, some subtle and some not, and toward Kinley-The-Sucker who's about to get a secret little gift swinging from my daft head, back and forth, back and forth, even if I'm the only do-do who ever knows about it.

I can't be sure, but I think my bird Ink on my right shoulder is laughing at me, at us both, the perfect pair of do-dos.

Chapter Six

THIS MORNING MARKS my least favorite of all our mandatory screenings–Gravid testing. And since early morning hours make the best time for finding Gravids–whatever the hell that word means–here I am, up before the blooming suns. *Screw this.*

I step into my booth, shuffle my feet as I grump around, and finally, in submission, drop my Levana cloth. Staring at the symbol, a blue disk with wispy cloud-like fingers swirling out around it, I can't help but wonder what it means.

Who designs such things? And why do I belong to Levana and not Salus like Baylor John? *Baylor, ugh.*

That particular fool makes me feel uncomfortable, leaving a metal, jagged cut in my mouth like a poorly sharpened rust-covered knife, despite the fact that Salus is the closest thing we in Levana know to a partner kith. With non-malicious indifference, we don't help each other out, but we don't hurt each other, either. We are, in general, crazy fast runners. They are unparalleled jumpers. We respect each other's talent in the Heats and occasionally acknowledge it as a clan by signing Levana in their direction after a big win to show our support or at least our absent hatred.

Once, I secretly watched a Heat that was so bad, so big, so powerful that Elder Khaan half made the Salus sign to their Elder out of honor for saving his life. Took both of those master alphas to slaughter a bastard of a dragon as a pair.

Damn, I was a bairn at the time I found the visor and saw the whole thing go down. What a glorious victory. The same battle that melted Elder Khaan's face. Small price to pay, I'd say.

First, he tamed the dragon with swirling balls of fire, and just when the rain started and put the fire out–my mentor most certainly doomed to die–the Salus Elder jumped over and slammed a blade of flaming steel through that dragon's skull.

Awesome. One day, I'm going to tame a dragon with its own fire. Won't that be fun?

But that's crazy…making someone else's sign. The thought sends chills down my spine.

Yet to be honest, Baylor drives me nuttier even though I can't figure out why. Why should I care if he's so sweet and simple? Why does one glance from him make me feel slimy? Like I owe him something precious, like I want to crawl under the sand and pretend it never happened.

What? What never happened?

Attempting to focus my attention elsewhere, on anything other than him, I catch the reflection of my body in the glass and stare. Slowly, I follow the long curve of my legs to where they join my groin. The tender smoothness of my pelvis draws out a want within me. It's almost like I sense it's a special part of my otherwise Ink-covered body that should be looked upon with importance. But even as the thought enters, I push it aside. *How ridiculous, Isla Jane. Get a grip.* Today is just too busy for thinking.

First, I have my Gravid appointment—terrible. Then I have the mouth scraper—horrible. I should still be snug as a bug in a rug for hours.

Then the other 53s, who are lucky enough to have an Ink allotment this week, have their appointments with their Ink dealers while I head back to the Foundry with the rest of the BRÉ red card brat pack to do the first cross and react tests with the new liquids from the virgin tissues. *Virgin?* Such a weird word. I wonder what it means. Anyway…

Tuesdays, like it's some incentive to do this crap work for the day, the red assignees always jump around excited about having the whole building to themselves, which is stupid since we never step outside of our general area on those days either.

As I pull my Gravid tube out, I hear a squeal of delight from down the hall. I guess we have a winner, winner, chicken dinner—Gravid to the right of me, four doors away. *Harley, you lucky creep.*

My ears, these magical horns, pick up things that others totally miss, like the subtle vibrations that announce a confounder's arrival during a Heat, like Harley's absurd squeal of delight. So not only am I the first to know that Harley Mae turns a pink strip, but I also estimate, with almost pinpoint accuracy, she's four booths down on the right side. *Bitch. Piss off, you.*

So I guess I will never see that know-it-all again like all the Gravids before her. *At least she will never slow me down again.*

Easily, I envision the smirk infect her round face like a virus and spread from her lips to her cheeks and then engulf her eyes before it moves on to her plain brown hair. The same boring hair which never braids smoothly, swinging back and forth excitedly in anticipation of the prize she has just won. Officially done collecting colored beads of hardly any value to her now, she dances the dance of the Gods. And her snooty nose, still twitching up from the viral load of her pleasure growing too fast to culture, will remain high in the air and no longer smell scaled biome elixirs.

What a snob. That pink strip buys her and her dish-face a life of luxury and peace. No more work, no more red cards, no more bacterial imbalance issues, no more wondering about the creatures and their slicing tusks or claws out there in the Frightening that will eat her if the bacteria on her skin don't eat her first.

Good for her, I think. But then I don't.

Something about the word "Gravid" makes me feel nervous. It's almost like I sense a lie in it somewhere. It tastes like a sweet square that falls in the garbage with just a faint hint of dirt. But none the wiser, I eat the whole stinking thing before anyone lets me in on the joke.

And it smells rotten, too, just like when Baylor, that gamma from Salus, swears he hasn't taken in a new bairn. I recognize that look on his faker face well enough to figure out he's covering up the truth.

I imagine his light brown eyes, so clear like acetone, oozing sweetness and clarity and honesty, and I shudder with disgust. Here I go again wanting to crawl in the sand from those eyes of his: so clear yet so thick, sticking to me like tar. The same eyes which give him away every time he tries to pull a fast one on me. That makes me even sicker than the innocence stamped on his tender face framed by his soft cheeks that surround his full lips.

Sometimes I swear he wants to put his mouth on me–disgusting. I am no square any more than I am a fish. *Whatever. That's his problem if he can't tell a lie to me and looks like a pillow that eats other people.*

As I think about lies and truth, my thoughts can't help jumping around. I try to reel them in, but sometimes it's hard. So I start wondering again.

Where do all the Gravids live after all the squealing about that freaking pink little piece of useless paper? I never see them again after the pink card. Surely they have to sleep somewhere, I realize. But nobody ever asks where because immediately all their Elders and sibs get double Inked and enough squares and boxes for five years.

I can't even imagine that–a whole five years.

Since, like most of us, I will only live to the good old age of thirty or thirty-five, that sounds like a very big deal to me. Although I can never share this with anyone else, I can't resist doing the math in my brain.

"That's about fifteen percent of all the food and water she will ever eat in her whole life," I blurt out foolishly, briefly forgetting I am not supposed to know much about numbers.

I scan around to make sure no one heard me. Even when I'm alone, I have to worry about being overheard. And the lights always flashing red. Have they caught me?

No metal gun splits open my chin, so I decide I must have gotten away with it, this time anyway.

Subtly, I press down twice over my chest to make a sign for Elder Khaan, as if he still lives, to show him I will do better keeping my secrets. As I do this, it dawns on me that I will never tell anyone if I turn anything pink, my new least favorite color. Because if one day the unthinkable happens, I want to be the first one to chew on the idea of a life of grandeur for a few minutes as I stare gratefully at that pink piece of luxury-offering paper, keeping my secret all to myself. Even if only for a moment. A moment inside another moment, perhaps?

For a minute, I ponder the meaning of the color pink. Blush. Fuchsia. Coral even. All these names I know that mean pink. But pink is just pink, isn't it? A little like red but not quite so dark and deadly.

So is it less, or should I say it's more? I just can't be sure yet.

Will a permanent pink card mean less or more of a life for Harley?

A life inside another life, maybe?

My thoughts, soaking in decaying pink, return to Harley's shouts of pleasure at her good luck. *I won't scream like her.*

I will do better than her, I swear it, with her boring brown hair and eyes that can't keep a secret if her life depends on it, better than her supposedly bright mind that has yet to impress me. I will keep it all inside–Gravid strips and Gravid stains, all for me, just like everything else.

Reaching up, I touch my fine plaits. They have held so many secrets too–ones for Kinley, for me, for so many. I guess Kinley won the big fat prize of another few months of disease-free life here in the City of Sick when I dropped that probiotic covered bead on her square last night.

Fool. It should have been her final night in the City, but she will never know it.

Well, I guess that makes me the fool and Kinley the bearer of my fool's gold. *Oh whatever.* I am so annoyed I could scream, but why bother? The bells ringing all over town would drown them out, so I just clench my teeth and growl as the folks cry out, "A Gravid. A Gravid. A Gravid, yeah!"

Who gives a crap really? *It's just a pink piece of paper.*

My face burns, red hot inside another layer of deeper, darker red–crimson, scarlet, rouge even.

I pull my womb cloth up and head to the mouth scraper, stomping my feet loudly. I feel almost better. Almost. Until I remember what comes next–the scraper. I hate the scraper; I really do.

Somehow, I make it to the BRÉ on time for the next round of gambling with my life. Once I get there, my stomach drops to the floor like I've drawn a useless poker hand without any face cards, because I am all out of gold now.

Eliza Rachel, that treasure who the monitors scanned twice yesterday, is nowhere to be found.

"Has anyone seen Eliza Rachel?" I ask, forcing the words to sound light and easy while they slip gently out of my flat mouth under my flat face as I sit down in my titanium seat and lock in. I glance round; so many positions are empty. Globes upon globes of titanium and glass that have nothing inside them. Empty–like cells without a nucleus, suns without a center, planets without a lava core, and oceans without krill to sustain the food pyramid. We are so fucked.

Melissa Beth, my cross and react partner today, answers, "Oh yeah, didn't you hear? She got a rest and relaxation assignment delivered to Enlil quarters last night."

I put my fingers over my lip and flatten my face further.

"You okay, Isla Jane?"

"Sure. Fine. You?" I look at the floor and imagine I have just tamed a two-horned dragon-like beast in a Heat with swirling balls of fire. Then I sincerely find my smile because that feels so much better than emptiness.

"Usual, I guess. Good news for Eliza Rachel, don't you think?" Melissa pushes her head back, and even though I can't see it, I know the Ethernet cable just climbed inside her simple mind.

"Good news?" I roll the imaginary bead I was just awarded for my kickass mutant monster slaughter in my hand and grin cheek to cheek.

"The resting assignment sounds wise." She blinks and moves her body slightly, and I know she is almost paralyzed by the machine.

"Wise?" is the only word my lips, frozen up like this, are able to form because I am losing my grip on the moment of peace.

"Sure. To be honest, she's been moving slowly lately. Hopefully, they can help her." Melissa shrugs and starts humming some tune. She doesn't realize it, but if I were a betting girl, I'd say she is soothing herself while her neurons sizzle. And as that robotic bastard integrates at a cellular level down her neck, through her spine, and across all of her major neurological synapses, her higher brain has no idea that criminals are robbing her of something no one should be able to take from her. But her unconscious mind is fully aware she is being violated.

She smiles at me even though we are almost enemies, and I give her the most reassuring glance I can. She swallows, and her shoulders relax, lost in the absolute lack of awareness of what is being done to her as she surrenders control of the only things she owns–her mind and body.

The pretend bead I just won in my imaginary Heat falls out of my hand and rolls out of sight like it actually existed before I lost it.

Melissa Beth's blind faith scares me even more than the idea of the medicals–the mysterious robed men I have yet to meet.

"Where are the medicals?" I want to ask but bite my lip instead. Trying not to taste metal again, I stop my teeth from going too deep into the soft tissues.

All day, I chew and chew on my lip, now more rubbery than soft, trying *not* to think about Eliza and where she has gone. But without fail, all I think about is her, whose absence contaminates my entire awareness while I cross and react bacterial strains, trying *not* to think about the sound the scanner made with her inside yesterday.

Can it be a coincidence? I don't know. *Please, Gods. Please.*

A few of my biome elixir combinations react today. Two of them change colors momentarily before they create minor explosions. Thankfully, I put them out before they really get going or the chief robot, the shiny, brand new but same-sounding bitch, intervenes.

With each reaction, overseer Steve rushes over all excited and foaming at the lips.

"What color, Isla Jane? What color? Any color? If you make the right color, we all get double-Inked," he squeals, rubbing his palms back and forth to keep them from shaking.

And double-skagged, too, you freak in withdrawal. I just grunt.

"Well?"

"Green, then went brown right before it blew," I say, hopeful for the others it is the correct reply.

He moans and places his hand over his stomach.

The monitors, watching us with their missing eyes, type in their little white machines and shake their heads. I hear one of them mumble, "Dead. As good as dead." He sighs and walks away.

At shift end, trying to *not* think about Eliza, the wrong-colored serums, and Mozek who seem to be hiding more than they reveal, I rush home. Maybe if I hurry fast enough, I can catch a few minutes of Heat simulation after racing up the seven flights of stairs to my flat.

Because of one of Elder Khaan's service medals, Levana keeps the honor of living in one of the best units on the outskirts of the city. And since we win enough Inks to maintain our position of status, I suspect we will always live here. Unless we outgrow it size-wise, of course. Since I am now the highest-ranking Levana who decides which bairns to take in, that will never happen. Never. Unless I go berserk Alice-fish out of control, anyway.

Blinking my eyes twice for effect, I am thankful they still close.

Time to turn my brain off and have some fun.

My sweet little pad connects into the central corridor for my grouping where we meet nightly for tabulation and simulations or to celebrate winning a Heat. And in case of a citywide emergency, it serves as the Levana meeting suite where the monitors can find us and escort us to safety.

"Safety–now that's a funny word," I scoff. When does a monitor ever display concern about my safety? And where could they possibly escort us? Out to another city on another planet? *Freaking jokers.*

Before he died, Elder Khaan occupied the central alpha suite to be more accessible for teaching the others how to use the simulators. But not anymore. Now it's mine.

And now what's left of him is bumping around in space. *Space–whatever that means.*

So as Levana's highest living ranking sib, I inhabit the quarters.

In my living space–a circle with a radius of about twenty meters–are multiple layers within layers just like everything in the City of Circles. Along one side of the outer ring are cabinets and shelves made of a hard material I don't really have a name for. Directly across from these storage compartments is my bed, a round, steel platform one foot off the white stone floor. Inside that circle are a few stools and tables and chairs, all as simplistic as possible to serve their purpose.

But the innermost ring, the heart of my quarters, is a collection of machines that belong to the whole family. These machines called thraex portals must weigh upwards of a few tons and are held in place by too many rods and wires and tubes to describe. I guess it is like a nest of robotic snakes that coil and loop around the most protected part of this nest in such a way that the devices are doubly encased. Machines inside machine perhaps. Who knows? Who cares?

But here is where I do my most important and rewarding assignment: teach my siblings to battle. Like Elder-Khaan did for me before these assholes took him from me. To honor him, I take the work seriously. Besides, if I don't, it is possible no one else will. And I'm a bigger fan of possible than impossible these days. In fact, someone has to care an awful lot, and that sucker happens to be me. But…to be honest…it is the one sucker job I like best of them all.

Now my prior mentor's job is my job. Despite the burden of it, teaching the bairns how to engage the massive titanium device–a much larger, self-contained version of the machine I use when working the biome elixirs–remains my one lasting joy. One even the skag can't take from me.

I know that stinking machine that transports us into conjoined consciousness of a Heat mind-battle almost as well as I know myself. Almost. Instinctually, I just get how it works, intuitively understanding how to make it do things. I feel it, sense it, alter it, and mold it into an extension of my body. Like I am it, it is me, like it always has been. So without even trying to explain my vibrational aptitude for controlling the thraex, I show the little ones how to follow suit.

Of all my pupils, one excels the most, far outpacing the others. When he connects in, I witness the same thoughts go across his face as mine. He is the same as me in the machine, inherently adaptable, able to function inside the portal device in a way that few of the others can even grasp.

Almost like he is part machine. *Part machine?* The idea sounds crazy to me, but apparently the Mozek are part machine. Machinoid is the proper term, I think. Rumor has it that's why they do not age, why they cannot die.

And according to Elder Khaan, that's where the idea of the implantor in the back of our necks came from. Using it as an interface port, they learned to communicate with us and understand our ways, translating our emotional thought processes through a complex connection inside the chief robots and recording it in some massive computer server. Although I have never seen it, rumor has it that somewhere in this city is a queen robot, sovereign to all the chiefs, who manages this massive interface of computers that acts like an internet of internets. Almost instinctually, I rub my neck and swallow. I don't want to meet this queen.

Back to my protégé, I bring my thoughts, and I feel better instantly.

During one of our sessions together, while wearing an acrylic glass observational visor so I could see and feel what he was experiencing, I witnessed him, from inside his own perspective, alter the structure of his holographic gladius blade. His subtle change made it much more effective by adding a curve and a hinge in the center portion of the blade.

Immediately, the six-year-old expert slaughtered his ten simulated adult opponents in less than four minutes. Outmatched, they were never able to comprehend the angle his blade attacked from. Unprepared and clueless, they crumbled to the ground; the session was over before it began. Awesome.

He called the device a sica and laughed.

Amazed he had discovered what Elder Khaan called the Dyer Principle without my help, I cursed the faulty simulator, trying to act like it was an error in the program. But I knew better; it was not.

His ingenious move reminds me of the first time I altered the way my legs functioned while connecting into my simulator. It was late, way past the sleep bell, and I was working one-on-one with Elder Khaan. Without thinking about how it might be impossible, I surrendered to my connection with the machine, rewiring my limbs at a subatomic level, making them move faster. Of course, I laughed thinking it was a trick to amuse me by my mentor.

Astonished, Elder Khaan threw his visor on the floor, and it shattered.

In between giggles and hollers, he made me swear to never tell my little secret to anyone with any authority and explained the theory of manipulating the inherent magic running through my blood via the Dyer Principle.

Simply put, place all my attention of the effect I desire in my imagination and then express some positive emotion or gratitude for my success in doing so, and voila, I've internally reprogrammed myself to be able to do it in real life just as I had imagined. He always said, *"If you can imagine it, then you can do it. The only question that remains is how to call it forth into physical manifestation."*

It sounds absurd when I try to explain it, but it works almost every time. Guess it works for Cale, too, that adorable little bugger.

I was maybe ten years old the time I figured it out. Cale is only six.

Bit by bit, I show the little ones how to modulate their nervous systems, too. Never understanding how or why, I augment their ability to race with a hint here or there.

My little protégé, Cale, is the fastest runner I have ever seen. In six more months, he will outpace me; I am sure of it. But no one, especially not him, ever needs to know that. He thinks it's just a fun little game and has no idea the power of his developing nervous system.

In six months… The time frame swallows me in Elder Khaan. *It will be six months since he died, next week.* I moan in pain, so lonely here without him.

I look down to my right ankle just as his disfigured face fills my imagination. Deep in my insides, I push back a spasm, almost like I need to cough or vomit. Then I hear his voice clearly in my mind. *"Don't you listen to them, Isla."* Dead or alive, he's still the only one who ever calls me this. No Isla Jane, no kith sign, just Isla. He said it with such sincere softness.

Without even trying, I see the familiar arch of his one good eyebrow as he scans my facial expression for information while he reads me like I'm a book. Not the picture book but the unedited, original, outlawed version. The *unnecessary* version no one can read because I must be full of words that only he bothers to try to understand.

Also without wanting to, I think back to one of those nights I tiptoed down the central corridor to find him just like Cale does for me now. Weepy-eyed and tender, I needed him to make me okay. As he cradled me tightly in his one strong muscular arm, my skin itching at the seam across my waist from my clothes, he sang me a song only we knew.

"So take these eyes,
    And give them sight.
    That search for you,
    On the hope you might.

. . .

My dawn. My only dawn.
My dawn. My dawn.

Your glowing beauty,
Framed in fight.
And precious rays,
Of warm delight."

The lyrics rolled gracefully off his wise tongue while his swaying made me feel safe, pure, and whole. His eyes, sparkling like precious jewels, covered me with a fine emotion I yearn to have again. It's the same feeling I have no word for. The unquenchable ache inside me that motivates me to search for the elusive answers to my neverending questions. All of them aimed at finding the same answer, the only answer that matters. The one I know exists. I am sure of it. But as of yet, I still don't know how or where to find it so that I can call it forth into the physical realm. Maybe it isn't physical? Maybe it's beyond physical.

And when the feeling of his smiling voice rocks me, I want to drift off to deep, deep sleep. The kind of sleep filled with overflowing dreams of comfort, so unlike my waking reality. The memory of the soft, soothing warmth of his bare skin against my tender white waist sends another one of those jerking motions through my body which reaches out to feel his supportive hold.

No one touches me like that anymore, tenderly with such encouragement and honesty. Shit, no one touches me at all. No one showers me with faith that somehow I will make the right choices, pivoting perfectly with all the best moves at the right time. No one convinces me that against all odds this will all be okay, that I am okay and worth holding on to.

On some level, I suspect he knew the answer I am still searching for; I am almost sure of it even though he never told me. Almost.

I finally arrive at quarters, unable to remember the journey home spent lost in reflection. But I must have run the whole way because my lungs ache and sting. Just as the sleep warning bell rings, I reach the top.

Quickly, I toss my squares onto the table for my sibs who seem to need them the most. They scramble out of the simulators, trying to regain control over their flimsy limbs, still battling over who gets what square. Miniature parmulas, wooden or iron swords, leg weights, confounders on the screen are all but forgotten.

The second warning bell rings. My sibs quickly offer the Levana hand sign, two fingers pressing down over their heart twice, and move on.

Cale Jacob, both the only Jacob I have ever met on this planet and my star pupil, gives me his best smile, which shines like a glorious sunrise out his titanium-gray eyes and announces that I will surely survive another day. Now that he is with me anyway. A flutter goes through my chest as he turns to close the door leading to his bare white corridor. He salutes me in his special, intimate way, and the feeling intensifies. My cheeks get warm, and even though I try to suppress it, a genuine grin spreads across my usually expressionless face.

Effortlessly, he returns the look, and I melt like serum all over the floor. Wonderful. That is Wonderland. The closest thing I know to truth or perfection.

Cale. His name reverberates through my being, and I shiver in the most lovely of ways. *Cale...I... Cale...I... Cale, you must know that I...*

The thought is incomplete but almost formed. *Cale...I...*

I sigh, deep and gladly, so pleased that Elder Khaan took him in when he was just a small youth. *Cale...I... Cale...I... Cale, you must know that I...*

At six years, he's already up to seven Inks. That, of course, I couldn't care less about, but for that adorable smirk of his while he swings his iron weapons like a master warrior, I think I would race up fourteen flights and hand over all my squares at once. Not to mention divulge every secret thraex portal trick I have ever acquired.

Cale...I... Cale...I... Cale, you must know that I...

He's going to be good in battle. Deadly, unstoppable, undefeatable.

It's just a whisper behind the heavy metal door, but I think I hear, "Heart you." Even though that's nonsense bairn talk, it makes perfect sense to me.

Unable to resist, the thought returns. *Cale...I... Cale...I... Cale, you must know that I...*

Softly, I put my two fingers to my lips and then tap them over my heart twice in return just like Cale always does. Next, I place them on the door, hoping that they might reach through the wall between us and touch him even though that's impossible. But then again, sometimes I've believed as many as six impossible things on the days I spend in Wonderland.

"Heart you, too," I whisper back as if they were real words.

Then I seal off the alpha space of the seventh floor of building Forty-Three B where I sleep and dream and hide my secrets in my clandestine City of Tricks.

Chapter Seven

WITH THE SWEET *"HEART YOU"* from Cale reverberating in my head, I seek out my medical book. As I flip through the pages, I examine each of the sections quickly to find the right one for Kinley. There are so many pictures that I always gasp when I scan the pages like this.

Finding the best matching section to examine the images, I see the word "liver" at the top of the page showing people colored the same yellowed-hue as her. *Great. That matches one of the shelves I walk past while working in Biome Repair Elixir all the time.* "Liver. What is a liver? Liver–one who lives. Guess Kinley is a liver," I whisper as I flip through the next few pages.

What strikes me as the most amazing thing about my book is how odd the photos of the people look. Every one of these fools from Home appears completely different with variety in ways that I have never even thought possible. And unlike all of us survivors, these humans have countless physical flaws. The proper word for such physical imperfection is ugly, I think.

Of all the 53s I know, none of them are ugly. In fact, they are all strikingly beautiful in comparison to these folks. Such a shame–people so doomed and unattractive at the same time. Yet even more incredibly, very few of these humans have more than one or two Inks. I thought, before the war, that most people had numerous Inks, but I just can't remember anymore. Why can't I remember that?

Little to no Ink. Ugly faces. Maybe we have been here longer than I realize. I think back to my robot who never tells me what year it is. Only the date. *Weird.*

After so many hours of trying to understand, I decide the only reasonable assumption is that they must be from a different, isolated part of Home that no one escaped. No one here looks like them at all. In fact, most of us look similar to each other: same colored skin, only a few colors of eyes and hair.

The dark skin that some of these humans have appears satiny and soft like a precious blanket. It is gorgeous and warm and soothing. Their eyes hold a hundred shapes and endless colors just like their hair.

Some even have red strands. *Red equals dead.* Must be really bad to have red hair.

Incredible. They have short and long hair too, but so far, I have not found a single braid in this entire text. Occasionally, their hair curls like the loops that mark the street signs in the Washing Zone.

If they lived here in the City, they would have to either be bald like the Elders and Ink dealers or have braids like me. And I can't even determine their class because they don't have any plaits, let alone complex weaves or beads to prove their status. And since they have few to no Inks to declare their valor, importance, and overall worth, I am totally lost to their status. Heck, for all I know, they are all considered the same class and carry the same rank (ladder, not stink).

I imagine this atrocity and shudder. Without my braids and beads declaring my value, I might as well be executed. They are the only things that keep me going. To be without them would be as horrible as making Elder and the hairdresser wax-shaving my head. The monitors can just kill me, please.

I glance back at my book and let it consume me again. Some photos show big, swollen bodies. Their skin rolling in ways I have never seen before, draping down on top of rolly-skinned thighs. Above this particular section, I read the term "obesity" and wonder what it means. I have never crossed any bacteria on any shelf for that. What kind of imbalance can possibly cause that? Is there a germ that might infest me and make me swell up with obesity–the condition of being obese? What does obese mean? It sounds painful. I try to break the word down into smaller parts but can't.

As I scan the section for depression, I can't help but notice the emptiness on their flat faces behind their gaping eyes. No matter what color or shape they hold, I see a penetrating sadness, a mortal wound so deep I cannot name it or hope to save them from it with all the stitches I have ever sewn. It looks like the feeling I experienced when the new Foundry magically appeared after blowing up. *No* trapped in a thousand more *nos* and coated in *nevers* plus a slap.

Ugh. If I could fix every one of those dropped expressions on their faces, I would. I swear it; I do. Even though I realize how futile and stupid it would be to help these Inkless people whom I have never met.

Shit, even if I risk a trip to the kill fields, I want to help them fill the intense vacuum inside. Then I can hope that maybe, maybe someone would care enough to do the same for me one day.

My cheeks flash red at the ridiculous idea, and curses start exploding in my mind. *Idiot. Fool. Jackass.*

Crap, I better get my act together. I have more important things to think about. Setting intentions like that will either–poof–turn me into a bigger sap like Baylor or shoot me out in space. *Space–whatever that means.*

Here comes Baylor's jagged knife again. I take a deep breath hoping it will keep all the sand from choking me when I shove my head in the ground underneath my feet. Disgusted with myself, I feel mad, frustrated at his innocence, furious with his clarity as imaginary dirt excoriates my tender eyeballs, exposed from my lack of eyelids. Ugh,

I'm such a fucking fish, and my bloated heart giggles at my mind because she has taken over and does not plan to let loose again. *I am so screwed.*

But there's something else underneath these raspy emotions, something that I don't know how to explain despite my best attempts. Preferring rage than this new emotion, I just go back to angry. Thankfully, fury makes more sense than the other feeling I can't describe, and my mind gathers a little more grip in this battle between its flawless logic and my wounded heart.

Returning to my book, I forget about Baylor.

Maybe it was something in their squares and boxes that caused them to roll out in such weird ways or look so sad before the Global War. I pull out tonight's square to inspect it. I take it in small, dry, flaky bites to make it last longer before I return to the page on depression.

My cheeks flash fire-hot again, and I change my mind, *woot, woot–score one for the brains*, deciding it wiser to let those fools wallow in their depression. I am not the cause of it, so why should I care what they suffer from? Besides, they probably deserve it for whatever they have done to end up in a remote section of Home: criminals, deviants, creeps. Irmin assholes like Jaxston Steve or the equivalent of it, I bet.

But despite my anger, at page one hundred and thirty-five, I stop dead in my tracks. I stare wide-eyed, attempting to make sense of it as my pulse increases.

The page-one-hundred-and-thirty-five woman appears about my age and has a perfectly smooth swelling just around her belly button. She glows, radiant as the power of two suns in one and full of health as she supports the round fullness of her body unmarked by any Ink. Even her eyes suggest peace and happiness as she touches this obviously diseased bubble that she holds with such affection. *No Ink. No Ink. No Ink. Unbelievable.*

How can a swollen deviant be so happy? She must be some other class from some far away country? But where?

And even though it's probably a disease I can catch just by going near her, my pounding heart forces me to want to reach into the photo and touch her just like Cale through the titanium door. *Impossible.*

Her beautiful swelling feels light and sweet just like when Cale says *"heart you"* under his breath, making me want to cry and smile and laugh all at the same time. *I want her impossible swelling to fill me like it fills her.*

And unable to resist the pull of it, a familiar thought returns. *Cale...I... Cale...I... Cale, you must know that I...*

Trying to soothe myself and simultaneously complete the thought, I reach down to my rising sun and think of Elder Khaan. If he were still alive, I would ask him why I feel so overwhelmed and full of wanting when I look at this woman. This lady who looks nothing like me yet makes me want to become just like her anyway. *Impossible.*

My pulse pounds like a drum in my ears with an intoxicating beat that I can no longer deny, and my pupils dilate even further as I touch her image again.

But then a rustling down the corridor steals my attention.

Quickly, I stash my secret book back in its secret place before I am discovered. For the book, I might get a public beating in the kill fields. Even if I promise I have never seen it before, they will probably tie me up and whip me while I beg for my life before letting me go. But for my letters in the margins, they will surely melt me on the spot.

I don't need any proof to convince me of that since I was there when they deactivated her bacterial balancer and necrotized Ashland Mae for a crime far less severe. When I flash back to that day, I remember thinking, *She is asking for it. How can she be so stupid? Everyone knows that writing your name equals...*

She was nothing more than a pile of rotten flesh and goo before I could even finish the thought.

I cough and swallow the slime in the back of my throat when I realize that I can spell my name along with twenty or so other words thanks to Elder Khaan.

Grinning proudly as though I thought of the brilliant hiding spot for my deadly treasure, I stash it away. In fact, I have no idea how this medical book found its way to this spot where it has remained hidden for who knows how long.

As the barely audible knock-knock pings my heavy metal door, I jump although I don't know why. I heard the undeniable vibration of those perfect pitter-patter feet about ten seconds before the knock came, trying to decide whether or not to turn back. Gods, I would recognize that soft shuffling sound anywhere. Even in the high winds of the dunes, most likely.

The same thought again. *Cale...I... Cale...I... Cale, you must know that I...*

Warmth infuses my chest as I open the door to view the sweet little body of Cale at my threshold, and the thought of being melted for it is lost on a spacecraft in a whole different galaxy.

With a nervous look on his face, he asks, "Can I? Just for a minute. Promise, Isla Jane, I already checked the flashing lights. No monitor."

"K, Cale," I answer even though I know it might mean my death because Cale is one year beyond the after-hours age cut off. So for the sake of being transformed into molten tissues, I should deny him. But with total abandon, I accept in this moment that I never will. Not him, no matter what the possible consequences. Besides, I already escaped my death twice with the blowouts earlier today. Why should tender little Cale make me worry?

If I fret as much as I should, my face might fall off from the pressure of it all. How much fear can one person suffer? Eventually, I just feel numb to it. So I decide if they find us together, we will be that much closer to joining Elder Khaan on the other side of this City of Fear. And is that so bad, really? Then I can finally just die like a good girl and stop obsessing about them finding my medical books and all my forbidden scribbles.

So I stifle my giggle, placing my two fingers over my lips to remind Cale to be quiet. Once the door closes again, I wink, but he looks away.

"What's wrong, little guy?"

"The wolf monsters came again for me, Isla Jane." A shudder courses through his tiny, little shoulders, too small for carrying such burdens. Big salty tears drip down his perfect cheeks, and he rushes into my arms to hide them.

"Oh sweet, sweet thing, you."

"The bad guys are bad, so bad. Those gnarly teeth, their howls, those chains, trying to bust loose."

"Oh, Cale."

"I'm so scared. Tell me I can stay till my heart slows. Make 'em go away. Please sing me Elder Khaan's song. Please. Please. Be your best friend." He looks up at me and winks.

I nod and recite the lyrics that I will treasure until the end of time. Cale's shiny eyes shut softly with sleep before I finish the first half of the first chorus.

Rising to put my ivy-Inked ear to my own door, the color the same as his precious eyes, I listen carefully. Nothing outside. The cold metal chills my ear, and a shiver spreads down my skin despite the warmth of the song that plays inside me.

It goes on.

"So take these eyes,
    And give them sight.
    That search for you,
    On the hope you might.

My dawn. My only dawn.
    My dawn. My dawn."

Elder Khaan's melody still plays so sweetly like it lives and breathes just for me.

After a few minutes of listening carefully down each corridor, I sneak Cale back to his room before they catch him in mine. As I close his door, the incomplete thought returns one last time. *Cale...I... Cale...I... Cale, you must know that I...*

Funny how an idea so incomplete almost feels complete. Almost.

Even though I should be, I'm not afraid to sway lifeless as a swinging message of warning in the kill fields before my few lousy years are up or to melt into a pile of dead tissue when they turn my bacterial balance off.

Really, what the hell do I care? Besides, legend has it that once my neck snaps or brain sizzles, there will be no more pain. And for that impossible moment inside a moment, the only moment that matters in all my years, I will finally be free from a life of misery and abuse on this planet. Wonderful. And then, like icing on the cake...whatever cake is...I will just be gone before they confiscate my rainbow hair beads, cover up what is left of my Ink, and shoot my gooey ass into space with all the other dead 53s. For a second, I laugh at the image of all of us just floating out there and bumping into one another. One big bump and grind party of death for the chief necromancer.

I mutter, "Can't have your cake and eat it, too," as if that makes any freaking sense at all. The absurdity of the phrase delights me, and I grin.

But then my face ignites, and my stomach churns. Surely the eyeless monitors will make me watch Cale die first, swiping away even my one fleeting moment of peace before I go bump in the night. Fuck!

Clenching my fist so hard that one of my nails lacerates my palm, a single drop of blood drips down my right pinkie, landing square in the center of my rising sun. Overwhelmed with grief, I want to collapse from the mere idea of Cale hurting because of me. *My fault. It's all my fault. I know it is.*

If only it could just be the two of us together forever. *Impossible.*

Slowly, I shuffle back to my room–my face flat, my eyes gaping, my sorrow drowning me like Alice's tear-river while I crumble into a useless pile on my bed. Trying to close what eyelids I have left, I turn over on my stomach and curl up like a bairn around my pillow.

Even though I am struggling to breathe, the first tear never falls.

Obviously, there is nothing and no one who can save me from this place. And if no one is going to save me, then who the hell is going to save Cale?

A thought, almost a subtle voice, pops in, but I deny it. *Impossible.*

Who the hell am I? I am no one. I am only one person. One Jane in a sea of useless Janes.

Perhaps we are all better off dead? Or perhaps there is another, better way? Right now, I am just too ruined to bother.

Who knows how long I wither and tremble before the oblivion of sleep mercifully takes over and gives me reprieve from the City of Impossible.

The next morning, I awake, dry and gasping with itching, irritated eyeballs, spewing curses while I prepare for my Ink session with my Ink dealer.

Stepping out of my quarters, I slap my cheeks twice on each side to get them pink and ready, and then I plaster a flat expression across my face. The corners of my mouth are heavy, and I struggle to draw them up to a level position. Then I remember who is depending on me to survive my Ink session intact: Cale.

Cale...I... Cale...I... Cale, you must know that I...

"Thanks Gods I am so happy," I fume as I step out the sliding glass entry door and into the depressing City of Sink.

Chapter Eight

EVEN DISTRACTED by my terribly itchy eyes, I can't escape the sensation that some-one, more than one someone actually, is watching me today. For the tenth time since locking in my Ink chamber seat, I glance quickly side-to-side over my shoulder to find no one, nowhere, except Jane-do-do, my bird on my right shoulder, always watching me. *Maybe I imagined it?*

Jane's rocket-like shape honors the owl, a beautiful and fascinating animal that lived before the war. I imagine how cool it would be to have a real owl swoop down and hoot at me while he flies by.

"Hoo, hoo," I whisper in Jane-do-do's honor.

And even though she's totally silent and utterly still, I know that gorgeous goddess of a creature could fly right off my shoulder if she wanted to. But being such a thoughtful beast, she stays to protect me. Guess she's a sap–all heart and no brain.

Subtly, I flap my arms twice to show her that I can fly away as well, if I want to anyway.

But…also like her, I'm secretly a royal spy from some avian world so much more advanced than these evolutionary flunkies who can't even fly, sticking it out on this horrific assignment from a top secret society that lives inside and underneath the walls. Out of sheer dedication to fixing up this shithole and saving all the poor little two-legged buggers who have less covert-operative skills than I do, I hold out to complete my classified mission. Some days, I even pretend to be a fish to make this charade more convincing for the bad guys.

The fairy tale, so lovely, cracks my weary face, and a smile breaks through my depression.

Reaching up to check my port, the metal ring in the back of my neck which allows my nerves to directly connect into my various machines, I take two deep breaths and count to ten silently because Gods know I am having way too much fun and might blow my cover.

Muttering, "Hoo, hoo," I focus on Jane-do-do once more, tracing her outline tenderly with my finger. I imagine it's pretty outrageous, but sometimes I really do think Jane-do-do on my shoulder watches out for me just like my rising sun does. The sun warms my front, but Jane-do-do guards my back. So while my rising sun pulls, Jane-do-do pushes. And together, the three of us keep going–back to finish another red card, back to that gut-wrenching Ink stage, back to building Forty-Three B for the sweet look in Cale's gunmetal-gray eyes, and back to steal more deadly drops to save the clueless liver named Kinley.

Maybe one day, Jane-do-do will fly me back Home, and we will celebrate our victory over these featherless fools.

While I trace the outline of one of my other favorite Inks, a purple flower from the old world named a lily, sadness consumes my heart just as my wings fail me, and I crash to the ground. *Thud.*

The petals, oblivious to the torture of this life, open up to me, sharing the impossibility of penetrating hope, a concept that no longer exists here. The colors, so lovely, so bold, so welcoming, mix and then drape and trail over my left flank like a procession of tender optimism. *Fools.* Clueless to reality, they are trapped in a past robbed of its future by the hate that destroyed our Home. I don't need a mirror to see where they go, these snake-like messages of beauty, because my grief already followed their wasted promises, flowing down my back like never-ending tears of acid rain.

I miss you, Elder Khaan. I really do. And Home, I miss you, too.

In a whisper, I confess, "Elders are supposed to be managing squares, boxes, and Ink. But not you. You were about something so much more, something so big that I can't find an adequate word. But I want to name it; I need to claim it and sing it out to the others so they, too, can learn the song."

I say this like he can still hear me. *Who's the fool?*

Like an over-soaked sponge that must be either dropped or squeezed, I start dripping, trying to find him and our song.

"Elder Khaan, the melody of you comforted me just like Cale's childish talk when he pats his chest twice, only even more. But the other 53s can't hear me, or better put, hear you leaking through me. They only hear my Ink, since without it they are dead, but remain deaf to the greater message, the beautiful lyrics, so oblivious to the value of the Isla underneath my Ink."

I might slap myself, but what's the point?

"All they want is Ink, Ink, and more Ink. Like I ooze for you and Cale, they ooze for Ink," I say. Damn, talking like this will surely get me killed. *Stop it, Isla.*

I wring my hands, trying to dry the innumerable holes inside me, but it only makes things worse because each newly emptied space just offers me more portals to suck up more suffering to add to the last. I might swirl like this for ages, but the light turns green to remind me that the Ink dealer attends my chamber next. I take a deep breath and climb out of the hamster wheel in my broken heart so I can apply a proper mask to my face. I want to stroke my hair, but I'm out of time.

The green flashes; he's almost here.

Unable to suppress my disgust, all my lilies clamp down tightly and retreat back into the buds that formed them in the first place.

I start counting again. One, two. Shit, what comes next? Three. Yes, three. Four. *Four.*

Four. The memory of my first Ink slithers in and slaps me from the past. Almost like time is an illusion and as long as I hold on to the moment, the moment still holds on to me. Perhaps one day I'll swing back and forth between the past and the present on purpose so I can avoid such terrible moments?

Four. I was four at the time, supposedly too young to remember. But I will never forget the first day when I was shown that Ink cannot be good, could never be my friend despite all the stories the Mozek teach us to the contrary.

I could recite one, probably *four* or more, but I refuse.

Flash. I'm four again. I woke up from my nap, strapped and confined, confused where I was, trying to move but unable. Some drug paralyzed my muscles. My eyelids, held apart by some cold metal device, remained open against my will. I tried to close them again and again. Small and too fragile to fight the pressure of the projector straps pressing on my neck and frozen in my own body, my mind decompensate.

The skag sedation coursing through my itty-bitty veins failed to keep me asleep like the other bairns while these odd pictures flashed in front of me, mostly too quickly to grasp, paired with a melody so gorgeous I wanted to play it over and over again. I dug into the sound, trying to ignore the images flickering, hoping against all odds that somehow I would be okay and survive this insanity.

I heard the vibration of the machine before I felt it on my skin. Again, I tried to move, tried to escape, but was helpless, trapped in my prison of coils and belts.

A presence, I can only assume now must have been the preliminary Ink dealer, stepped closer. I thought for a moment that some unsung hero would save me. But who the hell was I kidding? No one here ever saves anyone from anything.

The click, click, clicking sound of the Ink glove engaged, and I accepted that no one was ever going to save me. Immediately, an odd thought popped in about me saving myself. *Impossible.*

I tried to scream, but my vocal cords failed me. Terror washed through my tiny, fragile body. I struggled to kick, punch, break free, but it was no use. I was so helpless. Panic multiplied, and I thought that surely I would go insane. Then the needles started in.

The first puncture sliced me, and it dawned on me where I was: my first Ink session. I would receive no reprieve. Thousands of cuts would replace the first, so awful, so scary, so wrong for someone my age.

My child heart imploded and stained the floor with melted terror. My mind stepped up to the plate and cleaned up the mess while it convinced me that emotions cannot serve us, that logic is the only answer worth finding.

The Ink evacuator, a suction and irrigation system, turned on, increasing the vibration to the point where I wanted to explode. I retched, but something covered my tongue and filled my mouth to keep me from vomiting. I heaved again. Tears filled my eyes and dripped down my frozen face.

Just when I decided that I was dying, the sounds stopped. The clicking ceased, the pressure lifted off my chest, and the device left my mouth. Slime slathered down my neck, coating me with the scent of my own sickness. And the smell of it, my vomit mixed with my bacterial biome, was subtly different than before.

Tiny drops of my blood dripped down my neck, followed by a cool liquid that finally took some of the burn away. I was so afraid the adult holding me down would turn the machine back on that I did not move, did not open my eyes, did not scream, did not betray my lucidity.

I will never forget that day. *Four.*

So when I get Inked, I go somewhere else entirely. I'm like Steve, my overseer, minus his skag addiction, floating on planet Isla in the Galaxy of La-La.

Maybe one day, I will never come back. Maybe part of me is still stuck in between those moments in the past and the present as I experience it now. Who knows?

To fool my oblivious ID during these torture sessions, I hold myself perfectly still so that my Ink dealer won't keep upping my skag dose, trying to poison me with the drugs I don't want. The same drugs the others are literally willing to die for. Nor will he discover how much I hate his precious little Ink.

Hush, Isla. That's our greatest secret, whispers my inner genius. To the other 53s, the needle of the Ink machine must feel light and soothing with the colors bleeding yummy and good like tantalizing sweet squares underneath their skin while their hearts flutter and their pupils open up.

I remember Elder Khaan say, *"Any idiot can sniff out a skag freak by the way their eyes dilate under the sharp needle, Isla, moving with perfect mechanical precision, attached to the coils of the metal projector and all its tubes."*

Oh how I regret not having the foresight to ask Elder Khaan more questions about Ink, which he knew so much about. It's bizarre, now that I think about it; he understood Ink like he had worked with it in a former life on Home. *Did he? Maybe he was split between moments, between lives as well?*

The idea of a former life splashes me with a delight. A former life implies I might get a later life after this one. I rub the drop into my cheek and hang on to it. *Impossible. Or is it?*

If I could go back in time, I would ask Elder Khaan so much more, his half-finished teachings never quite enough to satisfy me while I still ache to grasp all that he could have offered so I can understand him in a way my mind can dig into forever.

Or is it my heart that will dig into him forever? *Silly fool, Isla Jane, it already has.*

If I had learned more from him, I would have even more of him to hang on to. And that pumper in my chest wants all of my mentor.

Inevitably, my thoughts shift to today's Ink stage with all those bairns and not enough kith Elders to go around. Since owning a finishing stick of flesh between your legs remains the one official rule about becoming the Elder of a kith, I don't worry about turning into a proper head of household. As beta, I am as highly ranked as possible for a female. The Levana sib next in line to be Elder is just too young.

So…unless we acquire a defector alpha male from another kith, which rarely ever happens, my clan is stuck with these beta braids for the time being.

But that Baylor wants to be Elder. I just know it. He might as well shave his head to make it official. *What an idiot, like Alice chasing that stupid rabbit that she never catches.*

But good for the bairns. Yet also good for me since then they will follow him and leave my fish-face alone.

Perhaps I will offer to shave his stupid, empty head for him?

The door slides open, and the air in the room gushes out. *Swoosh.*

I think of Jane-do-do on my shoulder and wish she could actually take flight because I would take a *hoo, hoo* over a *swoosh* any day.

But there are no *hoos* here, I'm afraid.

The ID, another hairless fool, steps in, and immediately I know something's up. Even though his features look similar, they are subtly different. His markings are identical, but this Ink dealer is not the Levana ID. His entire presence feels different. His feet sound as feathery as my wings as they shuffle lightly across the floor. Even his breathing is deeper and slower. I can almost hear his heart like it's just under his skin, open and exposed and waiting for me to shatter it. My pulse increases to match his. *Impossible.*

No hair, pencil-drawn eyebrows, and those uniformly purple eyes looking down on me with disdain to ideally complement his perfectly drawn beard. On every hairless extremity, he wears the 53 stamp proudly as if it's some kind of affirmation of superiority.

"Disgusting freak," I curse when he reaches down to touch my sleeves.

He pulls back, seemingly shocked how Inked I am for my age, but then sucks in enough air to loudly belt out the mandatory greeting. "Nice beads, Levana."

He touches my braids and then moves my head back and forth to prove that I have to let him. Although I can't say why, I think he wants to pull my braids down in some firm yet playful way.

As per protocol, I avert my eyes and roll my arms out in a position of submission. "Thank you, Levana Ink dealer. I allow it."

He probably thinks he recovers from his slip up, but he doesn't. I see it all: the surprise in his raised eyebrows and his circular mouth wanting to say something but holding it in, his nervous step, the constant checking of the flashing lights, his rapid pulse, the shifting glances about the room. If I didn't know better, I would think he expects someone to walk right out of thin air and catch him doing something naughty.

Quickly, he turns the corners up and flattens his forehead, presumably to reassure me that I've known him before. But I've never met this guy; I am sure of it. His flitter-flutter feet sweep softly toward me just like Cale.

Idiot. He's not fooling anyone but himself.

"Isla," he says with a pause before he adds, "Jane, beta of the Levana."

Suppressing my grin, I observe this subtle pause too.

"Yes, ID," I say as per our ridiculous script, acting like I have not noticed his surprise at my body, his difficulty completing a task as simple as speaking my name, his anxiety at being so close to me.

"Your request for the Ink is?" He slows his breath and fakes a yawn like I am nothing new or special to him.

Deciding to throw him a tiny, little trick, I say, "Just like last week. The same please." I yawn too, pleased as punch that this creep hasn't seen my back and has no idea why I do not wear any 53 or Levana stamps.

"Small, medium, or large? And section F or G?"

He's getting braver by the minute. Ha! The blooming idiot still thinks he has covered his screw-ups brilliantly.

Thrilled to continue the play of my little game, I add, "Large and G, of course," and inspect my fingernails as if they are as interesting as the collection of Ink that make up my anchor.

He turns me around and gasps, likely at the absence of stamps like the others wear so proudly.

"None of those crap-shots on me, which cover your absurdly hairless arms, chest, and back," I do *not* say. But boy, do I think it.

He's totally silent.

Congratulating myself on having him eating out of my palms, I give in before I get necrotized. "You remember the rose we spoke about last week? Large and in section G. Just like we discussed." I tilt my head to the side and ponder the loveliness of these split and uneven nails.

He relaxes while he digs into my words which release him from his discomfort by convincing him I have not even noticed he is new to me. And even though I am turned away, I sense his shoulders drop softly after the line of crap I throw him. *"Sucker,"* I say to myself as he claws his way back to okay.

He's smiling now; I can feel that, too.

"You can program the projector to Ink it, right?" I ask, thinking he will feel like an imbecile for one second more, which pleases me beyond measure.

But to my surprise, he answers, "Of course. I know a rose. By Ink glove, Isla"– another pause–"Jane. Okay?"

Now I'm the silent one.

"No projector for this one. It is too delicate to do properly on your lower back with the extra straps and hoses in place. Unless you want the machine and its skag, Isla"– same pause–"Jane. Of course."

Now I am the gasping fool trying to claw back to okay while my pupils dilate at the thought of a rose Inked by hand. Not because of the Ink of it but the lack of that Gods-forsaken contraption and its sickening skag designed to feed the Ink freaks like over-seer Steve and Jaxston, the evil tit from Irmin.

And the sweet, sweet smell of the rose's image in my mind envelops me, presenting the beautiful image to my heart, all rolled up and pumping out hope and joy to feed all the petals depending on it. And even something more powerful emerges within me, perhaps? *Impossible.*

No, not impossible. Faith.

All the hope in the world–impossible without faith to back it up and keep the ideal so strong and sure.

One by one, I feel my lilies erupt back open, so delighted to have a new friend en route, and I'm coated in those gorgeous little rose pricks to faithfully protect me, too. Maybe I am a rose?

Isla-Rose Jane. The beauty of the new name blossoms all around me in undeniable faith that somehow, someday even I will be okay. Even, I guess, if we never make it Home.

My heart goes into overdrive and kicks my mind right out of the driver's seat and onto the floor where she throws a tantrum.

The vibration of the machine ignites, bringing me back to this glorious reality, and I shudder with anticipation. Then I make my body perfectly still so my ID will not change his mind and strap me to the projector, that horrible device of destruction.

His fingers move up and down as he clicks the Ink glove in position. *Oh.*

For the first time ever, I am not afraid. I am excited. *Yes.*

When he pierces my smooth, white skin with his needle–one finger, two fingers, three fingers at a time–pleasure fills my cup and spills over the sides to prove it. And I can't help but wonder if this is what an Ink freak feels like every time they get done.

But I already know the answer. *Yes, it is.*

The ID finishes the wonderfully painful outline first.

Maybe I have finally flown…or perhaps swam…to the bottom of my rabbit hole?

He starts the middle shadowing next.

Perhaps I will catch a fuzzy rabbit down here?

The coloring, he saves for last.

This part hurts less, so my tired blue eyes fall asleep under his tender yet penetrating touch here in my Ink chamber, and I dream of a rabbit who leads me to a minty-breathed caterpillar who lives inside, yet between, these very walls. The queen is nowhere to be found, searching and searching for her lost roses.

Soon–too soon–he shakes me back awake to tell me my session is over.

The mid-section of my lower back rages with the glorious burn of my Ink, but for the first time in forever, this thrills me in a way I cannot quite name.

He soothes my skin with a salve, rubbing it in harder and harder until the burn is replaced with a glorious minty icy heat. The mint reminds me of something. My dream? The caterpillar, probably.

Wearing no gloves, his bare skin touches mine firmly yet softly, warm but cool. It's lovely but in a very different way than Elder Khaan's embrace. And although it feels like maybe I should, I do not pull away.

An Ink dealer has never actually touched me skin-to-skin before. Nor has a monitor, now that I think about it. It feels good, almost too good. Almost.

Unable to repress the thought, I wonder what it would feel like for his face to press into mine. Would I like it? Probably. I imagine inhaling his breath and making it my own. *Oh my Gods.*

He presses firmly into my back once more.

Thankfully, with the will of a fine warrior in battle, I remain silent and keep my face very still. Inexplicably, a warm sensation courses between my legs, the space pulsing lightly before I become aware of moisture gathering there.

Pride flashes across his flushed cheeks, almost hidden by his penciled beard, which he immediately represses. His breath becomes deep, almost like sighs of anticipation, and I sense his heart rate climb once more. The result of his work on me pleases him; I am certain.

Touching me pleases him, too; I am certain.

This oddity reminds me of his newness despite all his attempts to deceive me and convince me of his sameness, his smallness, and his lack of uniqueness. But why should he bother pretending at all?

Yet when he looks at me so fiercely this time, his tongue escaping to lightly lick his lower lip as he stares at me, I finally figure out that he's not only new, he's totally different in a way that the term "intense" fails to describe.

His eyes connect with mine, and he sees inside, not through, me. He sees the Isla minus all my labels: Levana, beta, Jane, 53. He sees the perfect nudity of my body minus my Ink. He sees the wounded Isla inside minus all the layers of pretend or protective indifference, the same Isla he wants to touch minus gloves, minus the projector, minus the confusion of skag while drawing out the moisture from within me.

Now I am the one who wants to look away and break his gaze because I realize I might feel more afraid of being seen than not being seen.

He needs to ask me something; I can feel it. So from my overflowing fountain of self-pity, I toss him another lifeline to save him–to save us both, actually–from drowning in the screaming silence of the awkward moment of aching need to touch once more.

"Because I've never seen one," I say, referring to the rose.

Looking confused for a second, he nods before answering back, "I have. Once. It was lovely, too."

I wonder what he means by "lovely, too."

Too… Like my other Inks, or what?

For a second, I think he is implying something more. But then I remember dealers don't say anything to 53s about anything other than Ink. That's the law.

But they aren't supposed to touch us, either.

And since we are really just talking about Ink, I let it slide weightlessly away from me without another thought. Even now, though, I know better. It is not weightless. It does not slide away from me. It could not because I am still wondering the meaning of such a simple yet complicated word like "too."

Too.

The heaviness of this short three-letter word crushes my chest, digs in, and rips my heart open before it stumbles and crashes with a deafening roar to the marble under-neath my woozy feet. Unlike skag, this "too" is a drug worth dying for.

But just when I think I might finally make my escape from that "lovely, too" of his, he lightly touches Jane-do-do on my right shoulder. He whispers so softly that I barely hear him. "Gaige. They call me Gaige."

"No second name? Just Gaige the purple-eyed and hairless rose maker who smells just like Elder Khaan did?"

Still intoxicated, I pretend I do not hear him and keep walking–walking away from his rose-creating fingers and needles, walking away from his impulsive glances and penciled eyebrows, away from the heat between my legs, away from his soft lips using words like "too", away from his Ink-covered bald head, his enticing colored face, his delightful touch, and his minty scent.

But most importantly, I walk away from those addictive eyes that see into, not through, me.

Terrified, I scurry back to the Biome Repair Elixir department where at least I understand the nature of the blowouts trying to kill me. For sure, this dealer, named Gaige only, represents a red card I can never dissect with my curious blue eyes.

Run, Isla, run, my inside voice warns, *before his words and his touch do actually kill you, too, you junkie.*

Still distracted by that bizarre thought when I arrive at the Foundry, I barely hear the explosion and smell the fire.

But then, I do.

Chapter Nine

NOW THAT I finally have gotten my act together, I instantly calculate this deadly boom originates from the far right side of the compound, the yellow-card region of the Foundry, Purification of Tissues. The side, which we less-than-lovingly call the Piss-POT even though none of us even remember what piss actually looks like. That place rarely kills anybody. Not today.

How long will it take to tabulate the death total? *Probably forever.*

No one will officially inform us of any specific details since they never do. *Asshole Mozek.* It's almost like they have no feelings, no appropriate connection to other beings. No heart, only hate. No kindness, only fear. *Psychos playing saviors of the galaxy. Nice. Seems reasonable.*

My head flickers back and forth, and I swallow the metallic drops of blood from my bottom lip. How long until it heals? *Probably forever.*

According to Elder Khaan, human psychos express the same brainwave response to an image of a table or a child. But torture a bairn and, all of a sudden, their brain waves go swirling all over the screen. *Maybe Mozek means evolved psycho in some language I can't translate.*

Back to the Pisser…at least disasters usually happen infrequently in the Pisser because despite those assignments being the most labor-intensive yellow cards, they are almost always the safest. Almost. Not today. The poor bastards.

Unfortunately, like a double-forked blade, less danger means less opportunity to earn Ink honors. So a yellow-card carrying 53 can usually live a few more days, but it's a life without any chance for upward mobility. With barely enough resources to survive and shanty, inadequate housing, most yellow cards seem to get assigned to the Pellonias, a group of outcasts who mostly keep to themselves. Rumor has it they compound their poverty by taking in more bairns than they can handle, keeping themselves constantly in danger of safely starving to death. Heck, I don't know whether to applaud or pity them.

After the exploding two thousand meters away ceases, I sense a vibration slow and then stop. Knowing that their large glass and metal globe has stopped rotating just like with ours the other day, I wonder if we will evacuate our area too. I start counting those around me so that I will be able to make sure we all get out. But after a few minutes, I feel the vibration of their globe return to its normal mode, and since nothing else significant happens, I assume the monitors have contained the blowout.

The monitors in my vicinity return to their tasks as if they don't know what just happened. But they do. I can feel their attention to the explosion slither across their blank faces behind their reflective glass masks before it falls to their boot-covered knees. *Thud.* Misery slides across their toes and leaves both an odor and a stain on the pavement, which they step in trying to convince me it's *not* there. The fools must think that if I believe it, maybe they will too. Or maybe they really don't give a flip? I'm just not sure yet.

Wondering what the monitors really look like under all those layers of gray metal gear, I spread my legs and open my eyelids for inspection. Once I pass, I enter the first scanner, pretending some of the very last living humans from the POT are *not* dying so close yet so far away from us.

To be honest, I try *not* to think about the heartless monitors always bossing me around and how much I despise them because I could *not* care less about their *not* feelings while I try *not* to step in the imaginary slime still clinging to their stinky gray boots.

If they hate me just because I'm human, then I get to hate them back too, don't I? It's only fair as far as I'm concerned.

After they test me, I have the honor of entering the Foundry trying so desperately to kill me again today. Lucky me, *not.* Bravely, I go to do what I do and hope I survive another red-equals-dead kind of day of concentrating those purified serums that some Pellonias just died for while they extracted them.

Whatever extracted means.

Trying to make a joke, I say, "What a Pisser." No one, myself included, laughs. *Not funny. Not good.*

Without explaining why, they quarantine off the twenty or so of us here today and march us one by one through a third scanner. This time, I am told to spit in a little white tub and scrape a small, dull blade under my fingernails. Finally, the machine clears my retina, and I'm allowed in. *Triple lucky me, not. Not good. Not funny. Not Wonderland. Total freaking madness.*

Once every few weeks or so, more than that lately now that I think about it, I look up, and a whole crew of monitors watches us BRÉ workers do our assignments. Then they furiously punch the keys on their little white machines like it's the most important event of the century.

Today is one of these finger-punching days. In fact, about ten of those creeps gather all around me while I step into my deathtrap, strap my arms in place, and allow the invisible connection diving down my port to invade my elbows and shoulders. The serum infusions and their various bacterial strains come through the small pipe, filling the clear little bottles, and I start my tests. Just like always, I remotely operate a large glass shelf of beakers and pipettes in the testing center, assigned to me by the chief robot. As she speaks to me from inside my own mind in her Gods-forsaken calm and monotone voice, she tabulates the chemical reactions and compares them to the observations I simultaneously make about the bacterial combinations.

Methodically, I cross them over. Intuitively, based on their interactions or reactions, I suggest certain variations, patterns, etc., and she usually obliges me. If an overseer, not too doped up on skag to speak intelligibly, asks me why I choose the combinations I do, I really do not have an adequate answer.

It's almost like I already know what will happen, like part of me designed this whole process to begin with. Almost. My inner voice, so proud of her little ah-ha moment, makes a suggestion. *Perhaps that's the real reason you keep taking these red cards.*

Occasionally, the bacterial strains react intensely, and the chief robot pauses so I can take additional tests of the specific mixture before placing it into a chromatograph machine. If one combination changes colors, it stops the entire line. Together, we then make three miniature bottles of the combination, which are immediately escorted to some unseen place by a whole troop of armed gun-slinging gray buffoons. Then I move on to the next strain and start over.

Boring, boring, boring.

"*What the hell are you doing?*" I almost ask one of the goons. But why bother? They won't answer me. Instead, I just bite down on my ruined lip to keep the words from coming out. I really don't feel like dying today. I am just too tired.

After all, the Mozek have just extended the red and blue cards shift by two hours a night. Next week, each kith gets two more high-risk cards per week.

As I cross and react two elixirs, both marked F, the monitors gasp like they just witnessed a miracle. One pink bubble rises to the top. "F...F...for the double Fools," I mutter. "Find something better to do. I would...if I could."

Nothing else significant happens, and even though the bubble disappears, the chief robot shuts down the entire assembly line to make extra samples of my mixture. I keep asking her why. Her response–total silence. *Bitch.*

Then the monitors type for what feels like an hour before moving on.

I overhear a monitor speak. "She's incredible. What if she's finally done it?" He moans under his breath and steps away thrusting his hips. "She's just like on the big screen. What I wouldn't pay for a chance to sponsor her ass in the gravaex. If I could afford her–"

I never hear the rest of his mantra because his eyeless counterpart punches him in the arm.

"Idiots," I grumble. Why he calls the machine a *she* is beyond me. He's never heard her voice inside my mind. Or maybe he means me? But that's impossible. Whatever. Who cares?

Returning to my samples, I cross again...back and forth, back and forth.

I might have asked the Pellonias, who are usually distant but nice enough, what

Purification of Tissues really meant years ago if not for the law that no kiths discuss their assignments with other kiths. And with all the little red lights flashing everywhere, I figure they are always watching us, recording us. So no one really understands what anyone else is doing all day long. The Mozek divide our lives up into so many little tasks that no one even sees the big picture. It's like a thousand tales inside of tales around here.

Do the monitors even know what these bacteria do? I doubt it. It's only because I can read the letters on the shelves that match my medical book that I have a clue what critically important strains I'm making or why.

Except for the favorite profound phrase of my overseer, Steve.

After making sure no one can hear me, I joke, being sure to slur the words properly. "It takes lives to save lives." I stumble for the fun of it. "All that remains of humanity is depending on you and me to turn our ruined bacteria around."

Like that pea-brain even comprehends his words, all covered in his 53 stamps. Like he's the clever boss of something other than a handful of workers who can't stand him. Yet if that minion steps out of line or I drop a bottle of our precious strains, I bet they necrotize him with me. *Fool.*

He's the top fuckface of us all. So in some ways, I feel even sorrier for him than the rest of us. That junkie thinks he's a leader, a mover, and a shaker. But all he really does is push around a bunch of 53s just trying not to die each day for a murderous boss. Pathetic traitor. Brainwashed monkey.

My overseer Steve likes to proudly list the names of all ten sections here at the Foundry like he's visited them. And since he ranks (ladder and stink) higher up on this crap totem than me, I have no choice but to believe him. My guess, though, is that all of his profound knowledge together is worth less than one flake of a sweet square, which falls in the recycle pod before some jokester trades it for crayons.

The thought forces me to laugh when I remember the time I played such a brilliant trick on Baylor after learning that he took in his thirtieth bairn. *Thirty plus now? Seriously, what a glutton.*

Everyone likes to share the rumor that if a kith leader survives long enough to take in too many young ones in a smaller building, his reward includes moving up to one of the top levels of building Forty-Four B, the most massive structure in our city that rises one hundred floors high, closest to the glass wall, just behind ours. I do not even know anyone who has ever stepped foot into that building, so as far as I'm concerned it will just be a rumor until Baylor takes his charity to such an outrageous level. Then we will finally see–rumor or not. *Thirty-two bairns, that joker.*

For fun, I am going to call him Baylice for Baylor-Alice, the supreme dough-ball. Soon, he will be asking me for squares to help him feed all those hungry Salus mouths. But thank goodness for standard issue drone wear or he will have to clothe them until he gets them all Inked as well.

If my mouth wasn't so dry and sore, I would stick out my tongue at him.

Besides, who really wants to live there, so close to the wall of separation and all the wondering that will invoke? But then again, the others don't seem to struggle with the mind swirling like I do. Sometimes, though, I wonder if they just hide it. None of the others know about my twisting mind. And it dawns on me that maybe they hide their searching too, thinking I'm not thinking, thinking all I care about is another Ink and skag.

But I'm not. I don't want Ink. I want out. I want answers. I want peace. I want the ideal I keep searching for but never find.

Cale's sweet little face fills my mind, and I smile. *Cale, you must know that I...I will always...*

On some level at least, Cale clues into this curious part of me when I scan his face to learn his mood and connect into his worries, trying to ease the fear his dreams bring to him in this unfeeling world.

Cale, you must know that I...I will always...

Why do I feel so close to him but not my other sibs, I wonder. Something special about him brings overwhelming warmth to me that the others do not. I sense his battles are my battles and vice versa. It's almost like he is a missing part of me, the other half of a puzzle I don't know how to complete.

And it was just like that with Elder Khaan, too. But he was an Elder after all, and I am not.

So why do I feel so clean and pure and motivated to ease Cale's suffering? *Cale, you must know that I...I will always...*

Why do I call him Cale, not even thinking the Jacob part of his name? And why does his face bring the words of Elder Khaan's special song to mind every time his tender-skinned hands reach out for mine like that? *As if a beta can be an Elder without a finishing stick. Wombs don't care. Elders do. That is the way it is. But not for Cale and me.*

For Cale, I am the equivalent of an Elder, but I can never say that out loud. That's another treason worthy of instant death–a beta trying to act like an Elder. Even I must admit the absurdity of such an idea.

I glare up at that pair of monitors, and they are still there just staring at me and rolling their hips around in circles like it's a move they plan to use in some Heat battle they will never have to play. To piss them off, I fight the dryness and flick my tongue at the two of them. And one of them, that ridiculous fool, drops his white device, which immediately shatters on the ground. Hoping not to get killed in retribution, I hold in my laugh and furiously lick my tongue across my upper lip like my prior motion never had anything to do with those two. A third monitor walks over and slaps the prancing pair.

"Stop looking at her," number three says and slaps them again. Guess he's the guardian of the guards.

Clearly, he's no match for the guardianship of Elder Khaan who, with thirty of us Levanas under his care, broke every Elder record of which I am aware. Until Baylor–now first in line for Salus Elder since they lost theirs at a blowout about ten months ago while he was dropping off some shipment of something. Apparently, he literally disappeared during the explosion, not a trace of him left, like he just walked right into a crack in the freaking wall. Now that's unlucky with a capital UN since he didn't even have a yellow card that day yet died in one of the blowouts.

It's almost like he was too good, too respected, too liked, too kind to be true, so something had to undo him. *Poof. Abracadabra. See him. Now, like that white rabbit, you don't.*

Maybe he was a spy like me? *Lovely thought, Isla.*

Same thing with my Elder Khaan who we lost in a freak accident as well.

At the time of their Elder's unfortunate demise, I expected Salus to challenge the Levana in a Heat retribution since most of the workers in our area that day came from my kith. But they did not, which is odd.

Bay-Alice-the-Sucker subsequently took over his grouping, feeding all his sibs with his chest Ink and just kept adding more. *Baylice, I love it.*

Smirking, I keep trudging along, ready to hear the marching feet of the monitors sent to retrieve the bodies from the Pisser. And now that I am far away from those three goons, I keep laughing hysterically at my own joke while I skip away from today's workstation, determined yet never able to forget the perpetual tragedy I see in this sorry City of Blink and You're Gone.

I get home late, too tired to move quickly tonight and still feeling deflated from today. I'm lost in thought, imagining who lived, who died, who shipped out for R&R? *Abracadabra.*

Like magic, Skylar has already powered down the simulators and cleared the alpha quarters for me. Perhaps she knows about the POT blowout and has saved me the trouble of trying to explain the unexplainable to our sibs?

My thoughts, jagged and piercing, are moving too fast to stop them. Here I go, diving down another rabbit hole, desperately seeking answers. When the monitors take the wounded away to Rest and Relaxation, how come none of them ever come back? And why do the monitors never tell us what happens? I never know if I will see someone again around here. And if a Levana sibling doesn't show up at quarters, I never hear why.

The not knowing drives me crazy. If my brain at least has some data to analyze, my poor broken heart can handle it better, handle anything, probably. But the uncertainty does me in every single time. Is my little one lost? Late? Shot? Hanging? Starving to death in some alleyway? I never learn at tabulation, either. I just punch in the little dots and put the white machine in the slot before it sucks up into its tube.

I hate uncertainty. I do. *But sometimes I hate certainty more.*

When I stole a glance at Kinley earlier... *Man, her liver problem...*

Certainly, the general repair strains have obviously failed her. Same thing happened with her brain cancer about five months ago. Each month, it seems, she needs a more specific bacterial strain to stay alive. Damn, I'm really not sure how much longer I can keep this up. Maybe she's not a liver. Maybe she's just a dier.

And part of me wonders if deep down Kinley suspects that someone is helping her because periodically she glances at me. Her eyes, wide open and full of hope, ooze a river of gratitude for just a second, and then she blinks and sucks it all back in. *Whoosh.*

Yet, to be honest, she's kind of tough because never once does she complain about her ailments to the others who walk on by clueless to her struggle while they search for another Ink, another square, another box, another whatever.

So for her own good, I keep handing her low level Washing assignments, where she covers her face with a mask to keep from burning it with the boiling hot water, or surely they would have seen her jaundiced skin and her yellow eyes calling her out like a diseased coyote in the night.

I bet we have mutant dogs out in the acid rain. My rapid-fire thoughts wander briefly to the Frightening and its unknown and countless dangers.

Even though I wish I didn't, I can still remember the day in school when we saw the photos of all the Volta initiates who found their way out there one night against all odds. With such safety barriers up and all, it's hard to imagine that they could have gotten so totally lost, especially with four of them together like that. They apparently made it past the winds of the dunes but lasted about ten minutes with all the mutated creatures waiting to murder them in the foggy sulfuric abyss.

In the picture, etched like a stamp on my brain, they were chewed to bits. One boy, missing half his face, just stared up at me from the photos with his one open eye. He wore a pendant around his neck that looked foreign yet familiar to me. The center part appeared to be missing, but I know the image; I swear it. And it begged for me to look closer at his blown face and see what wasn't there, to uncover how he got out there in the first place. He yearned for me to see him and experience what he suffered, daring me to finally answer his questions, too. And I don't really know how or why, but my gut tells me that his mind worked just like mine: full of what ifs and whys and an insatiable need to understand this world.

As I fall asleep for the evening, wallowing in all my not understanding, I lose myself in tattered nightmares where it is me in the photo. Only this time, I am wearing the pendant, and I am the one missing half my face, holding and shaking the precious trinket which has just cost me my life–a rising sun.

As soon as I wake–angry and annoyed–I return to my predicament. Or is it Kinley's predicament? I stick my tongue out and squeal at my stupidity.

One observant glance from the absent-eyes of a monitor, and off to R&R she goes, that yellow-skinned creep. So here I am devising another scheme to save her sorry butt, all smothered with a feeling I don't quite have the right word for while her sneaky ass slips in between the cracks in my mind all damn day. Or is it my heart? I just can't be sure yet.

Pissed off, I stand as far as I can from her on the Ink stage, yet there she is everywhere I go–drinking my blood like boxes and eating my brains like squares. And I could be wrong, but I expect she'll feed on me even more than I'll chew on the terrible idea of her and her fatal predicaments all day.

So after all of us Levana complete today's assignments without dying...thank Gods...I really can't help noticing that cannibalistic hound step in behind me on this main path back to our Levana quarters.

I holler out a few woops and make my sign–two fingers over the heart and press down twice. The others follow suit, and a few even laugh. It's been a good day as far as days go in the City of Usual Tragedy. And as we walk like a loyal pack of dogs back to our buildings to finish our leftover squares, drink our remaining boxes, and practice Heat in one of the simulators in the alpha room before the sleep bell rings, I take a few deep breaths and almost smile. I count quickly, hoping no one notices–no one dead, all forty-seven of my tribe accounted for.

Kinley whispers, "We all made it home tonight, didn't we? Must be tough deciding who lives and dies as holder of the assignment cards, beta Jane. I can't figure out why you haven't killed me yet. Maybe I'm next to die. What'd ya think?"

"Shut up," I say and wonder who really holds the cards around here. If I knew how, I would bark and run around in circles. Will that bitch be the death of me instead of the other way around? Especially if I keep giving myself the assignment card of helping her, that clueless predator. Is she worth all these chances I take on her? What's in it for me? And why do I keep helping her when she can never help me in exchange? *I hate you, Kinley. I really do.*

She hurries off and runs ten paces ahead of me.

So I think it again to make it official. *I hate you, Kinley. I really do.*

As if she hears my thoughts, she glances back over her right shoulder and that flagrant purple dragon Ink of hers to lock eyes with mine. Quickly, I pretend to wave another Levana over to avoid the intensity of the pain in those bright green eyes of hers. *Maybe I only mostly hate you.*

Those eyes, so common but so unknown to me, pierce me with their emerald fire. Their intensity urged onward by some unexplainable lighter fluid, determined to keep them open against all odds so...not in her favor.

But why? What is there to look upon in this bizarre world where she hardly lives before she dies? Why does she try so hard to keep moving forward where there is nowhere worth going? What pushes her?

What pushes me? Am I really so different than her?

I almost expect her to open her mouth and lick her wounds to clean them.

She should have died years ago, and I suspect on some level she knows it. *Okay, maybe I only hate you a little bit.*

Her words return to me. "*I can't figure out why you haven't killed me yet. Maybe I'm next to die. What'd ya think?*"

Shit, maybe she does know she is sick. Chills assault me, and all of a sudden, some part of me understands that this is the very thing that shoves her out of bed each morning and fills her mouth with such sarcastic and biting words. Words, actions, and behaviors she employs to disguise the taste of her misery which otherwise overflows from her diseased lips born to a life of overwhelming loss. *Okay, maybe I almost respect you. Almost.*

My trick apparently doesn't work.

She marches right back to me and steps on my right foot. *Hating you again.*

"Oh no. I'm so sorry, beta," she mocks and makes the Levana sign. Instead of twice, she pounds her chest three times.

I clear my throat and scratch my neck. *Yep, hate you.*

She rolls her eyes and says, "Such a good Elder, our beta. Oh, what am I saying? You're not an Elder, just a beta. I'm sorry, Isla Jane. Silly me. I must be dumber than dumb today. But we are so thankful for all you do. How about an extra square for a lowly ranked epsilon like me? An epsilon you have shown so much mercy to by not killing yet."

She pounds three times and starts to run away again.

I won't let her yank my tail. "No problem." I wink to top it off.

For half a second, she just stares at me. The corners of her lips turn down, and her lower lip quivers. If I didn't know her better, I would think she is going to cry. But that's ridiculous; this is Kinley.

I hand her a square and keep going. *Okay, like you an itty, bitty bit.*

Dead in her tracks, frozen from our interaction, she makes the three chest pounds again. *Okay more than a little.*

Everyone hates her and her selfish words. Yet never does she complain about the very thing she most desperately needs to tell them. Instead, she covers them with lying words to smother the truth in her eyes. Eyes good for nothing really but closing tightly as the monitors shoot her drone-covered butt out in the flat, dry sky of the City of Lies.

A city, twenty-two light-years from Home, so covered in Ink that we blindly over-look what it's covering up. Maybe it's time, it dawns on me, to ask what they are covering up with Ink. And why they want us to see only the images they color us with instead of the alternative. *Okay, like you and your dragon a lot.*

Chapter Ten

I STARE at Cale's back while he squirms in my lap, trying desperately to fall back to sleep after a bad dream. Back and forth he sways his feet; up and down they go, gathering speed to launch like a rocket off my lap into the sky. The silliness of the idea surprises me. Shockingly, it makes me happy for a fleeting moment to think he might make it back Home all by himself.

Then the image of a rocket shoots me back to the awful details I know about what happened to our Home:

Some years ago, just when the scientists from the Royal City, our Capitol, solved our limited fresh water and oxygen problems, several nuclear warheads laced with malignant bacteria launched inexplicably into the heavens on a silent and invisible drone and, in one fell swoop, effectively ruined us. The mutant microbiome aboard that devil plane, a war tactic gone wrong, was supposed to motivate the dissenters of the United Nations to join the recently assembled Global Nation in exchange for unconditional access to the cure–the F serum.

The only problem was that our president, some businessman who got elected despite losing the popular vote, had a brilliant cure that didn't actually work because the compromised strains aboard that plane interacted in some unanticipated way. And damn if the resultant form of the bacteria wasn't way more aggressive and way more explosive than intended. The affected humans, within hours of initial exposure, were as good as dead at the hand of their own foolish government. Needless to say, everything went super south from there.

The official account suggests the North Koreans with the help of a rogue group from Russia were responsible for the covert operation that did it, but really no one knows for sure. The effect of multiple nukes shot back and forth from both sides of this conflict met in the middle over what used to be a country called France and somehow knocked the axis of the planet off kilter by about one degree. Apparently, that's all it takes to ruin the world–a momentary alteration in gravity that alters the planet by one degree.

Out of nowhere, our otherworldly allies–the benevolent Mozek–appeared and used advanced technology to decimate the North Koreans. A few days later, their creepy mothership, a huge globe inside another globe, took as many of the survivors as possible to this place. Thus, here I am minus owls or roses or roosters, rescued from the vast nothingness of necrotic corpses left behind looking for that lost F serum.

Twenty-two light-years is so far away. Can you make it that far, Cale?

My throat tightens, imagining him gasping and flailing, unable to find air despite his best efforts while the mutant bacteria that scorched the remains of our beautiful planet eat him. The vision... It's worse than hearing about his nightmares.

Immediately, I reach down and stop his legs from swinging. I don't want him launching Home after all.

Scowling, I growl at the one 53 stamp that Cale wears on his back. From a distance, it looks like a black flower opening up its blossoms for a good sniff. But it's not. I hate it. *You don't fool me.*

As I inspect it more closely, I notice the petals are actually more like intertwined letters. From one side, the letters look like a B. But if I turn my head the other direction, an E pops out. Funny. I never noticed that before.

Once, I got the brilliant idea to ask Elder Khaan about his 53 stamps and the oil, which smelled like mint, that he rubbed on his bald head. His answer, totally lame, scooted around the truth so he wouldn't have to tell me a white lie.

I'm not sure why white is the word I choose because a lie is a lie is a lie as far as I'm concerned. Forgetting how pissed I am at the stamp, I beam knowing I could read his face like a book, too.

In my memory, Elder Khaan wears several 53 stamps on his arms, behind his neck, and on his right knee and thigh. But for the first time ever, I realize that if I loop a design over the intersecting bottoms of one of the Es and the Bs that they form the shape of a heart. Ink it in the middle and instantly I have a circle of connected hearts. He also wears several images of something like this but in more hidden places like behind the earlobe and under his feet.

Cale snores, and I jump back to reality. His legs, as limp and still as a sleeping lion tucked safely in his den, make me so happy I could cry. *Stay with me until I find the cure for you, Cale, and then I will make sure you make it Home.*

Oddly hopeful for some reason, I sneak him back to his quarters and tuck him in tightly. *Even if it kills me, I will get you one step closer to Home. I promise.*

As the door closes, I press my fingers to my lips, down twice over my heart, and then to the cold, metal wall to make it official. A funny rhyme returns to my memory. *Cross my heart. Hope to die. Stick a needle in my eye.*

Then as usual, I retire to bed tonight with my prickly thoughts swirling, like lionesses prowling and protecting her pack, despite how desperately I need to clear them so my body can rest. After all, tomorrow is Friday. And around here, we think we know why the monitors call it that. Fri on Friday. Fri must mean die because we always lose one or two of us red carders. So we will see who makes it through another Friday with the processed elixirs from earlier this week.

Three more Pellonias dead in the POT, best I can count at least, in a dying world. There are no livers here.

I start pacing and counting, attempting to quell the smoldering anger in my gut. Since it doesn't work, I reach for Elder Khaan in the back of my mind and pretend to hear the brilliant advice he has to offer.

I whisper, "Like Elder Khaan always said, Isla, follow your breath. That slows the swirling and empties your mind. "

Finally, just before the rooster crows, I drift off to a restless sleep.

In my dream tonight, I run.

I run from the creatures in the Frightening, racing away against all odds, certain of my impending death. Accepting that I cannot out run the horrific mutants, though, I decide to turn and face them. I dig my feet in, spin around, and attempt to stare them down with one last moment of dignity before they eat me like a square and drink my blood like a box.

But to my shock, what pursues me is not razor-clawed, one-eyed vermin at all. My attackers are nothing more terrifying than Elder Khaan; Tilly Raeanne, my old friend; Cale, holding a large pointy needle; and the new dealer named Gaige.

Mortified, I gasp at the image of Tilly, my friend I miss so badly that I can still smell her skin, reminding me of sweet squares all rolled up in a big squishy pillow. Softly, I lay my head down on the sweetness of her in my dream and rest my tired head and my guilty heart. And as usual, the memory of her reminds me of the empty feeling in my stomach I can never seem to fill since she's gone, since I'm the one who probably killed her.

Don't go there, Isla, I tell myself even in my sleep. *There's nothing but pain there, girl. She's here. See. She isn't gone.*

To my delight, all of them reach out tenderly for me instead of hunting me.

The shock of my odd situation startles and thrills me. Wanting to touch them so badly since they are not the monsters I imagined after all, I gladly stretch out my arms to snatch Elder Khaan's hand. But instead of flesh, I reach only glass.

As I smash one layer, another remains. Glass inside glass inside more glass. Trying desperately to get on the other side as my fingers scrape the thick wall without any lasting effect, I scream.

I call out for Cale, Tilly, and Elder Khaan. For a moment, I consider yelling out the new Levana Ink dealer's name as well but decide not to.

Then it occurs to me to look back, back in the direction I once fled. This time, much to my horror, I do find evil creatures poised and determined to consume me slowly and painfully as they rip me bit by bit. Only instead of animals, they are the eyeless Mozek.

Panting like I've just finished a Heat, I wake up. Gobsmacked, I realize this is the first time I have dreamed of Tilly since it happened, since I lost her, since I murdered her. Shaking and trembling, I wipe the sweat from my burning forehead. My heart pounds in my ears. For a moment, I struggle to recall where I am.

But then I remember: on this side of the universe in the City, on this side of Elder Khaan and Tilly in the divided City of Walls. In the City where it takes lives to save lives.

All of a sudden, I can't help but wonder whose life I am actually saving.

Chapter Eleven

MY SWEET, sweet Tilly. I miss her so. I swallow hard while her memory fills my mind despite my futile efforts to banish it.

"Tilly Raeanne, how is it out there in space? Did you finally make it back Home?" I ask, knowing she will never answer me, wondering if I will ever forget the day I abandoned her, my only real friend. *The day I might have saved her.*

Like a used-up weapon, I drop the thought on the ground right there, scattering the empty shells while the sharp smell of gunpowder coats me on the inside. I can't escape the pain of my self-directed fury, but I pretend to anyway. One day, unless they hang or necrotize me first, I will have to face this. *Face her.*

I stare at the tendril of the rising sun on my right ankle, surprised that it still shines for me, someone who forsook their best friend. Shoving my guilt down and swallowing hard once more, I remind myself that I can't change the past. What's done is done. *Or is it?*

"Shut up, you idiot," I tell myself.

Then I go about the business of getting ready for the day, Friday, my least favorite day of all. I apply lotion to my lower back where my freshly Inked rose tries its best to take hold so it can show its petals bravely to all that might look upon it, searching to find hope and faith. Like a computer virus, though, my dead friend's memory infects my mind and spreads its message of contamination to the rest of me instead. *So impossible.*

Still desperately hoping to distract myself, I purposefully think of roses instead of Tilly, my own judgment, or Fridays. And for the moment, I am not sure which sounds better: looking at the fine, satiny flowers or picking them apart while their thorns fail miserably to pierce my calloused fingers thickened from years and years of working the machines at the Foundry.

Or maybe painting the roses red? That sounds nice, too. Amused at such a silly idea, I laugh. The painting I will leave to another Alice, though. This chick has better things to do with something as beautiful as a flower.

A light scurrying from the corner of my alpha room catches my attention. Then I see the hind legs of a lady beetle bug attempting to disappear into a discreet crack in the wall behind one of the simulators. *Wish I could disappear into that wall too, you lucky bastard.*

Quickly, my feet launch over to inspect the situation. I have heard of these delicate, blind, little creatures, but this is the first time I have ever seen one in person. Because they are so rare here on this desolate planet where we have only squares to eat, they are fought over by the others as a delicacy.

Immediately, I begin wondering what I can do with it. Perhaps I can sell the sucker for some new ribbons for my lovely hair? But why is the little guy here, and what does he hope to find when I have nothing for him to eat but flaky squares of dehydrated protein and minerals? *Squares made from what?*

But then I shove the question away because I don't really want the answer, do I? Let's face it—nothing grows on this planet, so the possible sources are just a tad limited. *Don't go there, girl.*

I turn the creature over and back again—six legs wriggling back and forth, several Ink-like markings on its back, yellow-brown wings buzzing furiously to escape my grip. Definitely a beetle bug.

The specific details escape me, but legend has it that there is something magical about the clever creature sprouting a second set of wings under just the right circumstances. *No second set of wings for you, guy. You are modern day caviar.*

But then I realize how similar this bug and I are, both trapped in a world we cannot find a crevice deep enough to hide in and hunted everywhere we turn until something or hunger finally gets us.

I tell it, "Only you end up in someone's gut, and I get my thoughts ravaged on the big Heat screen while they try to cook me at the Foundry unless, of course, my bacteria eat me first." Mercy consumes me, and I add, "I think I will let you go, little guy."

Feeling a newly found compassion for this living object that might have allowed me to purchase who-knows-what, I take a closer look at it. But I don't really care what I could have traded it for. What more do I need?

As the question and the inevitable answer that follows it enter my mind, I push it away from me as far as I can. Involuntarily, my hands reach up and shove it back like a ball during a game of dodge ball.

"Fuck, Isla, why ask a stupid question like that anyway?" I curse and shake my head, forcing the question away until it resurfaces…which inevitably it does, each time more urgently than the last. I sit down on the titanium stool in the middle of this bare room and can't help but notice how my weight spreads to its legs, to the ground, the walls, and reverberates back down from the ceiling to where it came from. I guess everything comes back round.

Shit. Here comes the answer…back round.

Elder Khaan and Tilly, I need you. I need you both.

And forgiveness, I need that most of all. But that f-word, so slippery and dangerous, is just too hard to hold on to, so I reach for fuck-all instead as the priceless bug starts to wriggle and shake in my hand. Surprised there is so much life in the thing, I almost fall off my stool onto the cold, white marble floor.

"To be honest, I don't really want forgiveness, do I?" I tell the little vermin.

Why? Because underneath the first f-word, "forgiveness", lives the other f-word it always follows, "fault." I like fuck-all better than fault for sure. To prove it, I tap my feet and say it like a fool. "Fuck, fuck, fuck-all." But all I hear is *fault, fault, your fault for all.*

Fault slithers away from me like a snake. *But it was my fault.*

I hiss, "Fault." Holding the thing in one of my hands, I cover my own ears and rock back and forth on the stool to make sure the word coats every molecule on every wall. Then the creature escapes my pathetic grip and gets away too. But not before its wings flitter inside my ear like it is telling me a secret or something.

"What are you trying to tell me? I can't speak beetle bug...or can I?" I say and laugh at the absurdity of the whole ordeal.

The insect wastes no time and urgently moves on, probably totally oblivious to the second chance it has been given. I flick my ear, still ringing from those bizarre wings, and finally drop my hands in surrender that I will never figure out what the tiny thing was saying. Amused more than I have been in days, I giggle until I realize I have just pulled another Alice move.

Whatever. Who cares?

"Fuck-all. That is funny." I giggle harder.

Maybe I am like that Salus Baylor? And for the first time, the awareness follows that maybe, just maybe, that's not such a bad thing.

I can do so much worse than be like him.

I think I will be a little nicer to him later this morning when we stand arm to arm at the front of the Ink stage for another round. Perhaps I will even toss in a square or two for his mountains of mouths to feed. But even as the generous idea crosses my mind, I know I will not. That would be taking my charity way too far for one day.

Still curious, I bend over to see where that lady beetle bug disappeared: through a hairline crack, which extends up the wall about a meter and a half, just underneath the edge of the shelves that hold my three standard alpha quarter picture books and my animal book. I move the shelf over and find the top of the defect coming from a crevice that widens minimally. Just able to pass the edge of a stick in, I probe the space, which seems to extend even farther beyond that. I pound on the wall that seems solid enough. *Weird.*

My improvised instrument locates the edge of a piece of paper rolled up in a tight little sleeve. Carefully, I pull out the roll and take an even closer look.

As the image unfolds, I gasp and almost drop the parchment. Almost.

Not quite a photo but more like a copy of a photo, the ancient paper reveals the outline of something I have never seen before. In shimmering hues of gold, a male figure with closed eyes embraces and tenderly wraps his arms around a blond-haired woman with the same round-bellied disease the woman on page one hundred and thirty-five in my medical book suffers from. I try to find gray in her blond hair, hoping she undeniably resembles me in some unique way, but she does not.

Cale's words, *"heart you,"* swallow me while I stare at the image and stroke my braids. Unable to repress the urge, I put my two fingers to my lips and then point them to the photo that is so similar to the page in my book. Then I put my fingers on her chest and press down twice. My favorite incomplete thought returns one more time. *Cale...I... Cale...I... Cale, you must know that I...*

Unfortunately, his lovely grin floods my mind just as the Ink stage bell warns impending morning tabulation and ration distribution. Holy shit, I have exactly ten minutes minus one second to hide my new treasure, race down seven flights, and run a distance that typically takes me twenty minutes to walk.

Or I'm a goner out in space, and I'm never going Home–like Elder Khaan, like Tilly, and like Kinley and Cale without me.

So thank Gods for my rising sun which pulls as Jane-do-do on my shoulder pushes, making my patterned feet move faster and faster still.

I slam that gorgeous sun in my boots. Already, I'm running before I consider the potential consequences of what's happening.

There isn't enough time. I'm not going to make it.

Hopping on one foot and then the other, I try to make the boots stay in place in between strides. *I will never make it. They will all die without me.*

I sprint for Cale. I leap for Kinley. I race against time for myself and the dwindling chance to get to know myself a little better before I hang.

Moaning, I declare, "I still don't want to die. Not yet. I'm not ready. I can't fail them. Not like this."

Halfway down the stairs, I wonder how many seconds I have left. In the back of my disintegrating mind, I hear the Ink stage bell tinkle. It's laughing at me, taunting me, threatening me. But I cannot listen, or I will never have a chance of a chance to make it.

Panting, I holler, "Screw you. I won't listen. I refuse. Piss off. I hate you."

I race down the stairs, counting the flights as I go.

One, two, three, four, five, six.

My foot slips on the very bottom stair. *Bite me, slippery seven.* I tumble head over heels. Seven obliges my request, ripping open my shoulder, and I growl.

But since I do not have time to fall as my top half hits the pavement, I keep rolling. Then I catapult out the door onto the hard, cracked ground until I am back upright on my feet, which are still running even though the boot on my right leg is loose and threatening to trip me. Or worse, perhaps?

An undeniable rip sears through the same calf I had already injured. The wounded muscle has never healed from the first tear. Now I know for certain it never will, but that doesn't matter. It will just be another secret of mine–so many layers of secrets inside secrets.

Besides, while I'm in the thraex portal, I won't feel the injury. I never do. I never have, now that I think about it. In fact, my leg is always better after I Heat, which makes no sense to me.

Screaming more profanities at the stairs, I keep running, compounding the damage. It's my only chance inside a chance left.

I'm as good as dead, and I know it. I'm a corpse. A goner. The rope of my failure strangles me. *Fault!*

Then thankfully, everything disappears for me but three things: a blood-red Ink on my right foot, the hot, cracked ground, and the image of Cale's sweet face at the finish line, begging me to win this Heat for my life.

And his and Kinley's.

Time distorts. I pace my thoughts to delay guilt for being the source of so much suffering to come and the insanity of comprehending I could have done so much better. *Fuck-all!*

First, the red mound on my right foot rises like the fullness of dawn coming into view. Then, the gritty, orange sand scrapes the underside of my toes.

A tunnel, almost like a vortex of fear, envelops me. And just like in a Heat, I know I have two choices: win or lose, Cale or nothing, live or die, space or Home, fault or fuck-all.

My preferred choice obvious, I hear the sound of my heartbeat echoing in the tunnel. My ears fill with pressure, and numbness surrounds me. This void of disintegrating hope leaves only my beating heart to match the rhythm of the alternating sun and sand.

The rest of me goes into autopilot.

The red sun again. Then the orange sand.

The red. The orange.

The sun. The sand.

The dawn. The dusk.

And I am too afraid to acknowledge the third thing hanging over my every move. The only one that matters to me, really–his face.

Cale...I... Cale...I... Cale, you must know that I...

Lub-dub. Sun-sand.

Lub-dub. Sun-sand.

Lub-dub. Red-orange.

Lub-dub. Red-orange.

The dunes flash by me, and for once, I do not bother to worry about fences and the Frightening Zone just on the other side. I laugh at my prior terror of them–those boring adversaries that have nothing on the clock tick, tick, ticking away my last few moments.

And those who depend on me to survive.

I am almost there, and a splinter of possible success pierces my skin. But much to my dismay, my foot gets caught on the back stair going up to the stage. I'm so close now. Almost, almost there.

But it's not enough. I'm too close to die now.

I can't get up. I can't get through. My boot is stuck.

Help me, Elder Khaan. Help me. Somebody help me. Please.

Fuck-all, answer me.

I decide, like so many times before, I better freaking help myself.

I reach down and rip the boot from my foot. It flies, and I shudder from another ripple of pain slicing through my calf, probably useless to me now.

Time stands still.

I look around at an ocean of frozen faces, so many 53s who cannot see me. I am not up the stairs far enough.

I've lost everything.

Sensing the little hand of the clock move into position, I know I have but one tiny, little second left before I necrotize. A moment of eternity stolen by a computerized thief–the clock, my executioner.

I leap off my one good leg and do a half flip in the air, landing on all fours at the back corner of the platform. *Boom.* The hand engages. The final bell rings.

All eyes on the Ink stage turn simultaneously to attack me, still panting on all fours. They stagger back, pointing their fingers and gasping at the foolish girl who has all those mouths depending on her Ink-ridden sleeves.

The embarrassed lilies on my side crawl underneath my skin and tremble in shame. Jane do-do covers her face with her wing. One of the petals from my rose falls to the ground and turns to ash.

Yet, like a merciful rope dropping from the sky, a reassuring glance from Cale makes the others all fade in the background. Jane do-do opens her eyes and blinks. Cale smiles with confidence like he never worries at all because he believes I will always make it. Pride washes across his face for his faith in me, the one who will never fail him.

Cale…I… Cale…I… Cale, you must know that I…

The lilies think better of their traitorous retreat, and my rose blossoms.

Baylor breaks my interaction with Cale and grabs my hand to help me stand. A powerful emotion courses through me. It's a feeling but also a smell, both warm and kind, which feels certain in a world full of bad and uncertainty.

Then he walks me to my assigned position in the front right corner. Yet he says nothing, which says everything because I feel, not see, him smiling. And I feel, not hear, him applauding me for making it on time.

Maybe Tilly wasn't my only friend after all?

I hope I'm not the death of you, too, Baylor.

Despite the unbearable pain in my leg, I smile, pledging to give this ally of mine, in a world made of nothing but enemies, some of my squares. Maybe not right away but later after he forgets about grabbing my hand, when he forgets that I almost didn't make it on time today, crashed on my knees. When I forget that the lady beetle bug almost got me killed instead of the other way around.

I should have eaten the darn thing. But even now, I know it's a worthless thought; I will never eat a beetle bug, and I hope none of them ever eat me.

From the back, I sense the intense eyes of my enemy Jaxston tearing a hole through my Ink. He hates me; I am sure of it. He wishes I had missed the bell and been necrotized on the spot. *Ha, ha, you creep. Kiss this ass.*

Then the memory of the photo enters my mind again, and momentarily, I forget about that glare of his Ink-freak eyes, not dilated but angry and accusing that it's not fair and never has been that I always make front position on this stage, that my sleeves are complete, that the Levanas look for me, but the Irmin barely acknowledge him. That my feet move so fast, both in the thraex portal and in the real world, yanked to the front by my rising sun which has saved me again today.

Limping off the structure, my intuition tears my thoughts from Jaxston's hatred, screaming something is deathly wrong.

A terrible feeling overwhelms me, followed by an even more terrible sound. I don't want to know what it is. Really, I don't.

Then I am desperate to.

Chapter Twelve

NOT DESPERATE TO, dying to know. Dying...

Crap, have they found my beetle bug? Am I about to hang in the kill fields for almost missing the bell after all, or for the rolled up picture, for my medical book, for the stolen bacterial strain on my braid bead that saved Kinley from her liver the other night? *Impossible.*

It's not possible, not yet anyway. They cannot have found out. No way. The bug's too far gone. The picture's well hidden. And I know I made it on time. My mind reels while I search to uncover my fatal error. My gut cramps into a little ball, and my heart pumps so loudly I can hear it. *Lub, dub. Lub, dub. Lub, dub.*

I touch my neck, trying to slow the beating down, but the blade of a gladius goes right through and decapitates me. I'd blink my eyes, but what's the use? They are rolling around on the ground in front of this massive structure.

Will I ever be safe? Will these fucking Mozek ever stop trying to kill me while supposedly saving me?

Sweat drips off my palms and joins all the red blood gushing out my neck that will most likely feed the evil bacteria on my skin. *Red is dead.*

I can imagine it all now. Exponentially, my own lifeforce speeding up the very process of my biome digesting what's left of me as I crumble into a pile of nothingness out in front for all to witness. There is no serum that can save me now from that terrible sound. I'd lean forward to catch my own guts as they spill forth, but there is nowhere left to go but off the front edge of this gigantic steel stage. My bowel rolls like an infinity of snakes down four meters to red, hot sand below. There are no bars to hold on to. No beams to reach up to. I am so exposed as I flounder, my innards fileted like this.

I steady myself as best I can and take a deep breath.

Maybe the Ink dealer told the monitors that I played him like a fool? But how? I doubt it. He's the one who touched me, after all. *Gaige, it's your fault.*

His name falls like oil off my lips and oozes down my chin, which has finally stopping rolling back and forth on the ground to wallow in my pool of self-pity and fear. *No, it's my fault.*

For a second, I allow the inherent intensity in his name. *Gaige.*

The word opens my chest a little, so I squash it back in and switch to better feeling thoughts. Or maybe they are worse feeling thoughts; I can't be sure yet. Another deep breath helps, but only a little. And a little will never do.

Blood gushes past my feet and spills over the edge of the stage to warn the rest of me that I am really going over the side. *Fuck-all.*

Hesitantly, so as not to slip and fall in the oil or my blood, I glance over at Kinley while the sound gathers behind me. Following the first of several screams, I catch her bright green eyes, minus a yellow surrounding hue. She bubbles like an oxidation reaction and grins. Whew. If she's standing there smiling, then I am fine, about her and the liver repair strain anyway. I straighten my shoulders and dare to hope, but only a little. And a little bit of hope will never do either.

Almost invisibly, she nods to confirm that she is well and taps her chest three times. Three times just like the other day.

Suddenly, I understand; three taps is her way of saying thank you without verbalizing it, her way to reassure me she feels fine, that this disaster isn't about our secret dealings, that she's glad for me. But mostly herself, probably. *I hate you again.*

In that fraction of a second, I surmise she knows the *accidentally* dropped hair bead on her box at Levana gathering time the other night was no accident. She realizes I have saved her joke of a little life...again. Momentarily, I consider whether that's a good or bad thing. My inner goddess squeals, *Bad, Isla. Definitely bad, Isla. Now she will count on you too, like Cale. Only you can't stand her, so it will suck double bad.*

But Kinley's a survivor, a liver even, like my surprisingly clean feet, and I know it. It was the right thing to do. Thanks to my generosity, she takes a deep breath of sulfur-laden air and looks away. *Okay, hate you a little less again.*

Perhaps next time I will let her die to avoid the pressure mounting in the back of my neck. "*Screw you, Kinley, and you figuring out I saved your pathetic life. If you can call it life,*" I want to say. Instead, having forgotten all about my imaginary neck wound still spewing like a death fountain, I pace.

You have to stop this crap, Isla-Alice Jane, my inner bitch demands.

If I had eyelids, I would blink to prove that I still have a pair, but after all, they are still on the ground, right?

But then I remember Baylor's hand softly squeezing mine a minute ago while he helped me stand. *Maybe not,* I think. *I'll let it simmer for a while before I decide.* After all, I'm only twenty-one. So if I make it to the ripe old age of thirty-seven like Elder Khaan, I have a few more years to decide who I am before they kill me.

Elder Khaan always seemed to grasp just who he was despite their best attempts to distract him from his greatness and drown him in Ink. And I want that, too, more than anything, in fact–to be me: fish, Alice, winged bird, covert spy, beta playing Elder, whatever.

My heart snarls to remind my inner voice, so logical and sane, who is boss around here. I slam my heels into the hard, careless surface of the stage to remind it that I am not going over the side after all. And as my hope and faith gather just a little bit more inside me, I touch my abdominal wall to confirm it never ruptured at all. But it's still only a little more, and that will never do.

It's Friday, or die day, and that something, that awful sound, keeps creeping back into my cracked and swirling mind. Surely the only part of me worth listening to now is my heart.

My sixth sense shrieks that this is big. This is bad with a capital B. My earlier Heat against the clock is nothing compared to this, less than nothing even, like the dunes or the Frightening Zone.

The rest of my fractured mind, still refusing to acknowledge what is happening, pretends to hide in the safety of my quarters far away from here, so far away from whatever atrocity demands my attention so that I can safely examine the rising sun pendant hanging from my neck, or is it Inked on my foot? I just can't be sure yet.

As time freezes, I float with that thought for a moment–hiding with the lady beetle bug or, better yet, disappearing in my tunnel, unable to hear anything but my heart and waiting for this Friday to end.

I swallow and steady myself for whatever bad news tunnels my way.

It's pretty obvious this is not about me or I would already be fighting cuffs and ropes or sizzling on the ground with my decapitated head. Shit, I've been so worried about me that I forgot to worry about everybody else. Who will it be this time? What is that awful noise I keep hearing behind me? Why are the bairns screaming like that, like fingernails down a chalkboard trying to drive me mad? As if I can actually drive some-where I already am.

Skylar April, my delta, pops in my mind.

Next to me, in the family, her jobs are usually the most deadly. She can handle a red card like a pro, and yellow or blue card assignments almost insult her. Almost.

Even though she will lie and tell you otherwise, she's brilliant. I notice her observe things without saying a word. Yet, somehow, she managed to place lower than me in her Stain Heats. Last year, they banned her from the BRÉ after she messed up one of the cross and react tests. *As if...*

The screaming tries to get my attention again. I will not, I cannot, let it.

As per her usual red card, a low level worker in the DED, Skylar and the rest of her crew must do the first labeling of the freshly distilled combinations that come from us to them. The first blowout will probably be mine or for one of the other local workers, but sometimes things go wrong on the way to the next section for processing. The pres-sure builds up in the little glass bottles, and they blow as the low level DED heads open them.

I hate that. After the blowout, I always wonder, did my bottle do it? But we never find out who's responsible, so everyone takes the blame because no one does. Suspi-ciously, we glare at each other the next day, wondering whose fault it is as if we will ever figure it out. But we will not. The heartless Mozek cannot or, more likely, will not say. *Assholes, it's your fucking fault.*

I am truly convinced that knowing would be better. If it is my fault, then at least I can apologize, make amends, offer my squares, trade over an Ink…something, anything. But with the not knowing, I can only guess. And that space between sure and unsure tortures me like the straps of the Ink projector. *Double assholes, it was always you, always.*

Like my lip, I chew on the word "Friday" for who knows how long while time stands still forever in between those awful screams. What does Fri mean? Why do we use that word?

A real drop of blood drips down my lip and lands on my foot.

"Stop screaming!" I squeal at the bairns, but it's no use. It never stops.

It never stops.

All of this flashes in and out of my mind in the few seconds it takes for me to realize that the monitors have just shot a small child with one of their guns. As his blood, the same color as mine, spurts from the middle of his forehead, my thoughts return to the present moment.

The small and precious creature falls to the ground, and the necrotizing begins. I count the seconds, marching out the beats of what is left of my ruined heart to the saddest story I have ever heard:

One. There is no longer a face. *Two.* His neck caves in, and he gurgles. *Three.* The skin over his ribs goes first, and his lungs try to take one last futile breath. *Four.* There is no longer a heart to beat. *Five.* Once he had two legs; now he has none. Only a red puddle of goo remains.

Six. This little piggy went to the market.

Seven. This little piggy will never go Home. *I hate this place, this terrible place. I hate you, seven.*

What the hell happened to cause this? What had that little, grubby idiot done to be necrotized before his fifth year?

This little piggy had roast beef.

Swiftly now, Elder Khaan's voice comes through clear as day. *"Isla, ask yourself who is the grubby, little idiot here? Who really caused this? Was it the clueless youth? Could he really deserve a punishment so severe for something someone so small and innocent might do? Perhaps there was another purpose for this atrocity entirely?"*

And instantly, I know two things, other than my name.

The first is that there is no way he, that any child ever, deserves this. And the second is that I am in bigger trouble than ever before because I really, really care. *Well fuck me. This little piggy had none and never will. Oh my Gods!*

I'll be damned if the same expression spreading like fire across Baylor's soft and tender face isn't searing mine apart from the inside, and it's almost out for everyone to see.

Unable to hold back the tears, one falls from my melted face and mixes with the boiling drop of blood marking my foot to make it official. Red equals dead for the bairn who never had a chance, never even knew his kith, his Elder, his rank.

A second, a third, a fourth, a seventh, wash the blood away completely.

This little piggy cried wee, wee, wee all the way home.

Elder Khaan pops in my imagination again, standing there with one good and one twitching arm. He smiles but doesn't all at the same time.

Wordlessly, that devil says it. *"Pivotal."*

And now I understand exactly what he meant by that favorite word of his.

Doomed, I am past the circuit connector. I can't turn back and go the other way anymore. Everything has just changed.

The screaming stops, and everyone returns to their affairs like nothing has happened. *Nothing at all.*

The thought of Cale strangles me. *My little piggy, nothing at all.*

Cale...I... Cale...I... Cale, you must know that I...

Before I can stop, I scream Cale's name like the horrible red goo is him and he is nothing at all.

That's when I feel the stinging slap across the back of neck. Suddenly, I find myself staring at the pavement, trying to figure out how it could get so close to my face and why my head hurts so badly.

The vision of that bairn's melting returns. Numb, I feel, yet don't all at the same time, the first jolt of electricity shoot through my body. Outside, I hear nothing, but inside, I hear Cale begging. *"Save me, Isla. No one else can do it. Only you. You are my only sunshine."*

Just before I lose consciousness, I realize that we are the same, Baylor and I, and that I have always been an Alice just like him. Inevitably, a queen calls for both our heads and all of our piggies. The same red bitch who will never touch Cale as long as I am alive. Why? Because I'm going to chop off all ten of her toes and feed them to some mutant bacteria strains as growth medium. And if she doesn't die fast enough, I will eat them myself.

The last image I view in my shattered mind is a red rose, and I giggle slightly at the idea of painting it red even though I probably will never get the chance. Not now anyway, since I just announced that I need Cale like I do. That I screamed out in fear not for myself but for him. That he actually matters to me in a world where they don't want... No! They won't allow me to care about anything but Ink. I don't give a flying crap about Ink. Now it's out, and I'm done for.

"I will die before I let them get you," I want to say to Cale, but I can't speak because my vocal cords and all my piggies are paralyzed.

One last thought burrows in my mind. *Pivotal.*

And then just like that boy's toes, I am gone.

Chapter Thirteen

I WAKE UP, my head pounding. A few flashes of light come through my eyes which struggle to open, but the images are just too blurry to make out, so I close them and surrender to the overwhelming pain in my neck. I'm lost again.

Maybe it was just a bad dream? *Please, Gods, please...* Almost missing the Ink stage bell because of my bug charity, re-injuring my calf ligament, grasping Kinley's awareness, seeing all that goo–that puddle of red horror still painting me instead of the queen's roses. Me, the red card Alice, ruined because my thorns have failed to protect me and all my piggies from melting into nothingness.

And calling out for Cale. *Cale...I... You must know that I...*

Screw such incomplete thoughts. Gods, let me complete them, and maybe they can finally complete me?

"Help me, Elder Khaan," I mumble, the words as jumbled as my fucked up mind.

"Pivotal," he replies again, even though he can't because he's gone too, like it's some kind of challenge. My poisoned neurons accept the concept and fire too quickly to contain. Tripped up and disintegrating, they spin around searching for a new way, a better kind of thinking, and a different approach to survival here in the City where I have no guarantees.

And neither does Cale. *Cale...I... You must know that I...*

My heart pounds trying to steal my attention from my physical pain.

But it wasn't you, Cale. It wasn't. You're fine. I'm fine. Most importantly, you're fine. You're not dying. See, it isn't your blood.

My pulse rises because my heart knows I am listening now.

I keep telling myself this as if somehow that makes everything okay, as if somehow my whole world isn't crumbling before my eyes, as if my heart isn't bleeding for that stinking little one who I never helped, never knew.

Never even asked his name. Never, I condemn.

If I were strong enough to move my arms, I would reach up and gouge my own eyes out, those traitors. I imagine ripping off what's left of my eyelids and spitting at those wicked bastards that fooled me into thinking they were my friends but only blinded me to the power of my heart instead.

The power of my heart. What?

How long have I looked at the ground instead of meeting the gaze in the dead child's helpless eyes?

For Gods know how many days in a row. That's how many.

What eyes? They no longer exist.

Boom. I hear the murderous shot again and again and again. The same blast which has opened my eyes while simultaneously shutting his. I spin, dizzy from all the swirling in my brain because I realize that such an atrocity can just as easily happen to Cale or me or Baylor and all his bairns.

The image of the escaping lady beetle bug returns, and I shake my head slightly up and down to agree with her. I need to find a crack to hide in just like she did. A crack, perhaps, with a space inside it that no one knows about but us, one big enough for us all, one where no one will necrotize us. Maybe there I will finally be able to comprehend what she was trying to tell me.

Aiming to catch my breath, I wheeze and sputter, a thin string of mucous dripping off my lip. The pressure on my chest increases exponentially as my heart, pissed by now, keeps trying to make its point perfectly clear.

"I'm listening," I whisper. "I hear you. I feel you."

Before today, only Kinley could squeeze my chest like a beaker clamp, making it impossible to breathe from the pressure of saving her. But it's not just her anymore. It's also him, the dead one spurting red, and all the other kith-less bairns too.

Which one do I save by taking in? Which one do I walk past, selfishly knowing I am possibly sentencing him or her to death, squirting red, staining everything as they dissolve into nothingness? *My fault.* And like the blameless blowouts that murder the DED heads, I will wonder if I am the cause of the bairns' deaths? Is it my fault like with Tilly and her burning blue eyes still reminding me how I left her all alone to suffer and die?

Looking for someone to share the blame with, I lash out at Baylor. Could this all be Baylor's fault?

No, probably not Baylice, master of the charity case. He helps them all.

And now I will have to as well. Help them all, I mean, in order to survive this tragedy of unsure, trapped again in the land of the unknowing, despite the way the additional responsibility will wear on my Ink. *Fuck-all.*

But even then, can I really be sure which is worse–saving them or walking on by? If I take them in, then I will surely just fail them later, like Tilly. Not today, but maybe tomorrow when they feel safe and sound under my Inked wings, which have never flown despite my prior claims, made of nothing and nonsense. And is that better or worse, nicer or meaner? Because, let's face it–I am not a spy. This is no covert mission, and I have no idea how to get us all out of here safely.

So maybe it is best if I do walk on by, eyes peeled to the ground, refusing to see those innocent faces and hungry mouths, reminding them I survived as a lone child until Elder Khaan popped in with all his letters and numbers and songs. *So sweet, those songs he taught me about the dawn. So bright and beautiful that they still rock me to sleep each night.*

The bairns should learn to save their own butts like I did, my logic argues.

Or did I? Has my ass ever been saved?

"No. No, it hasn't," I tell my heart.

My mind flounders while the sound of a gun shatters my mind again. The crack travels down my neck port and spreads to my chest. Like mutant bacteria, it multiplies exponentially and infects my heart. My heart–the only part of me that really ever made any sense to begin with. *What? How crazy is that?*

Who am I kidding? I have never been logical; I have always been an emotional sap trying to survive in an emotionless world. Well screw that. I can only be who I already am. I jump into my heart and decide to stay there since I am already as good as dead. "Save me, my lovely little heart. Please."

I hear a click, click, clicking sound and know the gun and all the spurting will never stop. But just before I give in to it and declare myself completely insane, I realize the sound is really there click, click, clicking. *Just like the Ink projector.*

Where the hell am I? I try to move my arms but can't. *Oh no. Impossible.*

I don't feel the machine, but I hear it ticking endlessly. The echoing effect of mind-body disassociation takes over my ears, altering the sounds in and around me in a bizarre and yet, to my surprise, not entirely unpleasant way. My jaw, cranked down like a nut tight to a bolt, confirms the obvious–skag flows through my veins and numbs my brain. Now more awake, I can even smell the sick, sweet odor of the skag's evil juice coursing through me without my permission–really, against my permission–which no one ever asks because no one in the City cares what I have to say.

Except Baylor, my fellow Alice in a world of queens, and me, that is.

Or is it a white rabbit or Mad Hatter or disappearing Cheshire Cat? my internal voice asks, still clinging to the wormhole of her logic as the numbness of the skag takes over my mind once more, prompting me to question if my conscious mind has ever really been mine to begin with.

But the boom of the fire gun reminds me–it has–just before I lose myself again in the oblivion of a clenched jaw inside the infinite distance between atoms in another dimension.

When I wake up several hours later, still strapped to the Ink projector table with a huge 53 stamp all around my navel, I realize I will have to put back the scattered pieces of my mind like a puzzle that's lost the edge-pieces if I still want to think normally again. *But do I? Crazy, lost in circular logic, can be cool.*

To be honest, right now, I'm not so sure about trying so hard to regain my sanity. The hallucinations don't hurt at all, and I am moderately intrigued by the reprieve of total madness to stop the pain spreading through my chest. My heart beats fast and hard reminding me that the more it struggles, the more powerful it grows. *What?*

A cute, little mock turtle from the skag floats across my imagination, singing stupid sad songs about stupid things while he cries fake tears about problems he doesn't suffer, and to be honest, I can't help but find him amusing in his self-deprecating way now that I am so numb and detached. Yet even his outrageous melody sounds preferable to me than fire guns and bacteria determined to kill us all in this City of Nonsense. Or is it the City of Madness?

I have no idea how many hours pass while, like billiard balls, I ping between sleep and awake and crazy before Gaige comes back to unstrap me. Unlike the old ID, the new dealer touches me softly, like a doll that might break.

Once, so long ago, I had a doll, I suddenly remember. She was small and made out of wooden sticks which I found behind an abandoned, old building near the Pellonia quarters. I glued her together and put one of my drone socks on her top. With a single knot, I managed to give her a head with hair. When I gazed at her, I imagined her flowing hair so long and soft, draping down to the ground, unbuckled and unbraided like mine would never be.

Of course, like bairns tend to do, I named her–Kink, my stick and sock doll who I knew would see me through the first few years of life until I made some sense of a world that never made sense to me.

Even as a bairn, I suspected I was programmed differently than the others. So to escape from my differences, I started running away from this reality–and myself as well, I guess. Fast, faster, faster still because at least running made sense. I swore no one would ever catch me until I made it all the way back Home. As if some magical spaceship would show up at just the right time to take me back to my planet that was somehow magically inhabitable again, right? *What a joke.* But I am an awesome runner, and that serves me well at least.

To earn the Ink honors that saved my life, even if no kith wanted me, not yet anyway, I ran in child Heats before I had any business doing it, managing six Inks before I was five. *So young. Too young.* Unlike the other kith-less bairns who just disappear, one of the monitors, always the same kind female voice behind her missing eyes, brought me from one kith Elder to the next because of my overwhelming potential for speed. A few times, she said odd things about the sun, about how I was the most like her. As if a bairn could be anything like a monitor. It made no sense then–still doesn't.

As decreed by city law, five Inks and a kith affiliation by the age of seven are required for the right to struggle to live in the City under the roof of a habitation quarter or–poof–one day the bairns go bye-bye, never to show their cute mugs at another Ink stage.

"Kink, my sweet dolly, where do they go?" I whisper as if some unseen Doll-God will reply, because all of a sudden, I have to know. I have to, or I will surely freaking die. Because after this morning's horror movie, I'm pretty sure it's not an answer I want to hear, to be honest.

The whole concept of the helpful Mozek cracks a little further for me, and I decide that trusting them might just be the dumbest thing a 53 could do.

Shit, what makes me a 53 anyway? I remember Eliza Rachel's R&R assignment and realize I haven't seen her since she left Enlil quarters either.

But I must decipher the truth, so I ask the question again. "Kink, fucking answer me. Where do the bairns go if they don't make the cut?"

If I understand, then at least I will comprehend what I am saving them from when my charity goes berserk like Baylor's.

From a small corner way back in my head, I hear Elder Khaan warning that answers will surely follow the trail of dangerous questions I seem bent on exploring straight to my death. But I can't help it. These questions lead me helplessly from one to the next like an Ink freak looking for his next score in ridiculously dangerous assignments. And I sense I better be ready for the answers because just like today, the fallout's probably bad with a capital B.

The touch of the ID's hand on my skin burns me back to today. I gaze up into those purple eyes that look into, not through, me. *Gorgeous.*

Then I follow the sharp line of his nose until it reaches the dimple in the middle of his chin, visible even under that perfectly tailored beard. *So fine.* His lips, Inked along the outlines, move back and forth. This strikes me as odd, odder, somehow, than the fact that I cannot hear the words they are forming despite the echoes pulsing through my ears.

"Isla. Isla." Another pause and then, "Jane. Are you okay?"

I watch but cannot hear him speak. The elusive words bounce off the walls and ping around the room, making fun of the protons and neutrons still trying to form solid matter. Maybe there really is space between space, and even solid things are just as much an illusion as his words are right now.

Unable to hold it back, I laugh sadistically. "No," I say like I heard him perfectly. I want to add, "*And I never will be again,*" but I don't. I just look back into, not through him, daring him to ask me again.

He doesn't, yet he never looks away either. His expression oozes ageless wisdom like he grasps something important about me that I don't, like he wants to tell me a secret but can't. Unable to contain my sadness, I start crying.

Blubbering, I summon the courage to ask, "Did they do anything to–?"

But before I can add Cale's name, he cuts in with, "Yes," and my will to live falls to the floor with a smash loud enough to startle the deaf. Almost invisibly, he nods and then adds, "The bairn, Kalil, was necrotized during a public execution for his crime, of course. You must have forgotten from the high dose of skag required to sedate you."

My jaw locks asymmetrically, and I bite down trying to free it and stop the pain of a life I no longer find livable. Even if I could open my mouth to speak, I wouldn't because what's the point?

He adds, "Can you hear me or just the echo effect of skag?"

Did he just flutter one of his eyes at me? A clue I should figure out, maybe?

Then I notice the red light flashing behind me. Obviously, the Mozek are recording us. But aren't the dealers Mozek, too? Why does he bother to show me the light? Now I'm curious…

The IDs smell different, now that I think about it–more minty, less sulfuric. Maybe the IDs are something else, some other rank (both ladder and stink)? I just can't be sure yet. In a moment like this, could it really matter? Probably not.

So I grunt, "Both you and the echo, I think. And the little one's crime?"

"Stealing squares, of course," the Ink dealer Gaige, minus both the sulfur and a second name in his rank, says, "which is against their law."

Their?

"Of course," is all I can manage to say, still trying to disengage my jaw and successfully dissect the situation with my tripped up mind still so confused by skag, heartbreak, crumbling pressure, and all the pain oozing from the imaginary sutures in my neck from where someone reattached my head. *Guess their gladius never got me after all.*

But sure as death, I stink, infected with a disease that no bacteria can cause. Thankfully, the aseptic wound festers where no one can see it–on my inside, deep within my chest.

Like my beloved Alice, I wonder why it's always about the squares: Inks for squares, risking life for squares, stealing squares, kith families to ensure squares, bairns dying for them way too young.

Giving up on my jaw, I finger the 53 stamp on my front and accept that it's a small price to pay because they have not discovered my preference for Cale, thinking I care for the dead child instead. My punishment is for favoring him, the one I do not even know. *Did not even know–he's dead.*

Then it hits me like another swipe of the gladius blade in a Heat, severing my head again. If the monitors drug and bind me for caring about a bairn who they have already executed, then what would they do if they had a clue about how strongly I feel for the one who lives?

Cale...I... You must know I...I still...I will always...

Cale, who I will trade my every last square for, who creeps into my quarters so that I can rock, rock, rock away his night terrors and sing him songs so full of brilliant sunshine, whose battles are mine, and I will fight to the death.

In this moment, I realize that no one, not even Cale, can ever discover the truth of my preference for him and how completely it runs in and through me. Not of me, but from and even beyond me. Or surely they will take him away from me. The very thing I can never bear to suffer. Then he will be tortured for me, because of me, and most likely in front of me as I take my last gurgled, futile breath. *This little piggy has none, and it must stay that way.*

In my mind, I watch Cale place his two fingers to his lips, then over his heart, forming his special sign. His silly yet perfect words, *"heart you"*, stab me like a knife, deep in a place I have no name for. *Not yet anyway.* The space lives in my chest, through my heart, and even behind it. No, it exists beyond it, like it stretches from the front into a space too big for my mind to even grasp but never reaches back out the other side because it can't.

But soon, once my head clears, I will be able to control the expanding space inside my chest, making it smaller and less painful, like with Tilly and Elder Khaan, I'm sure. Gods, I hope so, at least. Because if I can't, I don't know how I will get up each day aware that I will have to look away from Cale and his, *"heart you."*

The monitors might as well freaking necrotize me now because I don't want any of their roast beef.

I think of Cale's flawless hands not yet thickened by years of handling red cards and all the poisonous assignments that will sear him outside, but mostly inside, taking away something they have no rights to and filling him with pus-filled wounds instead. His unspoiled center should belong to him only and not be for the taking or replacing, damn it. Not ever. Not from someone as pure and perfect as Cale. Or even from Kinley, for that matter, fuming spiteful words, bent on fooling us all that she is not covered on the inside with sores just like mine.

But my guess is that even if her body was colonized with a harmonious microbiome, she would still have gaping sores on the inside. Ones from this city, this alien place where we hand over everything to own nothing, to mean nothing, to be nothing, to make nothing worth making.

A world chock full of nonsense and madness.

And all of a sudden, it hits me that maybe it doesn't have to, that it shouldn't be this way just because the Mozek saved us from our decimated planet. That I should own me, Cale should own Cale, and Kinley should be the boss of which evil bacteria kill her and which ones don't. That I, that we all, deserve so much more just because and for no reason more than—just because.

Because we are all livers that shouldn't be forced to be diers.

How could this not be obvious to every living sentient being on this and every other planet? More time, more choice, more chances to make decisions like when to get up and what to wear or not wear or when to die or not die.

The spurting red coats me again, and I can't help but think about him—Kalil, the one whose name I would have never known if it wasn't for the boom still exploding my brain. It's time I face the fact—if it weren't for today's gun and goo club, he would have disappeared anyway without a kith or enough Inks like they all do lately.

Like I should have but didn't because of my wicked fast feet and determination to never give up even if I had to crawl through this rabbit hole and back out again. And the kind female monitor who presented me to Elder Khaan as well, I guess. I wonder if I heard her voice again, would I recognize it? Probably not.

But how will there ever be enough of us to get back Home if we keep dying right and left?

Unable to stop myself now, I surrender the illusion of any control over my disintegrating mind and let it crumble around me, not even trying to rein in my disorderly thoughts. I hear my mind snap and bow to my heart, seriously considering insanity a viable, superior choice once more. Snap, snap, snap, my mind snaps like poor little old Kink on the day the monitors discovered her hidden in my drones.

My doll, my precious little doll who meant so little to them but who meant so much to me with her sock hair that appeared so fine and perfect in my imagination.

Back when I was an innocent youth with ideas like I mattered, I was good, I was important to someone somewhere even if that someone was just a stick and sock doll named Kink who knew I was worthy just because. For no reason more special than—just because.

But now I know better. I learned my history lesson well about how little I deserve in the City of Impoverishment–just because.

Baylor, my fellow Alice in a world of disappearing cats, flashes in my memory now, and I think that he must get this, this part about how if he doesn't do something that no one ever will.

And for the first time ever, I see him in a way I never have before. I see a light around him, a goodness, a softness, a purity with open arms and smiling lips. Like my gorgeous lilies, it is hope that surrounds this picture of him, pillow-face and all, in my brain. *But hope for what?*

For a better day, a better way without squirting blood or clocks that hope to kill us for not being in the right place by the right time without second chances, because there are none here in this City of Never.

Except in Baylor. And now me, too, this Alice on a mission who fell through a hole without warning and landed in a screwed up world which makes no sense upside down, forward, or backward. The City of Riddles, rolling up smoking caterpillars chock full of skag and Ink that I never once ask for.

The dramatic side of me has taken over and kicked out my logical side for good. Here she goes–right down the drain in the City of Pipes that won't allow me to prefer innocent bairns like Cale and treat him special enough. But he is special, and I know it. Maybe only to me, but at least to me, who understands *"heart you"* for him in that place too deep and wide to measure.

Cale…I will always, without fail, no matter what…will always…

Shaking my head so hard my jaw unlocks, I finally comprehend that I will never control that space.

How could I? It is just too big. And that all along, I was fooling myself to ever think that I could because it is me, the real me, the invincible Isla inside the Isla who makes up the best part of this beta Levana named Isla Jane. If my heart had hands, she would clap because I really was, for once, listening to her message.

Cale's childish language speaks to me so much clearer than anything the monitors ever could with all their nonsense. Their normal words are worthless and mean nothing while they stand there all covered in their reflective gray getups, telling me who to be and how to die. *Such assholes.*

"Heart you." I *"heart you."* I *"heart you,"* I silently promise Cale from the me inside my space who knows so little yet feels so much, flailing in a world determined to destroy us with all its lack of choice, coated in Ink-covered lies, nothingness, and madness while it supposedly rescues us.

"But I will never tell you again, Cale," I pledge. I struggle against the straps across my legs and try to move my feet, but they are still strapped too tightly.

Tears wash across my coolant-blue eyes, down my angular face, and flood me, the real me that is, down a drain in the piping system. But no one sees them except for me. The tears are only visible in that place with no name–so deep, so wide, and so big it can hold Cale in me even though he's outside of me.

But he's not; he's inside too–forever.

And I do *"heart him"*–whatever that means.

Who the hell am I kidding? I know exactly what it means. It means everything. *Pivotal.*

I hear my heart clapping even though my hands are still, trapped in the machine that just Inked me.

Obviously, *heart* is the answer to this great big question wrapped in a question that consumes me. How could I have missed the only answer I may ever find worth finding? *Heart.* Now I'm not afraid of that queen anymore because there is nothing she can take away from me that she hasn't already taken, like Kink and Cale.

Certain of my next step, I accept what I must do. I have to tell Baylor, my fellow Alice, and try to hunt down the white rabbit with him, who will lead us right to the queen who's so set on removing our heads. That red bitch, sovereign of a city built on lies and hate instead of *heart.* The clapping gets louder so I move my arms and try to clap with my heart. The motion is clumsy but definitely an almost clap. Almost.

I reach up, my arms heavy, so heavy, and touch my throat, swallowing hard as I accept the burden this mission implies.

My physical heart beats so strongly for Cale that I do not even need to try to palpate it while it fills my neck and coats my brain in mission-driven plans. Too far to turn back now, I decide that even if I lose my head trying, I will do the best I can to make a better world for him and all the other bairns. For the tender-faced Baylor and the sarcastic Kinley as well. And even the bairns I cannot possibly name, who might potentially benefit long after I am dead and gone, along with all the other 53s who left this evil place because it wasn't worth living in. I would have been better off dead back Home.

Part of me is disgusted with this drama erupting from within. I try to control my theatrics, but I can't, damn it, because I want, no, I need a world where I can decide who I am. This beta Levana named Alice. I mean Isla.

Or I choose to die instead.

Because who cares to live this way? This way of nothings at all, this way of stamps and skag, this way of bloody showers and deadly bacteria for no reasons that can ever justify such horrid executions.

I look back up at Gaige and smile. The poor fool has no idea why. He probably thinks it's from the numbness of the skag. I guess in some ways, it is because this is the last dose I will ever take.

Or they will have to kill this Alice named Isla–just because.

He takes my hands from my neck and holds my fingers softly.

"It takes lives to save lives," I say, the words still slurred.

"Yes, it does," Gaige replies. He frowns and takes a full breath. And I am probably still hallucinating from skag, but I swear I can hear his heart too.

Like a platter of succulent lady beetle bugs, I offer my life up for the chance, even the chance of a chance of a chance, to look Cale directly in the eyes once more as I make sure he knows how special he is to me. Even if I am the only one smart enough to notice his value at a mad tea party where they keep changing the seats but not the place settings. Where round and round, like clowns in a circus, we circle, going absolutely nowhere at all.

I am Isla in a Jane body. I am beta Levana. I am undefeated Heat champion. I am me, the turmoil-driven me inside me who intends to go somewhere, finally.

Gaige places my hands softly in my lap and unstraps my legs, calling out my name once more with that pause of his. The memory of the phrase, "Lovely too," wakes me, lifting the haze of my funneling thoughts.

Intuitively, I sense that he knows about that place in me where he gazes into, not through, with his rose-creating fingers, and I finally figure out why.

Because it is simply too wide for him to see across.

I feel the mounting and undeniable urge to touch him again, to feel the smoothness of his penciled face against mine, which is crazy, I know; I want it anyway.

He smiles, making me want it even more.

"I will walk you to your habitation quarters," he offers despite the flashing red light of warning that it watches and records us. "You are too weak to walk on your own."

And I let him, every stolen glance at him intensifying the pull toward touching him and drawing him further into the space inside me. Yet, for some reason I can't explain, I fight the desire to run my hands across his hands as if my life depends on it.

The whole walk home, he says nothing. That Gaige without a second name has no words at all. But to be honest, I am glad for the not talking, because what would I say?

That I am broken? That I want to find comfort in his forbidden touch even though I just met him? That there is no me left to speak for or from? That I never cared for the one with the name I never knew until now? That the bloodbath has taken the one thing that ever mattered to me–not Kalil at all, but Cale–my favorite bairn, my everything in this world of nothings.

Yet somehow, by Gaige saying nothing and me saying nothing in return, we both say everything we need to about nothing in our perfectly matched madness.

And even though my hands never reach for his, I can feel his reaching back to rub mine once more. Though they never touch, I feel our fingers intertwined, soothing me like Elder Khaan's once did with his melted and ruined hand, which seemed so perfect to me.

I might fear Gaige is clueless to my suffering, and I have imagined him holding me without holding me, but he keeps stopping to let me rest. Yet I don't waste any words explaining to him what I can hardly explain to myself while I don't touch him, but do.

Eventually, he mumbles that my conditioning for showing preference for the dead youth will be a series of 53 stamps to assist with my improved reprogramming. "As you are my keep, I will personally escort you in the morning for your second session of mandatory re-Inking."

I want to scream for the treachery of such punishment, but there is no fight left in me for one day. And besides, like I keep telling myself, this is a small price to pay for keeping Cale safe and sound by my silence, by my looking the other way to act as though I couldn't care less. *Care less.*

Care less like I have always done for Kalil before today when he graciously opened my eyelid-less eyes, which will never close again.

Turns out, I am a Gods damned fish after all. *Ah, the irony.*

So I nod, not in agreement but in understanding that this is my sentence. As if I need one to remind me that I live a never-ending sentence here in the criminal City of Ink for crimes made of complete nonsense.

Once we approach the sliding glass entry to Forty-Three B, Gaige enters the code, and the doors open to allow me in even though I am late and should be punished for such a crime. But I won't be, not this time anyway, because of him. Then once more, I observe him peer into, not through, me before I return to my world that cannot be more different or more deadly than his.

Chapter Fourteen

JAXSTON, the Ink freak, eyes me suspiciously just before Gaige releases his grip on me. My arm burns hot like lava from the lack of my ID's touch, the nerves trying desperately to find his fingers again. Thankfully, though, Gaige offers me some reprieve by simultaneously giving me one of those looks of his–just a flutter of his eyelashes, which means nothing to anyone, other than me that is.

Oh my Gods. Touch me again. Please. I'm begging.

Unless…I have just imagined the whole exchange, which is totally possible, I have to admit. Doubt saturates me, and I shiver like my skin did the one time I ran out from the heat of the City of Broil into the frigid air of the cryo-chamber room behind the Foundry. But it wasn't the cold that made me tremble that time either; it was pure palpable panic and pain.

I have only been in the cryo-chamber called the Liebhorr once. Once was enough. It is officially off limits, and I am so okay with that. I never ever want to go back inside that building.

Lost deep in one of my thought sessions, I opened the back door, thinking I was somewhere else entirely. It was crazy though. I shouldn't have had access as far as I can tell. Swirling in my mind about new battle moves I wanted to try out, this greenish light flashed three times while it scanned my retina, and a little ball of sparkling light appeared. I was too surprised to get away before the glittery sphere moved right up to the space between my eyes and flittered back and forth. The odd sensation evoked a familiar remembrance from deep within me, which I have no words to describe. This lasted for what must have been seconds but felt like forever. The beautiful little ball called me Doctor, I think.

"Chief Officer of War Medicine," it said, "it has been a while."

Unable to do anything else, I followed the pulsating ball of light into a large room about twice the size of the BRÉ. There was so much green everywhere, which is quite strange now that I think about it. The ugly olive-tiled walls reminded me of a place I can't remember exactly but know I have been somehow.

But then panic got the better of me, and I quickly scanned the chamber, looking for a way out. Not because of the cold but because it hurt in a visceral way to be in there. Like knives slicing into my eyeballs and penetrating the center of my mind, I knew I could only tolerate being in that hall of unadulterated fear...or perhaps hatred...a few moments longer.

Wires and tubes made of what looked like archaic materials such as silicone and plastic, suspended globs of something meaty or muscular. These specimens, for lack of a better word, were connected by fine wires with clamps at regular intervals that dove into sacs hanging from hangers made of mesh and twine. The suspended bags made of a pale, almost flesh-like colored material, too many to count, lined the walls, but before I had time to touch one, I escaped. I had to listen to my own advice to make it out alive from what felt like impending neurological meltdown. Why? Because I had no other choice, preferring survival to my own curiosity this day when I was so unlike Alice.

Wondering where my certainty went, I try to reach back to before, back to yesterday. But this time, much like Alice, I am already a different person and can't. Suddenly, I am freezing, like whatever it was hanging in those slimy bags, even though I was consumed by molten fire a moment ago.

So I might contemplate fluttering mine back too, but what's the point?

Do I really want to know the truth? He can't really care about what I have to say about this, can he? And I don't want to embarrass myself by suggesting something as absurd as an Ink dealer trying to secretly communicate with me.

My inner bitch slaps me for being so stupid earlier. *Ouch.*

Since I'm not sure which is more painful, swirling in this doubt or finding out I'm mistaken about my new alliance, I ignore my internal critic and try to worry about things that actually matter. Like why is that Irmin and his dirty smirking mug in our building at all? Surely he's up to some trick.

Those Irmin creeps live in Forty-Two B, just one structure to the right, close enough to watch us and steal our meager possessions when we get distracted enough to leave them behind. And sometimes I swear they spy on us, trying to figure out why they can never beat us in the Heats.

Involuntarily, I reach up and touch my ears before I realize what I am doing. Then I remind myself to apply another layer of paint on top of that secret because losing it just might kill us all.

I click my tongue. "Yep. Uh huh," I say while stroking my hair beads next and twirl my braids around my finger. Jaxston, that piece of shit with skull Inks decorating his wiry neck, probably thinks I'm teasing him. But really I am just calming myself down even though I smile like I am enjoying this taunting display. I do not.

Why can't those jerks live on the other side of the city like Volta, the closest thing they have to allies in their ruthless predisposition of encouraging sinister behavior? The monitors couldn't have set up our living arrangements more perfectly to encourage conflict if they had tried. It's like a little Heat, day in and day out, but for real—no thraex machine, no shield, no weapon to protect me.

Then I consider maybe the Mozek city planners do it on purpose? Could it be to amuse them? But why do they want us warring, divided all the time, and who could that possibly benefit? I just can't be sure yet.

Not us surely, all distracted by hate and possibly injured in one of our trifle brawls outside the Orb where we are more protected at least. Here, in the City of Strife, not so much. *Assholes.*

Dragging my attention back from Jaxston, who is leaning so closely into the monitor that their foreheads are almost touching, and placing it on Gaige, I notice his head curves just slightly in the direction of my vile enemy while he points the other way. Gaige says something else that means nothing to anyone but me. Pleasure floods me and heats up my pelvis instantly. The imaginary burn on my arm starts sizzling and blistering.

I guess I didn't imagine the fluttering after all. *Yes, that feels good.*

Plastering indifference across my face like a mask, I act totally oblivious to Gaige's subtle maneuver. In fact, I scratch my ear and pace, obviously bored to still be standing there with him, a purple-eyed dealer of all creatures.

Of all creatures. The thought, delicious to my hands, my breasts, and for some unexplained reason, the pulsing space between my legs, feels wonderful.

While pacing, I observe my loincloth moisten and revel in the sensation. He has done this to me. I have no idea why or how, but I am certain I like it. I think he would like it, too.

I can't help but smile as I realize that underneath Gaige's sneaky and undeniably arousing caterpillar smoke, I hear two things. The first is that Jaxston is not my friend, which every idiot in town already knows. And the second is that Gaige wants to be or at least wants to pretend to be.

I tell myself that I don't actually give a flip even though I am not so sure that's true. Unless what he desires is something new that the monitors can turn against me.

My inner goddess shakes her finger at me like I'm an idiot.

But what can possibly make Gaige think I have anything worth offering him? He's an ID and so far above my rank (ladder, not stink) that none of it makes any sense at all. I am just a 53. Well, actually I'm an Alice born from too much pivoting, who wishes she could just be a 53 again but can't because she can't go back to yesterday.

Gaige doesn't know that about me, not yet anyway. How could he? I just found out. Or does he somehow? I just can't be sure yet.

Does he know something about me that I do not, something subtler than the color of my eyes, something more important than the flavor of my Ink? Is that what he observes when he looks into, not through me?

He points at the large clock on the wall of the main lobby in Levana quarters as we approach the monitor at the check in station to remind me that I have an appointment to meet him tomorrow.

"Yes, yes," I sputter and wonder where the lovely moisture went. My skin feels dry like powder-covered canvas. As if I could possibly forget my conditioning and repro-gramming, two words so heavy and dark, haunting me like the creatures in Cale's nightmares.

He sighs deeply, looking at me like he wants to say more but won't or can't.

Repeating myself, I say, "Yes, yes."

A funny look slides across his furrowed brow, and he half-winks at me. *What? What is he keeping from me now? How many layers of deception does he function from?* He walks up to the monitor and grabs the log book.

"Go on. I'll finish the log entry for you," Gaige says, and the monitor ignores me like I don't even exist.

Should I trust Gaige at all? *Probably not.* I should probably never trust anyone. Except trust myself to screw things up by playing Alice down her hole.

As I walk past the monitor and Jaxston, who were previously talking so friendly to each other, Jaxston glares at me. His tiny, malicious pupils try to figure out which part of me he despises the most. Which part of me he plans to rip off and eat, if given the half a chance, while no one else looks. *Creepy cannibal.*

"I am up for a black card later if you are willing to be the benefactor. I'll make it worth your effort. Unlike her," Jaxston says to the monitor and points at me.

Gaige coughs. "The entry is complete. We are finished here. I will sign now."

Jaxston groans, and I have to assume he is pissed that he has lost the monitor's attention for good. Does he know about Cale or my medical book or the words and numbers I know but shouldn't? Of course not. If he does, he would have seen me necrotized months ago—the day after I assumed the most prestigious suite in our Levana quarters six months ago, to be exact. *Elder Khaan, I miss you.*

While the monitor scans Gaige's retina, Jaxston forces me to the side. Smacking his gums, the creep says, "Why the hell are you just getting here, Isla, beta Levana? Shouldn't you be getting ready in your hot little head?"

I scowl and keep walking, avoiding eye contact with him. But that asshole grabs my arm and pulls me back.

"And why is the purple-eyed goon with you?" he demands as if I actually have to answer him. But I don't, so I just smile, shake him off, and keep walking, refusing to let his words dig in and hurt me.

Ready for what?

He rushes forward and shoves his arm out to stop me from getting away, his face coated in a few thin make-believe layers of pretend kindness. Then he looks in the direction Gaige just left to make sure I understand his meaning. Like I'm an idiot, he says, "Well, did the ID pierce your tongue? Why are you so late, beta bitch?"

What is he taunting me with? Why should I be anywhere but here?

My mind threatens to go overboard, wondering where else I should be, observing who knows what disaster.

Then he spies the fresh bandage over my navel. He has his answer. Yet I am still spinning helplessly for mine.

The fire in his eyes burns hot with jealousy at my new Ink. The same he would trade anything for.

"Ink freak, I hope you die during that black card," I say still smiling and fondling my braid beads like I couldn't care less. I stare him down and speak absurdly slowly like I'm talking with a bairn to display my superior rank (ladder, not stink) over his infantile Inks. He will not get under my skin. No freaking way.

He rolls his eyes and mocks a knife injury to his gut before he laughs. "You clueless little girl. As if you even know what a black card is. Stupid amateur. You have no idea what you are missing. But I do."

"Get out of my way, idiot, unless your alpha has sent you with some kith business to merit my attention, of course."

"Actually…" he starts, still staring at my bandage, saliva foaming in the corners of his mouth.

I can almost hear his thoughts. *More Ink, more Ink, more Ink.*

That's all he ever wants or cares about in this *care less* world, so unconcerned about horrors like the gun and goo club. Ink, the all mighty Ink, and skag with its slimy, sweet smell that numbs his brain and floats him out into the middle of a mad tea party attended by drunken mice full of burps and giggles who have all forgotten about finding their way Home.

Ironically, he hiccups, and I can't help but laugh.

Then the rodent informs me that as ambassador from Irmin, he comes to congratulate me for winning the opportunity to Heat tomorrow. How he knows this before I do, I cannot say. *Fucking rat.*

"On account of yesterday's events, perhaps you should invite that new pal of yours Baylor John," he adds, laughing while he drops on all fours and scampers about.

I stare past him and roll my eyes.

"I thought surely you would be in your thraex portal, prepping for some more gymnastics moves. Where did you learn to flip like that? Stealing Salus secrets now?"

I walk away.

"And I thought you were so honest. Perhaps we can be black card buddies, you and I, if you keep this up. They pay well for two players at the same time, you know."

They pay? What? That gets me, even though I have no idea what "black card buddies" means, and I turn around to face him. I think I better act like I enjoy my navel stamp a little more and grin from ear to ear while I touch my bandage reverently.

That shuts him up. For almost a second. Almost. But the creep recovers and pops a sweet square in his mouth like he already has enough stored for the winter.

"Black card buddies," he says and flexes his firm chest muscles up and down to some shrew anthem playing inside his head. "Double the fuck-me-fun. Everyone wins."

I gag, not certain why the behavior feels so sickening. *Wins? What?*

Then I remember what else he just said. *Winning the opportunity to Heat tomorrow. Oh no.*

Now so many will be punished for my tardiness, others I can't even name perhaps, and I will get to pretend I'm honored to Heat alongside the Irmin. Like I *win* something for almost losing with hours of pageantry and pretend battles meant only to amuse the 53s dumb enough to think they matter. *Ridiculous. When will all these backward illusions ever end?*

Now, at least, I get what Gaige was not saying, not sharing. He already knew, that bastard. And it dawns on me he must also know I would consider that a bad thing. *Impossible.*

How can Gaige possibly know the gallant award of being crowned the victorious verus means squat to me? I've never told anyone…ever.

Heats. The idea sends more shivers down my spine, and I climb in the Liebhorr cryo-chamber in my mind and zip myself up in one of the pale skin-like suits. Even though Heats are pretend, sometimes I wonder. *What if this were really happening? What if a warrior dies?* The urge to go completely still and hold my breath consumes me, but then I think better of it and decide that laughter is always the best medicine and climb back out of the Liebhorr of my frigid thoughts to set my trap.

Sardonically, I laugh and then flick my hair to warn that vole Jaxston that if he is my assigned opponent, he might as well hand over his cheese now because my sword intends to land at the most vulnerable place on his hairy neck.

He's back making eyes with the eyeless monitor, and I hear him whisper. "Black, baby. Please, baby. I want you."

I see the monitor, who's anything but sneaky, slip him another sweet square, which is totally illegal since we aren't supposed to even speak to, let alone interact with them.

The two of them flutter their long tails back and forth with delight.

Why would Jaxston behave like this–smiling, showing his muscles, and playing with his hair for the monitor? To get something in return, perhaps.

But what? Favor and sweet squares? Or insider information about us, about me specifically I bet, from that monitor who, unlike me, is allowed to have a preference? *Vermin.*

As this sinks in my involuting mind, I intuitively grasp that there is something critically important bubbling forth underneath my observation. A question that must be asked if I'm going to act like a proper Alice who hunts down the queen, sticking blades in her neck. Ha, ha, ha. Instead of showing her mercy, I chop that red witch in two and eat all her piggies for lunch. *Oh, even the thought tastes delicious.*

The question shoves its way to center stage of my swishing, swirling thoughts and wreaks havoc on my heart. Here it goes. I'm too far in and can only follow it now. Why do they Ink us? Why do they want me hooked by it, conditioned from it, assimilated by it, like Jaxston with his cruel, addicted pupils literally dying to dilate from a fresh stamp of it? What exactly is Ink, this coloring that decorates me, and why is my world built on, by, and for it?

Ink this, Ink that–it is a wicked obsession. And that's exactly how the Mozek want it.

Now that I have swallowed the bait, I cannot stop halfway.

I've reached the stairwell now and let the door slam behind me.

What does the stamp Gaige just stained me with really mean with those interconnecting Bs and Es? What is the stamp beneath the 53 stamp? Or even underneath the Levana stamp, for that matter?

Because there always is one, I am sure of it. Actually, it is the only thing that makes sense in all this nonsense.

Pressing my back into the cold titanium door, I let the chill of the metal spread down my back as my observations and questions gather speed.

It's the same with the Heats, too. What is the Heat beneath the Heat? What am I really competing, racing for? Who benefits from the pageantry of an illusionary battle in this pretend city inside the City of Ink?

It dawns on me now that I'm no different, not really. I slam my elbows into the door behind me and get ready to climb the stairs while my thoughts keep rising higher and higher to match them.

Why?

Because I'm always asking a question beneath and inside my question, that's why. And it's the same with my answers, too, I must admit. Taking them two at a time, I get to the top more quickly than usual before I realize how tired I am.

After I arrive at my quarters, I collapse from all those questions and answers, from fatigue, from submission, from fear, from pain, from the skag, from Gaige's eyes warning me about Jaxston's, both blinded by their eyelids.

I will have to prepare for the Heat tomorrow. Tonight, I crash.

When I instantly drift off to sleep, my long lost Tilly urgently takes my hand and winks while placing her finger across her lips to ensure my silence. Not sure whether to be afraid or excited to go, I follow.

Chapter Fifteen

UNABLE TO RESIST Tilly even in my sleep, I go. The whole time, she keeps tapping and shaking my hand to make sure I hold on tightly. Her eyes, obviously delighted to gaze upon me, light up and open with the excited urgency with which she leads me. Only she knows for sure where.

Oh no, not there. No.

But I have an idea where we are headed now and even in my sleep start thrashing about. I keep pulling back, a fish trying to escape Tilly's hook. I don't want to go, but she's got my lip now.

She drags me out of the water against my will.

Yet that look of hers, so sweet and innocent, makes me want to stay in the boat even though I don't really want to because I sense Tilly has something critical under her hull and will not be denied the chance to show it to me. So does Kink, the doll in my other hand, who winks up at me with her drone sock hair to remind me they never snapped her mast in half either.

"See, I'm just fine," the doll says and winks again.

Tilly squeezes my hand even harder to remind me that she is here as well even when I cannot see her with waking eyes and that she pledges to help me find my way back out the rabbit hole where life is clean, the water fresh, and all the boats travel with, not against, the winds of time.

"Home?" I ask her.

She grins. "Back Home where you don't have to look behind metaphors, underneath illusions, or in between the molecules of lies wrapped around partial truths to feel safe."

"Home." I sigh and pull the rusted hook from my lip and hand it back to her because, let's face it–she doesn't need it anymore.

Surrendering to her intensity, I lay my sleeping head on the softness of the smell of her, so fluffy and delicious, beaming while in peaceful slumber and willingly follow her as the lovely idea of truth infuses me with enough strength and purpose to face my greatest fear. But maybe it's something even more wonderful than that. *Hope, maybe?* My lilies get excited and start shaking.

Perhaps Tilly does not hate me, does not blame me for what happened, or maybe only partially blames me? I just can't be sure yet.

And even though I won't dare say it out loud, I do hope it. Oh Gods, I do. Maybe one day she might forgive me for what happened, for what I did. And I dare to hope even more than a little. Because a little bit will never do.

Maybe, maybe she will even forgive me for what I didn't do when I was such a stupid little minnow.

While I follow her through antifreeze-green meadows stretching in every possible direction, even up and between directions, an idea pops in my hypnogogic brain. If I can pull this Alice routine off, maybe, just maybe, I can make it up to my sweet Tilly with those eyes so clean and lovely.

"But how?" I whisper.

By making it up to yourself, my inner voice proudly replies. *Duh.*

First, though, I will have to figure out who is the Isla Jane beneath me, here where it takes lives to save lives in the City of Queen. Or is it Ink?

But then I realize I already know her. She is beta Levana. She is Alice. She is the eyelid-less, cold-blooded fish. She is the same me behind the mirror in melted Jane's pink eyes claiming her right to live as the verus champion in the center of the Gridiron, pulling down the walls of illusion and replacing them with only truth. *Me.*

Tilly says, "Don't you know that a life with no *heart* is like a ship with no sails? In fact, if you take away the heart, nothingness and timber is all that remains."

"Yes," I say and float down a river in a place from Home called Scotland.

Still clutching desperately to that beautiful image, I wake to the slam, slam, slamming of Skylar April, my delta, beating her fist on my door. Like a wave of fire, a volcanic eruption of fear spreads from my heart to every corner of my body. I don't bother to check the rate, knowing it beats over two hundred times a minute.

Instantly, a layer of sweat coats my brow and drips down my breast to warn me–the Heat has officially begun.

Section II: The Heats

Your glowing beauty,
Framed in FIGHT.
And precious rays,
Of warm delight.

Chapter Sixteen

I ROLL over and take deep, slow breaths with my head buried in my pillow. Determined not to betray my nervousness or answer my lower ranking sib too quickly, I lie here ignoring the pounding on my door while that drop of sweat sneaks down my stomach. Then I remember the hate in Jaxston's evil eyes, drowning in pleasure at the idea of me losing my head and Gaige not telling me about it. The Heat is today, not tomorrow. Today. Now.

The drop reaches my toes and just stays there. Maybe I should get up?

As my delta, my lifeline in battle, Skylar preps, encases, and then releases me from the thraex, my portal into battle, on the other side of a fight. In a troop Heat, where all ranked members of an entire kith fight, she will serve as my second in command–me number one, her number two. So, I guess I better not piss her off too much.

Yes, I should get up. *Crap.*

Taking another deep breath, I imagine stepping completely naked into the thraex portal vault, pulling out the location probe from the back of my head, and applying the solid Heat wire. The titanium-encased tube will click into position in my neck and bury countless electrodes inside the base of my skull. Then they will travel down my spine and out into all of my peripheral nerves, which control every part of my body. At that point, I'll be more the property of a Mozek computer than myself, I guess. *Piggies locked and loaded.*

Shivering despite my sweaty brow, this chilly feeling would probably make me wonder what's the muscle ball connected by all those wires in the slimy bags in the Liebhorr if I had the time. Thankfully, I don't and go back to warmer thoughts instead. *Get up, you drippy little piggy.*

In my imagination, I sense the weight of my computer-generated parmula, a simple circular shield, in my hand, protecting my chest from the imaginary ax, sword, or trident of my rival. The cold steel of my preferred gladius blade, the same used in gladiator battles of old, firm in my other hand, begging me like an Ink junkie hunting for more skag to deliciously end this as violently and viciously as possible.

I can almost hear the chants of thousands drawn into the disgusting display, booing, hissing, screaming, but usually demanding, once I have kicked my opponent's ass, to abstain from the final deathblow. Missio–a gift of mercy meant to drag out the fun and humiliation of my rival in supposed compassion that is really just good old-fashioned pity. *Get up. Get up.*

"A pretend death would be better than pity," I mutter.

Skylar and her pounding stop momentarily like she knows exactly what I am thinking about. *Impossible.*

Rarely can I remember the crowds asking for death of a warrior. The last about a year ago, I think. I try to remember the verus champion who won. Was it Baylor? Yes, I think so. But as for the one who lost, I can't recall. I'm not sure I ever saw him again, now that I think about it. *Get up now. This little piggy has an appointment with a battle-ax.*

Strapped in my thraex portal, I will feel every cut, slice, and blow that injures the projected version of me on the gigantic screen of the entertainment Orb inside the Gridiron where we hold the Heats. Thankfully, even if I bleed or suffer terribly inside my thraex, it's really of no grave consequence to the real me because once I'm out the other side of the Gods-forsaken contraption, I emerge intact.

So even though I have never lost my head, if one day I do, I will be well prepared for the queen trying to kill me. My hands go to my neck and rub before I realize what I am doing.

But I have never lost. Today will be no different.

And even though the entire battle will take place only in the joined consciousness of my fellow warrior and me, the rapture of my thoughts on the floating, misty canopy for all to see makes me feel exposed in a way that words fail. My nervous system betrays me, sharing the only thing I've ever really had any power over–my thoughts. And if the Mozek can display the images in my mind like a motion picture for all of the Heat enthusiasts to witness, then certainly they can uncover every single secret I keep hidden in this brain of mine without much more effort. I cringe, looking right and left for soap to wash my dirty little secrets.

Skylar marches in just as I stand to open the door. I recall showing her the code once. Once is apparently enough with this lady. Hand on her hip, she gives me a look to say, *"What the hell?"*

"Okay, okay, I'm up."

She brings over two fresh boxes for extra hydration and starts my rub down for prep. All of my beads, one by one, she places in a bead box in order of my preference. I remember telling her that only once as well.

"You screw up your cross and react tests? I don't think so," I almost say. Instead, I say, "Thank you."

Talking a little too loudly, she jovially braids my hair, multiple braids within a braid, in a tight circle around my head that starts on the right and finishes at the top. By the time she's done, I am gorgeous, my skin glowing, my hair as shiny and beautiful as a jewel on my grayish blond crown. No one does hair like her. If I had time to ponder such things, I would be curious where she learned it. *If...*

As usual, she chirps her classic brand of small talk. *Chirp. Chirp. Beep. Beep. Ugh.* Thankfully, she waits until the hair-sprayer kicks on before complaining about the DED and how useless those overseers are.

"I thought the BRÉ was bad, Isla Jane, but I was wrong. These idiots don't even notice which bottles I open and of which ones I dispose. In fact, if I were to swap them, no one would ever notice. Maybe I shall if you keep sending me there. Ha. What do you think?"

Shrugging my shoulders like I'm listening to her or actually give a crap about DED assignments, I say, "Huh. I guess. But they might melt you for it."

Doesn't she know they record everything we do? She seems so much smarter than that.

Luckily, once the spray is off, she returns to more trifle topics. *Chirp. Chirp. Beep. Beep. Ugh.* When she's done rambling about nothing drizzled in more nothing, the silence sounds even more awful than her crap talk.

Unable to take it any longer, I start in with my own ridiculous comments to match hers. "Has the editor posted the Libellus? I expect a Binary, don't you?"

She laughs knowing I already know better than to ask her such stupid things. They will hold off posting the document announcing the kith of my enemy, the terrain of our battleground, the confounders, and our available weapons of choice until it is too late for me to do any kind of valuable prep work.

"Soon enough, but not soon enough," she says in her riddling sort of way.

"We are all mad here, aren't we?" I reply, feeling a little sassy myself, so slicked up and gorgeous.

Still laughing, she escorts me, like a prisoner minus the cuffs, to the track.

As I step into the warrior entrance that opens into the catacombs beneath the Gridiron, I get an answer from one of the posted signs littering every wall in this City of Distortion. The Libellus states:

Level I: Porus-Orbona
     Level II: Camena-Agenor & Janus-Hora
     Level III: Finale: Levana-Irmin & Luna-Volta & Salus-Suadela.

So a graded Binary, where pairs battle side by side, mounting in difficulty and probably declining in weapon options. *My personal favorite. Great. That I can do!*

But then I remember how many people are being punished because of me. I count them—eleven. The same 53s, oblivious to their punishment disguised as a gift, who will completely forget all about the little spurting bairn Kalil murdered by the Mozek gun and goo club. *They've already forgotten, I bet.*

But not me. I see the lies hidden in this "gift." An old memory returns to me from a lesson with Elder Khaan—the Trojan Horse.

I won't forget you, Kalil, my inner voice pledges.

As the opening ceremony begins, the ground shakes from the powerful drums, the booming trumpets. Holographic rose petals fall from the sky, waiting for the damned dozen to enter.

Out of, actually underneath the main entertainment Orb and therefore unable to watch in real time, I have to imagine the events as they occur or can choose to view via a remote observational visor. Unwilling to miss a glimpse of Cale, I place the visor on and revel at the effort put into our glorious display. It's crazy, but sometimes I think every creature in the galaxy must be watching for the frugal Mozek to invest such massive efforts on a program like this. And even though it's obviously aimed at making us forget about the dead and spurting brat, I smile knowing Cale is amongst the chosen ones during the opening ceremony.

Again I make my fiduciary pledge: *I won't forget you, Kalil.* Then form my Cale's special sign to seal my pact.

The decorated bairns covered in beautifully colored armor, march into the center of the Orb in real time and space to play their roles as lighted Virions, saber-like swords, appear magically in their excited hands from the conjoined laser lights that brighten the dry sky. I hear the bairns giggling, easily able to pick out my dear Cale from all the others despite his elaborate coverings while he bubbles from behind his ornate mask. Oh he must be so pleased to be chosen as the representative of Levana. With as much honor as this place can afford, he acts out his part of the dramatic battle, recreating the inciting events of the Global War that decimated our Home.

The anthem plays louder and louder. *Boom. Bam.* More fireworks. The anticipation mounts exponentially, and Cale, just like all the others, literally twitches back and forth.

When the crowd can no longer suffer the teasing, a great bell rings, and the ceremonial fighting of the bairn mock Heat ceases. The supposedly defeated youth, as scripted before they came out, collapse to the ground beneath the feet of all the vindicated verus. All of the bairns drop their masks simultaneously.

Then the crowd, who must play their role too, cries out in mock compassion for missio. At the last possible moment, right before the defeated are decapitated, a band of twelve golden-robed droids assume the central position of the floor, holding hands to effectively interrupt the impending slaughter.

A penetrating light emanates from underneath each central droid who then blesses the shoulder of each kneeling victorious verus with an olive leaf. The losers wail in pretend defeat, hoping to escape their execution by offering the robed band of robots a decorated bead of great beauty. The twinkling babes, both winner and loser in each pair, demand a merciful outcome by shaking their heads and clapping in agreement that the defeated must be spared for the good of all. The droids submit to the will of the masses and accept the beads as tokens of proof of their manifest destiny–superior race over the bairns who have been so foolish to fight to begin with. Then all the contestants, champion and defeated alike, bow in awe of such a display of compassion, good will, and unified purpose.

The crowd goes wild in approval.

Then the robed droids, still shining brightly, descend beneath the Orb's base while the others from the mock battle all stand, drop their protective gear, and display their beautifully decorated skin. Each of them wears the sign of their kith, hoping to please the Gods for favoring them as they finally assume their fated rank (ladder, not stink) beneath the clever golden robots. The bairns then make their appropriate sign, and the cries from the crowd deafen out any other sound.

A holographic audience, which I suspect has been added for its glorious and impressive effect, sitting behind and even above the 53s vastly outmeasures the thousand or so 53s in the Gridiron. The projected visitors bang their seats and play hand held instruments as each of the bairns is cuffed to the child next to him or her in the pageant. As a single line, they, too, descend to the catacombs beneath the stage where they will be unchained and returned to their kith members.

Sometimes, I stare at this insane projection of the visitors while the bairns parade around. Some wear bizarre observational visors, have forked tongues flickering out of their abnormally shaped mouths begging for a bloody fight, odd colored knobs around their necks, horns on their heads, metal plates sticking out of their skulls, gold masks and robes. It's all so strange. I can't help but wonder why they look this way. Where do the images in the Gridiron come from? Are they real? Are they fake? Who cares, really?

Answering my own question, I announce, "I do, actually."

The drumming becomes almost unbearable, and with one final spasm of release, the freakish mob goes insane, and the real Heat begins, starting with level one and increasing in intensity until the third level or finale—me.

Skylar nods, and I know it is time to enter my portal.

I step into my thraex portal, a smaller self-contained version of the massive glass and metal contraption I use in my cross and react tests in the BRÉ, and I feel the vibration of its circuitry engage. The outer glass seals itself as Skylar punches in the proper codes on a white panel she holds in her hand, and I sit in the metal seat and surrender to the inevitability of the next several hours. She smiles and nods her head to remind me that she will be here when I return.

Why?

Because I always win. I always return. She will wait right here for me.

With a measure of ambivalence, I replace my location probe in my skull's port with the Heat wiring, allowing it to plug into the deepest place within me—my mind. *Does it know about the space so deep and wide within me?*

The electronic bastard climbs inside my brain, contaminates my nerves, penetrates my muscles, and poisons my defenseless organs. Instantly, all my piggies are paralyzed.

The two inner titanium doors beneath the glass casing activate, and I know what comes next as well as I know the two parts of my own name—Isla Jane.

The first door of my thraex portal rotates into a closed position. *Isla. I am Isla.* Then the second follows suit. *Jane. I am Jane.* The safety latch engages, and the three layers become one. *Isla Jane. I am Isla Jane in a glass encased prison.* Trapped, I am unable to undo what is happening to me until the Heat is over and Skylar lets me out.

"Sure am glad I didn't piss her off earlier," I would joke to calm myself down if my tongue worked. But it doesn't, so I just shut up. It is pitch-black now, and I have no idea if that is from a simple lack of light or that my eyes no longer work.

If I hadn't survived this freaking process a hundred times, panic would saturate me, paint me in misery, and ensure my total decompensation. Instead, I silently and motionlessly laugh at the idea of Skylar too furious to let me back out.

"I think I will be a little nicer to her later," I do *not* say.

The pressure inside the unit increases exponentially until a penetrating buzzing sound fills my ears so powerfully that I swear I can not only hear but see it. I try to blow out my nose and pop the bubbles in my ears. The sound returns but no describable visuals yet–only wavy lines and flashes. Falling too fast to measure the distance, my stomach drops, and I get unbearably dizzy. Just before I pass out or vomit, everything stops moving, and I go completely numb.

At this point, the machine owns total access to both my mind and body because I am nothing more than a character trapped inside a virtual video game. Only saving grace here is that I work my own controller. Well, sort of, anyway.

I can feel again, only this time I know it's the holographic version of me responding. Even though the movements of the projected version of me seem fluid enough on the three-dimensional hammock in the Orb, they are nothing in real time because I am still paralyzed in my thraex, directly connected to the portal. Just like during Heat practice, the simulated version of me disengages from the straps and clasps that hold the original me in place, and I prepare to enter Folding, a transitional room that takes the projected version of me into whatever place I am going to next. And if I didn't know better, I would buy the whole charade. This video bitch I'm operating certainly looks and feels real enough. In fact, she looks and feels exactly like me.

Sometimes, I wonder which version of me is more *real*.

I pinch myself for such a stupid thought. "Ouch," I holler, genuinely surprised that it hurts and reach up to feel my skull: no port, no locater–cool. Still grumbling even though I am thrilled that metal is gone from my neck, I place my digitally remastered eyeball to the first scanner, followed by the second so the doors open.

Now I am truly helpless until the Heat is over.

At least the machine's controls are easy enough to manage. I think, *Exit,* and my body steps out the exit side of the thraex into Folding almost as if I am real and remain untouched, unharmed, inviolate. Almost.

The flashes intensify until my vision finally returns. *Thank Gods.*

Unable to resist, I look back at the thraex portal, and sure as shit, there I am. Both of me–here and there. Only the other Isla looks still, thin, and lifeless like a bag of flesh and nothing more. I bet just like the Mozek, she has no eyes at all. *Creepy.*

The unnatural heat of the powerful machine my *real* body is attached to courses through my nerves, and I shiver both from the heat and the lack of it in this odd room. *Nope, not thinking about Liebhorr bags or the other me or lack of me. Move, piggies, move.*

The longer, the deeper my physical body stays connected to the thraex portal, the more distracting the sensation becomes. Eventually, it becomes painful, intolerable even, testing my physical limits, determining the ultimate time I can fight in a Heat and remain conscious.

Do the others feel the same misery from this contraption?

"The others are my enemies in the entertainment Orb, and I don't care how they feel, duh," I say for the benefit of my heart.

I am only concerned about myself. But since I'm not so convinced of my cardiac reserve, I think it again just to be sure. *I am only worried about myself.*

And even though the monitors assure me that the Heat wires do no long-term damage to my *real* central nervous system, I don't believe them. Each Heat takes longer to recover from. One day, I am pretty sure my muscles will not come back, and I will remain split–trapped out of my own body, unable to escape the machine's effects permanently.

Would that make me a ghost? "Shut up, you stupid sap." My brain assumes control and slaps my heart in the face for being so stupid.

A ghost, what?

Simultaneously, the twelve warriors, including me still laughing at my split person-alities to match my split bodies, step into Folding where several of those eyeless Mozek and twelve Interval Riders, the chair-like devices that transport our projected bodies into battle, await our attention.

We place our right hands on the Heat participant plaque and say the mandatory oath. "I, the damned, undertake to be burnt by fire, bound in chains, beaten by rods, and slaughtered by the sword."

Once pledged in, each of our projections sits on the appropriate Interval Rider seat, and in less time than it takes to blink, we are in the entertainment Orb, standing on our invisible hoverboards above the assigned globes of doom we ride into battle: shiny balls made from pure Bloodstone, which Elder Khaan told me is the opaque form of something called Chalcedony Quartz. They are impressive dark green stones that almost look black but get their name from the red flecks or streaks that resemble blood inside them. Once, I overheard him say to the Salus Elder that Bloodstone is mentioned in something called a Christian scripture and was associated with martyrdom. What-ever that means. With a radius of six feet or so, each Bloodstone is etched with the theme of its rider's kith. For us in Levana, it is the image of the Levana symbol–the same wispy finger-like projections, ever so faintly blue with gold speckles, that tumble outward from a folded core. The Volta kith rider is marked with two parallel arms of stacked circles. Each kith, of course, has their own symbol–all unique and probably symbolic in some way I have yet to decipher–which matches the design on their womb cloths.

Then we circle the perimeter on the self-propelled massive stone to entice the audi-ence to support our particular kith's cause.

Once in a while, an entire section stands to salute us as we ride by.

After a few minutes of us screaming and flailing and them standing and sitting, we dismount our globes and *blinky blink blink*, we are back in Folding.

We maintain our positions arranged in order of our battle level, which leaves Baylor John, the pillow-face, and me seated next to each other, as usual.

While we both fidget around trying not to talk to each other, I wonder what will happen if I ever refuse to say the oath. Does a monitor nominate me for the goo of the month award? Probably. Who knows? I'd ask who cares, but my gills would start flapping, so I flick my forehead and just blink a few times. Obviously, I'm not ready for the answer. I always say the freaking stupid oath, don't I?

Baylor grins at me although I don't know why. Maybe he likes this circus act of ours? Maybe my hair looks funny to him without all my beads? Maybe he really does want to lick me? *Gross.*

The Interval Rider chair straps magically appear, locking tightly around our wrists and ankles. *So totally unnecessary, you idiots.*

I laugh imagining my projected image escaping while the monitor inspects my throne for integrity. How long will it take for that puffy idiot to catch me in here? How far does this Folding room stretch? What does Folding mean? Where will I end up? I am pretty freaking fast, after all. Then I remember he has a gun and can necrotize my body still trapped in that damn machine under the Gridiron, waiting for Skylar to let me out. Surely the *real me* is in no condition to outrun him, so I better just sit here. *Well crap.*

The Mozek anthem plays, and I know level one has begun. I blink, a screen appears in front of me, and I watch, curious how this whole process works but knowing I will never understand it. Baylor giggles, and it takes me a moment to remember that I do not hate him while I imagine him licking me. I gag.

After circling atop their Bloodstone globes and then facing each other in the center, two level-one warriors face outward, calling out, "Hail, Chancellors of the Mozek. We who are about to die salute thee."

The opponents reach their assigned starting positions.

After one final bow of mock glory, the first round spins and spins, going nowhere at all. What a mad tea party for the two tweens—Porus vs. Orbona epsilons, twelve or thirteen years old at most, fighting their first Heat. This should be the fastest and probably the most amusing round for the crowd. *Blubbering novices.*

Orbona kith members are usually moderately fast, I admit. But their real talent is hiding. Porus, honestly, I know nothing about, so I can't really predict who will win this fight—too many unknowns to compute the odds with accuracy.

Holographic rain, only mildly severe, pours onto the Orb's floor. Good. I hate the rain. Let them suffer it instead of me. That still leaves sleet, snow, tornadoes, and vicious natural disasters for them to bless me with.

The Orbona epsilon turns out to be pretty clever after all by kicking mud in his opponent's face. Unlucky fool, the Porus, has chosen a visored helmet with a high crest and feathers. Between the soggy plumes and the mud, he can't see a thing. So a few minutes later when the Orbona slings his weapons out from hiding behind a large boulder, the Porus never even sees what slices him. A wide-based sword, somewhat short with a fine tipped edge fillets the backside of his right thigh deeply, probably ten centimeters in length or so.

The doomed sucker flicks his mud-drenched helmet off and drops to the ground to put pressure on the crimson stream pouring out of his leg just in time to find the same sword pointing to the nape of his neck. Battle over–after only ten minutes or so. Brilliance really, for such a beginner.

I am almost impressed. Almost.

While the crowd goes wild at the Orbona's efficiency, Baylor and I snort at the same time. We will have to keep an eye on that kid in the future.

Twelve figures shrouded in deep red robes at the far end of the Gridiron rise and simultaneously raise their hands to the pair of warriors in an oddly and disturbingly synchronous manner. It is as if all twelve are duplicates of just one. I can't help but notice one empty space amongst them. *Twelve...but there should be thirteen?*

The crowd squeals, pointing up. "Let him live. Let him live. He's too young, too simple, too primitive to kill."

The robed figures turn their thumbs up in mercy.

The Lunesta, the voice of fate inside our heads who announces all formal comments during the Heat, bellows out, "Missio."

The crowd chants, "Missio, missio, missio."

The Lunesta drowns out all other sounds and speaks directly into our minds. "Verus of this completed round one, take the bead of your choice."

What a gallant but ridiculous charade.

Level two–here we go:

On one side of the Orb, the Camena delta emerges about one hundred meters away from the Janus delta. On the exact opposite side, the Agenor and Hora deltas march around like they have already sealed the deal against their enemies before the Heat begins. *Fools, you will pay for that.* The buggers even share a clapping and whooping session.

Their self-inflated arrogance shocks me. Put me up against either one of those princesses any day, and we will see who prances about like a fairy on the other side of that fight. I yell, and my spit splatters the screen those two twats keep flitting across. Baylor explodes with laughter again, only this time I don't bother to wonder why. Besides, I don't care, not one little bit, so I growl at him too. That shuts him up. Well, almost.

The girls pull my attention back, and I holler a few times before I just shut up, too. The four of them are gorgeous, so glittery and fine with their movements as they gather approval before the battle by flowing and moving like Gods. And the drums, powerful and intense, act like a concoction of wanton numbness that heightens yet also lessens my ability to respond to the lightness of girls' dance of death. Like magic, the spell infuses me with desire. For what exactly, I cannot say.

My heart beats harder and faster in perfect timing to the sound of the audience, thousands of others just like me, drumming with teeming and mounting anticipation. And I want to be that beat, to own that drum, to be the source of my, *I mean their*, impassioned audience as well.

My brain slaps my heart's face again because it realizes that the alluring effect of the Heat is working on me, too. My mind argues with my heart for a moment, but thankfully that oh-so-generous mind of mine allows me to watch a little bit longer. After all, I am next, and this is almost like practice. Almost.

I hate to admit it, but damn, it is exciting–the gallant pageantry, the beautiful globes of Bloodstone doom, the flawless physical specimens on the screen that keep pulling me in and away from the mundaneness of my usual life. It tastes dangerously special, and instantly, I want more. Wanting, no, needing their promise of something intangible to be real even though I, of all people, know how false it is. Mesmerized, I can't help wondering which weapon, which shield, each one of those little chicks plans to employ. And honestly, they are so freaking tempting that I don't dare look away–skin simmering in their oil preps, hair pinned up in a bun, and body frosted in too many Inks to count.

I lick my lips.

But then something happens. Disgust creeps in as the call goes out, and they follow all the rules like such good little girls.

The little females say their little allegiance to the Chancellors, hoping with crossed fingers for the little drop of cheese promised to them. All of a sudden, I don't want to watch them anymore. They make me sick. The once-powerful females become nothing more than trapped little vermin again, powerless to rage against a machine this big. And both they and I shrink back into our usual nothinglessness once more. The effect of the Heat dissipates, and only frigid disappointment remains.

My brain, such a snob, reminds my heart who has always been the smarter one in this mundane world, and the foul taste in the back of my mouth multiplies. I spit once more and turn my head away from the screen.

I'd watch more intensely, but what's the point? I already know I can kick all four of their sixteen-year-old asses, and they are nothing but inedible gears in a watch, ticking away these precious minutes I will never get back. Boring, minus any flavor at all, the way they play this game like they are told to. Shame my backside is so slippery on this metal seat because I think a nap might be nice.

Then, I hear gasping terror infiltrate the Orb, and I have to look back. In fact, I'm already turned around despite my best intentions not to grace them with any more of my peppery attention.

"Oh my Gods." I scream.

Baylor laughs a third time.

The bad luck. I can't even imagine the odds.

Chapter Seventeen

SUCH POOR PICKINGS. If they weren't so annoyingly cheesy, I'd almost feel sorry for them. Almost.

The Camena, paired against the Agenor–the first of the peacock twins–has chosen the capture net and trident. But unfortunately for the Agenor beauty, the Hora–her twinkling twin in the other battle on the other side of the Orb, bears the only shield large enough to fight it off. Such bad luck, the same heavy shield that might save the Agenor serves the Hora not while she runs from the rapidly advancing spikes of the ball-ax that the Janus, her assigned opponent, swirls around her head like a pixie stick.

A parmula, small, light, yet effective, would be so much better!

But if they were to switch? Can warriors switch instruments once they have chosen? I just can't be sure yet. It has probably never been done before. *Probably.*

I flash back to the time Elder Khaan tamed that dragon with the fire swords and try to remember where the blades came from, but I was so little. Did I swap them only in my mind? *Probably not.*

Oh my Gods, if they actually pair up as a real team, they might defeat the advancing rivals instead of being caught in this unfortunate web of their own foolish making. *Impossible. Or is it?*

To top it off, the confounder makes its timely arrival. If I wasn't next, I might feel a little sorry for them, so ill-stocked, as the first of a million fuzzy spiders with scorpion-like tails spew from the sky. Eight-legged drops of terror from the downpour quickly scatter, drenching them in fear on top of failure. Screaming fills the Gridiron, both in the Orb and out. I try to laugh but can't because, for once, I am speechless.

Guess I am wrong about the whole no-rain-repeat theory. Bugs are apparently not subject to the usual rule. Thunder claps, and more creepy crawlers, large and getting larger, emerge. Terrified, the two little flies actually lose their useless weapons while scrambling to the center of the Orb, aching to find protection where there is none from a spider as wide as they are tall.

Sitting on the edge of my seat, for once I am thankful for the straps holding me in place. Without them, I would be climbing to the top of my mechanical throne, betraying my almost absurd paranoia of spiders. Almost.

I hear Elder Khaan's voice in my mind. *"Tarantupions can't hurt you, Isla. They look scary with all that hair and that spiky tail. But if ever faced with a choice between that and one with a red stain on the underside, take the fuzz-tail combo and run. Red equals dead. Got it?"*

Red equals dead.

Trying not to look at that huge spider, I think about the color red for a moment. Other than my cards, the sand here, the two suns in the sky, and the Chancellors' robes, no one nowhere wears it. No red Inks, as per law, on anyone, except me and my foot.

Chills race down my back like they do every time I observe something important. I hear Elder Khaan again in my mind. *"Red equals dead. Got it?"* Another chill follows, and for a moment, the thought of the cold, cold Liebhorr pops in, but I refuse to let it take hold and decide the big, hairy spider isn't so bad after all.

Calmly, I look back at the screen. Baylor never even registers the chilly fear that crawled up my leg and into my brain before I banished it.

The girls, though, have obviously missed their spider lessons. The more creepy-crawlers, the more chaos. Now that I have recovered my dignity, I have to stifle a few half-formed laughs. From this side of things, the whole ordeal is almost funny. Almost.

But then another chill assaults me, so intense my right foot twitches, and I wonder. *What's about to rain down on me?*

Baylor, quiet as a good little mouse, says nothing.

The monitors hold back the second layer of confounders. Wouldn't want to waste any holographs, would they? Finally a true pair of allies, the defenseless twins stand back to back together, forgetting momentarily how much they hate each other. Obviously they hate spider monsters more.

Both the Camena and Janus approach from the flanks, swords and teeth bared, acting more like a team than the flit and glitter Gemini twins, and I stop watching because, let's face it—what's the point? This level two grade ends before it even begins, just like the first.

I drag my dry tongue across my dry teeth and taste nothing, nothing at all.

Within minutes, the robed Chancellors stand, granting their pretend pardon to the star-crossed weapon girls still shaking from arachnophobia.

Bugger of a life, this Heat business, I have to admit.

The Folding alarms chime in preparation for the finale—me.

My straps unlock. Here we go.

Baylor and I exchange glances. An urge to sign him like a fellow Levana swallows me. I place my fingers over my heart, pressing down twice. *Levana respects.* He shoots two of his right fingers in the air. *Salus returns the respect.*

Invigorated by his response, I assume my position on my Interval Rider, ready to rock the stands. Grade three, the end of this little pity-party commences: Levana-Irmin and Luna-Volta and Salus-Suadela as paired and parallel opponents.

Blink, I'm in. Or is it out? I just can't be sure yet.

Since the Orb is a globe, our starting positions divide the space in six equal segments like spokes on a wheel. As we flit and shimmer to gather the audience's favor just like the others before us, the center cage descends into the unseen domain below. Upon its return, several appliances surface for each of us to choose from.

We salute the Chancellors, and instantly, a thick, hazy wall isolates us from the others in our grade. Unable to visualize our enemy's selection until it's already too late, we each stand there and make the best decision we can with such limited information. Considering the prior display, this disadvantage shocks no one.

To get myself in the mood, I chat myself up. "I am gladiator. I accept this challenge." But not for their pretend morsels. That's my secret. I fight for me.

As always, I select the traditional helmet, a simple parmula to shield my chest, and the light yet effective gladius blade. Never once partial to the unusuals, the forked swords, twirling axes, ropes, nets, and every other sharp or deadly weapon one could imagine, I accept that at the end of the day, I am just an old fashioned gal.

Acting like I almost believe it, I make my pledge of allegiance to the Chancellors... who will never be the boss of me even after they've killed me.

I flip my metal headgear into position and bow.

An Irmin gamma, my opponent, wastes no time. In seconds, he is on top of me. This huge asshole, Lerner Steve, flinging a gladius, same as mine, leaps to the right side of me and starts trying to knife me. For a second, I ponder how similar we look sporting the same gear, how much he also looks like that creep Jaxston who bears the same second name of Steve, and how hard the poor audience must be struggling to decide whom to encourage, whom to condemn. Then I wonder how the Gods can tell any of us apart. From a distance, we must all seem the same. *Impossible.*

About twenty seconds go by, my thoughts lost in a swirling pit of who's who, before I remember that clanging in my ears comes from my steel blade sparking against my enemy's.

"Get back in the damn game," I command. Thankfully, I do.

Behind me, the central cage descends again. Great. I can't wait–the first confounder en route. *Wonder what the Mozek have in store.*

The first of countless flames shoots out of a living fire pit and partially burns my right arm. So thankful for my reflective armor that just saved most of my freaking arm, I decide slashing swords to the left side instead of the right seems to make better sense. My less than clever opponent agrees as the fire seems to ebb and flow like my breath.

For a moment, I think about Baylor, hoping his armor is the non-heat conducting version like mine. But why am I worried about Baylor of all things while this Irmin asshole keeps advancing? With a superficial slice to my flank, Lerner Steve reminds me I have bigger issues to focus on–his intention to slice me into itty-bitty Islas, to be exact. So even though I hear the others battling, I decide to hone in on the gigantic vermin spewing curses and slimy saliva at me.

I throw a few names back his way right when I break my position and get away. I am fast, way faster than him. So instead of away, I run toward the fire pit and simultaneously acquire a better view of my video game landscape.

Scanning the perimeter, I see rocks as high and as far as my eyes allow it in every direction. The ground under my feet, packed and hard and perfectly smooth as marble, feels like it has been buffed smooth to perfection. The mounds of rocks, jagged pyramids rising from this glass-like base, are marked with lines that I can only assume came from the pressure of some massive dissolving force running between the walls.

It hits me—water, the universal solvent, a knife disguised as liquid, must have done this. And the possibility of clean and safe water in every direction as far as I can imagine pleases me in a way that words fail to describe. Off to the far right side, maybe a thousand meters away, I see a sign that says *ARIZON,* but the last letter…or perhaps letters…has been swept away. *Swept away, too. Impossible.*

Halfway to the fire pit, I start jumping like I belong in Salus. It feels so good that I laugh even though I'm still running. For the fun of it, I do another high jump, somersaulting over the raging flames while flipping my blade in the air. As I land safely on the other side of both of my unworthy adversaries—Irmin and fire—my hand catches the hilt of my sword, and I bow for the benefit of my attentive audience so swept away by my brilliance.

I'm not sure who's more shocked by my move—me, the Irmin, the audience, or Baylor. All eyes lock on me, the Levana who has just leapt into and over a fire. Dumbass or commendable move? Who knows. Who cares.

My chest puffs, and I say, "I do, actually."

The second confounder, right on time, shows up. Reptiles—terrible.

A pitch-black racer snake slithers over my foot, obviously wanting to seek shelter underneath my armor to escape the hot, piercing flames of the fire in the middle of this massive canyon. Another reptile, one with orange markings on his chest, falls from the rocks above, landing on my head. Shivering but determined not to lose my weapons, I grip my blade tighter. One of the armless vermin slides down my neck, and I suppress the sickness gathering in the back of my slimy mouth. Running away from fangs makes perfect sense to me, so I go with that plan instead of puking. Besides, even a fire flipper like me needs both arms to hold my sword and shield to fend off that giant Irmin still trying to make his way around the fire. I squeeze my instruments tighter still, laughing sardonically while I join forces with the wormy devil under my armor. Maybe this snake and I can become true friends, true allies. Maybe the more I help him, the more he helps me. *Helps me,* such a lovely and bizarre idea.

For the fun of it, I spear and then toss a poisonous rattlesnake which just hissed at me toward my human opponent. Maybe that Lerner Steve grows hungry for something other than squares these days. Shame…he passes on my culinary offering in lieu of slaughtering me, still stumbling as quickly as his clumsy, gargantuan feet can move since the fire took out a few of his toes. Sword slinging, he advances as fearlessly as a barely walking bairn, utterly unaware he's stepping into yet another trap. My sword glows with mature anticipation.

Not sure exactly what intention drives my movement, I sprint directly toward the fat-cheeked Salus named Baylor John. But then it dawns on me that the Irmin goon and

I must look exactly the same from afar. Only difference is that the smaller one of us moves fast and graceful and the other stomps around heavily and uncoordinated.

Will Baylor recognize who is who?

Even if he gets a half-decent look, probably not.

Enraged by the possibility of looking like as big a buffoon as the Irmin, my face flashes red like the fire pit. Suddenly, I realize not only do I *want* Baylor to know which one I am, I *need* him to know. Yep, even if he will lick me for it later. That crazy idea returns. *The more I help him, the more he helps me.*

My lily Ink erupts underneath my armor and oozes warm affection for Baylor and the possibility of our parallel victory over these fools. The slithering snake, now that I have gotten so used to him, forsakes me for some more terrible place to roost because I am way too innocent for his tastes. *Traitor. Guess he was nothing more than a pretend savior. But that Baylor...I wonder.*

The ground rumbles as more cliffs and crevices suddenly appear under Baylor's feet, quite effectively distracting him from recognizing me. My lilies, doubting my reserve, clamp down and consider betraying me, too.

Immediately, I fling my helmet on the ground as hard as I can muster–first to lighten my load and second so that the crowd at large, and by default Baylor, will know who's about to be the grand champion of my Binary. My lilies reopen and start clapping, and the thought flips around. *The more he helps me, the more I help him.*

The Irmin, offended by my arrogant display, hollers behind me. He spews threats about how he plans to hang me up by my toenails while he guts me for the crowd. *Maybe he's kidding?* But then I see a net hanging over his arm and decide I should probably take his curses somewhat seriously. My lilies agree.

All things being equal, I prefer to keep my abdominal wall intact. Like I said earlier, I am an old fashioned kind of girl, so even under pressure, I like to keep my shit together.

Simultaneously, the Suadela gamma disarms Baylor with a deadly rope. What are the odds? Either way, not good for Baylor. Perhaps they can string us up and eviscerate us together? Not my idea of a good time. And even though it won't kill me, I am pretty sure the whole experience of being gutted like the fish I am is one I can do without. I don't have time to ask him, but my instinct tells me that Baylor feels the same way.

I decide, just like the time I smelled the Jane melting, that surely I can move a little faster than this. In full thraex assimilation mode, I willingly push the device into the sub-anatomic portion of my nerves and muscles. The temperature increase exponentially, and I know I am fully synced.

Time to show these boys what a little girl power can do. *Help me.*

Tossing my parmula aside, I bare my shimmering chest. The crowd roars and claps to a beat that forces my arms in the air to move in time with them. Damn, I have them now. Or do they have me? I just can't be sure yet. *Help him.*

More disembowelment threats surface from my drooling opponent.

Rolling my eyes, I shimmy my shoulders to tease the house. The drumming intensifies, and I think I might explode. I have to admit that I almost enjoy holding the entire Orb's attention like this. Almost, anyway.

A chasm in the ground opens, and I lose my footing. Distracted by the crowd, I must have missed the confounder's subtle warning. Almost falling into my demise, my nails catch the rest of me just in time. More earthquakes erupt, and boulders tumble down on every side of me.

Sword in my mouth, I climb back up by the skin of my teeth. I can't help but imagine the cinematic value of my predicament. Nice.

Unbelievably, he's almost on top of me, that disgustingly slow Irmin. His crashing blade lands a centimeter from my nose just as I stand up tall to leap once more, now that I am so good at it, right across the canyon. Even nicer.

Still determined to literally get under my skin, he follows suit but barely misses the other side. The poor bastard's bones crunch from the impact, and I see part of his ragged leg bone before I quickly look the other way. I swallow hard, but saliva gathers in the back of my dry throat.

The crowd hollers in delight.

I growl once more, and the saliva slows down.

The audience roars back.

Then I scan for Baylor. Not good. He's down, his enemy poised above him for the kill. He has seconds, at most, to surrender. *Help him.*

While the Suadela lassoes the thick steel-wool rope with small barbed spikes around his head, a memory surfaces from the last grade–the star-crossed weapon fairies and how much better they might have done to swap instruments.

Impossible. Or is it?

The idea, so absurd, so novel, so *not* like a rat in a maze…I decide, what the hell. I don't need any cheese. *But Baylor does. Help me.*

With snakes falling from the sky, me sprinting like a goddess across the tumultuous ground and all, who's going to notice, other than Baylor and I, if we sword swap? Probably no one. *I just might…help.*

The ground rumbling again and pointed snake fangs piercing my left ankle spur me on to action. *I will.*

Instantly, everything disappears but three things: a blood-red half-circular Ink on my right foot; the erupting ground under my feet; and the image of Baylor's face, minus barbs, holding a gladius to his enemy's neck in victory instead of the other way around.

I go into autopilot and allow my body to perform in a way that even my mind cannot grasp. Only my heart, that glorious bitch, has a clue what I'm doing.

Time alters almost to a total standstill.

First, the red mound on my right foot rises like the fullness of dawn coming into view. Then, the rocks and sharp corners scrape the underside of my toes. A tunnel, almost like a vortex of terror, encases me. I know I have two options: win or lose, save or kill, help or be helped, fuck-all or fault.

My heartbeat echoes in the tunnel that only it knows how to travel. Pressure and numbness fill my useless brain. This void leaves only my beating heart to match the rhythm of the alternating sun and sand. The rest of me surrenders everything to the machine integrated into my nervous system.

The red sun again. Then the ground.

The red. The rocks.

Death. Life.

The sun. The canyons.

The dawn. The crests.

And I am too afraid to acknowledge the third thing hanging on my every move, the only one that matters to me right now, really–Baylor, my dear friend.

I shoot two fingers in the air. *Salus, I honor you. I will save your ass.*

Lub-dub. Lub-dub.

Lub-dub. Lub-dub.

Lub-dub. Lub-dub.

Lub-dub. Lub-dub.

The cliffs and crevices flash by me. I no longer bother to worry about snakes and fire pits on the other side. The subtle vibrations of the field guide me, allowing my intuition to maneuver me safely through the obstacles.

Just as the enemy's rope encircles Baylor's neck, I reach him. I toss over my gladius. Airborne, that glorious blade of steel twirls once, twice, three times, landing perfectly in his hand. I simultaneously somersault, finishing on all fours, one hand on the hilt of his sword, now mine. My battered calf muscle, suddenly so strong and whole with purpose, tightens, preparing for my next maneuver.

A python as long as I am tall rises up behind me to strike. Quickly, I swivel to face him. In one glorious swoop, I chop his hissing head off his green and purple body. The fangs, previously poised to impale my left shoulder, miss but even from the ground keep twitching in my direction. Only moderately hopeful that the liquid spurting out its neck and onto my chest can't hurt me, I take a deep breath as I toss my borrowed blade away.

Is the snake poisonous? Knowing these Mozek, the odds are pretty good that nothing has ever been in my favor.

A few more seconds pass before I realize that the only person not frozen from total shock is me, except the Suadela gamma, of course. He's panting and, despite Baylor's sword at the nape of his neck, still holds on to one piece of his tattered rope for dear life.

For dear life.

The old saying appalls me, slamming my gills against my overheated neurons. How much have we forsaken the concept of *dear life*?

This is no *dear life* that I am forced to barter for what? Ink and skag.

Screw that!

I, well the projected Isla, at least, battling in a mock war, killing mock reptiles for a mock prize to honor a band of red-robed men in a mock world that pretends to help us, glow red with fury, ablaze from the flames of my judgment.

Got it. Red equals dead. I am red. I am fucking dead.

I stand here for who knows how long exploring that burning thought before I hear the previously silent crowd burst into scalding applause. Baylor walks over to me, cautiously at first and then more quickly. Grabbing my right hand with his left, he raises it in the air, our fingers intertwined around our single, shared gladius blade. *Help him. Help me.*

Half-Levana, half-Salus. *Two halves finally make a whole.*

Why? Because helping him does help me and vice versa.

The crowd claps furiously, and my ears ache from the loudness of their approval. To bring the audience to the point from which we will never return, he takes it one step further. He places two fingers to his chest, presses down twice, and then shoots them in the air twice. *Levana in my heart, Salus in the sky.*

We are not Salus, not Levana. We are Salvana.

Unable to resist, I return the fiery gesture as sweat drips down my back.

To say the stands explode pales in comparison to what we witness. Rose petals litter the floor, and the cries–so passionate, so strong–deafen me. Right before a needle injects me with skag, that is.

My pupils dilate, and my heart slows, almost stops beating. Almost.

Is it the real Isla or the projected version of Isla floating off to the land of oblivion? Are you flying? Or is it me? Who is me? I just can't be sure yet.

A voice pops in that sounds like one I've never heard yet have always known. "Sweet baby girl, I will bring you Home. I will bring us all Home. Hold on to my voice because this version of you is the only way that we can undo what has been done." And momentarily, I am reminded of a monitor so long ago who took me from Elder to Elder. *Impossible. Or is it?*

Baylor's painful screams drag me back to the Heat, and my last venomous thought before nothingness steals me lingers like metal in my mouth and echoes through my ears. *Mock, m...m...m...mo...mock you. That's impossible.*

Chapter Eighteen

I WAKE up late the next day feeling partially drugged, not caring much about anything. I've almost forgotten about my Heat last night. Almost.

The last few scenes from my dream dissolve because of the flashing of the laser UV light. On and off it flutters back and forth before it finally gives in and goes out with one last disorienting flash, no fight left in it–like me.

I notice not one but two new braid beads on my nightstand, knowing I should smile and wonder if such a lovely little gift means I crowned verus after all. Or something better, like double verus, perhaps. But I can't. Thinking requires too much will power, and I am all out of power after giving it to Baylor last night. Right before the Orb stole it from us both and turned us back from strong carriage horses into the scampering mice we started as, that is.

Where's my fairy godmother now?

Stifling the memory of his cries of pain, I try to go back inside my mind without thinking a single freaking thought. *As if...*

For as long as I can hold on to the illusion, I pretend I am still gliding through my dream state, immersed in that place so deep and wide amongst all the green fields going on and on in every direction forever. I sweep my smooth hand above the cool blades from the bountiful fields of joy and feel the life force there that overflows with wisdom and oozes safe tranquility. The soft, easy-to-look-at light augments the humble breeze of perfection that cools everything to the ideal temperature. Beautiful. Gazing longingly into Tilly's fading smile, she fills me up, like usual, in a way a square never has. She fits me perfectly, like usual, in a way that a glass slipper never will.

Then I remember the final thing she said in last night's dream. Something about two superimposed versions of me while she grins back up at me from the corridor that, thanks to me, she will never leave. The idea, so preposterous with an alert mind, intrigues me. Did she mean the bigger me inside this little me? Or did she really mean

147

two of me? Do I have some long-lost twin I have never met–the two of us separated and living in different dimensions or far apart galaxies?

The thought would usually make me laugh, but my head hurts too much for such trivial pleasures. Yet, somehow even after her demise, Tilly twirls round and round in my mind. Or is it my heart? I just can't be sure yet. Dancing like a ballerina to a back-drop symphony of white flowers that infuse the glorious air like musical notes, she speaks sweetly, amused as if nothing else matters more than our fun, the exploring, the climbing, the spinning circles of our infinite waltz. *Gods I miss you.*

I shake my head back and forth, hands over my ears still aching from the booming, the collapsing, the echoing of the terrible loss of her. Then I abandon what's left of her, as per usual, and return to the memory of last night's Heat and both Kalil and Cale. All my moments of failure drip endlessly from the sponge in my chest. My hole-filled heart soaked eternally in the same stink-covered guilt keeps leaking so it can become empty. Empty enough to just keep absorbing more, that is.

My fault. The insufferable guilt of being less than someone needs every time they need me. *Always my fault.* I keep tossing my brain around, hoping to find some thought worth thinking. *No, no, no. Impossible.*

When I finally stop thrashing, I notice Gaige sitting there just watching me. He squints trying to get a clearer view. Obviously from the expression on his face, I am the most curious thing he has ever seen, and honestly, I'm too tired to care. Certainly, I should be afraid of this Ink dealer and all his secret layers of smoke, but I'm not. Fear requires too much energy.

"There was a problem," he calmly says, his words still hanging on that dimple of his, "at the Levana Ink chamber. So you are coming with me, Isla"–his predictable pause–"Jane."

Raising my eyebrows, I say nothing. My lips, peeling off in layers, are too chapped from last night's skag injection and its lasting emptiness that always follows the numb-ness, at least in me anyhow. Disgusted and full of spite, my head throbs, so I rub my temples, trying to soothe my face back together.

The Ink dealer hands me two white pills and a fresh box of the cleanest liquid I have ever seen. *This is no 53 box.* I take it in with one big swig, and both my thirst and the pain bumping around in my skull disappear immediately.

Yet the oddest part of the ordeal is how the whole exchange seems perfectly normal to me–Gaige in my room, him offering me things for the complaints I do not say out loud, me taking his treatments without any fear he is planning to harm me.

My heart skips a few beats but keeps going.

Why would I be afraid of this box and the pills he offers me? Would he bother to poison me if he can just necrotize me? I think not.

Perhaps this Gaige who looks into, not through, me searches for something inside me that I don't have to offer him. Or anyone else either.

My pulse quickens.

It makes no sense for him to kill me now. Even in this mad, mercury-laced world. If he wants me harmed, I am already dead. So I let the details play out. It's amusing, sort of.

I think he is trying to help me. Or does he want me to help him? I just can't be sure yet. But that is surely a question worth asking myself later, assuming I'm still around to ask it.

My cheeks flush and my respiratory rate increases with every kind gesture he offers. I bite my flaky lip, feeling more and more annoyed. Seriously, how can I possibly pay him back for his fluttering lashes or walking me home late, probably carrying me home unconscious after the Heat last night, the pills, the box? The list, long and getting longer, reminds me that some debts can never be settled.

But then I realize how absurd the idea is, actually. The whole concept implies and then completely depends upon a future no one would dare promise me in a place like this City of Debtors. *Impossible.*

So with bemused defeat, I eventually decide to find the whole scenario more and more amusing. And since how I react to things is the only choice I get to make in this life of absent choices, I choose the superior of the two options from my perspective: detached surrender over rage.

Lovely, I'm too tired for raging after losing my shoe at the ball.

I feel better immediately–like me on any other day, like it's not this day, two days after Kalil, one day after Baylor's screams. *My fault.*

Gaige takes the fresh bandage off my front side and inspects a new Levana stamp I cannot remember receiving. It is excellent, beautiful actually, making me wonder why I've always refused it.

The wispy finger-like projections, ever so faintly blue with gold speckles, tumble outward from a folded core like elven whispers of divine devotion I could never resist. The gorgeous outline, perfect and fine, forms a teardrop of serenity that portrays an emotion I possess no words worthy to describe. It is like a gift folded within a gift too precious to own, so it can only be held briefly before it must be gifted forward. The only way to own it, I think, will be to give it away.

I am speechless from the Ink's effects so far superior to the efforts of my prior dealer who was known for his excellent skills. But this purple-eyed king named Gaige creates works of art that are so untouchable, so unfathomable, that they must be handed over in order for me to hold on to them.

Over and over, I finger the delightful design, and eventually, he places his hand on top of mine and traces the Levana stamp with me. Like I am crazy fast, he Inks crazy good. So if we team up at an Ink Heat, I guess we would be one crazy pair to beat. The thought makes me smile for the first time in hours and what feels like days, maybe even weeks.

In response to my expression, a look goes across his face, a brightness of idealistic harmony, which comes from behind, no, beyond his eyes, more purple than purple now. I stare at the color too perfect to be named. The color, the look, a deep yet light purple I have never known before but would never attempt to label with something as useless as a word. I know better, this rose with no thorns, scattering my petals across the floor and around my toes as I melt amongst them. Barely able to breathe, I want to sit down so I can take it all in because now I'm begging to hold on to one more second of his gorgeous face standing over my gorgeous Ink before I finally release it. *Gods, please save me.*

So lost, hopeless to ever find my old self again, I just sink into his expression. It professes how much he knows me. Better yet, has known me forever–before the first clock ever ticked and after the last clock ticked, too. His look oozes inside me, heals my sores, and dries my tears. Yet it also keeps the perfect mystery of me honored and validated through its one innocent, intimate glance, which I can finally see because he shows it back to me through his purple, too gorgeous to name.

Still speechless, I just glow. My chest sputters, and my moisture gathers once more in a guttural physical response that needs no explanation even though I am utterly clueless to its meaning or source. The urge to draw him in, whatever that means, consumes me.

Slyly, but completely, he smiles back from a place so deep and wide he probably cannot name it, either. So instead of waiting for him to label it, I show it back for him to see. The purple color oozes inside him now, hopefully healing his sores, drying his tears. Only this time, the purple looks bluer than blue because it comes from behind, no, beyond my piercing sapphire eyes.

For a moment of eternal bliss, he rests inside the deepest part of me, and I catch my breath, finally at peace inside him with this look, this smile, this place, which is so simple that I can't hope to describe the complexity of the layers inside the layers of it.

Impossible.

I want to blink, to glance away but don't dare, not being sure I will ever see this clearly again.

And now I know how a magnet feels, pulled in an undeniable way into those eyes of his that actually want, no, I think need to really see me. To see the most authentic me beneath and inside and throughout me in a place where we all stand champion together. Because here there are no verus and no losers, just us, the victors of all the pure intention that ever mattered in the multiverse of universes.

As a chill climbs from my brainstem, out my spinal cord, and disperses its zing in every muscle in my physical body, he takes my hand and guides me step by step through the motions of walking until we are out the front door and heading straight for the building I have never entered–Forty-Four B, the one closest to the thick glass and all the wondering it will invoke in me.

Dizzy, I reach for the ground, trying to pull myself back together again before he sees the swirling mess of me. But who am I kidding? Even a fool would see what he's done to me even though I don't have a clue what that even means.

After Gaige enters the code and we step through the retracting glass and metal door, I run into Baylor and his gang of bairns happily moving and scooting the few things they own around in cardboard containers and white cloth bags. Baylor grins at me with that tender full face of his and nods. So I suspect he knows perfectly well that I finally recognize his value, his clear intention beneath his actions in last night's battle. The unforgettable Heat where we fought not side-by-side but as one side and burned some enemy ass together. His smirk gives me more than I could have hoped–assurance that his screams were short, maybe even erased by the skag's amnesia.

He touches his fresh bandage to show me that he knows about mine.

"Forty bairns now, eh?" I say.

"Forty-one."

"Disgusting." I snort.

"Yep. Terrible," he says, his smile too big for his fat cheeks and dribbling off his chin.

Rolling my eyes, I snort again, and he just laughs as he walks past, subtly touching his fingertips to mine. And I am so thankful for him and each and every single one of those babes who shall not gush crimson under his watch this day or tomorrow that I consider grabbing hold of his wrist and licking it. Like he can read my thoughts, he shakes his head and gets back to work.

Boy, I am glad to call him friend, this Baylor named Alice, too. Tilly is right. About there being two of me, that is. But not *two*, she means *too*.

Too.

Baylor is one, and I am one, and so are Tilly and Elder Khaan, and maybe even this Ink dealer Gaige who holds all the fragmented pieces of me steady as we walk past so many flashing red lights, so clueless to the nameless colors inside. *Red equals dead. Or does it? I just can't be sure yet.*

Unable to resist, I laugh at all my nonsense. Yet it all makes perfect sense to me. Of course one plus one plus one plus one never equals four at all. My math, so useless, means nothing because of the *too*. Because they care, *too,* and they must know I do, *too*. And they know I know it all now, just like them.

Silently, we all nod in agreement, choosing to see things so differently than the others do in our caterpillar way in this City of Smoke and Mirrors. So I follow him, this Gaige of mine, even if he is only pretending to be my friend. My ID who isn't my ID but is, *too*. And *too* is far better than three or four.

We travel through a series of hallways, some curving this way, others curving that. And much like a tree in a forest on some deserted planet, I am lost. But then I realize I never can be lost here with Gaige because he knows the way. And if he does, then I do, *too*.

Spinning, I keep my cyclonic thoughts to myself because I am no good at speaking while I'm thinking. And what could I possibly say anyway to this purple-eyed king who shows me the way? Try to explain all these *toos*?

I don't think so.

We finally come to a stop at the opening of a large room. In the center is a projector, which looks different but similar to the one in the Levana Ink chamber. The steel coils shine. The snake-like tubes and hoses are new and fresh, made of obviously superior materials.

He shows off his glance again, so purple and blue. Then he silently guides me to my seat. He makes the motion of locking me into place, but doesn't. Although, if someone were behind me, they would be no wiser to the false clicking and locking of which only I am aware. The fake moves are recorded by another flashing red light behind me that always records us.

I think surely he will spare me the skag; I've simply had too much. Of all people, he knows that I might not recover from another round draining me.

"No," I mouth, my eyes pleading desperately for his mercy with cries that my lips are not allowed to utter in this City of Gags.

He clenches his jaw tightly, and the corners of his mouth turn down. "They told me it would take some work to convince you to trust me. Don't you think I know better than…?"

My heart trembles. The looks…did they mean nothing? Fog, coming from my imploding mind, settles in the center of the room, and I can no longer see his face. Or can he no longer see mine? I just can't be sure yet. Shit, if he isn't any different than the rest of the assholes running this terrible place.

Baylor too, probably.

I've imagined it all. *Too?* As if that was ever possible? What *too?*

Surely this is proof I should only count on my own compassion like the cold-blooded fish I am. So weak and foolish, will I never learn that no one cares about me? That no one ever has. I drown in self-pity while Gaige loads up the roaring machine with its hoses and tubes. Disgusted, I sputter a few curse words.

For a second, the champion in my chest gathers strength again, trying to hold on to hope that things might still be different. But my mind just shakes this head back and forth, feeling so sorry for all the wasted effort during this internal battle of mine. The duel inside an Alice who refuses to listen to sad songs from the mock turtle anymore, who resists any more skag juice, who joins forces with Baylor in the Orb to fight not as *two* sides, but *too* sides as one.

I'm fucking done. I won't hear this madness. I just can't because I have enough sadness in my song already. My song longs to be so much prettier instead of foul. My lyrics die to overflow with sunshine instead of dark deception while we sing them together as one side instead of side-by-side, unconcerned about one another's plight.

Elder Khaan's melody flows into the holes in my spongy heart, replacing every-thing else. He adored me; I know he did. Surely that was no lie.

Even though he's gone, he sings to me:

"In a sea of blinding darkness,
You are my shining light.
Without your rays,
There's only night.
Will you rescue me,
And set things right?

My dawn. My only dawn.
My dawn. My dawn.

. . .

So take these eyes,
   And give them sight.
   That search for you,
   On the hope you might.

My dawn. My only dawn.
   My dawn. My dawn.

Your glowing beauty,
   Framed in fight.
   And precious rays,
   Of warm delight.

My dawn. My only dawn.
   My dawn. My dawn.

In a sea of blinding darkness,
   You are my shining light.
   Can't you see?
   Won't you be?
   The dawn that overcomes,
   So big and bright.

My dawn. The only dawn.
   My dawn. My dawn."

To me, these are the only lines worth singing. I will hear no others. I won't survive them with so little left inside me, obliterated by my emptiness.

A single tear gathers behind my illusionary eyelids, which my heart sucks back up quickly, feeling unworthy of my own salt, and scorns such a simple yet impossible desire. Why pretend I need more tragic lyrics when I already wear a thousand secret sores inside me?

The me beneath me, all covered in rose thorns, cries out in defeat.

I cannot hang on anymore. The queen wins. I will do the dying, and she will eat all ten of my piggies. The cool blade of the gladius screams welcome to the nape of my neck and begs that someone finish this charade already. Really, I don't even care now that I have seen how different things could be. I don't want this meaningless existence any longer–this way of nothings at all where they take Cale away from me because not having him is my only way of keeping him.

Well screw that, and screw me. And while you're at it, screw yourself, you Mozek!

And now the evil queen steals Gaige's look from me as well because that witch smashes it on the floor and names it *purple*. But I am done with colors so plain that I can label them. They mean nothing to me if I am covered with skag. I give up and let the *too* fall away from me in a haze of addicted confusion and pain. What use is *too* in a world that floats away on a river of madness?

I look back at the projector, a plan forming more perfectly in my mind. I see the controls which manage the pack of needles. I can easily disengage the tiny blades, removing them for a different, entirely more diabolical purpose than Inking. But when Gaige turns around to program the device, he leaves an extra needle grouping on his Inkstand. So to accomplish my goal, I won't even have to remove the one from the machine. *Perfect.*

I glare at the swirling tentacles of the contraption, like a titanium octopus bent on hooking me behind the dilated eyes of an Ink freak that I will not become, will not allow to squirt out of this Isla Jane who could be so much more if only she was allowed to choose something better than nonsense melodies and skag Ink showers.

I won't have it. No way. Not anymore.

While he prepares the projector, I sneak the needle pack into my boot whose sole is good and strong, the upper leather edge barely covering my rising sun–the same one I don't recall picking. I crave it so badly my mouth waters–not for skag but for the dawn in Elder Khaan's song, the same sunlight gloriously peeking over the top of my boots. That beautiful solitary ball of fire that sings me songs without any sadness at all as all songs should be but can't be...here in the City of Sea Monsters.

The supple leather boots cradle my rising sun like Elder Khaan once cradled me. They, the boots, are the one fine thing I own. I remember that I won them the day I sacrificed the skin on the bottom of my left foot and the back of my right calf while recovering a burning pink bottle of biome elixir serum for the monitor who screamed for it. He shrieked as if his, in fact everyone's, life depended on it.

I shudder realizing it was the same type of pink-colored bottle that ended up murdering the other beta Jane this week.

Reality melts, and time stands still. Chills zing everywhere.

That first bottle ignited about one year ago, I suddenly recall. How could I have lost the memory? At the time the second one blew, I thought the bottle was new. But it was not. It has already tried to kill me before. Almost did, *too*.

All these *toos*, they just keep twirling around like puzzle pieces that don't fit together in some maddening game–no rules, no instructions, no way to solve this never-ending riddle which has no possible answer.

Or does it? I just can't be sure yet.

I thought the boots, a gift from the screaming monitor, were to protect my healing limb so that I could keep working the red cards after my injury, the one that never intended to heal. And now that I think about it, I have to admit that they should have sent me to R&R like they usually do after blowout injuries, but they did not.

"Why?" I mutter. It is almost like they rewarded me by not sending me to a medical.

"Because of all the pink, I guess," I keep mumbling.

A bell rings inside my brain, louder and louder. Or is it inside my heart? I just can't be sure yet. But most certainly, this is a question worth asking and answering *too*.

The memory must have faded because of all the skag they dole out around here in this hazy, backward world.

But why?

To numb me? Make me forget?

I just can't be sure yet.

For a second, I consider if answering this question about pink bottles holding precious serum is worth holding out for. Do I take the skag and the stamp in exchange for a chance to discover why, or even a chance of a chance of why?

Nope. The only chance I am looking for is Cale. Pink bottles are useless to me, Alice or not. But maybe not. I just can't be sure yet.

Gaige turns back toward me with the skag hose, carefully taking his time to hook it up without squeezing me too tightly. Then he flutters that look of his and says, "Hold on, Isla...Jane. This will make you a little dizzy."

Fire shoots out my nostrils. "I don't think so," I say, still scheming to use my needles. The ones that will finally free me from all this crap in my world minus Cale and his *"heart you."*

Without hesitating, I finger the spot on my neck that exposes the beating of my heart and know this is just the place for that pack of needles. Even a small puncture will do the trick. The instrument I need is right here in my beautiful boot, calling my name.

"Alice," the devious plot whispers. It's a good name for me, I think.

To prep my skin for the new Ink stamp on my chest, Gaige opens my front supportive gear. He pauses for a second, taking a long and gasping breath. That expression of his starts in again, swirling purple and blue behind, no, beyond our eyes, and consumes his face.

The purple crayon snaps like a twig in my hand.

Tenderly, he lifts my breast like it's a precious bottle of life-saving bacterial strains that might save us all, or at least him. He begins his work, slipping on the Ink glove and engaging the foot pedal, followed by the deafening click, click, clicking of the monstrous mollusk. The skag hose shrieks out a complaint on my behalf, not wanting me as much as I am not wanting it. The Ink evacuator sucks in and out cool liquid, planning to vacuum back up the residual Ink and tiny intermixed drops of my blood as he paints his art on me.

I smash the blue crayon into oblivion with my fist and prepare to die.

But just before I reach down for the miniature blades, he places his hand on mine in such a way that I have to stop and look once more into those blue, I mean purple eyes of his.

Then without a word, he unhooks the skag hose so quickly and swiftly that the flashing light will never notice. But I do. *Impossible.*

Thank you. Help me, and I'll help you.

Forgetting all about my needles, whose calling out to me falls on deaf ears that can only hear his silence, I gaze into his colors, still firm and strong and unbroken in my hand. I suck in the precious air around me hard, trying not to die from the impossibility of what this might mean. *No skag.*

He begins his work on my body, so perfect thanks to those rose-creating fingers of his. *No skag, ah!* Another of my delicate petals opens up and falls to the floor from the pleasure of him and his hands, minus the skag, plus the *toos*, purples, and blues. All of it *too* complicated to name just like me–Isla, Jane, Alice, 53, all of them unworthy to describe the simple complexity of who I am.

He smiles subtly, but I keep my face like a mask so as not to betray my joy.

Did he always know I had the needles? Probably. Like maybe he even left them there for me on purpose, expecting I would make my devious plan, even before I did, like he most likely figured out I would make Baylor's sign in battle before I did. *Impossible. Or is it? I just can't be sure yet.*

Obviously, he must see me from inside my own eyes, maybe even clearer than I do, already understanding something I am still trying to learn. Why? Because he already knows the girl who meant to take the heartbeat from her own neck but would not because his hands would stop hers first.

And I am sure there will be no more skag for me, ever. He will honor my choice. And one day, Gods be merciful, I will decipher his words about trust, a concept as foreign to me as a healthy bacterial biome.

My purple and blue eyes dilate from the glory of it. The choice, I mean, to choose for me–who finally matters to someone like Kink always knew I would. My heart skips a few beats and then keeps going.

Gaige I... You must know that I...

The wonderful choice showers me, fills up all my holes, and washes me clean while it takes all my contaminants and replaces them with something right and good that drips from me onto the floor and fills the room. But unlike Tilly, who won't come back, this flood raises me up instead of drowning me.

And I just can't be sure anymore who all my intensity oozes for and why and how. But does it matter?

No, probably not because it just is, just because, and for no reason more than that.

As Gaige continues, I drift off to a place of half-sleeping where Tilly finds my hand. But this time, I am not afraid to take it because she is my friend no matter what I did or even what I didn't do. Here, where I live in the City of Roses smelling so good and fancy and coated in hope and faith underneath my lovely thorns for the first time in forever. My lily Ink opens wide to nurture me, and I suckle it fearlessly.

Then Tilly takes me back to the day when the unthinkable happened, her hand in mine like we have only ever had one pair of hands between us.

Chapter Nineteen

WE ARE LITTLE BAIRNS AGAIN-MAYBE seven or eight years old at the most. And that grin of hers which smells like perfection, happiness, and purity reminds me why Tilly is the best friend I've ever had. My only friend, that is, before Baylor and maybe Gaige now, too.

Tilly looks at me the way only she ever has–in kindness. Raising her eyebrow, she dares me to be my most authentic self with her teasing expression. Certainly, she needs no words to explain this because I understand her perfectly just like I always have.

In a flash, I see a silver wire extend from her chest to mine and then disappear. She bubbles, laughing hysterically like it's the funniest thing she's ever seen. After she finally stops giggling, she nods her head and creases her left eyebrow again to make sure I've understood the message.

I nod, agreeing completely, like the concept is as obvious as the treachery of my every waking moment. She grins, the smile way too big for her face, at how connected we are by an invisible wire that can't ever be cut even if we wanted to sever it.

Why?

Because as any idiot fish can see, we are intimately intertwined in this rabbit's game forever. To take it one step further–if I win the whole stinking Heat to get back Home safe and sound, she wins. Another step–even if she were to be our champion instead of me, then she would hand the honor over to me because she prefers to watch me win rather than to win herself so we can both win, *too.*

Too. Too. So many toos. Thank you, Tilly. I... You must know I...

And I wonder how she grasps this profound and idealistic concept at such a young age when I am still so clueless about things like *"heart you"* and spaces so deep and wide while I only bother to worry about simple stick dolls and sock wigs.

A tear slips down my half-coherent cheek as it dawns on me that this is exactly how I feel about Cale. All the same, so full of *"heart you"* and songs that wouldn't dare pretend they are sad because grief is impossible in any tune that we would sing together tied up with our invisible wire. Our joyous melody blending perfectly just like colors in a rainbow all fuzzing into one another at the edges that somehow change without me realizing they are changing. Then, without drawing any attention to the shift, they are just changed, matching perfectly right at the same time, *too.*

Ah…blue making purple, red making orange and then looping around until blue surfaces once more in a never-ending circle of undeniably gorgeous colors. As per usual, I push the analogy too far: perhaps we 53s are just like the colors inside and beneath the colors which are all somehow the same. Yet all somehow different, each one of us depends on the others because we are not possible without the rest. Almost as if we are all colors within one single clear or white color holding all the other colors perfectly together in a rainbow of overlapping connection. I just can't be sure yet, but this is exactly the same as my *"heart you"*–blending one into the next, rolled into one big clear *"heart you."*

Tilly shakes her head and giggles at me getting all tangled like a spider in the web of my thoughts like I always have, unlike her who just exists in the truth of who she has always been. She never needs questions and answers like I do, life so simple and clear to her. And I suspect this very contrast makes us such a perfect pair.

Still laughing, she starts walking to the place where I lost her, abandoned her, killed her. She blows a sigh forcibly out her nose and shakes her head *no.* That's not the way she sees it, apparently. Not even close.

I hang my head and drag my feet.

She blows another hard sigh and says, "See for yourself."

Instantly, I am inside Tilly's eyes looking back at me, feeling her feelings, thinking her thoughts. Darn, if they aren't as clear and pure as the box Gaige gave me earlier. Unable to resist the beauty of it, I gulp down the purity in her mind, the simplicity of her thoughts, which are so unlike mine always doubting and wondering and needing to figure things out. Because, unlike her, I do not already know, and even if I do, I still have to go through the motions to prove it by asking why underneath the why.

Flash. I'm back in time watching it–the day I have spent more than a decade trying to forget–happen from inside her eyes that couldn't have seen it more differently than I did:

We played our game of hide and seek like we always did on special days away from sanctioned responsibilities as youths. Daring one another to be braver and braver than last time, we explored the corridor of some building I didn't even recognize. Somehow, though, we found our way inside a space in one of the walls. So on our hands and knees, we crawled through spaces almost too tight for bodies even as small as ours to fit. We marveled at the adorable and lively beetle bugs wiggling about, never having seen in real life one of the few living creatures that naturally inhabit this planet. They seemed cute, like pets. Almost.

Oh my Gods, how have I forgotten all of this? The bugs, the pink serums. How many freaking memories has the skag robbed from me?

We followed the bug dance which seemed to be leading us somewhere very important. Or maybe not. I just couldn't be sure yet.

The game felt more dangerous by the minute. We kept pushing on even though we heard the roaring of the pipes beneath us. Deeper and deeper into a part of this building we traveled. Or were we still inside the wall? I'm still not sure.

We came out underneath the structure inside a secondary structure beneath the massive building, or maybe still in the wall somehow, which opened into an even more massive central room. This new room was filled with large metal containers and doors, too numerous for me to count, stretching down endless hallways. Behind some of them, we heard sounds that we did not understand.

A weak cry called out. It was smaller and weaker than a normal bairn cry. There was clicking, booming, smashing, things falling, doors slamming, loud and harsh mechanical sucking sounds.

But worst of all, there was screaming. *Gods, help me. Help us all.*

I hated this place immediately, more intensely than I could have ever despised anything. Way more than Irmin who seem like best friends, infallible allies compared to this. Way more than the thraex wires burrowing into my deepest thoughts.

A crash startled us, and we were terrified. We shook furiously.

Were we discovered? Or had we discovered this place? I couldn't be sure yet, but it must surely have been against the law to be in this place, probably punishable by the unthinkable.

Shockingly, no one came to shoot or necrotize us. Yet the fear, palpable and thick, continued to mount. Neither of us opened our mouth, too scared to speak or even utter a whisper. Something there was bad, very bad with a capital B, too bad to even acknowledge. We both intuited we must get out immediately and run away as far and as fast as we possibly could, never returning to this terrible place, to this interval in the wall.

It stank like rotten squares, garbage, hurt, terror, misery.

An idea, familiar yet distant, popped in–abuse.

Dropping all worries except survival, we ran side by side until I see myself sprinting ahead through Tilly's panicked eyes. Even at such a young age, I was wicked fast, faster than she.

I hear another scream, Tilly's scream. Only this time, I feel her terror as the scream erupts from deep within her, and I see the horror through her eyes as I watch myself running away. *Oh no. Please, Gods, don't make me watch this.*

She slips on something sticky and red near one of the large metal containers, which is partially open, and falls in. *Red equals dead.* Another scream, only more muffled this time, escapes her throat. Immediately, I feel her lungs fill with the biting smell of the liquid inside the vat. Her nose burns from the sulfuric fumes that swallow her gasping breath.

This time, I am the one breathing the pungent air, unable to fill my lungs now melting like the wax we use to seal our test tubes at the Foundry and then later, Kalil's toes. I keep looking back out of the water at myself still running away from the gray tub of whirl-pooling liquid that is not good and is not clean. It burns when I breathe it in, so sharp and penetrating like liquid knives held by billions of evil bacterial strains.

My legs go numb. There is no more pain. And I know instantly, just like she did, there are no more legs underneath my melting lungs. I mean hers. *It's her, not me, in the evil water.*

Tilly was already gone, already ruined, already dying. *This little piggy went to the market.*

And her thoughts, previously so clear and simple, start to flash back and forth. Images rapidly fill the screen in her mind, alternating too quickly to be understood. So I accept this and just take in what I can, knowing these are her last living thoughts. *This little piggy stayed home.*

She shows me bits and pieces of her life. Or is it lives? And honestly, words fail my lousy attempt to dissect the images. But for her, I will try. For her, I will try anything. *This little piggy had roast beef.*

I see the drawings of a child. I cannot say if they are hers or belong to someone else, but does it really matter? No, probably not.

Some of the drawings are bright and lovely, filled with the images of things I have never seen here in the City of Mutants, except in the altered versions sometimes used to confound a particularly dangerous Heat–horses, dogs, tigers, elephants, birds, and even mice. And the flowers, cartoon after cartoon of roses and lilies, surrounded by rainbows, balloons, trees with bright green leaves. The images keep coming–meadows, mountains, rivers, clear, blue skies, smiling faces, and hearts. But weirdest of all, the same letters over and over: l-o-v-e together in a combination I do not think I have ever seen.

Love. This little piggy has none.

Normally, I would question where the pictures and letters come from, but right now, I don't have time to think about things like that. I watch, completely focused on her, before the images and what is left of her slips away forever.

Then I see bairns holding hands with Elders and what must be older female sibs. I infer they are female from the curve of their breasts and the shape of their womb cloths. Some images are dark, and I do not want to see them. But to honor her, I do– flashes of cuts and scrapes, slaps, tears, more and more pain.

The same idea returns–abuse.

Many images I do not understand but only recognize they are pictures of hurt–her hurting. There's just no worthy way of describing them.

Finally, small bairns, smaller than I usually see in the City of Minis, all lined up in little plastic containers, crying and crying like they will never stop. One by one, they do, though, when they submit and give in, abandoning their futile complaints since no one ever answers them.

This little piggy cried wee, wee, wee all the way home.

All of this I witness from inside her eyes that still look back at me as the hot, thick liquid knives cut her down into nothing.

I stopped running, buckling around to search for her. Finding her drowning in the water, I backed away from her in horror, thinking only of my own selfish skin.

I was disgusted with myself and spat on my own foot, so brazen to bear this gorgeous Ink that I do not, will not, ever deserve. *My fault.*

She shook her head *no*, assuring me she was not done yet.

With a single innocent yet piercing glance, she reminded me there was nothing left of her to save. Then she went completely under the liquid, her final sound nothing more than a gurgle.

Next, I heard the sound that made me run away from her drowning in the liquid, abandoning her used-to-be-so-gorgeous face.

The boom, boom, boom of the fire gun startled me.

Just after I escaped around the corner, multiple monitors and a trail of little ones came out from behind all the booms. The line of them still screaming, the bairns wailing, crying, begging, falling into the knives.

One at a time, each forced to watch all the others before them melt in the liquid that washed Tilly away. Or did it raise her up? Now that I know about the wire, our magic string of silver "*heart you*"? I just can't be sure yet.

Without a doubt, I would have been executed if they had caught me in the proximity of this atrocity, this abuse. Thankfully, they did not. Clueless to the massacre I had barely escaped, I stepped back out of the space in the wall, still running from the fire gun.

And now it all makes sense, all this nonsense. Why the boom of Kalil's execution affected me so—my previously repressed memory of Tilly's death. There is simply no going back. *Pivotal.*

I place my two fingers over my heart for Tilly, so generous with this vision even after her demise. Fuck-all, it has never been my fault. That honor belongs to the red liquid she slipped on and then the nasty water, not pink but gray, trying to cut us all.

As the dirty rainbow of pain swirls, I can't help but wonder about all the colors beneath the colors and what they mean. All this red, all this gray, all this pink, trying to kill me, kill us all, actually, in the City of Death that is supposed to save us.

And now I find the answer to the question about the bairns and where they go without kith affiliations or enough Inks. They go down the dirty drain where Tilly is, but isn't.

Waking up gasping, I am forever changed. The next obvious question presents itself: Why would the Mozek kill us? Who are they actually saving? What is really going on?

Until the answers show up, I have a plan for as many bairns as I can take, who won't need invisible wires to survive all the gray water because of me. As for the liquid, those fluid bacterial needles and spikes of abuse, I have a plan for that growing beneath my plan, like fire underneath my mind.

I open my eyes fully and look into, not through, Gaige, startling once more from all the beauty in the colors inside those eyes of his, full of blues and purples, which are almost beautiful enough to cover up the gray liquid I remember now. Almost.

Wow, what if he knows about it, too?

Is that why he is helping me? *Holy shit. Is he a spy?*

I would ask him, but how do you ask something like that when a red light is recording every word you say?

Silently, I thank Tilly who I realize is still helping me win so that she will win so that we might have a chance of a chance of a chance for us all to win this mad Heat to escape the song of a mock turtle. The song I vow I will no longer sing or listen to ever again now that I recognize its treacherous tune.

Then I tug on Tilly's wire and giggle softly to myself on the inside right where I am certain she will hear it perfectly. Because she lives there inside that space so deep and wide that hears my thoughts, feels my feelings, and shares my heart trying so desperately to get out into a world of confused turtle songs. Here in the Gods-forsaken hellhole where it takes wires to save wires from all the deadly stains in the City of Liquid Knives.

Perhaps it's time I do something more than just think about that.

And maybe it's time to find the way out of this rabbit hole.

Chapter Twenty

WHILE I'M STILL THINKING about the delicious idea of escaping through a crack in the side of this rabbit hole, my Ink dealer takes me back to Levana quarters. Silent as usual, he speaks to me without speaking. Then he goes inside with me as if I need his protection. *Protection from what?* This seems odd because the only one I need protecting from, other than myself, is the queen of the Mozek fuckfaces, who isn't here. Or is she? I just can't be sure yet.

Maybe this Gaige knows more than I do, but I can't risk asking if the sovereign of the evil monsters watches me, can I? So like usual, I say nothing back, and he replies with more silence. Subtly, he nods at the light near the stairwell. Shocker. It's red. *Red equals dead.*

He slams the door to make sure I notice. I nod back.

Once in the stairwell, I whisper, "Red equals dead."

He nods again but says nothing as usual.

There are no red lights on any of the walls the seven flights up. But in a few corners, I see a momentary flash, like a sliver of a flash of a color that is almost green but not quite. Yet the color disappears before I am sure it is even really there. The next time it happens, he pauses and puts one finger over my lips and his other hand over my eyes. He holds me still like this for a moment until I feel the flash happen again. With closed eyes, the color is a brilliant, deep, and lush green that molts into a color I can best only describe as anti-green before my field of view is white again. Ha. I can feel and see the flash better with closed eyes than I ever saw it with them open.

Not even sure what I mean, I say, "Thank you."

"Welcome. Keep moving. They are timing you."

Still too afraid of her, I ask nothing about the queen. Why would I? Now I am sure she is watching, and besides, words are basically useless to the two of us.

When we step through the stairwell exit door, he slams this one too. Probably so both the queen and I will notice.

Yep, there it is–the red flashing light on the other side again. He points to it subtly like only he can with those speaking glances of his, helping me figure it all out without a single word and a double door slam. *Slam! Slam!*

I also can't help but notice Gaige is breathing normally while I'm panting like I just ran a Heat. How is that even possible? Is his body some kind of machine? Does he spend his entire day walking up and down stairs with his muscular body covered in handsome Ink?

Jealousy, one of the manipulative vessels the queen uses to run this world, gnaws at my stomach. I want my ID's strength, his throbbing legs, his firm arms, his infallible lungs to claim as my own because, damn…I sure could use that kind of power in battle. I would be unstoppable.

How can he be so strong? I squint my eyes taking a good hard look at his ripped back, his thick neck, and that jelly in my gut takes another nibble of me.

But Elder Khaan taught me a long time ago that jealousy is like a bad strain of bacteria–the more medium I give it to grow on, the more it will flourish and take over the whole petri dish of my inner mantra. So, I try to think about something else instead because, let's face it–I already have way too many holes inside of me to start playing with envy and its destructive properties.

So…

Why is he doing this to begin with? Is he building trust like a big muscle between us, planning to crush me with it later? Or is he tying me up in his wire, preparing to cut me when I least expect it? Is his friendship real? Or is he just another layer of illusion? I just can't be sure yet.

Is he even here? Am I drunk on skag and imagining this all? Am I paralyzed in my thraex portal and this whole scene plays out in my mind, projecting onto some screen to amuse thousands in the Orb?

My mind gets pretty happy at this point because my thoughts are swirling at full intensity just like it likes.

And what if this whole existence known as my so-called life is just a game inside a game inside another game? Would that be total nonsense or complete madness? Or something even worse than that? I just can't be sure yet.

Shit, just like Alice in her Wonderland, nonsense is the only reality I experience. Unable to stop now, I keep racing down this track of thought. But more importantly, that a big difference exists between madness and nonsense.

I take it one step further just for the fun of it, probably, as per usual, too far. But never too far for me…

After everything is said and done, every level of this video-game life conquered, every card dealt, every hand won, every rabbit hole explored, I don't want either nonsense or madness. But if forced to choose by the evil bacteria growing on my poor skin and poised to kill me, I will gladly accept the former over the latter any day. Nonsense–so preferable to madness, it turns out.

Fuck m…m…m…mmmm…madness. Madness is for the mad, and I may be crazy, but I am not mad.

For the first time in forever, I also realize the clueless monitors forgot their little turtle song is a fake tune whistling bullshit Dixie. After so many verses, more than seventy I bet, they actually believe their own lie. *Idiot madmen.* If I didn't hate them so much, I think I might feel sorry for the puffy gray fools in their suits spreading sad song lies like a contagious strain of bacteria. *Wow. Chills.*

Could hate be nothing more than a manufactured bacterial strain? If so, then surely I could find the cure for them. Until I remember the boom of Kalil's fire gun and the necrotized goo that they offered him instead of his ten perfect little toes, that is. *I should have protected those piggies.* My hate, so much bigger than my sorrow, washes away all traces of my sympathy for their evil insanity even if it comes from nonsense first. Heck, it's not my fault they were just too stupid to stop it from evolving into the madness that inevitably follows. Fuck the madmen; let them die of their own disease. The one they gladly give themselves. It is totally their fault, not mine.

Why?

Because nonsense, just like a prodrome of illness, might proceed and then lead to the disease of madness, but the critical thing is that it doesn't have to. We, as creatures with clever minds, always have a choice about being mad or not. And as any fish-of-a-person like me can see, the beauty is that we can always take a rotten choice back and choose again differently, more responsibly, the next time. We can vaccinate ourselves with nothing more than the intention to be clean and clear and uninfected. So...*Fuck the m...m...m...mmmm...madmen.* I say let's quarantine them instead of saving them.

My mind returns to Gaige in present time, strutting around my quarters like he built every cabinet, every shelf. Effortlessly, he finds the things I need without my asking and without his looking for them because he already guesses what I need and where to locate them. But how? Did he download the map?

Who cares, really? Not this Alice. Or do I? I just can't be sure yet.

Who the hell am I kidding? Of course I do.

This whole scene should scare me, probably. But it doesn't. And that seems odd, too, but not odd enough to bother me, which is the oddest part of all.

Unable to pull away my gaze from his handsome body, I admire Gaige's physique. Unlike last time, though, I deny the temptation to get all jellified. In stark contrast, I choose to be firmly pleased, realizing, of course, that his strength is mine and accepting that maybe, just maybe, it always has been. No longer envious at all, I offer up only gladness because the wire between us holds us together so strongly just like between Tilly and me, Cale and me, Baylor and me. So many silvery cords of lifeblood uninfected with even the slightest trace of madness. Is each wire a new wire or a strand within one big wire? Surely I cannot say. But I can feel it, all of it, embrace and support me as it branches out like the roots of a tree, that gorgeous masterpiece of nature—a tree.

Oh, what I wouldn't give to climb one of those trees that once grew right out of the ground before the terrible strains of hatred parasitized all the goodness back Home and replaced it with addiction, jealousy, madness, necrotizing deaths, and the Frightening on this horrible planet.

I sigh, not hard like Tilly but deep and low.

Focusing my mind on my curious dealer instead of the fallen trees, I admit that there must be so much more to him than meets the eye, as any fool can see. Gaige moves gracefully about my room like he owns it, like he is more an instrument than a visitor, like I am just a tree that can never be lost in this forest because I planted him to find me in a secret place eons ago.

I pick my chin up off my chest and close my mouth.

Where does he come from? And why? Why does he smell of mint leaves like Elder Khaan did instead of sulfur? Why is he helping me but pretending not to for the flashing red lights? And why is he allowing me to make choices?

As if I deserve such importance, such value, in a life made to teach me the lesson that I don't matter, can never matter because I am filled to the brim with mock-turtle lies. We don't even have the truth of who we are after being tricked into buying our smallness, our lack of value as we see ourselves through their missing, mad Mozek eyes instead of our own. For a moment, I stop to ponder if we are the saviors and they are the victims but then decide I don't give a shit unless it helps me get back Home, twenty-two light-years away from these lies. Such obvious lies even the writer of the song knows it. At least used to, anyway, before he forgot he changed all the lyrics and made up this ridiculous, much more sinister verse.

And somehow with Gaige's help, despite the false lyrics, I figure it all out: that I, the Jane named Isla, am valuable for no reason other than—well just because. Not because I am Levana or beta or verus—just because. And I am full of wires and *toos* and *"heart you"* all rolled up inside the most gorgeous of rainbow-white wire. *Isla, I... You must know that I...*

Yet I had to see it in the white color of his eyes shining back at me to see the whiteness inside of mine. Perhaps Gaige is just a mirror. Or am I the mirror? I just can't be sure yet.

But I do know one thing, seeing now what I never could have seen on my own but was always there waiting patiently for me to remember. I am beautiful. *Isla, I... You must know that I...*

I... You must know that I... The same incomplete thought now crosses over every boundary in my mind that never mattered and aims to fill every hole inside my spongy heart that was never empty with the one cure that never existed until I will it into existence right now. From Cale to Gaige, back to Tilly, and out through myself.

Isla, I... You must know that I...

I take my new braid beads and roll them around in my hand while he prepares my simple meal. They are not ordinary, these beads, to say the least. Inside, they have a crack, a fissure, a place made perfectly for holding a drop of liquid. They open with a little hinge. Instantly, I understand the gift in them, the power of them, the secret use I will have for them. Or do I? I just can't be sure yet.

Gaige watches me silently and nods expectantly before he brings over another clear box of his from a shelf that holds many of them. I have not put them there, but somehow they are there on a shelf behind a slit in the first shelf like they are folded in between the molecules between the shelves. *Impossible... yet not...somehow.*

I gulp the clear box down while he clips the beads in my braids. Then he takes off my boots along with the stolen needle pack and places them in the closet like there are no needles hiding in them.

But there are, and we both know it. I look in the closet just to make sure but cannot see them. I guess there's a hidden crack in there as well.

"Rest," he says, followed by another one of his, "Islas." Only this time, he doesn't bother with the pause. He calls me, "Jane, my Jane," which is even weirder than the "pause Jane" business.

So am I his Isla Jane? Or his Jane Isla? I just can't be sure yet.

I say pretty much the dumbest thing possible. "Okay."

"Baylor," he says, "is safe. But not Jaxston, that black card asshole. Baylor John's eyes are opening like yours. He has had enough red Ink hadrons to stabilize."

I turn my head to the side, confused like I've just woken from a dream and can't recall the day or year it is. "What?"

He grimaces and adds, "Expect another Libellus, Jane, that lists you as a warrior. The Mozek are not finished with you yet." He clears his throat.

"Shocker, huh?" I nod with certainty yet remain totally confused by so many weird words that make no sense. Finally, he leaves me alone.

I go over to inspect my mysterious shelves after the purple-eyed king leaves me to my thoughts–all swishing, all swirling around who I am and who I can no longer be. Now that I know better, that is, about which songs I will no longer hear and, more importantly, which lyrics I will sing loudly enough for all the others to learn.

Damn it. Like Gaige shows me, I intend to show them.

My cabinet, full of squares and boxes which do not belong there yet are there when I reach in between the shelves, gives me courage to say it out loud. "Impossible."

No longer just a thought, I give those ten magical letters the power they deserve and say the word a few more times to make sure I hear it clearly. "Impossible. Impossible. Impossible." Ten lovely letters for my ten little toes.

Pivotal, that gorgeous goddess inside me confirms and points her feet.

Then I take it one critical step further. If these hidden gifts can arrive unnoticed in some secret way in a crack between and somehow inside my shelf, then surely items can go out the same secret way, minus all the watching little red lights. Items like Cale and I, to be exact.

Pivotal. I'm dancing now.

To further my amusement, I say it louder. "Impossible." Or is it possible? I just can't be sure yet.

Tomorrow starts a new week. Undeniably, I plan to take in many more bairns and train them in the thraex, secretly teaching them to battle with novel approaches. So I guess I, *too,* will be moving to Forty-Four B and all the wondering it will invoke.

Besides, I have always liked Baylor, right?

So having the Salus clan as our new neighbor sounds like a pretty good deal to me. Yep, even if it forces me to suffer endless wondering from living so close to the thick glass and fences that protect me.

But what exactly are they protecting me from? Or is it really keeping me from something? I just can't be sure yet.

All of a sudden, it hits me like a ton of bricks because I am sure. Part of me always has been. I am a prisoner. We all are.

"Impossible!"

Dropping to my knees from the weight of the idea, sickness spews out my mouth and litters the floor. My brain spins looking for good news as the acidic slime coats everything in my putrid disgust.

My heart begs me to hang on, to take the next logical leap, to complete the thought, to find the mother-of-a-glorious-gift always hidden somewhere within the bad news. *Wait for it. Wait for it. Wait for it,* my heart encourages.

Thankfully, I find the shit-covered jewel worth holding on to: if things are going in and out through folds in the space in my shelves, then there must be somewhere else worth going to, somewhere outside or even inside this prison. Maybe even some place like Home.

Possible.

And that's exactly where I am going. Somewhere else. "Gods damn it."

As for the medical book and the photo all rolled in the beetle bug crack, we will see. *"I will find a way to save it, Elder Khaan."* I stand, dizzy from my new awareness. Obviously, it is his book after all, of course. And I haven't found it; it actually found me from the hidden space inside the City of Sneak.

As I lay my weary head down on my bed, still spinning from confinement of and simultaneously liberating possibilities for escape between the molecules of the chains that shackle me, the slip comes under my door.

The next Libellus, just like Gaige said it would, trying to kill me.

I laugh, leaving it where it lands, knowing Skylar will be right behind it. *She can pick it up.*

It takes about five minutes before Skylar's feet come marching. She doesn't even bother to knock. "This is your fault, Isla," she says, shaking the declaration at me. Spit flies out her mouth in little drops that shower me.

"What," I demand, "is your freaking problem? I'm the one who gets to bear the brunt of the burden. What do you care? Do my hair, plug me in, and you are done. Get over it."

I wipe my face even though her saliva has dried. Unfortunately for her, she slips on some of my vomit. She stifles a laugh but then gets all pissy again and starts sputtering more rain showers.

"Look!" she shouts, trying to shake my gut-slime off her toes. She smacks me on top of the head with the paper and grunts. Funny how the paper, not my secretions, is the source of her disgust. I can't help but laugh at the irony.

I examine the paper closely to decipher the picture image–the Levana stamp surrounded on all sides by Mozek seals. The central red ball of the official Mozek image spins atop thirteen small stationary golden dots. Each dot, like the top of a lower-case letter "i", leads down one of the arms forming the pyramidal throne upon which the red ball reigns supreme.

Counting the total number of balls again, I can only hope they are a clue: thirteen little balls in each of the thirteen larger images. Surely that is no coincidence. But thirteen what? Planets, cities, strains of evil bacteria? I just can't be sure yet.

But I want to be sure, sooner rather than later, so I ask the question again. "Thirteen what?" Then I look at the picture once more. On every border, the Mozek seal surrounds Levana. No, the image feels way too hostile for something that benign. The Mozek seals imprison Levana seems more appropriate. Better yet, quarantines it, which makes perfect sense to me under the circumstances. Spread infectious hate that kills 53s, but quarantine novel partnerships that save them. *Clever, mad creeps.*

The intention is clear, the result deducible without much more effort–Levana kith vs. the Orb. Or better put, the Orb vs. Levana? I just can't be sure yet. Or can I?

All clan members old enough to wear an alpha, beta, gamma, delta, or epsilon label, in other words the entire force of Inked Levana members, will fight against the Orb itself as a troop. Us, unprepared and possibly even unarmed, against an opponent with every upper hand poised to slaughter us in one fell swoop. *Oh my Gods.*

"Have you ever wondered, little lady," Skylar asks, "what happens if you die before your wounded body makes it back to the thraex portal?"

"No. I mean... I never... Except that dragon battle with Elder Khaan." I see him in my mind, wounded and perfectly imperfect. *Oh my Gods.*

"Maybe you should, Isla. Not you. You are fast. The crowd loves you. But what about the no-names like me, the slow ones like Oiya, the ones you roll your eyes at in practice, the ones like Destarta who never even come to practice? Because they are the ones I am talking about."

A thousand responses scuttle through my brain. None are worthy.

She's right. I have done this with my little sword swap with Baylor. *My fault.*

At the crack of dawn, Skylar and I wake the others, the twenty-two Levanas whose death sentences are to be served up because of my little hand holding in battle. It doesn't take a rocket scientist to know where this little mission plans to take us–down. Or is it out? I just can't be sure yet.

I lock the door and get *down and out* to business.

We have six simulators, which means each Levana will have about three turns before the Heat begins. Skylar and I will take shifts in the chief thraex, wearing our visor so that we can instruct in situ. The other will guard the room, practicing hand-to-hand combat in real life as a second station. The third station, hydration and refueling, will make use of all those extra boxes and squares on that shelf inside my shelf. *I'll be damned.*

For a moment, I wonder if this is why the supplies have made their way secretly here...not for the future bairns at all but for the troop Heat? But that means Gaige already expected this would happen, that I would swap the sword before the battle occurred, that my whole kith would suffer the consequences.

How the hell? That's impossible. Or is it? I just can't be sure yet.

This train of thought makes me dizzy, so I drop it like an ax. Only this time, it slices my foot in two. *What if...?*

Why haven't the Mozek already killed me?

Wouldn't that be easier on us all? A bad square or some bizarre explosion like the one that killed both the Levana and Salus Elders, perhaps? The choices are endless, really. *Chills everywhere.*

"Is that what happened, Elder Khaan?" I scream, unable to hold it in.

"Shut up," Skylar responds. "Now. Right now!"

She points to the red light, and I begin to grasp how little I understand the City of Evil. *Get back to work before you lose it, girl.* Thankfully, for once, I take my own very good advice.

We start with weapons first, going over the pros and cons of each helmet, sword, and shield. I recommend the usuals and discourage the unusuals, of course, since I have such a proclivity for tradition and all.

Then I turn away from the red light and whisper some of my most guarded secrets. Like how I will my legs to move faster, how I let the thraex machine activate my muscles from inside my nervous system, how I slow my thoughts, actually clear my mind, and focus on *one thing* only–the outcome I intend to bring forth with my motions. Elder Khaan called manifesting the *one thing* the Dyer Principle, and I share this priceless and ageless knowledge with my family.

At first, they laugh at me, blowing the whole thing off. Then Skylar reminds them the last troop Heat was so long ago that none of us can remember it. We have no idea what is about to happen, and the Orb will play on our deepest fears. The Mozek will use our ignorance against us, and we have about a one-in-a-million chance of winning. But if we do win, no one will ever forget us or challenge our status again.

They shut up and get down and out to business.

I wonder how she knows this right before I remember that she supposedly screwed up her cross and react tests and was subsequently demoted to other red card assignments, that is. My eyes wander to her right foot wrapped like always in a decorative bandana that bears the Levana symbol. *Could it be?*

"Underneath... What's underneath?" I am dying to ask her.

Instead, I say, "You...um..."

She tosses her ankle about. "Did you say something?"

"Nope," I say because words are useless to the two of us. I mean *too* of us.

In this moment, I decide to trust her with every bit of knowledge I have ever acquired. We are one team, she and I–one Levana, one ocean, one glass wall, one color, one wire, one beta, even though she pretends she is delta.

As we head to the gladiator entrance, all of us lathered up and gorgeous, I whisper in her ear the secret I swore I would never tell anyone ever, because this may be the last chance I will ever get to explain how Levana always beats Irmin. Or should the Gods favor us in this case, how Levana will defeat the Orb.

Chapter Twenty-One

SKYLAR LAUGHS while we strap in.

To my shock, she actually laughs so hard she snorts like a pig. "I figured," she says, taking a full minute to gather her composure enough to complete the sentence, "there was no freaking way you were actually that talented."

I laugh back, minus any snorts, and wiggle my toes. Then I sign her like Cale— fingers to my lips and press down on my heart twice. *Levana in my heart, Levana in my space so deep and wide.*

She returns the sign and smiles genuinely from her space so deep and wide where she finds the hot and beautiful silver wire connecting us eternally as friends. She strengthens our titanium attachment with her attention to the goodness inside me. Or is it her? Or is it both of us at the same time? I just can't be sure yet.

She twirls her ankle. I flash my piggies.

The opening song plays, and we both gasp, reoriented to the total lack of goodness in store for us. Thankfully, I'm too busy to start swirling thoughts about crap songs and crap turtle lyrics.

The re-enactment ceremony of the bairns begins. The rose petals fall. We lock each other into position. The youngest stays behind to let us out on the other side. Or is the Folding the other side? I just can't be sure yet.

After surviving the disorienting fall into the Orb, we, Levana kith, take our places on our Interval Riders and, in the blink of an eye, arrive in the great and powerful Orb, say our pledge, and prepare for the Heat of a lifetime.

"Did you hear that?" I ask Skylar.

"Maybe? Feel it, more like. The first confounder?"

"Exactly." We run the lengthy perimeter of the game board.

Like a pawn, I can move in any direction in this game of chess. She goes one way while I go the other, gathering up the others, egging the crowd on by slinging our knightly swords, bowing our bishop-like heads, bearing our chests, displaying our Ink. We, this Skylar and I tied up in our wire of intertwined intention, are stronger together than the sum of the whole. Instead of adding, we multiply; I am sure of it.

"Remember," I tell my sibs once we are all back in one grouping, "they are going to play on our fears. The more afraid you are, the more they own you. Do not give in to the terror. If you feel nervous, look at me. Look at Skylar. We can do this."

They whoop. They holler. We all sign Levana and step forward as a pack.

Immediately, the Orb darkens. We are unable to see the audience, blocked off from anything that might remind us this is a holograph. We might as well be in the middle of the Frightening Zone. Then I realize, effectively, we are.

Unable to resist, the thought rooks me. *A Frightening inside a Frightening.*

I suspect what's already coming next. In fact, I can hear the black trickery advancing. I glance at Skylar who nods, hearing it too.

Mutant creatures are heading our way like in the Frightening, and before the complete thought even fully registers, the fog settles in. Lightening crashes. Eerie sounds erupt.

The Frightening!

"Oh my Gods, help the white team," I mutter.

Skylar punches me.

Several Levanas cower screaming, utterly immobilized by their fear. Others cry. Even I have to admit the effect is impressive. This outscores any nightmare I have ever suffered. *Cale... But Cale has... If only Cale were here.*

But wait. I do not mean that. Even if he knows exactly what happens next.

Scanning my memory, I try to recall the black visions he has shared with me in the past, searching for anything that will give me, the cause of this to begin with, an upper hand. Guilt threatens to consume me, but I won't allow it. Or surely we are goners. I will have to connect to my fury instead of my fear or my guilt, neither of which can possibly help me. Or the others, more importantly.

"What do we do now?" one of my epsilons asks.

"Kick their little, creepy butts."

The joke lightens the mood, and several of my clan laugh.

But then the sound of crackling twigs stops them. Something, Gods only knows what, lurks behind us. I scan the perimeter, trying to find some information about our surroundings.

On the ground a few feet away is an ancient sign with letters that spell "Beware the center of this haunted Romanian Forest." In a circle, perhaps a thousand meters across, only we live and breathe, nothing else–no snake-like trees as on the edges, no vegetation, nothing. *The Orb within the Orb.*

Whipping out my gladius, I take the lead, flagging the other Levanas behind me. A black-masked figure floats out. His sword and shield are unlike anything I have ever seen–alien shaped and made of foreign materials that I cannot hope to name. I try to find his eyes, but they do not exist, like deep portals of darkness, perhaps the original source of the hate in the universe. His feet hover over the ground like he is lifted on some invisible support structure. Not sure if he is another 53 or merely a projection, I battle anyway.

The demon's motions, so fluid like smoke, are almost beautiful. Almost.

Craning my neck around, while I fight, I sense that others just like him are close by. I can actually feel them before I see them. They feel like a void of blackness, a great, dark nothingness that wants to rook the source of every possible emotion out of me. My heart beats in time with his motions and pulls to the edge of my chest wall. My lungs spasm, and I cough, almost unable to keep breathing.

"Cale. Remember Cale," a familiar voice says, subtly entering my mind, the same from my last Heat after the skag floated through my hazy mind.

"Are you real?" I ask the voice.

"Very real. Unlike them," it says.

Skylar jumps in and takes on the noir monster next to me. So do two of my most talented deltas, accepting the evil challenge before the voice speaks again. Am I crazy? Is it crazy? Maybe we are both crazy? I just can't be sure yet.

I can't help but notice that several should-be-fatal blows pass right through the center of my opponent. *You aren't real. This isn't real. It's a nightmare, the only nightmare, a decoy, fear in physical form.*

I drop my sword and stop fighting.

My three partners, shocked, start yelling at me–the sacrificial pawn.

"Trust me," I say. "It's not real. They won't, they can't hurt you without you buying into the fear."

I really hope my theory is a good one because the dark knight's blade is about to slice me in half. It goes right through me. But I do not buy into the terror, the illusion, so I remain unaffected and remember a story Elder Khaan once told me about portals of darkness.

"Perhaps I am already dead, you fucker."

The images instantly disappear.

The same voice whispers, "Oh you are so fine," but I ignore it.

Several of my kith start signing and hollering.

"Shush," I shout, looking at Skylar. "Are you thinking what I am thinking?"

She nods. "It was a distraction."

"Yes, but more importantly, why?"

Then I get my answer. The first bolt of lightning crashes about one centimeter from my left foot. Thankfully, I lift my foot, sparing it from the fire now igniting the ground as the subsequent lava stream erupts, spreading dangerously fast. In seconds, flames engulf the north side of the forest.

"Lightning-lava!" I scream. "Run as fast as you can! Follow Skylar!"

I am the main enemy they are trying to kill. Surely they will aim most of the attack at me. If she can take them away, away from me–the source of all their suffering–they will fare much better. *My fault.*

Oiya cowers. She is the slowest, and she knows it. I grab her hand. "Remember what we talked about. Zone it out, and focus on the *one thing*. The thraex portal will operate your legs for you. You just have to stop resisting your own power. Get out of your own way. I believe in you even if you do not."

She pauses, trying to find the nonexistent doubt in my eyes until a lightning bolt igniting the ground behind her motivates her to get moving.

Standing there a while longer, I hope to gather the brunt of the attack while the others escape. I raise my hands in the air, flicking them toward me twice. "Bring it on, you piece of shit."

I spit on the ground and slowly wipe my mouth.

In response, they honor my foolish request.

I lose track of time at this point, which seems to speed up and slow down simultaneously. Hoping that every attack upon me gives the others another chance to escape intact, I succumb to my tunnel, my vortex, and my zone. Willingly, I give my physical power over to the machine contaminating my nerves and muscles. The temperature behind my neck increases dramatically, confirming that the thraex has gone deep, so deep within me.

Fully synced, I leap gloriously high in the air, higher than possible in real life, to avoid the molten bolts from above. With remarkable speed, I climb the burning tree-like poles around me, jumping from one to the next and then back down to the ground to avoid the flames. Running in every direction, I weave in and out of the red streams of death, still flicking my hands toward me, urging them on. *Yeah, baby. All attention on me, thank you.*

Kindly, the Mozek continue to oblige me.

This must be what hell looks like. "Maybe I am already dead."

In perfect timing, the wind increases, and the electrical lava storm mounts. By now, Skylar and the others should have reached the far side of the Orb. Hopefully, things look cooler over there.

Who knows how many bolts almost reach me before one finally does. A terribly painful sensation that words fail to describe sears across my back, and I suspect I am seriously wounded. Callously, I brace myself like a king and pretend nothing bothers me. They cannot know I am injured, so I will never tell.

Besides, what's one more secret to a royal old fish like me?

For a moment, I wonder, if this burn takes me down, will they call the Heat off and leave the others alone? Probably. Almost certainly. Almost. But can I really be sure yet?

I blink twice and laugh at the absurdity of my predicament.

If for sure it would, I would gladly step toward the bubbling inferno spreading along the ground toward me and allow it to engulf me. The final nonsense joke is on them: me–winning by losing, the Orb–losing by winning.

But I can't truly be sure, can I? Those devils are raging bastards, after all, who very rarely function from logic and reason. Could I possibly predict the response of psychopaths? No, probably not.

If I am wrong, then who will lead my kith out of this Heat? Skylar is good, better, more intuitive, far cleverer than she realizes. But is that enough to finish this? Unfortunately, they need me. Damn it. The irony infuriates me, which, to be honest, is probably a good thing since I could use some pissed-off.

My little molten party must finally get boring because it suddenly stops. The Orb must be trying to figure out a more exciting way to kill me. Great. That sounds like fun, *not*.

But then a new, more terrible awareness assaults me–maybe the other side of the Orb, the side with the other Levanas, is now more exciting. While I still have the chance, I go to find the others, hoping against hope they are all okay. I should already know better; they are not.

Like it lives in my head, I hear the voice one more time. "Good girl."

I can hear the howls, growling, and screams from here with my flawless ears. I start running. *Why am I always running?*

My feet take off, and I allow my body to go into autopilot and do what even my mind cannot grasp. I slam that sun in my boots, make a Levana sign, and whoop loud enough so that the entire audience, but most importantly Skylar, will hear that I'm coming. Already, I'm sprinting, leaping before I consider the potential consequences of what's happening.

There isn't enough time. I'm not going to make it.

I hop on one foot and then the other over the lava streams around me, trying to make the soft, supple boots that I love so much move faster.

Going even deeper now into the machine, I will the program to sync lower, more completely within me. I have never been so deep. But it's now or never. *Or I will never make it. They will all die without me.*

Infused with purpose, I sprint for Skylar. I leap for Oiya. I race against time for the chance to get to know me a little better before I'm gone. *I don't want to die. Not yet. Not like this. I'm still not ready. I can't fail them.*

Halfway across the chessboard, I mean Orb, I wonder how many seconds I have left. In the back of my disintegrating mind, I hear the howling again. It's laughing at me, taunting me, threatening me. But I cannot listen, or I will never have a chance of a chance of making it. I won't listen. I refuse.

I race past several chained up monsters trying desperately to get loose and chew my sibs to pieces. I count them one by one as I go past. *One, two, three, four, five, six mutants.*

Are they tigers? Are they wolves? Or some radiation-ruined mutation between the two? I just can't be sure yet.

My neck burns intensely from the Heat wire, the lava-blister keeps spreading, the heaviness of my guilty mind threatens impending insanity, but I refuse to listen and shout, " Screw you, seven," at the largest of the mutants blocking my entry to the pen. *I'm really starting to hate the number seven.*

And since I do not have time to fall, as my shoulder hits the pavement while I leap over him, I keep rolling until I am back upright on my feet. My calf injury feels strong, surprisingly so, considering what I'm doing to it. I might wonder why it never bothers me in the Orb if I had the time. It's almost like the Orb heals it. Almost.

I can just barely make out my kith safely crowding inside a central pen, but they must be able to see me because I hear their hopeful whoops and hollers urging me on to victory, to reach them, to finish this. They bang on the walls furiously to encourage and invigorate me.

That's when I hear the chain break. *Shit.*

The seventh monster roams freely and creeps toward me. Ten meters away, his saliva gathers as he seemingly prepares to eat me. His long, pointy ears, shaped like the blade of my sword, perk up as if listening to the beat of my delicious heart. That snake-like tongue of his licks his leathery lips, and drool puddles between his huge paws. He scratches his nails, razor sharp, on the ground once, twice, three times to gather grit. His mane, dark like a wolf's, forms a line of needle-like points down his arched back. And his coat, striped like a tiger's, shimmers as beads of sweat trickle down his muscular legs, wholly preparing to pounce me.

I can almost decipher his thoughts: *kill, hunt, eat, dominate, decimate.*

His pack howls urging him on to victory, to reach me, to finish this, just like mine does. And as much as I might wish that like earlier with the ghost-demon this putrid mutant and his pointy teeth won't hurt me unless I fear him, something tells me my brilliant tactic will not work twice.

The voice returns. "It would be wise to kill him quickly, Isla, but even wiser to use the power of the Orb against itself."

Against itself?

Imagining the brilliant entertainment factor of this gore, I feel the crowd's obsession with me, horrified by what's about to happen but unable to look away. Secretly, they delight in the prospect of witnessing my mutilation. The violent nature of humanity begs for release. I am that release.

The fog lifts.

Considering the purpose of this grotesque display, I am not surprised in the least. The Mozek don't want anyone missing the bloodbath, do they?

I imagine Skylar lifting pieces of me back into the thraex and infer she is spot on. If I am chewed to bits, then I will not be coming back for another round. As the large metal cage locks over my sibs, keeping them from helping me instead of the other way around, I snigger. I hate to admit it, but it's almost humorous. Almost. They, my kith, were the second distraction–the decoy all along.

Brilliant. The Orb uses my greatest strength and weakness against me–my own kith. Clever Mozek creeps. I might applaud them except there's a tiger-wolf stalking me, planning to eat me.

Cale's face floods my fragmented mind, giving me stronger purpose.

Plan B emerges right on time as usual.

Two can play at this game. *The Orb against itself, huh?*

As I run toward the monster, the red mound on my right foot rises like the fullness of dawn coming into view. The gritty sand of the Orb scrapes the underside my toes. A tunnel, almost like a vortex of power, encases me. And just like in every Heat, I know I have two choices: win or lose, fear or *heart*, Levana or nothing, eat or be eaten, verus or loser, impossible or possible.

I hear the sound of my heartbeat echo in the tunnel. My ears fill up with pressure, and numbness surrounds me. This void leaves only my beating heart to match the rhythm of the alternating sun and sand. The rest of me surrenders completely to the circuitry of the thraex.

The heat is almost unbearable now, both in my neck and on the field. I don't have long before I collapse–both the pain and the temperature too great to bear. But somehow, I keep going because I am so afraid to acknowledge the third thing hanging on my every move. The only *one thing* that matters to me right now, really–Skylar's face congratulating me, congratulating us all on a second chance for life when we step out of the thraex portal, totally intact, minus any chewed up pieces at all. *Lovely.*

The voice is right; if the Orb can use my weaknesses and strengths against me, I can do the same. *Orb against itself. Yes.*

Just to be sure, I listen carefully one more time before I make this wager for my life, for all of Levana life. Clear as day, I hear the monster's heartbeat. I dissect his murderous thoughts, focused only on ripping me to shreds, from mine and accept that we are intimately intertwined in the same device, the same program, the same holograph. The same wire perhaps?

And much like Cale can make his new blade by willing it to have a hinge in the middle and calling it a sica: s-i-c-a, I can fucking un-make one by willing it in reverse and call it a acis: a-c-i-s.

I walk confidently up to the monster, look right into his devilish red eyes, and lie down on the ground in front of him. When he lowers his matted head, his foaming jaws open wide, salivating with the anticipation of tasting my blood, I reach up gripping the putrid and clumped fur of his neck and swing up and over him to mount him and his spiky back. Thankfully, his fur parts under the weight of my thighs.

Then I ride him like a true king on a devastated horse of terror.

The monster, now my monster, my mutant chariot, gallops to my commands around the perimeter of my Orb while my crowd goes wild. The twist ending pleases the audience almost as much as my demise would have. Almost. The entire audience raises their arms in the air, begging for missio, demanding the entire Levana kith be set free.

Without knowing why I feel undeniably inclined, I rip off what's left of my clothing. Slowly but surely, I climb onto my knees and hold my arms up to the sky as my minion gathers speed. I tell my slave beast to run faster, faster, and he obeys my every command as he marks the full perimeter of the Orb with our combined power. On my way back to the start, I can't help myself and place my arms straight out to the side like a T or cross and stand fully erect on his back. It is as if there is a large stabilizing wooden structure behind me and my hands are nailed to it, not in submission but in absolute victory as I rise, rise, rise up to show them just how fucking beautiful my naked body is.

Just as the remaining creatures, still chained and spewing hate, descend into the floor, the metal gates open. My kith runs out to reach me as my monster's final lap comes full circle. I dismount the creature while Skylar showers me with approving applause, and the roses fall.

Still teeming with a thirst for vengeance, I stare at the twelve robed men at the top tier of the Gridiron, knowing they have no other option but to crown us verus. When again I notice the grouping seems to be incomplete, it hits me. Thirteen minus one makes twelve. One of the figures must be missing.

I smell the rose petals and frown. I, the red Isla Rose Jane, covered in spikes, still plan to rip their twelve pairs of hands apart while they pull away from me.

And just when the Chancellors lift their thumbs up to declare, *"Let them live. Mercy. Spare Levana,"* I bow slowly, oh so slowly, and then take out my gladius, give it a hinge in the middle, and slit my mutant wolf's throat to spite all twelve of them. If possible, I would kill the monster eleven more times just to be totally clear with my intention. *Check.*

Damn shame such loyal monsters can only die once.

I bow once more and wipe my hands in the bastard's blood now dripping down my arms. Red is dead for him too, I see.

My fellow pawn's blood travels down my raised arms, leaking into my boots and coating my toes with proof of my fury. And for half a moment, I regret my decision to kill him twelve times. His coat is so fine and lovely even if his breath smells horrid. But I remind myself he wanted to eat me a few minutes ago and decide I made the right choice after all. I turn the blade back into a normal gladius and throw it on the ground for everyone to see. The metal echoes through the complete silence of my shocked audience.

"Well done," the voice says. "I exist in Unum. I call myself the Augur."

"Get out of my head, Augur. I call myself verus."

She laughs.

Disgusted at them all–the Mozek, the speechless crowd, even the weird voice–I wipe the blood across my forehead like a red mask of death and walk out of the Orb before the robed Chancellors get the chance to dismiss me. Or am I dismissing the Chancellors? I just can't be sure yet. Or maybe I can? *Let Skylar take the God's-forsaken bead.* I am weak and shaking, my body pushed further than it ever has been, but they will never know.

Once I reach the Folding, I collapse on the ground, not sure if I will ever recover from this Heat stroke.

At the top tier, twelve robed figures stand. They can't help but notice one of their positions remains empty. Because they know only logic and have forsaken the concept that emotion holds measurable value, they make the next logical conclusion: the 53 represents danger to all that maintain the concept of war as status quo and is therefore already a dead harvest walking.

Chapter Twenty-Two

TILLY LEAVES me alone while I sleep tonight like she knows I will need my strength back for what's coming tomorrow. Her absence confirms the feeling I already have—that I am about to jump off a cliff, a precipice I can't turn back from because there is no way back.

And I might worry about this if it wasn't for all my newness. This version of me, so unlike the prior version, who is full of hope at the idea of being like Baylor even though a week ago the same thought would have sent me running. I giggle imagining my prior self screaming out Kinley's sarcasm and picking fun at the very thing I now aim to become. So, maybe I have already jumped. I just can't be sure yet, can I?

Yes, I can.

And since I have already jumped, what's another hop to a little old fish?

On the other hand, the lady from page one hundred and thirty-five will not leave me alone. She wakes me up inside a dream inside another dream and smiles at me just like Kinley does. Before she sucks it back in to cover up her gratitude with illusions, pretending she has none of those sores on the inside that she keeps hiding from everyone, that is. *Poor Kinley.*

Trying not to think any more about Kinley's doomed piggies, I give the book lady all my attention, hoping desperately to at least understand her better. She beams back at me like I'm helping her and that sweet swelling in her belly, like she already owes me before I jump off my cliff, like my cliff is built of too many piggies to count. Inexplicably, I understand it is also her cliff and that maybe, just maybe, it is the only cliff.

I wiggle my toes, so close to the edge of everything I have ever known, and just chew on that for a few minutes. *The one thing I should focus on—piggies.*

✧

The next morning's Ink stage goes well. No one cuffs me, beats me, or puts a fire gun hole in my forehead before my own bacteria eat me. Honestly, I can't figure out why not. Surely I am dead goo walking.

Acting more brazen than I should, I nod toward two bairns. And Baylor, grinning cheek to cheek, takes one more.

Jaxston, his jaw clenching and popping, throws me looks all full of hate while he tries to figure out what we are up to. The black Ink on his neck, a row of skulls with pits for eyes, keeps staring at me as if there is something going on that eludes him and might cost him another dose of numbness.

So to rub things in a bit, I show off my new thigh Ink, my award for winning the troop Heat, even though, as far as I am concerned, it just proves how fucked up this place is. My whole kith, thrilled with this little gift, welcomes it. In contrast, I hate it. But Jaxston, that dome, of course doesn't know that dirty, secret, little detail. Just a bit, I taunt him with the very thing the Mozek torture me with. Not too much, but enough.

His clicking and popping increases while his skulls light on fire.

But then I remember my choice for no more skag which Gaige honors once more, hiding it for the second time from the flashing red lights. So maybe I will think more fondly of my new Ink, making it a symbol of sorts, a symbol about turning weakness to strength, about infusing absolution with choice, about finding myself by getting lost.

My first new bairn, Craven Larsen, is about five years old. Doomed for Tilly's liquid knives, it makes sense to save him first.

The second, too quiet and shy to speak, refuses to tell me her name. Feeling sappy and sweet about it, I tap her on the forehead while she looks at the ground. "Fine by me. I will just call you something else until you tell me your real name."

She whistles.

"Whistler it is."

But then best of all, Alexis Lynne, a three-year-old with short braids and two home-made foil hair beads, shrugs her shoulders like she couldn't care less about being or not being picked, being fed or not being fed. The fake beads in her hair, twirled aluminum scraps, catch the rays of the sun and glitter back and forth like real beads. Her clever and original transformation of such waste into value reminds me of our innate wires and spaces so deep and wide that I snatch her up, *too*, almost against her fiery will. Almost.

Determined to prove that she will never need me to help her, she spits on the ground and cries out, "Whoop, whoop." Forcing eye contact, I show her the Levana sign to prove she belongs to me.

She spits again. This defiance and her proud face make me laugh on the inside. On the outside, though, I just spit back at her when she tells me, "Isla Jane, I don't want you." And then she takes my hand tightly in hers just to prove how much she means it.

But I know better, so I say, "Yes, but I do," and spit right on top of her spit.

With her perfect little piggies, she rubs both our spit into the hot, dry sand and twirls those adorable beads of hers. And I am sure, if I have ever been sure of anything worth anything, that she wants me as much as I want her not to be broken by this terrible place. As much as I want Kink, my sweet, precious doll, not to be broken even after they shatter her in pieces to convince me she isn't real, made of nothing but sticks and socks.

Raising my left eyebrow, I say it again. "But I do."

Alexis locks eyes with me and swallows hard. Finally, she smiles. Deep inside me, Kink smiles too because this time, I remember more quickly that she cannot shatter, and she will always be a real doll, always more than sticks and socks.

Cale, who I so desperately want to reach out to, just stares at me, furrowing his brow. I can still hear him knocking from last night...even now. The thundering proof he still crept down the white corridor looking for the comfort I could no longer and cannot ever allow myself to offer him from his loneliness, from his night terrors, from the mad song of the City of Dirge.

Cale...I... Cale, you must know that I still...

I glance away instead of running to comfort him. Damn. I can only hope that deep down inside he realizes this is just an act. But how will I help him do that while the red lights tie my hands behind my back this way? When what he can never know is that I waited on the other side of my icy cold door, *too.* My ivy-Inked ear stuck desperately to it, waiting to hear his pitter-patter feet yet hoping that he would not come last night more than that he would. Because if he didn't need me anymore, then there would be nothing to turn away from. If he didn't come, it would not break me to not open the door, not rock him, not sing him happy songs made of dawn instead of lies.

But he did come.

And I sat there, trying to disappear like a grinning cat, ears first so I would not hear him as he needed me like that. While I needed him back, maybe even more than he needed me, tears streaming down my ashen face as they drip, drip, dripped to the floor under the door that I couldn't open, having to deny him in order to save him.

Cale, you must know I... You must understand that I...

Cale–the one I wanted to answer more than all the others combined but could not and therefore would not and simply cannot ever again no matter how badly it rips me apart to refuse him.

That same one who looks at me right now as if I never sat on my side of the door, crying like a bairn myself for so long after he left to convince him I never even heard his knock. Clueless to my suffering, he's unaware that I am the only one left still sitting here soaking from the misery of denying him, drowning in a river of my own tears long after he goes back to sleep. His night terrors have become mine, forcing us both to toss and turn. But never do I find relief, reaching further and further across time and space to reach him. Yet my heart, so much wiser than my mind, already knows my hands can never be mine again until they are holding his.

Get over it, Isla, my logical brain demands, oblivious to the truth that I am so full of good advice that I will never follow.

So I look away from Cale as if I couldn't care less. The pain courses through me while I rip the scab off this treacherously deep wound that will never heal until it bleeds me dry. I turn from all that my *"heart you"* means only and always for him and grasp her hand instead. Alexis, that is. The same one who doesn't want me, but does so badly.

"Cale, I want you but can't tell you. Don't you know that?" I shove, shove, shove my pain down and out and cover it with mock-turtle lies. Or is it soup? I just can't be sure yet.

Spitting on the ground again, I make my Levana sign in anger–not to Alexis or Cale but as a pledge that I will make this right someday, somehow.

"Why is there so much wanting?" I want to scream in this world where we are not allowed to want, yet do anyway, of course. In fact, we starve for it–the *"heart you"* I feel for Cale probably more intensely because of the not allowing of it. It's almost as if we already figured out that we deserve better than this for no reason more than–just because. But we aren't brave enough to say so, to demand so. And this self-condemnation becomes the most painful punishment of all because in the end, we do this to ourselves. We sign the evil contract which keeps us from the very thing we need to keep going, living, and breathing. It is everything. It is *"heart you."* It is *the one thing* that can ever fill my gut of jelly, my spongy heart, my sad songs, my never-ending space inside, behind, and even beyond me.

Cale, suffering from the rejection I offer him instead of an outreaching hand, lurches away from me and lacerates me with the shame of my failure to be the one who will never desert, never forsake him. My entire body shatters as an irreparable line of destructive deceit travels like a bizarre prion infection across my Ink lines and spongifies my brain to match my heart.

Cale...I... You must know that I...

But for the sake of Cale's survival, I cover up my mad cow's mind with a big fake smile while I grip Alexis' hand back, trying desperately to pretend it is his and we are on the other side of all this nonsense back Home. Besides, today we start the Stain Heats, and fuck if that isn't going to hurt even more. *Oh, Cale...I... You must know that I will always...*

I think of our wire, the one that goes from me to him forever through all time and space. Then it travels on to Tilly and out the big tree that grows inside of that place of mine so deep and wide instead of dying in the putrid soil in this awful place where nothing grows. And even if it can grow, the fucking Mozek turn it to goo instead. Yet inside of me, there lives plenty of fertile soil made of *"heart you"* to feed our wire with. And I imagine Cale grasping that wire with his hands wrapped sweetly in mine and tugging back on it to tell me he sees it so clearly from inside my blue eyes and back out through his.

But he doesn't.

He doesn't know about wires and trees.

So I have to hope that I learn it well enough for the both of us until I can teach him the new lesson I am mastering.

And when I relieve the queen of her corrupt head, I hope he will forgive me and these ivy-Inked ears, which will never disappear, will never forsake him after all.

Why?

Because I'm not a cat. I never have been. I'm an Alice-fish, damn it.

Flapping my gills, I watch the monitors walk across the Stage, so different in their sameness. Or is it so same in their difference? Who knows and who cares about all of those idiots full of the mandatory mad belief that we 53s don't matter, that we are less than them because of the Ink stamps on our skin or the braids in our hair.

One of the monitors turns around slowly and looks directly at me behind those eyeless pits that seem to contain something new in the space I can only usually describe as nothing. And even though I know it seems impossible, I am certain the attention thrown my way by the monitor is intentional. The monitor turns its stinky head to the side, and if I didn't know better, I might say I feel compassion or curiosity or even reverence coming from behind those once empty eyes. But in another flash, the presence is gone again.

The Gridiron trumpets cry out, startling me back to reality. And I know they have begun–the season's Stain Heats. Cale is in grave danger, and these bound up hands, thorns or no, cannot protect him from all the colors planning to kill him.

The monitors line up the bairns and begin the march to the Primary Stain, which will set things up for the next week of Stains, the outcomes of these mini-Heats determining which bairns can accept which colored cards. Those same bairns who will now get to risk their lives every day doing their work for the monitors because they mean so little.

But I know better.

Obviously, I can read the words in my medical book that matches the shelves at the Foundry. And it dawns on me just now that without me, the monitors are actually nothing, do nothing, make nothing. They don't even have a clue how to do the cross and react tests, and Gods know the overseers are too drunk on skag to remember. We teach the new workers. And then the new workers teach the newer workers and on and on. And even though I can't say for sure, I bet the other departments do the same thing. All of this undeniably suggests we are more critical than I can imagine. And as usual in this mad world, things stand perfectly right–upside down and backward. Or do I mean perfectly wrong? I just can't be sure yet. Yes I can.

We, the important ones, serve them who mean nothing singing upside down and evil tunes to teach us the only lesson strong, painful and wicked enough to keep us chained without chains or imprisoned without bars. The *one thing* that benefits them is how we view ourselves: how small we believe we are, that we are worthless, we mean nothing, shall deserve nothing because we make nothing worth nothing.

When, actually, we make everything.

I stare at the monitors and discern a whole new level of cruelty in their empty eyes. An intentional mechanism they build to trap us, eternally ignorant in our suffering while simultaneously and indefinitely distracting us by our Heats. Then the real kicker, they hook us on the only reward they offer–another dose of skag death. And us idiots, we buy it all hook, line, and sinker while thinking we are working for precious Inks to maintain the good to bad ratio of our Ink affected biome, clueless to the lies of the Ink beneath the Ink.

Really, we are less than prisoners. We are slaves.

We work for manipulative monsters and then die for them. Foolishly, we hand all our power over to them, battling in made-up wars that keep us too occupied to figure it all out. All of this we do in exchange for something as worthless as Ink and numbing skag, trying to hook us, assimilate, condition us, so it can reward us with more punishment we don't want to begin with as they claim to rescue us with biome protection from ourselves. Yet they have us on our knees begging for more. Brilliant. Terrible. Wicked.

Trapped in our vicious cycle, we keep trading our lives for Ink, losing for winning, over and over and over. Our entire existence–one big lie, one massive illusion made of deceit, one Gods damn huge pot of mock-turtle soup.

I accuse the holographs in the Orb of being false, but now I realize they are so much more real than everything else here on this weird little planet ran by these weird little Mozek.

Gaige's words flood my awareness. *"They said it would take a lot to convince you to trust me."*

I mutter, "Of course it would. The only thing I know is lies. All lies."

Stomping my feet, I can't help but wonder. *Who are they, Gaige? And how do I find them?* I ask the questions twice to be sure the answer starts heading my way quickly. *Who are they, Gaige? And how do I find them?*

Alexis squeezes my hand one more time before she runs off with Craven to join the band of bairns heading full speed ahead for the Gridiron, hollering and whooping in delight. And all the sorry I ever felt for the monitors is so far gone that I will never find it again. But even if by some crazy chance I do, I promise myself I will toss it aside like I don't see it at all, walking on by with my eyes peeled to the ground, away from them and their evil ways.

A funny little song Elder Khaan sang pops into my mind. *"Three geese in a flock, one flew east, one flew west, one flew over the cuckoo's nest...O-U-T spells out...goose swoops down and plucks you out."*

"But how the hell do we get O-U-T?" I cry.

Silence.

"What goose will pluck me out?" I demand.

And not sure if I am imagining it or not, that Augur's voice returns. "Silly little goose, you will." Then it is gone again.

I look at my foot and grumble. "Ink this, Ink that. The Mozek made up the whole wicked obsession." And my hate grows bigger and deeper as the crevice within me widens so much it becomes un-crossable no matter how hard these wings flap.

The Stain trumpets sound, and the drums beat, calling for more dead bairns, more suffering, more turtle songs of sad little lies.

That voice is right. If I don't find the way O-U-T for all the piggies, who ever will? "There are no other geese here," I honk. Besides, if I get my way, there will be no more monitors singing their backward songs even if I have to take them down one by one on my way to the queen's castle. Like a deck of cards, I will watch them quiver at my feet instead of hers–the beheaded queen, victim to my gladius.

And I will laugh as I paint their roses red with their blood and goo instead of them painting mine. Me–all covered in spikes that will tear their bloody hands apart while they pull away from me and my hate, totally minus any sorry for them. Them–to whom

I will give no more missio. They–the keepers of the turtle songs and Ink–who hide their nothingness by blinding us to our greatness.

As the first Stain begins, I realize that not only are the bairns racing this year but also the monitors, all puffy-gray with their lies. Lies which are not white like nonsense but are black, too black to see through, like madness.

Determined, I smile, planning to replace those terrible lyrics with bright yellow sunshine instead. And before I even realize it, I am halfway through another verse of Elder Khaan's song. I step forward and take the hands of two more bairns I do not know and tell them they are mine.

Anja Rebecca makes the Levana sign back for me while I pull a square from my hair and hand it to her. She has gorgeous dark brown eyes that will see her worth from inside mine now. Giggling, I lift up Stiner Zadiah and kiss him on the cheek which shall not spill red from a fire gun or turn to goo.

Baylor laughs. I may be imagining it, but I think I see him make the Levana sign right before he shoots two fingers in the air to make his sign. Half-Levana, half-Salus, it's the best sign ever, except Cale's of course.

I cry out, "Hoot, hoot, whoop, whoop," while I thump twice on my chest to gather up my bairns. I do sound a bit like a goose, I think.

Baylor calls back sounding like one too. "Whoop, whoop, hoot, hoot." He claps to gather up his bairns.

The little ones loudly slap their hands on their legs to the beat of his call. It is a lovely song that I will hear and that I will join. Supposedly, he directs this celebration to honor the excitement of the Stains. But I know better. The other Levanas, clueless to the significance of this event, join in and, for the first time ever, walk not side by side but as one side with Salus to our assigned seats.

While I shine from the joy, the possibility of our alliance, he bounces and beams the light back, making me shine even brighter. Then he laughs obviously, to me at least, at the color of hope oozing from behind, no, beyond my eyes. The same eyes so full of rage that refuse to see these black lies any more. Here, where it takes the dawn rising to finally see through the blindness that no longer conceals the real City of Ink.

Unable to resist, I say one thing to him. "I am no slave."

"You never were, Isla."

I can't help but notice he says it without any other name attached to it at all.

Chapter Twenty-Three

CALE, alongside thirty other bairns, lines up to Stain in pairs. *Thirty? Why so few? So many fewer than the year before.*

I try to remember my Stains and struggle for recollection beyond a few minor details. I won first out of the hundred or so battling, and Skylar wasn't far behind me. Closing my eyes, I try to dig out more details, but they are too lost to retrieve them.

All of a sudden, my fear for Cale returns and takes over once more. The drums beat, and my heart flips, my breath short and gasping.

I squint, unable to look but dying to see as I wish I can go back to the safety of my previous blindness. But I can't. Not anymore. All tangled in our wire, I know what is happening before it happens because I see it from behind, no, beyond Cale's priceless eyes.

He flips his golden mask into position, bows, and assumes a traditional stance for battle. His opponent returns the gesture.

The bell rings. The trumpets cry out, and drums deafen the crowd.

I count. One. *This little piggy.*

Before I get to two, the curved blade of Cale's transformed sica finds the soft spot of an Enlil bairn's neck. Round one–over for the other piggy before it even begins. The olive leaf crowns Cale the verus champion.

The monitors rush out to acknowledge him, punching data into their little white machines. This may have been the fastest first bairn battle ever.

I have taught him well, too well, probably.

My heart jumps out of my chest and soaks up all the pain on the floor because I realize that the only thing my brilliant protégé wins today is loss. I have done this. I know I have. I hang my head and click my tongue. *I wish this little piggy stayed Home.*

Baylor grabs my hand swiftly but briefly. He crumples his brow in sympathy. No, not sympathy, empathy. His two bairns win as well, also in record time. We simultaneously plaster fake grins on our mugs any intelligent observer can see through.

Not only do the verus bairns earn new Inks and therefore exposure to skag addiction, but they also win the first three positions for tomorrow's leg of the Stains. Gods knows they will surely win tomorrow, too.

"Screw that, too," I mutter.

Baylor reaches for me, and for once, I can tell he needs me to save him like he saves me on the Ink stage. I squeeze his trembling hand. He squeezes back for dear life and marks out the seconds. He counts, "One, two, three, four..." Just before he gets to ten, he lets go.

"So I'm not the only one who can count," I offer, trying to lighten things.

"Oh, Isla Jane." He sighs. "How will we do it?"

Back to Jane, huh?

He looks nervously right-to-left and then behind us to make sure our conversation goes unrecorded, unnoticed.

"I don't know, Baylor John, but we will find a way," I quietly reply, thinking of the various things we might do to save Cale and Baylor's two bairns.

"But they turn so fast. There are so few left. They take them all now before... And sometimes it only takes one Ink." He buries his head in his hands. The same hands that want to reach for mine again.

"There are so few now. And the ones that belong to outside kiths? How do we reach them all before they do?"

His voice quivers through repressed moans, and his use of pronouns confuses me. *Them all? Before they do?*

What? Them all? What? My cheeks flash, and my mouth dries.

My heart slaps me. *Yes, all them piggies.*

Cale has always been my main concern, saving him my only realistic goal. Sure the theoretical idea of helping all the bairns with the medical book lady is in here somewhere, but it's a pipedream, really. Baylor actually wants to save them all. Who is this guy? What motivates him?

He grabs my hand again, and his twitches move from him and back out through me. And once more, an emotion wells up when he touches me that is too big for a simple description like fear or anger. The feeling, big and warm, smells sharp yet sweet. Another follows this grand emotion which is also too big for a simple word, but the closest ones I have are *regret* and *shame*.

Regret what? What have I done? Or is it not done? I can't be sure yet.

"Isla, I..." he stammers, searching for a word that he doesn't have, either. Probably because it doesn't exist here in the City of Forgotten Words. But it does somewhere else deep inside me, and I almost have it. Almost.

I know one phrase so integral to the incomplete thought that keeps coming back to me. *I... Baylor, you must know that I... I still...*

Cale gave me one to borrow for now; I will pay it forward to Baylor. So I finish the sentence for him. "I *heart you*, too."

He flounders, speechless for what seems like an hour but must only be five minutes because the other Stains just finish.

"Exactly," he offers, and a single tear forms, which I quickly wipe away.

I blow air sharply out my mouth and replace the fake smile with a real one.

"Do you remember, Isla Jane? Do you remember it all? Do you see me in your dreams as I see you in mine? Do you see him? See her? Do you remember what happened when we…?"

My smile disappears. What the hell is he saying to me?

Stunned, I have no response adequate for what he asks of me. So instead of even trying, I say, "No."

The same feeling too big for a word as inadequate as "regret" rises up and paints my face. I might clench my jaw, but the paint is too slippery, and my chin slips back on my sternum. Usually, I just stamp out feelings like this with anger, but something tells me it won't work with Baylor anymore. My defenses, too far down, are permanently breached.

What do I regret so badly? What happened that I don't remember?

"Isla Jane, no matter what occurs or how this game ends, you must know one thing. There is nothing, nothing you can ever do that will make me *'heart you'* less. And there is nothing, nothing that can ever make me *'heart you'* more than I already do, either."

How this game ends? What does he mean? What does he know that I don't? *"Baylor's eyes are open,"* I remember Gaige say.

This must be so much bigger than I realize. What are they keeping from me? Has this Alice mission ever really been my decision to begin with? Who is this Baylor, and what does he expect from me? Why does he think I will agree to it? What does he know about me that I do not?

And who is *she*? *Alexis*? Who is *he*? *Cale*? *Baylor's bairn*? *Who*?

As everyone else at the Stains claps in the verus' honor, I quiver. Terrified of all the layers of answers within the layers of questions I seem bent on asking, I switch views, trying to observe the deeper meanings of the Stains–the Stains beneath and behind the Stains–from inside Cale's eyes. Yet I only end up wishing he could see from inside mine instead. And like a reflection in the mirror, I see myself in him on the day I won my first Stain and every Heat since.

It's almost like our bodies are made for working the thraex and playing warrior. Me, Cale, Baylor, and even his bairns too, I guess. I can't help but wonder if they are like Cale and me, able to manipulate the machine and modify the holograph with nothing more than an intention. Yet even more importantly, why?

Does Baylor have the answer, understand how we do it, or grasp the importance of why it matters so much? Is it some advantage related to our biomes? Something else entirely? Does he teach his bairns like I do, knowingly on one level yet clueless on another?

Shaking the jumbling thoughts from my head, I try to focus. So I get up and walk away, burying all my thoughts in Cale even if my shallowness will embarrass me again later. *So Cale must have a chance,* I argue with myself, *to make it out alive and awake and aware like me.*

Another thought slips in before I can squash it. *Like Baylor?*

Or not like Jaxston?

The year after I crowned verus of the final Stain Heat, Jaxston won the olive head-piece that led him straight down a pipe filled with skag to his own personal gray pool of liquid knives, still slicing and cutting him. He lost for supposedly winning, but surely he might have actually won more in his defeat. *Those freaking creeps.*

Yet all Jaxston, like so many of the others, wants is more and more of the very thing that eats him from the inside. Soon, if not already, I suspect he will be only skag residue with no Jaxston left inside at all–hooked, conditioned, assimilated, emptied like his barren neck skulls, convinced the queen remains his only friend instead of his evil enemy.

But why do I care? He's not my problem. Or is he? I just can't be sure yet.

So why do I feel so sorry for him even if he is an evil bastard conditioned for eternal misery?

Because that's how the Mozek want me to be, I realize. That's why and what makes Jaxston my problem. Oh the irony. I will have to hold all the wires together to hold any of the wires together. Or will they hold me? *All the little piggies go Home or none of them do.*

Damn it, and now Cale, too, despite all the *toos* I want for him instead. And if the monitors succeed, how will I teach him about wires and *toos*, that white is white and black is not and cannot be no matter how many layers of paint on top of paint on top of paint they coat it with?

I close my mouth because the paint tastes as terrible as the Mozek smell.

Crack. Like an earthquake, the paint splits my Alice ears until they bleed, victim of the fire gun. To be honest, though, at least there is mercy in the speed of the gun's murdering ways that never once pretend to be anyone's friend. So it may be evil, that shooting contraption of violence, but at least it is no liar, like a Heat, like Ink, like a monitor, like the fucking bacteria on my skin, like the song they teach us and make us sing to others so we will believe it too.

I flash back to Elder Khaan's statement about believing anything if we hear it enough times despite all evidence to the contrary. *Mind warping madmen.*

Clapping, I kick my feet and slam my chest, not twice like a Levana but three times like Kinley. *"Thank you for the brain wash, you lying assholes."*

She's right; sarcasm does have immense value.

And now that I'm clapping along like the other 53s, I take notice of what exactly the monitors are doing. They are taking notes, typing into their little white machines that are flashing red lights. They nod from one to the next, convinced they speak truth instead of only madness.

Maybe they heard the lies seventy-one times as well?

One of the Ink dealers steps forward to take Cale and Baylor's two bairns, leading them away for their award–the Ink, the skag, the sad song of lies. *Reprogramming. Conditioning. Contamination. Brainwashing.*

But the one thing I can't help but notice is that this ID who takes Cale so swiftly by his sweet, un-ruined hands, glances quickly over to Gaige, my ID, with one of those caterpillar smoke glances I dissect apart so easily with these curious eyes of mine. Is this good? Or bad? Or somewhere in the middle? This secret between them that should not be spoken out loud because a queen hovers over them, watching their every move.

And I'll be a fool if he isn't expecting me to be wondering this very thing because Gaige then shares the secret look back for me to see, saying nothing and everything all at the same time.

He must know. Oh my Gods, he must...

He must know what I am thinking, fearing, hoping for against all odds. Like the whole tribe of caterpillars is in on the secret now, he glances at Baylor next, exchanging nods while they both appear to stare in opposite directions. *Impossible.*

What happened? What do I not remember? What have I already done?

Unable to stop myself, I mutter, "Stop it, Isla. Stop it right now."

This time, thankfully, I take my own advice. So to keep me from asking any more questions, I allow my fascination with Gaige to distract me instead.

For the first time ever, I let my eyes follow the wonderful curve of Gaige's handsome body past his violet eyes, down his pencil beard-covered dimple, and across the curve of his perfect neck. My eyes wrap around his broad and sturdy shoulders, into and even through his chest. Delightful warmth courses through me and gathers between my legs. The glow expands–opening, pulsating, welcoming inside a wanting of undeniable urgency. This urge feels like *"heart you"* only hotter, more intense, and coats me with a hunger that I already know squares can never fill. He is so physically flawless that I wonder how he could possibly be real. Perhaps the Gods themselves designed him just for me to stare at.

My pulse quickens, and my eyes dilate like a skag junkie. So I stop my ardor for the sensation right there, sure of the question that is the most dangerous of them all for me. What does Gaige want from me? And what the hell do I want from him in return?

Honestly, I do not even try to see into that space of his so big and wide for an answer because it is too large to see, making it easy to miss in its entirety. I know it is. It can only be experienced in the moment, coursing through every fiber of my being. And why would I bother trying to see something that I already understand as perfectly as my name or the color of my eyes?

Then I glance across the stamps on his muscular flanks, down his solid thighs, and behind his firm and intense calves. My stare drips, pausing slightly at his groin, and spills onto his feet as the heat in my pelvis intensifies and moisture slicks the inside of me.

Gaige I... You must know that I...

Unable to complete the thought, I follow the dripping liquid from me and allow it to ooze onto his feet–his feet which are covered in supple leather boots. Oh my Gods, the exact same as mine. His almost completely cover over a tattoo. Almost. It is also the same as mine.

The same as mine. The same as mine. The same as mine.

An Ink with one ray of sunshine cradled by the top fine edge of the lovely leather that spreads onto the sole of his boot that hides a rising sun, the same as mine. The glorious ball of fire I can't recall picking which peeks and sneaks and winks and hopes for a view from a secret within a secret in the City of Mystery.

Pivotal, my internal goddess pumps, knowing perfectly well that my synapse has decided which way to go. I cannot turn back. The rising sun shall guide me now, straight out of this dark rabbit hole and back out the other side of not-wonderland. Chills everywhere.

And of course, I have the answer to another question of mine.

Gaige's *they* must also be my *they*, Baylor's *they*, Skylar's *they.* The same *they* who must live somewhere else. A pull so powerful, so encompassing, returns: *Home.* Home–where we will take Cale and all the other piggies, where we will drink clear boxes and gulp down clear choices about who the hell we are.

I am so sure of my revelation that I do not even bother to look at Baylor's right foot to confirm my suspicion. The rising sun, he will have one, *too*, of course.

Oh my Gods, how have I doubted it for so long?

The song, lessons, words, numbers, wires, Elder Khaan's words of wisdom. They are all a message, a preparation, an answer to a question I am finally ready to ask.

What exactly is the rising sun? *No, that's the wrong question. Not what, but...?*

Before I get the chance to ask the question properly, a monitor, fire gun strapped to its side, brings over a Libellus demanding my attendance as the object of amusement and distraction in another Heat, immediately. Obviously I go because dying sounds pretty crappy to me right now when I'm on the brink of something wonderful. Or is something wonderful on the brink of me? I just can't be sure yet.

Chapter Twenty-Four

SKYLAR IS NOT PLEASED, not at all. To be honest, I can't tell whom she's more furious with–me for putting myself in this position or the Mozek for doing something about it.

We do not have much time. So as the trumpets play, she hurriedly prepares my body. Shaking her head over and over, she says, "This is no ordinary Heat. The troop was a warm-up. You know that, right?"

I smile sardonically and widen my eyes. "Really? You think so?"

She rolls hers. "Don't you think they want you dead now? Dead for showing them up, dead for the rare chance that you might actually have the power to bring the full essence of the prime Jane forth to dominate them?"

Essence of the prime Jane? What?

I raise my eyebrow, and she looks away. She smacks her lips shut and turns back around. Like with Gaige, her eyes fill with sympathy. She knows something about me that I do not, doesn't she? Or maybe I know something she doesn't know? I just can't be sure yet. But what? A fact I am still learning, probably.

She speaks again slowly. Carefully choosing her words, probably.

But before anything meaningful escapes her scholarly little mouth, a monitor arrives and drags me away. "Come with me or the Chancellors will deactivate your biome codes and necrotize you."

Maybe one day, Skylar will finish the lecture. Who knows? I will have to worry about that later. Right now, I have bigger problems, other nuggets to fry before the twelve robed ones fry mine.

The gray goon locks me in the thraex portal. For a moment, a flash replaces the emptiness of its eyes and then is gone again. The spinning of the device commences. I disengage as usual. Then I look back at my prior self–so lifeless and crumpled, still wondering why the Libellus is blank. Its declaration makes no sense at all. Until I step out of my thraex, that is.

Blankness.

Nothingness.

Barren wasteland, like an eternal frozen tundra. *Like a dimension inside the Liebhorr would look.*

For the first time, I am completely alone in the center of the Orb. I look up expecting to see the crowd, but they are gone. Am I lost inside the Gridiron? Or is the Gridiron lost inside me? I just can't be sure yet.

The transformation amazes me. It is almost too good to be true. Almost.

A gray, cloudy barren horizon replaces the stands. Nothing exists besides a frozen wasteland in every direction–absolute winter, packed ice, pure, vast absence of anything. I should shiver, but in this nowhere, I feel nothing.

In the Orb, I feel everything–the wind, the rain. If this is the Orb, shouldn't I feel the cold under my feet? What exactly is the molecular makeup of the odd surface under my piggies?

I bang my foot to test the material for weakness, for information.

Nothing but color-less, temperature-less, meaning-less ice.

Can the other 53s see me? Is anyone watching? Am I alone? Is this an illusion? Or is the City of Blink and I'm Gone the illusion, and this freezer is my only true reality? Honestly, I cannot say.

No grate or box appears.

No weapons exist for me to choose amongst.

Nothing follows more nothing.

I listen for the subtle sound of the confounders. Silence. I stand still for probably ten minutes before I start walking, open and utterly exposed, in this void of a landscape. This must be an illusion, a holograph. Surely I am still strapped inside a machine inside a machine hidden in a tunnel beneath the massive Gridiron like always. This nothingness cannot possibly be new.

Even as I tell myself this, I already know better. I have never been here before. Probably no one has ever been here before in this City of Nowhere.

Does my fear shoot across the three-dimensional screen and amuse the masses? If so, I am not proud of my projections. Actually, I am embarrassed by my dwindling composure.

Do the twelve robed men stand? Are the Mozek even real? Maybe the Chancellors are nothing more than a computer program I designed hundreds of years ago and only this place will ever be real? *Impossible.*

I shall have to slap myself if I keep this bullshit up.

Why do I not swear the oath? And the hand plate, where is it? Where am I? Where is this nowhere? Will the twelve decide thumbs up or thumbs down without giving me a chance to prove my valor?

My hand gets ready because my anxiety is getting old.

The crowd must be getting bored. That cannot be good. If there even is a crowd.

Ah! Chills everywhere. Still perfectly warm inside, my scary new reality condenses and turns my thoughts to zigzags of icy panic. My breath shallows and quickens. I have never been alone before. What if no one lets me out of nowhere? Will I die in the thraex? Have they effectively buried me alive in my body paralyzed by the same cruel machine that overtakes my mind and incapacitates me to do anything to escape this life?

My face preps for the sting of my slap to stop my nervous breakdown.

I am fucking trapped in a sarcophagus in my own frozen Liebhorr of a brain. And whatever those clumps of specimens hanging from the ceiling in that freezing room were, if they were good, they have left my shell of a body permanently now. All I have left is fear. Pain. Terror.

Trembling, I fight the urge to scream.

Finally my courage pulls through. *Smack!*

"About time, you stupid bitch," my brain tells my spongy heart because I know full well that even though I'm dying inside, I don't want to give the Chancellors the pleasure of hearing me voice my impending insanity.

"Okay, over it," my heart replies. Reaching up, I press two fingers into my steel jaw to stop my teeth from chattering. I roll my shoulders and pop my neck.

"Well thank Gods," my logic replies, and I plaster a classic veneer of indifference on my face, a look I have mastered so well it no longer scares me because, let's face it– by this point, nothing should scare me.

No expression to match the nowhere. Perfect. Almost, anyway.

I consider laughing now but decide it's best to just keep my face flat. Why betray that I feel totally vulnerable to exposure, to an attacker, to the loss of my delightful mind floundering with the possibilities of *what if?*

I shall not scream. I will be brave or at least look it. Those thieves shall not steal my last shred of dignity. Something reassuring returns to my inner awareness: self-respect.

Walking onward, I stomp my feet every ten meters or so for effect.

The voice returns, shaky at first then louder. "You are so lovely."

"Screw you, Augur," I say since I am pretty sure the voice is not real at all.

"So lovely," it says again.

Sticking my tongue out between my fingers held in the shape of a V feels like it will clearly sum up this feeling I have for my circumstances, so I make the gesture twice. My face cracks slightly.

The last stomp sounds like a drumbeat, and I decide that's something.

Feeling even stronger, I reach my invigorated hands up in the air and shout at the top of my lungs. "I will not fear you!" I bet that will get someone's attention. I almost smile with anticipation. Almost.

But nope. Still nothing.

So I try again. "Screw you, Chancellors!"

Silence.

Maybe I am really alone? Have they mistakenly transported me into the wrong circuit, the wrong program? Is this an error? Intentional? Does a chief robot eternally trap me, locking my mind between thraex synapses, forever poisoned with inaccurate code to match my flawed bacterial biome?

Without a reference to judge it by and no response from my environment, time loses all meaning. My racing thoughts compound the discomfort. My hair, pinned up in a tight bun, offers no relief.

To spare myself some agony, I decide to try some distraction to pass the time. After all, if I'm lost in my own mind for all eternity, I might as well have some fun with it. I add a few claps to the stomps, hoping to add some kind of song to this nowhere. My face cracks further.

Behaving this way goes over much better than the alternative, and I let my long gray-blond hair fall down my back. I throw the pins on the ground and kick them to and fro. Playing both sides of this pin-football game as Kink, the sock-doll, swaying my locks back and forth, I will be damned if I am not gorgeous.

Flowing hair, slick bronze skin–shame I cannot see both sides of my reflection. I am lovely twice; I am certain. Guess the Augur is right. *Lovely, even more lovely.*

Maybe this program is better than a regular Heat, I think.

Then the ice shifts. Or maybe I shift? I just can't be sure yet.

Stomping my supple boots against the cold uncaring ice, I do another series of claps and listen again. I feel dizzy for a moment, and then this time, I hear the subtle humming. *This is an illusion. I am in the Orb. Thank Gods I'm no longer stuck in nowhere doing nothing.*

Something slithers swiftly under the buckling ground, the same ground cracking and shifting underneath my feet. *Shit.*

"Alone with myself wasn't so bad," I mutter.

I should learn to keep my mouth shut. Too late now.

The crevices widen. Water replaces the ice.

Still no weapons.

No armor.

No shield.

No gate.

Just ice, water, and something slimy skirting the water.

I decide to run; running usually helps. Not this time.

In seconds, I am under the ice. And unlike up above, now it is freezing cold. The intensity of the gelid water takes my breath away. Swimming furiously fast, I try to keep my piggies as warm as possible and to not think about the other thing in the liquid with me–the sea creature from Loch-nowhere.

Then I see them. Not one but three alphas swimming toward me, all armed with breathing gear, tridents, swords, and a massive red and black net.

"Assholes, I am no fish!" I want to scream. Instead, I hold my breath. *Three alphas? Seriously?* Why do these creeps always make me fight men? Right now, the sixteen-year-old peacock twins sound nice. Where are those blimey tits? Safe and sound in the distant stands, laughing at me while they play the bagpipes, I suspect.

I dive under the alphas. If I can run fast, I can swim fast, too. My real problem is that I have to keep coming up for air while they do not.

It doesn't take long for the inevitable to occur. The three—one Volta, one Irmin, and one Pellonia—gang up on me like this is a game of shinty the poor little girl. Deciding to use the one advantage they have, other than being bigger, stronger, and more numerous than me, they drag me underneath the water to drown me.

With my last gasp, Cale's face takes over my mind. Surely he is watching this, witnessing me suffer. I make a brave face, almost smiling, trying to give him hope for me. If he still cares about me, that is. Then I go perfectly still, trying to save my air as long as possible while I drum up an escape.

Hello? Plan B? Hello?

The Pellonia places his gladius to my neck while the other two tangle my lower half in the net. The Volta pierces my right hand with the center spike of the trident, essentially pinning me to the spongy surface that lines the bottom of the icy bin.

We must be twenty, thirty meters down in this pool thousands of meters wide. Even if I get free, I will not have enough air to make it back up. The Volta, obviously the one leading this bully session, generously puts his mouthpiece over my nose. Apparently, I have not suffered enough for his tastes. He retrieves an extra oxygen device, snapping it over my face now that I am helplessly and safely entangled in their web. Something tells me kindness is not this bugger's primary motivation. *Fucker.*

He plans to kill me slowly.

Painfully.

One little itty bit at a time...while the oxygen keeps me conscious.

He reaches down and whips out a short blade with three smaller spikes, shaped much like a fishhook, I imagine. Goes in nicely, comes out really badly. *Very effective for killing fish.*

I shudder, and my stomach flips.

For a moment, I wonder why that Volta hates me so much. I have never met him, never done him wrong personally.

But then I realize he despises me because he's supposed to—that simple, that true. The seventy plus doses of dope and turtle soup makes him do it. His previous Elder abhors me and my Elder before me because they always have. And because his kith detests the image of Levana stamp, in exchange, I get the honor of hating his clan back. Voilà, without having to actually do anything, the Mozek spread that bacterial infection of hate from one of us to the next for no reason more than—just because. And clueless, we do it to us for them.

What madness. What insanity. Judging me by my sign is as absurd as judging me by the length of my hair, the color of my eyes, the tone of my skin. His fury spawns from nothing but brainwashing madness because the jackass buys the deception hook, line, and sinker and plans to freaking kill me with it.

I laugh again, the sound garbled by the mask, since I'm about to eat the hook, not him. Oh, the irony.

Shocker. He is not amused.

The madder he gets, the more the mutant strain of hatred multiples inside him. Hoping to snare me in its evil plan, too, the contagious bacteria try to convince me to hate him back, but I refuse. Why? Because I know how this clever disease spreads–via permission from one host to the next. Sympathy almost wells up inside me for how the Mozek trick him. Almost.

But with hook-knives in my face, it turns out I'm not quite as big an Alice as I usually am. I laugh again. Well sort of, anyway.

The Pellonia, a few meters to the right of me, glances away, avoiding my eyes. This is not his plan. He doesn't want to do this. He knows better than to think that turtle lies will satisfy the thousand holes inside his heart. If I have the luxury of more life with more time, perhaps I will ponder this later. Could this Pellonia be like us, Baylor and me, just wanting a way down and out of all this madness?

Elder Khaan's song about geese returns to give me courage.

Starting with my jawline, the Volta makes a shallow cut with the sharp point of his miniature sword. My eyes lock with his and never stray.

Tilly laughs from inside my space so deep and wide, calling me Home. "Not out, Isla. Go in, in with me. In is always better than out," she says. She will keep me strong.

I honk once more, the sound mostly mumbled by the air mask.

My eyes might see the red stream of my blood polluting the water around me, but my heart does not. That glorious sponge soaks up antifreeze-green meadows and purple too gorgeous to name. So distracted by the beautiful imagery, my projected body feels absolutely no pain while he cuts his design–a Volta stamp with two parallel arms of stacked circles–across my face, which like paper cuts, may hurt, may mutilate, but will not kill me.

He's just warming up.

His eyes, red with hate, smile more than his lips.

My face remains a mask. He cuts again, and I remain perfectly still.

Clearly not pleased by my lack of response, he takes my air away to punish me.

Suffocating inside, the pressure in my chest crushes me. But even though my lungs thrash about from my terrible desire to find one last breath, my body remains motionless. Tilly keeps me still.

Just before I pass out, he replaces my air. To be honest, whether this is good or bad, I cannot say. I am almost gone anyway, locked in a Loch for the damned.

Next, the creep paints my arms with razor-blade strokes of hatred.

A fresh stream of crimson pearls coming from my right arm intermixes with the frosty water. For a moment, I cannot help but surrender to the awe of the glorious color. The rouge, so powerful, so strong, so full of life and vitality, swirls all around me in miniature designs, dancing death's masterful finale. Graciously, despite his total lack of grace, the Volta butcher takes the internal beauty of my physical body and displays it magnificently for me to see. Beautiful. I am mesmerized by how not dead this red seems.

Sounds I cannot decipher fill my ears. A voice echoes around me. "Trust me. If you survive, I can show you how to fold into Interval. Do not die, Jane. Do not die."

Is it the made-up voice? Are the Gods finally calling me home? Will the great king of all Levana appear to greet me, or Elder Khaan, or will I just be gone? Who can say?

By this stage, I am sure Baylor, Gaige, and Cale watch every moment, every cut. So I try best as I can to hold my face flat. For a second, I get lost wondering what Skylar must be thinking. *I will probably miss her, that chick.*

Suddenly, the Volta jerks back, his body ripping apart in numerous gnarled pieces while a scaly sea monster swims back to retrieve the floating fragments of his innards left behind.

My blood, the scent of my blood, has brought this Ness-of-a-mess on. Turns out my tiny cuts kill after all. They kill the Volta who enjoyed torturing me so much. Turnabout is fair play, I think.

The irony is quite profound–my red equals his dead.

Dark green oil, most likely poisonous, oozes off the monster's gargantuan body. Its eyes, replaced by red pits, scan for another victim. Snorting debris out of a horned snout, the creature bares a million teeth that guard its black forked tongue. Countless legs wiggle underneath its writhing body in delightful anticipation of a morsel of this fish named Isla.

Oh my Gods, I think that piece of shit actually thinks I am a fish.

I blink twice and gather my bloody wits.

It lurches.

I move.

It swivels.

I turn.

It lurches again, this time making contact with my face.

My breathing apparatus shatters, but my net breaks loose, so other than the spike nailing my hand, I am finally free.

I am without viable oxygen but almost free. Almost. Free like the Volta's guts that are just floating in little pieces all around. The water stays a dark crimson and brown, not gorgeous but horrifying, from the spillage of his innards. I cannot see, literally blinded by the shit that blinded him for his entire life.

In all the fecal confusion, the sympathetic Pellonia frees my hand and swims away unscathed.

Yet still I have no air. Plenty of crap but no O2. *Impossible.*

My hypoxic body spasms. I am drowning. Already almost dead, in fact.

Only the Irmin, cowering like a bairn behind a boulder, and I remain on this seafarer's menu. I have no air but plenty of steel. The Irmin has no weapons but plenty of air.

Either we, my cowardly enemy and I, help each other or we both die. Me, the second square for this creature. Him, the third course of scrumptious 53.

I see this blinding awareness strike us both simultaneously.

As the serpent turns back around, I raise the trident.

That viper bitch licks her lips with her forked tongue, preparing to consume me. I return the gesture since I like my slimy tongue better than hers.

Marching quickly through my previous success in such life and death matters, I consider the following: I do not have time to go into full thraex mode to change her plan for a murderous meal. My little mutant mind trick from the matted wolf creature in my last Heat will certainly not work out so well if I am already half-digested, so…

Here I am starving for plan B–like usual.

The Irmin coward remains nowhere to be found. Shocker.

The monster, all ten meters of her nastiness, thrashes about in excitement, ready for her next sweet square–me. I swallow hard and prepare to lose my tongue.

I am totally out of air now, already effectively dead, to be honest.

My thoughts come through cloudy from the lack of oxygen. For a moment, I forget where I am, wondering why this water appears so murky. Then I remember–the freaking bloodbath and all the Volta's bullshit.

Another spasm shoots through me.

The Irmin, his choice clear by this juncture, prefers we both die to a partnership with me, his rival. What an idiot, so willing to chop his nose to spite his ugly face. If I can find the time, I'll surely help him accomplish such a clever feat because my zigzagging half-dead neurons conclude that maybe this imbecile deserves a senseless death to match his senseless life. In fairness to all that is good and fair, I can only hope he suffers immensely from the pointy teeth of the serpent's mouth while she nibbles slowly on him, making it as prolonged and painful as possible.

If not about to die, I might feel guilty for my vengeful thoughts. Might…but probably not. After all, I am half-altered, my brain sizzling behind my newly found eyelids.

Time's up, Isla.

I remember Skylar say, *"This is no regular Heat."* She's right; this one is a real drowner.

Final joke offered up, I giggle and prepare to be lunch.

Deciding I would rather be gone before the first crunch, I welcome a large wave of water into my lungs.

For a moment, I suffocate again. Visions flash before my eyes like a brilliant electric storm from the old days back Home. Suddenly, I remember. I remember the glorious scent of rain in the air. My first memory. *Thank you, Gods.*

But, Gods, this whole scene is just an illusion, a holograph. How can water drown me if I don't believe in it?

It's a lovely thought really–detached amusement via genuine introspection instead of blubbering fear. I think I *"heart"* her, that brilliant piece of work inside my mind always screaming about what is and isn't so pivotal.

"Pivotal," I mouth in her honor.

I know the water isn't real. It's just an illusion, so how can it hurt me if I don't let it? I decide not to. *Impossible.*

Completely immersed in liquid, inside and out, I feel another seizure coming and clench my fists. For the sake of the audience, who must be on the edge of their seats about to watch me convulse like a fish out of water, I try to be as still as possible. With all the strength I have left, I say slowly and clearly, "None of this is real, not even you. I am an arcade game the Chancellors play to distract and amuse you."

I smile, closing my eyes and allow my final lucid convulsion to take hold, waiting for Tilly to claim me as the scaly horror defeats and joyfully eats me like sizzled steak.

Honestly, I am glad for it. This game tastes like charred flesh.

For a moment, I come to freezing and trembling in a room empty and ill definable like the Folding.

Then I am gone again. Perhaps I am finally dead.

Section III: The Rising Sun

In a sea of blinding darkness,
You are my shining light.
Can't you see?
Won't you be?
The dawn that overcomes,
So big and bright.

Chapter Twenty-Five

NEXT THING I KNOW, I wake up lying on my couch alone and shivering, my long gray-blond hair wet and sticking to my shoulders. The memory of the smell of rain returns and instantly settles me. *Home.*

Maybe I am still Home, and all of this has been one long, terrible nightmare folded within a single string of time inside some hidden dimension that is so small I hardly ever notice it. Maybe the dimensions do not go one, two, three, four and on to ten. Maybe they go in a different direction, from five to negative five. Maybe less really is more. This time anyway. Whatever time is.

Silly me, I am still five or six years old, just resting from playing too hard in the rain, and the past fifteen years have been nothing more than a long, evil dream condensed in the past hour or so. Perhaps time can fold as easily as space in another dimension if one knows how. *Impossible.*

But then the memory of my battle returns and pulls me away from such a lovely, if utterly impossible, thought, and I shiver again. My chest deflates, and my mouth fills with a sour taste.

Did Cale suffer watching my seizure? Where is Skylar now? Will I ever see that chewed up Volta again? And what about the Irmin? What has happened to him? And the Pellonia, does he still breathe? Maybe I am actually dead. If so, is this really my couch, or is it merely a projection of my couch in some waiting station swirling and flitting between strings between molecules and anti-molecules, between past and present, between impossible and possible?

Twirling a wet strand of my hair, I tell myself that surely one loses memories and wet hair once dead.

I hold on to both my hair and this string of spacetime and try to focus my thoughts. Paying more attention, I hear something rustle in the simulator room.

Maybe I am both not dead and not alone? The Grim Reaper comes to finally claim me on my own couch recreated in a video game to amuse assholes.

Ugh. Or maybe I am guarded by a band of eyeless goons who plan to publicly necrotize me for the crime of winning the battles they make me fight? *Freaking idiots.* If I could, I would choke them with this string of spacetime.

But since I have made the whole idea up, I try to go back into my itty-bitty fold and disappear. But that doesn't work either, so I decide I better figure out what the hell is going on in this place.

Testing my not dead and not alone theory, I make a few observations. My chest rises up and down, so I really must be alive. My ears register more bizarre sounds. More proof. I pinch my skin, and it hurts. *Crap, definitely not dead.*

I see Gaige come around the corner. Okay, he's better than a band of goons. Now I am getting somewhere worth going. Alive and with him and that delightful dimple. But how long has he been here? Shit, how long have I been here?

He sits down and touches me softly, pulling me back to awareness by tenderly tracing the outline of my intact, un-ruined face. Then he stands to leave after pointing to the three beads on my table.

"*I am verus thrice,*" I think but do not bother say to him.

I should ask him how I survived the Loch of Terror, but I am just too tired to move my lovely tongue that much.

Right before I lose consciousness again, another observation burrows through my wasted brain: wet hair and a memory from Home, two firsts.

I awaken, who knows how many days or hours or months or dimensions later, and go back to the Ink stage like nothing ever happened. When I get there, no one cuffs me or makes me the next victim of the goo and gun club. And much like always, no one explains anything.

I take my cards and pass them out to the sibs who need Ink the most. Skylar winks and takes the only red in the stack before I get the chance to take it myself, so I go back to my room to rest and think and rest some more.

How have they not murdered me like Kalil? There must be another reason. Some motivating factor more valuable than my death, perhaps? Or is it less expensive? I just can't be sure yet with these jerks.

My most reasonable theory is that they must want me terrified by keeping me in the dark. So I decide not to oblige them. Besides, what would they do to me that they have not already done? Throw me in a freezing pit with a scaly monster, perhaps? The thought makes me laugh for what seems like the first time in hours, maybe even days or weeks.

Feeling much stronger after practice, I push the others out of the simulators so I can do what must be done for me, for them, for Cale.

I pack my few belongings in a cloth bag, knowing the notice will come soon enough that it is time to move. And I will have no time to prepare, so I prepare now in advance.

"How will I hide my medical book and photo, Elder Khaan?" I ask as if he can hear or see me.

At first, I scoff at my own stupidity, but then I remember he can see me from inside that space so deep and wide and back out of my eyes. So I go take a look in the mirror so he can see me better, and I smile, full of sunshine.

The strength in my reflection surprises me, and I wonder what the others, who look through my eyes, see in me.

Do I look the same as the other Janes? Or different in some way? A way that only I can appear, perhaps. Do the others smile like I do with just a slight wink of my right eye? Does the sharp line of my nose please them? And what about the high forehead hiding all my swirling thoughts? Or the arch of my eyebrows, so thin and fine? Or the length of my muscular neck? Or maybe the intense line of my collarbone that mimics the clear lines forming inside of me?

"Clear lines on which to base my clear songs so I can see clearly how to sing the best lyrics for the others like you did for me, Elder Khaan," I say to both my reflection and my mentor looking back out through my eyes.

Gratitude floods me on so many levels that I stumble backward trying to sort through all the complex layers of the feeling resulting from drawing boundaries within, so simple yet so gallant and grand a process.

Why have I not seen them before?

Blubbering, I thank Elder Khaan for the letters and the numbers he has given me but mostly his song about the dawn–such a beautiful melody that plants a seed of my mission inside of me so many years ago, a lovely combination of notes about a rising sun, which he feeds with his encouragement like squares and boxes of warm sunshine. Concepts he fosters in me about how much I shall matter to someone worth mattering to other than a doll named Kink. And how much they shall matter to me in return.

This seed of his grows deep within my fertile space with strong roots, branching out, growing exponentially. So even though I cannot remember touching a tree, I do own one: a tree, big and strong with beautiful flowers colored brightly with hope and intention, a tree centered in goodness, waiting for a chance of a chance of a chance to grow taller and even more beautiful.

All the nights of extra work make so much sense to me now. Elder Khaan understood the only way to save me was to offer me the tools to save myself: learning to read, to count, to ask questions, and on occasion even more importantly…to not ask them. These things and seedlings built from self-value, so much more motivating than necrotizing bacteria and pools of liquid knives, acted as the only things mighty enough to remove my invisible shackles from my imaginary turtle prison. The one I never knew existed until I first could see my value as I, not the Mozek, assigned it.

The irony rattles me and fills me with hope that no one can steal. Only I can show myself how precious I am. I take it one step further–the only thing more powerful than fear is hope. Wow.

A beetle bug crawls across my foot. Is it a sign? Am I right on the mark?

He tickles my rising sun to tell me so even though the blind, little bug can't see it. Funny how he shows me something that he's unable to see on his own.

I take my womb cloth off now and inspect my bare skin, finally understanding why it is so beautiful to me. The clear skin–minus all the Inks the Mozek use against me to chain me, to imprison me, to shackle and condition me– is so fine and lovely because it covers the only free parts left of me.

The idea hits me like a brick. The Inks brand me their slave.

This smooth, white skin screams freedom to me: freedom from black lyrics and freedom to see who I really am–an Alice-fish, never once a disappearing cat, and certainly not an animal to brand.

I stare at my 53 stamp, determined to decode it. If I am a 53, then there might be 52s and 54s. But 52 or 54 what? Planets, cities, kiths, worlds, spacetimes, strings, dimensions, strands of mutant bacteria, Homes?

And the symbols, the intertwined B and E, must mean something too. Hmmm. B? E? The answer floods me like Alice's own tears nearly drown her, so simple, so obvious in retrospect. The biome elixirs that I work with every stinking day–BE. The 53 stamp marks me slave to the biome elixirs. *Assholes.*

But why? Why save me from a dying world and place me on another? Other than to serve them, maybe? *Slave traders.* Chills attack me head to toe. I can accept that I am a minion, a serf to the biome elixirs, but maybe I am not alone and maybe so far less alone than I could have ever dared to hope. Maybe 52 or 54 *worlds filled with piggies to save?*

Unable to resist from the hope flitting around in this slave's heart, I follow the beetle bug because I also remember what the voice said in my last battle. *"Do not die. I will show you a way into Interval."*

The bug goes down, down into the alternate space where I lose Tilly. And again, like with Kink, this time, I recognize more quickly that I can never lose her. That she still exists here, perfectly safe inside the core of me.

I place two fingers on my right hand to my lips, kiss them, and then place them twice over my heart as a salute, a signal full of wires, toos, and *"heart you"* for her and all the others inside my space so deep and wide forever. And unlike it usually does, the sadness of my losing her does not cut me down and make me smaller. In fact, it lifts me up larger.

Why? Because I could never lose her or anything else, for that matter, that *"hearts"* me so much, living here forever from inside and behind, no, beyond my eyes.

All of this sinks in while I follow that sightless little bug, that silly white rabbit in such a hurry, toward the ventilation fan. Before I can see it, I feel the anti-green flash of the space inside the wall.

Suspicions confirmed, I take off the ventilation grate and begin my journey down where I don't want to go but do all at the same time. I blink and am surrounded by a metal tube that I also suspect will lead me farther into the place I ran away from all those years ago, where I never wanted to return but must now to save us all. Why? Because just because and for no reason more than that, which is good enough for this 53. Surely I plan to pay this gift of awareness forward, like the page-one-hundred-and-thirty-five lady, hopping on board, bound with the other blind bugs for the journey to the bottom of a pit of madness underneath, inside and between, no, beyond the dirty City of Stink.

The voice subtly returns. "Good girl." And for the first time, it occurs to me that it is the same voice of the monitor who took me from one elder to the next so long ago.

I roll my eyes because I no longer need someone to tell me I am good; I already know that. "Piss off, you. Tell me something I do not already know," I say, and the voice laughs before it trails off.

I should probably be afraid, but I am not because it dawns on me that even if I don't make it back up from my quest to the chopping block, it will all be okay. Why? Because I'm in someone else's space now, too. And I will be there forever, able to see the sunshine inside them instead of black lies wrapped up in a wire I can never untangle because it can't be untangled, ever.

The idea, so delicious, fills me in a way no square ever dares and guides me more brightly down this metal tube than any light on my path ever shows me anything.

When I finally reach the bottom of the shaft, I see more than I might have ever imagined. An entire world lives and breathes underneath the City. Or is it between the walls of the City? I just can't be sure yet.

Machines.

Buildings.

Rectangles that travel, hooked to one another, shooting past my view along a track of some sort.

Endless clear glass tubes that open and close, flying up and down.

Needless to say, I am speechless. Words, half-formed, just dangle from my lips, but they are too incoherent to turn into sentences. Gurgling, I sound like I have just been necrotized. I pinch my skin to make sure it's still solid. Yep, I'm here, not a clump of goo left behind. *Left behind. Oh my Gods, how long have we been left behind here?*

As I emerge from my tube, I step into a large chamber, the same one I now remember from my dream. The one that leads to a pool of liquid knives and doors where bairns scream and fall to the ground. The same place where they must plan the evil of the Ink beneath, no, beyond the Ink to stain me hideous colors so simple I can name them.

This central room is so large I don't have the words big enough to describe it. It stretches farther than the Orb inside the Gridiron and higher than building Forty-Four B. My mostly unobstructed view of this inner city allows me to do the watching for the first time ever, minus flashing red lights as I become the red light of warning. The flash that watches and records without and even against their say.

"Red equals dead, you slave traders," I whisper.

I might sit here for hours and not take it all in.

Two hundred meters away from me, smack dab in the center of this space almost as big as our entire city, rises a glass-walled structure. And even though I can't hear what they are saying, I can see people on the other side talking. I deduce these must be our monitors because they still hold their white devices from the Stain Heats.

Squinting to make my eyes see farther, I watch some monitors come through a sliding glass door from somewhere up above. Then they travel through a double set of machines just like my entry scanners where their bodies are probed and examined just like mine.

The third machine I would recognize anywhere–the mouth scraper. I hate the scraper. I bet they do, too, especially the hideous grating sound the awful contraption forms while it swabs the inner side of my lower lip, searching for clues about the inside of me.

And that wretched machine, making me feel so exposed, probed, violated, what does it search for? Data, information, the genetic problems on our bacteria like Kinley suffers, perhaps? And that Eliza Rachel suffers…suffered, I mean?

Or maybe something worse? Something that might jump from a 53 to a puff if they didn't wear suits to protect them?

But why are they using it on the monitors? And who is they? The Chancellors? Or maybe someone I cannot possibly know.

But who? A silly little song Elder Khaan once sang returns. Something about a cookie jar even though I have no idea what a cookie is. *"Who stole the cookie from the cookie jar?"*

"Who, me?"

"Yes, you," the soft female voice says.

"Couldn't be."

"Then who?" she asks and sighs.

"I don't know. Please tell me," I whisper.

"The queen," that same kind, little voice inside of my mind whispers back.

It's the queen. She is testing her pack of cards that quiver at her feet.

"But why?" the voice replies.

To see who will fail her little test that is anything but little. It is big and bad with a capital B.

For a moment, a question I am not yet able to stomach raises its ugly, little head. Is there any space or time outside of the City at all? Maybe the salvage processor goes somewhere else entirely. Maybe, maybe not? Maybe there is only a pool of liquid knives and goo? And since the implications of the deception this trail of thinking leads to terrifies me, I drop it like an ax. The same ax which keeps barely missing my right foot colored by my rising sun. The one I can't recall getting.

But the same as Gaige's.

Growing more nervous by the minute, I stop hunting for answers right there. These are questions I am not ready to answer, not yet. Soon, knowing me, I will anyway; I am sure of it.

So I force my disbelieving attention back to the monitors tested for the benefit of an invisible queen. I watch them like they usually watch me, realizing she probably watches us all.

And like a fish, for a fraction of a second, I start to feel sorry for them again, examined and probed and trembling like this. But then I remember all the hate I feel for them and their evil, black madness, which is so much more intense. Like unrecyclable waste, I let all the empathy wash off my dirty hands, flushing the trash down the piping system. Why? Because, after all, it's just a load of crap-coated madness.

But since that really isn't my problem anymore, I focus on the things that are. The racing bairn who will die working for these backward liars. And Cale who I cannot let turn into another Ink freak juicing for more Inks coated in skag, such a disgusting vehicle of manipulation.

Ink this. Ink that. I decode this wicked obsession.

These fools pretend I am so different from them, but any idiot can see I am not. Except for my non-sulfuric breath and my name, of course.

For a minute, I get swept up in the storm of my thoughts again, trying to figure out what's in a name. What is the value of it really? Am I not the same with or without this name Isla Jane? Which could have just as easily been Rose or Jane-do-do or Rising Sun like my Inks. Or maybe even Cristin or Jen or Vanessa or Nicky. And my 53 designation could be 42 or 17 or 1. Or maybe not even a number but just a letter. Or like minty Gaige, no second name, number or letters at all.

I come to the only reasonable conclusion. The name–be it Isla or Cale or even Gaige, with or even without a second name–means absolutely nothing. It is nothing more than a symbol, a useless series of letters. What matters lives underneath the symbol, just like with questions and answers.

What the name stands for is the only thing that matters.

Yet now I have no name to name it with because just like the purple inside Gaige's eyes, any name will only shame it.

But why is that?

To confuse me? To distract me?

I don't think so.

Perhaps the Gods want to make me find the only answer worth finding: the name beneath, no, beyond the name and the answer beneath, no, beyond the answer, just like the color beneath, no, beyond the color.

Oh I can go on forever: the same with *"heart you"* in my place so deep and wide through the rabbit hole inside of me, the same I am pretty sure leads me to the Isla beneath, no, beyond me.

Before I pass out from thinking so intently, I dismiss my little philosophy class, returning my brain to my chilly smooth-walled tube. As I place my flat palm on the sidewall, a shiver races down my spine just like Cale raced earlier today but lost for all his winning.

Thank Gods I finally remember why I am here to begin with–to save Cale.

Then I notice a monitor's gray suit for the taking, very close to the opening of my shaft, and I steal it gladly, knowing exactly what I will use it for.

I thank the Gods for another tool in my arsenal against the Mozek gun and goo club. Like the bead in my hair with the fissure made for holding liquid bacterial cures or liquid killer knives and the needles hidden in my lovely closet for stopping the heartbeat where it pulses in my neck. Now this suit too. I reach up, rub my neck, and swallow.

Ah, my neck, this neck made for hanging, underneath heads made for chopping, to stop Heats made for losing and black songs made for spreading infectious lies.

Pivotal, that champion inside me screams.

Delighted, I travel back up this hidden way beneath the City of Liars where it takes cards to worship queens, kings to pardon them, and Islas beneath and beyond Islas to defeat them all.

I blink and am back where I came from. But just after I close the grate, I hear the bang, bang on my door. A loud voice bellows, "Why aren't you answering us, 53?"

I clasp my hand over my mouth to keep from hissing, *"Because I've been spying on you in the city inside the City."*

Thankfully, my grip is tight across my lips, and the slippery words do not get the chance to slither out.

Chapter Twenty-Six

"OPEN THE DEADBOLT NOW. If you are an enemy of the City, the Chancellors will necrotize you. You don't want to seem like you're hiding something, do you? Open the damn door!" the goon declares.

Pretending I am Kinley, I consider saying, *"Yeah? How you going to make me? Shoot me?"* But then I remember the nothingness left of Kalil, so I just shut up instead. I can't pretend to guess how long they have been knocking, so I'm not sure how terrible my predicament.

Quickly and quietly, I toss the suit into the subtle green flash by the grate, and it disappears from my sight. I slump to the floor, hoping to appear unconscious while I come up with a reasonable excuse that sounds a little better than, *"Been busy figuring out your little scheme here, you vicious liars. How's the mouth scraper treating you eyeless creeps?"*

The thought of actually telling them off sounds so hilarious that I almost laugh. Almost. But as they laser off my deadbolt, I decide they must be serious about chatting it up with me, so I better get it together. After all, I'm not sure I want to find out what being eaten by my own microbiome feels like.

I've lost all desire to laugh now.

The door slams open, and they march into my quarters, slinging their weapons of mass distraction.

Feeling more afraid than jovial now, I press my forehead down hard, trying to remember if I closed up my shelf in front of the hidden compartment inside my shelf. Do they know about flashing green lights that are easier to feel than see? Probably.

Will they discover all my precious secrets? Probably.

The list of my crimes saturates my mind: squares, boxes, needles, books, Cale, Baylor, the suit.

For sure I'm getting the goo treatment.

Damn it all. If I die now, all the bairn taking will have been for nothing. So instead of afraid, now I'm feeling pretty pissed off because I'm about to melt, left whistling a lying backward tune instead of the truth. And that totally sucks because the Mozek, not I, screw it all up, upside down and inside out, too. These idiotic turtles mix up the lyrics to fool us on behalf of a ruling tyrant while they Heat us to distract us, Ink us to addict and condition us into the nothings we are never meant to be. And now that I finally know it, I'm done for.

Well shit. Screw that.

If it didn't stink like their breath so badly, I might be almost amused by the humor of it all. Almost.

So here I go looking for that plan B again.

Why am I always looking for plan B?

Maybe with the element of surprise, I can take them down? Then what? Drop them in the liquid knives? Should I fight? Or stay down and play stupid?

I just can't be sure yet.

Before I have time to choose, the monitors, squishy with stinking rot in their puffy suits, rush over and pick me up. Looks like I'm the one diving into a pool of liquid knives instead of them after all.

Where does all the swirling gray liquid go? I start to ask my inner voice, but I stop myself.

Yet a moment later, I think better of it. After all, I'm about to die, again, so how can a little question hurt me now?

Where does the liquid pool of knives go? Where did Tilly go with it?

To make things worse, my internal bitch actually answers me. *To the same place we all end up–Rest and Relaxation. Duh, Isla.*

All the while, since I'm still trying to find a way out of this disaster, I keep my eyes closed tightly, hoping against hope that I will come up with something, anything that might save Cale and Alexis. And let's face it–as a side effect, me.

They shake me and throw me down on my bedding surface.

Still I fake sleep or something even worse.

The smellier of the two gray suits takes my pulse.

Plan B, nowhere to be found, evades me. My mind flounders, but since I can't stroke my beads to slow down my pulse, I bring my thoughts back to something good like Elder Khaan, which might help.

One lesson Elder Khaan taught me takes over my brain. When I was seven, he told me about an ugly snouted, nasty creature called a possum. With a creepy long tail sticking out the back of its wiry-hair-covered rear end, this of all possible things consumes my brain.

Hello, plan B. I'm still here. Let's forget the super-sized rat thing.

But nope. It's useless; all I have is the possum. And this, of all potential solutions, flashes in and out of my searching little mind.

Flash. A possum–a nasty, disease-ridden monster that might live out there in the Frightening Zone under all that fog.

Apparently, this daft rodent thing possesses a knack for convincing other even stupider things hunting, chasing, or trying to eat it, that it has died. It rolls over and acts like a rotting corpse until the predator leaves. Then it just gets up and walks off alive and utterly unscathed because it expects no self-respecting animal will eat scavenger fare.

Utterly unscathed, it survives–unbelievable, brilliant even.

Guess it isn't so stupid after all, my inner goddess, so proud of herself, announces. I feel the burn of hot blood infuse my motionless face.

Okay, plan B, you have to be kidding. Possum? Really? This is the best option we have? Seriously?

Possum. I'm playing possum. So I might as well play for my life, I guess. So this possum named Isla, minus an ugly tail, doesn't move when they pinch my toes and kick me to see how I will react. I play it well, too well because I start to believe my own little trick about sleeping safely, about how these puffy turtles won't discover my plan to scatter them like a deck of playing cards.

Limp bodied, I allow them to toss me side to side and force my eyelids, mouth, and legs open, probing me for clues they are too foolish to find. Silently, I watch from behind, no, beyond my eyes while they try to figure me out.

"Oh my Gods," one of them, the girl I think, finally says.

Silence.

She starts in again. "Yep, she's a sleeper."

Like somehow this is a good title? Whatever the hell sleeper means.

But I'm not. I'm an Alice playing possum.

"A sleeper?" the other monitor, a boy, I think, asks, kicking me in the ribs for effect. I do not flinch.

"Yes, with a delayed and prolonged response to the skag, obviously, you fool," the chick declares. And she's right; he is a fool. Not for knowing nothing about sleepers but for turning his nonsense into madness.

The female slowly traces and then painfully twists my nipples, hoping to make me squeal. But I will not; she can't make me. No way.

As she finally lets her evil grip go, she adds, "Which is good...for us. Bad for her but very good for us."

"What do you mean?"

"Exactly what we need to climb the ranks and cut years off our prison sentence in this fucking hellhole soaked in recycled human rejects. Might even translate into a few extra doses of juice for us both, Quentin."

"Uh?"

"Especially her, everyone's favorite beta bitch, of all the 53s. She, Isla-the-Great Jane, a sleeper. What are the odds?"

"Huh? How's that?" the dumber male asks.

Guess I've found Tweedledum and Tweedledee in this rabbit hole. What are the odds?

Honestly, I am glad for Tweedledum's ridiculous question because otherwise how am I going to figure out what I have just gotten my stupid self into? Unable to reel in my fishy thoughts while the twins carry on their foolish conversation, I ponder which one of the three of us is actually the most stupid of all–me playing possum or one of these two monitors kicking and punching a defenseless sleeper.

My internal voice giggles, still thrilled the nipple trick didn't get the best of me, and decides. *Him, of course.*

So...I'm pretty sure the biggest idiot is the deeper-voiced puffy-boy who keeps asking all the questions of the softer-voiced puffy-girl.

Ms. Nipple Twister continues. "Like Jaxston of the Irmin. He's a sleeper, totally hooked. When that Ink junkie goes too long without skag, you know how he gets. He's willing to do anything to get it–anything–and I mean anything. Even...you know... voluntarily playing the black cards. And now her too, in withdrawal, this deviant Isla Jane."

She kicks me again and then curses. "Guess who's playing a whole new kind of warrior for the Mozek now? I can't wait to watch them chain her up and fuck her until she bleeds. Disgusting Humanite."

Humanite? What's a Humanite? Until I bleed?

"So?" the stupidest one of us all asks.

I listen hard; I need the answer too.

"They thought," the lesser of the two idiots explains with one more swift kick to my groin, "that she...this gray-blond-haired verus bitch, carries some magical bacterial cure insider her. The same one they can't seem to duplicate in the Foundry."

"Who gives a fuck about her genes? She's a video game."

"Seriously, you're a dumbass. Ugh...you know, the same genetic alteration the prime Jane Dawn intentionally mutated and hid inside her own fucking DNA before the first harvest, protecting her from the skag's effects to implement the necrotizing sequence."

"Oh, okay." *He is so not okay.*

"They thought that this Jane named Isla was immune to the Ink's effects in this weird-ass city because of the weird-ass color of her ridiculous hair. Seriously, the Ink is my least favorite form of anchor administration in all these bizarre as hell cities."

"Oh."

All these cities? It takes the memory of stroking every precious strand of Cale's hair to keep me from jumping up and strangling her while I make her explain what she means by this. *All these cities.*

"Oh," he says again, slowly drawing the syllable out like it's a long word. If I grabbed his finishing stick, I bet he'd have more to say. I can almost hear the dead space between his two neurons firing in opposite directions and sticking to the cobwebs in his empty skull. Heck, maybe the space in his head is the missing tenth dimension that Elder Khaan told me about.

"Fuck, Quentin. You know how the Mozek masses, especially that experiment in Marxism, Chancellor Jaziah, love this version of her. Posting her bizarre Ink-covered image everywhere like a lovesick puppy. Disgusting."

"Oh," the dimwit boy says for the third time, raising his voice at the end, more a question than a statement. I seriously consider killing him for it.

She goes on. "You are stupid, aren't you? No wonder they caught you stealing skag. Dude, they give the shit out, and you steal it. Idiot!"

"Hey, easy now. You were explaining…"

"Ugh, you never read the mandatory manual. Idiot! The same bacterial genetics the Mozek modified to make it easier to manipulate them all. The numbered races, I mean. They thought this tramp might be immune like the prime Jane, and that could upset everything in the entire amusement park."

Amusement? Park? My fingers are twitching because I am so about to choke them both and slam their heads together in front of the camera outside my door to make sure everyone sees it. Cale's hair keeps me still. Thank Gods.

The dumbest one just goes silent as if those two nerve cells in his evil brain just exploded from the strain of the thought.

And for a moment, I start to feel sorry for him, the idiot puff who can't even comprehend what a pawn he is, what evil he does for his horrid queen. Then I remember he plans to kill me every minute of every day. And worst of all, he plans to kill Cale and Baylor and Alexis, and he has killed Kalil. At least he might have; I can't say for sure. So I assume he has so that it feels easier and lighter to hate him so much instead of feeling sorry for him, the clueless imbecile.

Yep, just checked. Zero sympathy left here. Choking them sounds nice again.

Cale. Cale. Cale. I think it over and over to hold me steady.

While I'm thinking about this, sleeping like a possum and licking my wounds with a raspy tongue, I attempt to avoid hearing the words she says. And I try even harder not to decipher what they mean.

The prime Jane? What the hell? Skylar's words return. *"The essence of the prime Jane forth."*

In a lesson, many years ago, Elder Khaan explained the prime numbers to me. Not much, but enough. So even though I do not wish to apply a satisfactory meaning to the titty-twister's words, I already know what she means. The prime Jane infers the first Jane, a Jane un-divisible by another Jane because she is the original Jane.

What the hell? *Don't act so surprised,* my inner voice scoffs.

Picking up speed, my thoughts threaten to implode. *And if there is a first Jane, what does that make me and all the other Janes? Janes number 53? Or 52? Or 2?* Somehow, I don't get particularly fuzzy feelings about this two, which is not my kind of too.

Titty-twister's words return. *"The numbered races."*

Perfectly still, while trembling terribly on the inside, I shatter as my rose withers inside me, dying around the other words spewing from her nasty mouth about people trying to hook us, like Jaxston on Ink skag. And now I am supposedly addicted, too. I mean, two. There are no toos here with these two.

To be honest with myself, I already know the Mozek's intention is to hook us on skag. But it feels so much worse being certain.

I hate the Mozek queen and her entire army of monitor playing cards.

"So what next?" the dumbest one asks.

"We tell the Director of Park 53. He will promote this bitch to higher leveled assignments and then upgrade her location probe to overseer level. He will reprogram her opiate receptors and then bathe her in skag to keep her a deeper and deeper sleeper. And we will use her to control all the other 53 creeps.

After all, the Mozek masses love her like she is some kind of juice celebrity, so no one has the authority to just kill her outright anymore, do we?"

"Unfortunately not. Should have on the stage the other day, huh?"

"I say let's make her work for us instead. A champion minion. Awesome. I'm liking this shithole of a prison ward sentence better all the time."

"And?"

"And what?"

"What if she doesn't play the blacks or whites like Jaxston?"

"Then we will stop her skag supply. That will hurt her inside bad, so bad now that she's a sleeper. And if that doesn't fry her brain, we will kill her Ink dealer in her place to remind those mules—freaky half-human, half-Mozek criminals, that the monitors still run this park.

And then, one by one, we will take away everything this Jane bitch has ever cared about or loved bit by bit while she watches it play out on the big screen of the Orb until she does play along."

She starts laughing, flicking and pinching my right nipple once more while she foams madness from her disgusting mouth. "As if these freaking sub-human creepy 53s can even love something. Reject robots covered in flesh, stink, and mutant bacteria that don't even know the word love. Ugh. Clueless, fucking fools."

The other idiot bellows back. Surely this is the funniest thing he has ever heard. But then he says, "Careful touching her skin like that. You will accidently contaminate your Achillean suit with the 53 park bacteria. And if you do..."

Gasp.

"Neither the Humanites nor those wimpy Curonites in City 161 have the anti-strain. Every idiot knows that."

City 161? If I could scream, I would. City 161? *All the cities.* What the hell?

Turns out, maybe he's not the dumbest one after all. For a moment, I feel sad at the loss of the possibility of finding the tenth dimension...or perhaps the negative fifth dimension if I start counting backward...in his noggin.

Immediately, they stop laughing, getting out of my quarters as fast as they can while, unlike the gigantic rodent in Elder Khaan's lesson, I do not walk off virtually unscathed.

Bummer.

It also turns out I'm no more a possum than a grinning cat. But I am still an Alice, so I jump right through the looking glass, straight through the center of a black hole to an anti-dimension made of hate, minus any sorry at all.

I might shudder from fear if I had any left, but now there is only spite inside of and through and behind and even beyond me.

I listen for the caterpillar smoke fuming out of my ears, raging through my mind inside my *creepy sub-human* brain that does not know how to *love*. Whatever this word I have never heard before might mean.

That internal monster shakes her little indignant finger at me. She wants to say it; I know she does. *Pivotal.*

Pursing my lips, I try to shut up but can't. "Bitch," I say, not even sure who I am speaking to or about. Surely I should be afraid because I am in terrible danger, more than ever before. But I'm not; I am pissed thinking about their plan to use me, to make me their tool.

Still unable to shut up, wide-eyed, I add, "Oh, shaking in my boots."

But I would rather die than sing a verse of their turtle song spreading their lies, so I grit my teeth instead of trembling, looking for another plan B to augment and amplify my anger instead of diffuse it.

Maybe I am good at playing possum, I affirm, still smoking. Surely I can find a way to turn this around and play another game. Why not? Why should playing turtle be any different in this City of Zoos?

Plan B, minus any more vermin, makes a timely arrival, as usual, while I inspect my superficial wounds. If they can use me, those idiots, then maybe, just maybe, I can use them. Especially now that I see the truth behind their stupid, empty eyes that fear my 53 park microbiome. Whatever that is.

Time to find out, I think.

I wink, waiting for my inner voice to answer all the questions I ask her. The answers are coming fast; I am sure of it.

Then, for one tiny moment more, I consider feeling a little sorry for the gray idiots in their Achillean suits because I'm pretty sure that behind and even beyond the fear in their eyes, there remains nothing, absolutely nothing at all.

After the millisecond passes, I place my fingers to my lips and twice over my chest to salute the reflection in my mirror because behind my eyes live something so much more powerful than nothing. In fact, it's everything.

Perhaps that's why I wink when I smile. So I can hold on to it longer. The thought, so full of sunshine, makes me wink again.

Chapter Twenty-Seven

CALE KNOCKS AGAIN TONIGHT. It's very late, yet I do not, no, cannot answer him and his pitter-patter feet.

"Isla," he says softly as only he can, "I won today. Did you see? I won."

And even though it's killing me, the supposed sleeper of an Ink-freak junkie, I clap my hand over my mouth to stop the words from coming out. Words like, *"Yes, Cale. You were so fast, faster than me. But you're too good, too good to win...so don't you win, my sweet, sweet Cale. It will only hurt you. They will send you on red cards."*

So instead, I say nothing. And this nothing, unlike with Gaige, really means nothing.

"Isla?" he whispers again. "Why won't you answer me?"

And still I say nothing instead of, *"Because I 'heart you' too much, Cale. Because if they know how much we depend on each other, how you need me, and how I need you back, they will hurt you or kill me to hurt you deeper. And I can't let them just like I can't let them blow you away. Lose the Heats tomorrow, Cale. Lose. Because I can't live in a world made for losing you when you win."*

In my mind, his gold mask flips in place, blocking the beauty of his eyes, replacing them with metallic holes filled with nothing but portals of darkness. The same vehicles of evil nothingness that destroyed Home. *Boom!*

I think of my needles once more and how it might end all this losing for me and painfully accept that even if they are the only things that can help me escape this mess of mine, I cannot use them. Not yet. I'm still not ready to die. Not like that.

Because if I spare myself, I will be no different than the queen, selfishly hurting Cale yet only serving myself through my death–a piss-poor, crap shot move, a lowly escape planned perfectly by a coward too afraid to face her queen.

And I am not afraid of that twit, not one itty bit.

For Cale and all the others too numbed by the turtle song to even realize they have a villain trying to behead them, I can't back down now. I can't play out a quivering plan built by flimsy cards as if I'm an idiot twin instead of a brave Alice. I am an Isla, damn it, who's willing to keep this turtle zoo for Cale.

Ah Cale. Without him, there will be no use for fake songs for me anymore, only needles sharpened for stopping hearts that no longer want to beat in a world minus him.

I tighten the grip of my hand even firmer across my mouth, shoving down my truth and covering it in turtle soup for only him–the Cale part of me who I cannot, no–will not live without.

So, again I help him by not answering, not crying out, not opening the door, not rock, rock, rocking his gorgeous locks to sleep on my lap that aches to soothe him.

And instead, I deny him.

"Isla," he says one more time, minus all the Jane business. Just Isla, no pauses, no "my Jane" like with Gaige, just Isla like with Elder Khaan.

And I understand why Cale says just Isla. Because my name is just a name, after all. The Isla, merely a symbol for something far greater than it can ever adequately describe. Those silly letters are a joke: I-S-L-A. *As if...*

And he needs no long or fancy name to call on me, the real me, who always waits for his summoning. The same one who *"hearts"* him so much, all tied up in his wire because even as young as he is, Cale senses that he speaks to the Isla beneath, no, beyond this Isla from behind my blue eyes. And he needs no name to call me by because I am inside him, and he is inside me. My name exactly the same as his even though the letters and sounds try to convince us otherwise.

As if a Cale ever exists to call out or a separate Isla ever lives to answer him back when really looking through both our eyes and back out of that tree-filled space inside us where there only is we.

Nothing else is even possible.

With just a door between us, I kneel with my head pressed against the cold, hard floor. If there was a way, I would slide my fingers under the door to reach his. I would call out his name–Cale. But I can't. I can't even say his beautiful name so unworthy of him.

And for a moment, I swirl even further down my tunnel of thoughts about names. Actually, the categories of names we learn which really never matter at all once we learn the name beneath, behind, and even beyond the name. So really the name's only function is to avoid confusion about which part of me I am speaking about because we are all one great big, beautiful metallic wire. And maybe that infinite space of connection and inclusion and completion is the missing tenth dimension where everything exists as one with everything else.

Then I think even more deeply about the John parts of me, like Baylor John and Elder Khaan, too. His second name was John, I think, before he accepted Elder and forsook his prior name to represent kith solidarity. All the Johns I know are sweet and tender like Baylor, like Elder Khaan. I connect with them more than the others immediately.

I can't help but wonder if I have a special wire with them. One that rolls all around me before I am ever aware of it in this lifetime from inside this space so big and wide before I even learn about spaces and wires or the true value of a name–not in the name at all but underneath it.

I slam my head on the floor, but the thoughts keep gathering speed.

Could it be that I know the Johns before I meet them and already assume the best in them? Could I already be certain what goodness lives behind the name that describes one part of me that I hold so dear? Could this be why I experience so much regret? Perhaps I almost remember something crucial. Almost. Almost close enough to the surface of my mind to grasp it.

Have I always known John? Has John always known Jane?

My John. My Jane. My Cale who is my only Jacob. My "heart you."

My love. My love. My l-o-v-e. My love.

The puff's word slices me open, and I bleed like an impaled animal all over the floor, slipping in my sticky red warmth as the oh-so-obvious-in-retrospect meaning sets in.

I *"heart"* them, I love them, for a thousand years.

Before the Global War or even today and will heart them tomorrow.

For Gods' sakes, I will love them for a thousand more forevers. As long as there is any planet to live on, any world to live in for forever and even beyond an infinity of forevers. My loves.

Even if they, the Johns and Jacobs, I mean, try to hide it under countless layers of cracking paint colored from misery and nonsense because they forgot their true name. The one that is the same as mine. The only name that ever means anything at all.

Baylor–my every John.

Cale–my only Jacob, my every Jacob.

And I cannot answer him back or he will die.

Oh my Gods, how will I survive this?

"Did I do something wrong, Isla?" Cale whispers through the closed door between us, reminding me where I am. And just as my heart jumps out of my chest to reach him, he adds, "Don't you want me anymore?"

And I tap, tap my head while my mind breaks into numerous ragged pieces like shards of a shattered glass beaker that will never come back together. Shit, I'm too far gone now. Freezing and shaking, I am unable to warm myself because all the sunshine has deserted me, and the nature of my being splits in two.

Suddenly, I realize what I saw that day in the cryo-chamber and why it hurt so badly. I saw this. This. This kind of pain. And so insane in this moment, I could imagine the whole thing, but here comes the voice again, so kind and slow and almost crying in her own misery now. "Darling little one, now you see what they have done to you. Done to us. Oh, my Jane."

Too devastated to reply with anything else, I tell her to go back to her own hell. And I think she does because she is gone. Gone like Cale.

So…as my eternal punishment, I shall live forever in the Liebhorr of my personal hell, frozen in two pieces separated by such cruel clamps and tubes that separate my bloody heart from my empty shell of a body. Still exsanguinating, my last drop of blood falls on my rising sun, and there is no me left to speak of because I disappear as I splinter all around that red globe. No, actually, I desert it, and I have only hazy gray pools of cold misery left to replace it because I am nothing but a shell in a bag in the Liebhorr now. My heart just died.

"Why don't you want me anymore?" he says again, but I can't hear him because I am just a ghost. As if it is possible to not want him, this Cale, chock full of sunshine, which I must abandon in order to save.

To whom I must scream "isn't" when only "is" can ever be true.

"Then I don't want you anymore either," he says. The words muffle as he chokes on them. Underneath his voice, I clearly hear the pain, the hurt, the suffering, the injury that I cannot ever undo. And it all makes terrible yet perfect sense in a world over-flowing with so much backward nonsense.

He walks back down the hall not shuffling lightly but dragging his precious wounded piggies that lost today and will mostly likely lose again tomorrow when he fucking wins. I cannot save him. Help me, Gods.

Screaming into my pillow, I hate myself for wounding him like this, hate the world even more for giving me no other choice, but mostly I hate the queen who turns me traitor against the only thing I want to turn to–Cale.

I envision the wire without any clamps coming from inside me and trailing down the hallway to reach him.

Comfort him.

Cuddle him.

Cradle him in a thousand layers of *"heart you"* made of my sunshine for him. But he will not have it. He is done with my love, my wires in this City of Wire Clamps and Cutters.

I don't know how long I lie like this, screaming and crying rivers of salty tears that pour from a million sores festering inside me, the Isla whose name means nothing to her now, until I lose my mind in the oblivion of sleep.

Tossing about restlessly, I try to find comfort where there can be none until the pressure of Gaige's hand on my Jane-do-do tattoo wakes me. He pulls me back from my dreams of terror. Nightmares where Cale wails for me but I can't reach him because my hands are tied behind my back, entangled with wires that cut through my flesh. Drip, drip, dripping, I ooze my final drops of blood all over the floor.

Furiously waking in a haze of confusion, I struggle against the wires to reach Cale, but he's not there. Only Gaige and I remain.

I say nothing, like usual, to Gaige. And in return, he says nothing back.

A look of sympathy washes out from behind Gaige's eyes and onto his face. It's almost like he knows about the dream. Almost. But how could he?

Calmly, he slips the gifted braid beads in my hair like I will need them and their double purpose today. "You have fifteen minutes before the bell. I let you sleep as long as possible after..."

I swallow, gathering myself, and struggle to the bathroom. From across my room, I hear him say, "You are stronger than you know, than you even think possible. If only you knew what you have done in the..."

He coughs awkwardly.

Cale is depending on you, I remind myself. *Get your butt in gear.*

And so I do.

Quickly, I apply my womb cloth, slip on my soft leather boots, and adjust my hair beads. I rub my gorgeous hair up and down for the soothing effect and swirl four beads into a unicorn's horn in the front. If I can't leave it down, then I'll pretend I'm a magical creature instead. Or is it pretending to be me? I just can't be sure yet, can I?

Gaige hands me a square and one of those clear boxes of his while I approach the door. "You know," he says, "you are...I mean...would be even more beautiful without that hair. It's just hair, Isla."

Just hair? I scowl. In response to his insult, I slam my beastly hoof on the table which shatters into a million pieces. It feels great. So great I don't care if I will die for it. In fact, I can't help but laugh at the absurdity of it all. *Just hair.*

Brushing my hair back, I say, "That table was just glass."

Gaige laughs and gently touches my *just hair* beads. He leans over me, his monstrous height offering me protection no one can truly offer me in this place. He places one of my beads to his lips and looks away.

He wants to tell me something but doesn't. Instead, he places his fingers over my heart and presses down twice. "My Jane. Isla"–that pause of his–"Jane, I still love you. I think I always will."

Not sure what to say, I say nothing.

I'm thinking too much about that word–love. And since I'm no good at talking when I'm thinking, I keep my mouth shut. Yet I do not look away.

I need to do something and feel it call my name like a siren. *But what?*

Placing my head to his throbbing chest, I twist my rainbow-beaded horn into his neck back and forth, back and forth. Then I place my fingers to his lips, press them over my heart twice, and finally summon up enough courage to find his purple eyes once more.

Like usual, words are utterly useless to us two.

That same pulsating warmth gathers in my core. Wet and getting wetter, I yearn to pull him closer to my center and make my body join in some way with his. I want to bring him inside me further as if that is possible somehow.

Suspecting the gesture will symbolize that want growing inside me, I press my breasts into him firmly. My cheek brushes his softly while my eyes try to see inside, behind, and beyond him. I know it's insane, but the urge to fill myself with him consumes me further. Or is it fill him with me? I just can't be sure yet.

Either way, the notion terrifies me.

So instead of sticking around any longer, I trot out the door as fast as I can. The door slams shut behind me.

Rearing up on my legs with determination, I fight the desire to turn around and go back, back to him and his blue, I mean purple eyes that look into, not through me.

I hear him picking up the glass while I go around the corner. Unable to suppress it, I grin and laugh sinisterly.

Pressing two fingers to my lips as I gallop, I imagine pressing them firmly to his. Almost instantly, though, Baylor's face replaces Gaige's in my vision. Inexplicably, shame washes over me, followed by terrible regret.

Regret for what?

Surely I cannot say.

Inspired by my regret, I hot hoof it even faster to make it to the Ink stage on time, to not let Baylor down, to not look at Cale, to not turn to goo. *So Gods damn many nots.*

How odd that I do not think, *Why is Gaige in my room? How does he get in? Why does he stay in my space after I leave?*

Until I reach the Ink stage, that is. Then I find out even though I do not want to.

Chapter Twenty-Eight

THE FINAL INK BELL RINGS.

I avoid Baylor's eyes. Even though I am looking the other direction, I feel them boring holes into me. Guilt eats at me like a square, chewing me up and spitting me out.

The monitors type in their little white machines to compute tabulation. How many of us are missing? Who knows? Do I even care? I wish I could say no, but by this point, I'm not sure of much anymore but my mysterious regret.

The monitors dole out the squares and boxes. Baylor looks expectantly, hoping for me to take more bairns, but today I just can't. I look away again, unable to meet the sweetness oozing from behind his clear blue eyes. Or are they brown? I can't tell anymore.

I remember his words, *"How can I save them all?"*

He is so much more than me, his intention so much higher. If I am a unicorn-fish, what does that make him? A dolphin, a mythical whale, a phoenix?

I will never be as good as him; I see that now. A week ago, this would have thrilled me. Instead, my bitterness sets in and enrages me. How can I look back at him and his need for me to be so much more than I am?

For Gods' sakes, I'm too wounded to help him. I can't even manage to help Cale, let alone help Baylor save them all. How can I possibly offer salvation to the innocent ones when all I do is hurt the people who mean the most to me? To say I'm broken with self-disappointment is no exaggeration. It's the understatement of this century. I wish time is an endless loop in the tenth dimension. If so, then I shall find it and freaking do better next time.

So when the monitors cuff me and march me to the edge of the Stage, I do not bother to fight back. Maybe next time I shall be better, be more, be worthy of the Ink on my cracked hoof. Maybe next time around I shall rescue all the piggies, even my own broken piggies.

A pack of eleven monitors encircle me and take turns slapping me with a vengeance too intense to be impersonal. Unable to maintain eye contact with the crimson hue that replaces the pits of their previously empty eyes, I just stand there dumb and dumber like the puffy twins. Honestly, I don't even care what I have done. I don't even bother to ask why they are beating the shit out of me.

In shock, the other 53s stare at me–Baylor, Skylar, Jaxston, Alexis, the new bairns whose names I haven't learned, even Cale.

Avoiding their eye contact too, I just laugh inside, remembering the shattered glass table. I am one sliver left of the whole, and I will cut everyone's piggies with my glass while I rip them to pieces with my thorny hands and spear them with the horn on my head.

Gaige, that total creep, must have known this would happen all along. I bet if I look at the eleven fuckfaces slapping me, I will see his purple eyes looking out of one of their faces. He's one of them, after all, isn't he? So the act, the look, the words, the lips, all of it such a freaking bullshit charade.

Secretly, I hope for a quick death this time. If I can start the sequence, I will initiate my own necrotizing. I am finally ready to die and meet with my wicked queen. Without Cale, without his love, truthfully, I have nothing left to live for. Even Baylor offers me only regret.

Busy wallowing in my own misery, I try to ignore the other 53s and their suffering at the loss of me. All of them looking for a reason, an explanation, something, anything so they will not be the next 53 cuffed and turned to goo.

It dawns on me now this is one of the monitors' most powerful weapons against us. The not knowing, not telling. Just like with the blowouts that kill the DED heads. The uncertainty this demonstration feeds acts like gas on the always-growing fire of terror blazing inside us all.

I try to blink, but my eyelids are missing. I flail my gills, looking for something, anything I can do to make it better, to help them all.

But what? What?

I hear that twat inside my brain before she even starts. *Pivotal.*

Maybe I can offer one last thing to Baylor, to them all, it seems–certainty.

Maybe I am stronger than I think? Not a sliver but the whole piece of glass from before I shatter, the rose and not just a thorny stem, the entire unicorn and not just a horn after all. Because maybe even though I'm already broken, I have always been whole. Like Gaige, that traitor, claims earlier–so much stronger than I realize.

I think about the ocean like it once existed before the polar ice caps, full of life and promise, melted from global warming. Before the Global War when the frigid water soaked up some of the altered bacteria and killed the tiny suckers called krill, which previously fed the entire aquatic base. Before the oceans flooded the continent called South America, before the Mozek transported some of the surviving humans to the City on this Gods-forsaken planet.

If I take one drop of the ocean and isolate it from the rest, will it not still be the ocean? Yes, a drop perhaps, but the ocean nonetheless.

I laugh again, observing the glass table fracture in my memory once more. Me, the sliver but the whole thing, too.

So complex yet so simple.

This City of Ink yet the whole universe, too.

I roll my head back and forth, back and forth, displaying my beaded horn, my power, and my rank. I do not roll my arms over in submission. How can I in cuffs like this?

I am a rainbow of sorts, just like I am an Alice. I am ocean in one drop. I am glass table in one fragment. We are the universe in one City of Ink.

Inside my mind, I hear the tension mount just like in the Gridiron. The drums of the Heat gather, and the wires burrow down my neck port and invade my nerves. This battle with the monitors stands to be no different, except I'm finally going to die.

The weight of my parmula coats my chest. The gladius feels sharp and cold in my hand. I am gladiator and will accept one last Heat.

I will not leave the other 53s not knowing. They will be certain that my wire reaches out for them if they are willing to tug back on it. They will witness that I am the ocean, the table, and just like each of them, all of humanity in one 53.

I gaze up and meet their eyes. All of them so blue from inside mine.

Fear saturates them, but I will not show it back for them to see because it isn't real. All of a sudden, I realize the only thing that is real, that has ever been real, is *"heart you."* I mean…love.

Love.

Love.

Lovely.

So instead of cowering, I giggle at the absurdity of it all. Because after they kill me, I will still be looking out from behind those beautiful eyes, the colors too gorgeous to name. Blue? Purple? Brown? As if these words are even worth speaking.

They cannot kill me. It's impossible. Only I'm-possible

I am invincible. I am wire with no clamps at all. I am ocean. I am table. I am humanity. With or without Gaige's allegiance. With or without Elder Khaan's song.

I lock eyes with Cale, my only Jacob. Nodding, I aim to assure him that I have always loved him, that I will never forsake him, that I am still the only one who will never fail him.

Pivotal, my inner voice delights.

I shall not die in vain.

He puts his fingers to his lips, then over his heart and presses down twice. No one sees this—only me. I mean every me.

I sing our song. Elder Khaan's song. Cale Jacob's song. Baylor John's song.

No one else ever needs to know our secret—that I belong to the rising sun, his dawn. I always have. I always will.

I sing:

. . .

"In a sea of blinding darkness,
    You are my shining light.
    Without your rays,
    There's only night.

Will you rescue me,
    And set things right?

My dawn. My only dawn.
    My dawn. My dawn.

So take these eyes,
    And give them sight.
    That search for you,
    On the hope you might.

My dawn. My only dawn.
    My dawn. My dawn.

Your glowing beauty,
    Framed in fight.
    And precious rays,
    Of warm delight.

My dawn. My only dawn.
    My dawn. My dawn."

I could be wrong, but from inside my mind...I think I hear, *"Heart you, Isla,"* just as the metal fire gun smacks the back of my head.
    And then I am gone.

Chapter Twenty-Nine

WHEN I COME TO, I am confused, my tender jaw is out of alignment, and I have a raging headache. Totally alone, I am facedown, naked on the frigid, marble floor. There are at least ten new bruises on each of my arms. I reach up and touch my face. One eyelid is swollen shut. The other feels almost absent, nowhere to be found by comparison. The irony makes me laugh, and I almost blink my one good eyelid. Almost. Instead, I cough, and a string of bloody mucous drips off my swollen lip onto the spotless floor.

Red is dead. Or is dead red? I just can't be sure yet.

Unable to resist, I rub it in small circles on the floor. I do this until the red blends into the white, leaving only a pink stain. If red means dead, what does pink mean? Pink stains look a little like red but not exactly. So is it more than dead—super dead? Or less—anti dead? I'm still not sure about anything pink, like pink strips and pink serums which started all this crap to begin with.

Since no one explains where I am or what anti dead can possibly mean, briefly, I consider licking the pink stain to see how it tastes. Yet for some reason, perhaps a sliver of sanity or good judgment, I decide against it. Besides, Gods only know what poisonous substances they clean these floors with. Might alter my biome into mutant bacteria trying to kill me.

I stifle the laugh and examine my surroundings.

My cell is small, maybe ten by ten meters at most. The walls, smooth and barren, glow an eerie white. No furnishings, only a small metal square in the center offers my beaten ass no place to rest, so I take the hint and sit down, moaning and groaning from the fatigue and pain in my limbs. The air cold, so cold, sends a thousand shivers down my backside, and I cannot help but think of the Liebhorr. All the while, one red light beep, beep, beeps away the moments of cold nothing. I almost expect a sea serpent to buckle the floor. Almost.

I shiver at the thought of battling a Heat this wounded, the most I have ever been hurt, actually.

For a moment, I wonder if I'm really here. Is this some hallucination from skag? Am I dead and on the other side of Cale's gray eyes, needing to figure out how to look out? Am I back in the no-where of my mind, the no-where of a locked freezer of the spacetime. Hell, I hate being no-where. Or is it no-when? I can't be sure yet.

Shit, I think I would rather be dead if this pain in my head no-goes away or I no-stop making bad no-jokes. Maybe yes, maybe no?

Still no-one shows up to list my crimes here in the no-where/no-when.

I am here for no-one knows how long. Days, hours, weeks in this loop of time in the no-when. How long no-when lasts, this no-body named Isla cannot say.

Bored out of my mind and absolutely sick of my own word play, I reach up and find my braids thankfully intact. I uncurl my unicorn horn and march them out, over and over. Unable to resist, I take my newly won fissured beads out to inspect them further. On the underside, I see a symbol–a letter probably. "J" in some fine language no-one besides me can read?

Then it dawns on me that there is no-way that I look terrified enough to force a reaction from the assholes watching me. I am way too calm despite my beaten body, and I certainly don't look like I'm in withdrawal from no-skag.

A clever plan, not made of flimsy cards, begins to surface in my deceitful, vengeful brain. Time for some caterpillar smoke, I think.

I start shaking, just a little at first. Then I fidget back and forth on this ridiculous stool, stand up and pace, stomp, and breathe heavily. Next, I wail, knowing perfectly well the flashing red light records my image and my pretend moans of gut-wrenching pain. And those fuckers see this fake Isla but are oblivious to the Alice-fish beneath, behind, and even beyond me so determined to take down their queen with the black lies and pronged hooks she teaches me how to use against her.

Pivotal, my inner voice sings while the song about the dawn plays in the back of my mind for Cale.

Then I lean over surreptitiously, hold my stomach, and stick my finger down the back of my throat to induce vomiting.

Immediately after my heaving meltdown, the monitors come in, confirming my suspicion. If I'm afraid, sick, and desperate, then they think there is no-way that I will argue against whatever assignment they offer me.

That means they are more terrified of our refusal than we are of their punishment, that brilliant inner genius assures me.

"Jane, named Isla, confess your crimes," the gray idiot demands, throwing a brown powder on the vomit.

Thankfully, the stink of my gut disappears.

I blubber, snot spewing across my chapped lips to make my act convincing. Then I bury my head into my arm and wail even louder. But really, I'm searching for an answer–the one that will satisfy us all. Here I go on a perpetual quest for plan B in this loop of no-time again, which hopefully looks more attractive than the last possum routine that landed me here to begin with.

"Leave out any details and you will be necrotized for treason," he threatens, shrinking his hooked finger back into his fist to prove it.

I think of Kinley and her bacteria rebalanced by the stolen strains, my medical book, returning late with Gaige, my new band of bairns, the boxes, the broken table, the beetle bug, the stolen a kill...no...a kill e-in...Achillean suit, the flashes I know how to follow in between the spaces of this place. All the countless crimes I commit every day because only obeying imbeciles is legal here in the City of Stupid Rules.

I flash back to the other day–the puffy twins I fooled by my possum act, the words she said about Chancellors, prime Janes, microbiomes, love, subhuman rejects, and numbered races–and my resolve grows exponentially like bacteria in the petri dish of my putrid heart.

After all, I'm an Ink-freak sleeper. *You will do anything for more Ink*, my inner voice reminds me. Well no-shit!

Plan B surfaces–this time covered in bugs instead of huge rats.

"I saw a beetle bug the other day but did not report it," I say, hoping this will suffice. Of course, I skip the part about my new photo from the crack inside the wall and the woman, same as page one hundred and thirty-five with the rounded abdomen.

Those idiots jump on the hook I offer them like no-hungry fish with half a brain ever does. Over and over, way too easily, they gulp down my insect. So, I reel them in helplessly, and they are obviously clueless to the way fish hooks work–bad going in, infinitely worse coming back out.

Once, many years ago, Elder Khaan told me a story about fishing, and I return to the memory of his story now, unable to resist the pull of the conversation's black hole inside my mind.

Flash. I am a small child–four or five at most–peering into the cyclone of how I recall the story.

Suck. I'm through the hole and back out the other side of the memory where Elder Khaan's eyes lit up as he read me the same picture book again. Somehow, I exist in both no-times at the same time–past and present.

He followed the pictures and said the rhyming words, "Red fish, green fish, slow fish, quick fish."

Like a funny song, it made me giggle.

"Fish?" I asked, having never heard of them before.

He bellowed again behind the damaged skin that acted like a mask constricting his face. I heard pleasure in his voice and watched the distance grow in the soft, golden sparkling of his eyes clearly telling me he was already leaving the present and going back in time.

So now in this no-time, I am in the present as I currently experience it, my own past and even Elder Khaan's past all at the same time. Perhaps some-time I shall consider whether or not all of time is nothing more than an illusion and perhaps the tenth dimension is where all-times or no-times exist all at the same-time.

"You don't know about fish, Isla. But I do. Back before the Global War stole the beauty of our Home planet, we used to sit on things called boats and put rods in lakes–big holes in the ground full of water."

I nodded, egging him on. I had never heard of any of these things but acted like I understood because I knew this was going to be good.

"And for bait, we would put a bug or a slimy armless creature called a worm on a hook at the end of the string coming out of the rod."

I tried to imagine the absurd little device and the bizarre creature but couldn't.

Tears welled up in his eyes. At first, what seemed like overwhelming sadness filled them. Then I realized it was not grief but the memory of something powerful that brought him to a place where he couldn't contain the intensity of his emotions. A hole, much like the black hole that brings me back to this very memory of witnessing him having his own memory, inside him opens up for me to look, allowing me to travel deep within him, down to the very best part which is his truest self.

Surely it is one of the most beautiful things I have ever seen—me looking through his black hole while peering inside of my own black hole. Ah!

This time, though, I realize it's the same hole, the same space, the same story inside of me—so deep and wide that is so undeniably beautiful. His story is mine, mine his, all of them the same, really. Why? Because all the memories and stories have always been tied up in a big ball of wire about life and love—the very thing this city's existence lacks by taking the individuality, the luster, the choice, the experience of living and replacing it with the no-where in the no-when for so many no-bodies.

Much like I always do, Elder Khaan gets off track for a moment now, telling me about the importance of keeping stories alive for the next generation. Even if we might live forever, we lose ourselves if we lose our stories. In the olden days, we once wrote them down because we still knew how to do such things. This is why I must practice my letters and words behind closed doors just like he told me to.

He went on to tell me how his Pee-Paw described this one magical fishing excursion. At this point, I didn't interrupt him to ask more details about his Pee-Paw because I didn't want anything to stop him from telling his story. Apparently, Pee-Paw and five other amateur fishermen, frozen like fools, planned to reel in some slimy, scaled creature they never intended to actually eat…just catch and release.

Anyway, this day, the fish apparently spawned everywhere. There were so many trout they almost jumped in the little boat. Here, there, everywhere. And the six of them couldn't unhook them fast enough to stay ahead by throwing them back.

So they all started laughing, roaring and rolling so hard that the boat started rocking. Two of them stood up to reel fish in at the same time—the wrong time, of course—and their boat flipped over on them. Half drowning, half-frozen, his kith members climbed back in the boat and got down to the business of catching more fish—catch and release, more catch, more release.

But Pee-Paw decided to just watch them. Why? Because the watching meant much more to him than catching and releasing the useless fish, which were just an excuse for them to spend time together.

Elder Khaan kept laughing like he was there in the memory. Which, I guess in some ways, he actually was. Like maybe he fell in the water. And I feel like I'm there too even in my memory in present time. Which, I guess I am in a way.

Salt threatens to well up in my eyes, remembering Elder Khaan overflowing with joy at this silly little memory that belonged to someone he always called Pee-Paw. But I refuse to cry, so I make my face flat and expressionless so they won't see my private bliss, which I will not let them steal from me, no-more.

I shudder inside yet remain motionless, half-drowning and half frozen, and make myself an unbreakable vow. One day, I will try this game called fishing. I will rock my boat, and I will purposefully fall over the side. Somehow, under the water, I will find Elder Khaan and his Pee-Paw, and we will laugh together watching all the others play the game of togetherness.

I never even hear a word the idiot monitors say, but what's the use? It's all lies anyway. I think I'd rather play fish in my mind with Elder Khaan. I nod at their stupid words, reeling them in. They jump in my boat, and I catch them, minus any plans to release. Capturing the slimy little turtles, I have no intentions of letting them go. The charade goes on for who knows how long in this no-time. Hours probably.

I cower.

They lie.

I crumble.

They feel superior.

I quiver and shake.

They convince me to be an overseer at the Research and Development Division, or RADD, which directs the work of the BRÉ where I usually go.

I convince them I don't want to.

For retribution for my supposed crime of withholding information, they will only forgive me if I complete this new assignment to their satisfaction. If I can prove I deserve it, they will turn my skag supply back on, maybe even better than before.

Begging for mercy, I ask for skag, anything for more Ink skag.

In exchange for access to a limitless supply, I will spy on the 53s that work in BRÉ and RADD. Each sordid detail I report will win me Ink honors and more squares to feed the growing band of Levana bairns whose lives depend on my rank. And the information will win the monitors an opportunity to necrotize someone new, spreading their flames of fear, which heat up the turtle soup they poison us with.

Hesitantly, all coated in pretend terror, I concede to the arrangement because of the Ink I supposedly want so badly to color me as the skag blinds me, numbs me, and effectively annihilates me. *Whatever*. Fools buy it all.

For fun, they slap me around a little to convince me how lucky I am and that surely I should be so fucking grateful for barely surviving from their overflowing mercy. But in truth, I suspect they celebrate how lucky they just got.

And as usual, everything here flows backward, covered in nonsense. They lose by winning. I win by losing. Such a stupid game for stupid players.

"Oh, one more thing," they say, handing me an overseer's womb cloth to replace my Levana one. "You will be working closely with your new best friend, the Irmin named Jaxston. He is already part of our team of inside strategists. You report to him after the Ink stage tabulation and resource distribution tomorrow."

Silence.

"For now, you must attend an appointment with your Ink dealer in Forty-Four B to complete your overseer level reprogramming. Your new overseer location probe will be implanted."

"Excuse me?"

"Shut up or the deal's off. You are expected in less than twenty minutes. Do not disappoint us, Jane, named Isla. Or the consequences will be severe. For your entire kith and the Salus, too."

"Consequences?"

"Shut the fuck up, I said."

"Yes, sir." Somehow he doesn't realize I had to disobey him to oblige his telling me to shut up. *Idiot.*

"One mistake and they all die while you watch. Then you die slowly and painfully as we gradually necrotize you."

Oh my Gods. What have I done? My whole kith?

I reel back thrashing. Now I'm the fish, and they are safe in a boat.

And the Stain Heats, day two, will start any minute. Who will protect Cale if I am busy getting Inked, busy playing a little turtle spy?

Baylor. Baylor will. I know he will.

Jaxston? What? My partner. My ally? What could be more terrible? *Boom, smash, crash.* I hear my plan B explode all around me. What have I done? My kith–all of them dead. And Baylor and all forty-plus of his bairns?

A new location probe? Why?

Being responsible for them all. Me dead is one thing. But them all? Like Tilly? Guilt-covered stink oozes from my pores. I can't stand my own odor. In one fell swoop, I will murder everyone I have ever loved.

To say I'm terrified to fail them doesn't come close.

Then I hear the Stain Heats bell ring and realize that this is all a joke, a little fluff of nothing compared to my fear of losing Cale–the one who matters more to me than all the other no-bodies combined in this no-life of a life.

Chapter Thirty

"LEVEL TWO OF THE STAIN HEATS," the Lunesta declares. The call sounds inviting, happy, and joyful. It is not. Why? Because instead of running toward that liar's voice, I must race the other way.

As I pace toward building Forty-Four B, I count. Out of spite, I say both the alphabet and the first one hundred numbers out loud. I spit them out, actually. Then I rub my hair to calm me down again.

Then everything disappears for me except for three things: a blood-red half-disk on my right foot, the hot cracked ground, and the image of Cale's sweet face at the finish line, cheering me to win this turtle Heat for what's left of my precious piggies.

And his. And Kinley's. And Baylor. And this time, now that I understand the importance of my mission, all the others' piggies, too.

Just like Baylor, I ask, "How will I save them all?"

Chills race down my back.

Time distorts as though somehow I am trapped in one string of time that moves more quickly than the others, and I can still barely hear the bairns celebrating in their spacetime, which is no longer synchronous with my own. I wonder if I move fast enough and somehow jump from one string to the next, can I return to the moment before this very moment so that their experience of this never occurs? Or better yet, can I return to the sentinel moment that led to this inevitable moment so that even I will never have to suffer it?

They go on whooping, hollering, signing back and forth across lines that will one day define and divide them. If only…I can prevent it all or at least undo the damage by reminding them that we are all the same in that space, that lost tenth dimension so deep and wide where only…or perhaps every…we exist, and that child is child…not Levana, not Salus, not Irmin. If so, then keeping this turtle zoo will be worth it. Even if I die, it will be worth it. But what if I fail?

I try to deny my hearing, hoping to delay the guilt of being the source of so much suffering to come. If I fail, they die. Not only one bairn but every bairn. So many, so unfair. And I will carry the burden of knowing I could have done so much better by all those adorable piggies.

First, the red mound on my right foot rises like the fullness of dawn coming into view. Then, the gritty orange sand scrapes the underside of my pink toes.

A tunnel, the same vortex of fear, encases me. And just like in every Heat, I know I have two choices: win or lose, past or present, all of my Cale or none of him, live or die, verus or loser.

Holding on to my one...or perhaps every...string of altered spacetime, I hear the sound of my heartbeat echo in the tunnel. My ears fill up with pressure, and numbness surrounds me just like always as I enter this altered vibration. Or does it enter me? I just can't be sure yet.

This void leaves only my beating heart to match the rhythm of the alternating sun and sand. The rest of me goes into autopilot once more. Or is it every-pilot? I just can't be sure yet.

First, the red sun. Then, the orange sand.

The red. The orange.

The sun. The sand.

The dawn. The dusk.

And I am too afraid to acknowledge the third thing hanging on my every move, the only one that matters to me, really: the every face–Cale's face.

Lub-dub. Sun-sand.

Lub-dub. Sun-sand.

Lub-dub. Red-orange.

Lub-dub. Red-orange.

The Gridiron rushes by me, and yet again I do not bother to worry about fences and the Frightening. I've lost all terror of them and the kill fields, those boring adversaries who have nothing on the clock tick, tick, ticking away my last few days in reprogramming before I ship out to play little spy. The same evil clock proudly ticking away the last few days of the bairns' freedom.

Unless, of course, I can fool the timepiece first. Or is it last? Who can be certain in a second like this?

I think of Alice's white rabbit and his pocket watch. If possible, I might ask him how long a second is anyway. But why shall I bother saying something as ridiculous as that if I already know the answer–sometimes, just one forever. Or do I have that backward, too? *Ah, too!*

I am almost there–to Forty-Four B, to the new location probe, to the new Ink, to my new piggies. I list out the number of bairns I know by name now. There are so few yet so many of them. Or is it only one? I just can't remember anymore.

Then I count out the days: one, two, only two more left. There will be three days total of Heats to indoctrinate the bairns in the sport the Mozek abuse to entertain and eventually divide them.

At the end of each event, they tabulate the scores. The highest-ranking bairns assume the first takeoff positions for the following day.

Today, Cale and Baylor's two race in front. Each win for them means another double-Ink and access to one more tool for survival–extra hydration boxes, energy supply, or weapons to fight off the others. Or maybe even secret information on how to avoid a deadly obstacle.

I might wonder what instrument Cale will chose, but I already know the answer– probably the curved bladed sica. The one he alters in the thraex, the machine he can manipulate in his mind.

His beautiful mind is built perfectly for this game. He is way too good at it–same as me. Same as me… It's like the same gift I have runs through his veins too, like I gave it to him because he is an extension of me, as though he has always been an extension of me, just like the lady with the rounded abdomen whose cliff is my cliff and who pays me forward so I can pass the currency on.

A knowing, a memory, or more like an anti or parallel remembrance, bubbles forth. Something important, something that ties regret to Baylor. It makes me want to collapse and disappear in the red sand.

In terrible pain from the thought of it, I almost stop running. Almost. It weighs down so heavy, so dark, so big, like with Tilly. It smells and tastes exactly the same– like I murder Cale, like I kill Baylor, like I intentionally kill them all.

The silly pig song plays in my mind once more. *This little piggy had none.*

But how can that be possible? I haven't killed them. Not yet, anyway. So why do I feel like I already have? Like I own the fault here instead of the Mozek? For all of it– the City, the Heats, the liquid knives?

And this little piggy cried wee, wee, wee all the way Home.

I can't carry the heaviness anymore, so I look from the sand on my feet as I loop around the edge so close to the glass that separates and imprisons me from the dunes, the Frightening, and finding our way back Home.

The Gridiron lights up with fireworks as the event begins to distract me like all the others. The booms sound identical to a deadly weapon, and I can't help but wonder if it is a celebration or a massacre or both at the same time. If so, then who is the party really for? Surely not the 53s. Maybe the Chancellors?

I step through both entry scanners in Forty-Four B, trying not to throw up more stinking gut rot. The machines assault and violate me. And much to my dismay, the only thought piercing my mind when Gaige takes my hand on the other side is, *I did this all. It is my fault. I deserve this abuse because I already killed them all and will always kill them again.*

Unable to escape my own hatred, I think about the Heats as we walk, silently as usual, to the Ink chamber.

Each second and third placed winner in today's Heats will be awarded one Ink and a meager advantage over the others. The lowest ranked bairn will not be invited back for the following Heats. They will be sent with the medicals, although I'm not sure why. How will Rest and Relaxation help them do better next time?

Unable to stop her, the goddess inside my mind provokes my continued thoughts on the subject. *Isla, you know perfectly well why. Think about it.*

Oh my Gods, seriously?

All of a sudden, I suspect what those words really mean, what they really hide. The losers will go to R&R, where we all go according to Tilly, where her body went down the blooming drain.

The lowest ranking bairn does not come back because the liquid knives made of acid murder them. *Assholes.*

In addition to mounting rewards for those left, as the days go by, the Heats get harder, more dangerous, more deadly. *Double assholes.*

Each Heat, longer and more competitive than the last, will kill more. By the end of the Heats, the surviving bairns will all hate each other, supplied with a lifetime's motivation to battle each other, to avoid friendship. Effectively guaranteeing they will never work together to find their way out of this hellhole because their hearts and wires are ruined by clamps and cutters. *Triple assholes.*

Then after the final Heat, the Mozek dole out the assignment card levels. The higher a bairn ranks at the end, the more deadly but prestigious the cards he can run. And also the more possible Ink honors, rewards, resources, addictions. So if Cale wins the whole thing like Jaxston or I, by the time it is over, he will have essentially managed his basic needs yet simultaneously isolated himself from friendship and assured himself of skag addiction. Brilliant. Terrible. *Quadruple assholes.*

Confined in here, I am powerless to protect him.

Gaige, sighing and huffing the whole time, straps me in the Ink projector, bringing me back to being a four year old all over again. All my stolen choices smash and scatter across the floor. What choice? There is none here in the City of Whips and Chains.

Speaking of belts, is he really about to do this to me?

I guess so.

Chapter Thirty-One

PANIC CREEPS IN, and my pulse quickens.

I give Gaige a look of, *"But you promised."*

He looks away nervously, obviously injured by my fierce and accusing eyebrows that demand he change his treacherous ways.

I hate him for it. He's a lying piece of shit like all the others.

He bends over acting like he's checking the instrument panel. Instead, he places his fingers briefly to his heart twice. I'm too disgusted to willingly apply the meaning of his ridiculous gesture. *"Levana in my heart. You in my heart."*

I see but do not acknowledge. I refuse. I also refuse to feel nervous or at least look it. Clearing my throat, I roll my eyes.

He straightens back up to face me, his eyes digging in hoping to find mercy in mine that isn't there to be found.

"This isn't part of my plan," he whispers.

But I will not consider his pleas or give him my forgiveness. I break eye contact, refusing to lock glares with those eyes determined to look into, not through me while they betray me. What does he think I am? An idiot, a glutton, a sucker for never ending abuse? Screw him.

He lays the projector's Ink table down flat quickly. Too quickly. Startled, my eyes search for reassurance in his. Then he makes that same face–the one I want to hate more than I actually do.

The straps firmly clamp across my limbs, rubbing painfully into my cuts and bruises. My cuffs hold my wrists down tightly, too tightly. My chaffed legs spread just enough to expose the opening inside of me under my cloth. Chills assault my ass as the cold steel table sends goosebumps down my legs and back up again.

Am I angry, disgusted, afraid? Or am I excited? Honestly, a little of all of the above, I think. Or is it below? I just can't be sure yet, can I?

"Maybe I need a new plan?" he asks.

I grunt and then wonder what he means.

"Plan B, perhaps?" he says. He raises his eyebrow, obviously planning something I don't quite have a word for. But the idea of it is familiar; I am sure now. Trying to suppress it, I feel the warmth within me take over and cloud my thoughts, soften my hatred, ease my disgust, lubricate away every bad thought I ever had about that creep.

Crap.

Honestly, I'm gripping helplessly for my anger with my gnarled teeth at this point, trying desperately to keep my hold on it. I snarl as my intensity oozes out of me and moistens my womb cloth, but unfortunately, the only response I get is a bigger grin on that face of his.

Creep.

"Oh yes, Isla"–he pauses–"Jane, just say it. Say yes once."

If I had access to my hands, I would reach up and touch his penciled beard…right before I slap him. Then I might wrap my legs around his back and…I don't know… pull him toward my body. But I most certainly will not say that word he wants me to. I might think it, but I won't say it. *Yes.*

"No," I say, my voice raspy and low.

He traces the outlines of my superficial wounds, his touch as soft as the underside of my tongue. He whispers, "You mean yes. I know you do."

His words remind me of a connection I can't place but want to, want to wrap my legs, maybe my entire body around. I want it so badly that I am willing to melt like elixir for it.

Tenderly, he caresses my imperfections like he wants to make them heal faster or even replace them with tenderness instead. It's almost like he thinks they are his fault to begin with, and I bet that if he learns how to go back in time, he will stop them from ever happening.

Maybe he's only mostly a creep.

"Say yes, baby, please," he whispers again. And the *please* drips off his chin and lands on my toes, the same piggies no longer trying to get out of these straps. I consider stepping in his tempting *please* then but decide that maybe wrapping it all around me like one of these firm leather belts sounds far more interesting. Part of me gets angry at the other part of me wanting to do such a stupid thing. Partially pissed at my wet anticipation of his continued attention to my skin, I shake my head. "No," I whisper.

No, he's just a creep like the rest. I try to think it twice, but honestly, my grip on the whole idea is slipping through my fingers, much like his *please* is slipping through my toes–all so much quicker and slicker than I care to admit.

I notice the subtle red light flashing and know the Mozek are watching us. He has no choice but to leave the straps in place even though my bruises keep spreading from their pressure. The Mozek intend to record this whole session. Shocker.

Maybe you're only mostly a creep, I suppose.

Yet still I plan on hating him for it even if my body switches teams and joins him against me.

242

"Bastard," I say.

He takes the sting but says nothing. He just stares at me and raises his right eyebrow higher. Another grin, bigger this time, follows. Then his tongue escapes, flittering around like a lady beetle bug from a crack in the wall, excited by the possibility of escape, and scuttles across his tasty lower lip.

Shit. I'm in big trouble, and it's only getting bigger.

Yes. I push the word away and replace it with a no. *No.*

I hear him in my mind. *"They said it would take a lot to convince you to trust me."*

I shake my head again, flushing the delicious thoughts of chewing on his tongue from the deepest pockets in my conflicted mind. I will show no tolerance. Yet, for some reason, I feel the folds of my womb swell and prepare themselves to gather him. For what exactly, I can't be sure.

Or…will he gather me? I just can't be sure yet. *Yes, I can.*

Damn it.

Swiftly, he kicks on the skag machine. Even though I am looking away, I see him shake his head back and forth. *No, no, no,* just like I do when I'm torn inside, about to pull an Alice move against my better judgment.

He whispers, "Fuck it," and disconnects the projector. Then he trails his finger around my navel, sucking in his breath, now more raspy than mine, and holds on to it for dear life. But it's not his finger in my mind, it's his tongue and his dripping mouth fluttering across my wounded skin as those wings take flight. Cleaning my skin, healing it, evolving it, molding it, transforming it, owning it. Or is it owning me? I just can't be sure yet.

Yes, I can.

He subtly unstraps my hands, leaving me unchained except the bands across my legs. Grabbing the Ink glove next, he clicks it into place and groans. That groan follows the *please* from earlier; only this time, it lands right between my flexed thighs.

No projector. Thank Gods. Perhaps I should offer him some mercy after all? My thighs relax briefly. But then I decide not to, and they tighten even more firmly because, to be honest, I'm not the merciful type toward lying bastards.

He connects then swiftly disconnects the skag hose fast, so fast that I can't be sure what is happening. The roaring engages when he kicks the foot pedal one more time. I close my eyes, not sure if the skag is coming or not.

No skag. Please, no skag.

Then I remember I am supposed to be hooked on it. So I think of what other things I am hooked on. One thing surfaces–his eyes, so purple I cannot name their color. Well, a few others as well, to be honest. Like his penciled beard and that groan still swirling inside me.

It's all coming back to me. *Shit.* Oh, the way his eyes make me feel.

But I'm just playing Ink-freak junkie, right? So I decide to toy with the image for a while, which isn't even close to showing compassion considering my circumstances. It's just self-preservation, really. Or is it?

Even now, I know better. But since I have let my guard down, I am useless. I'm already too far in, unable to follow my own advice. My softer…or perhaps wetter…side wins again. *Alice.* I condemn and compliment myself, dying to rub my hands up and down his yummy face.

Purple, purple, purple–the color infuses me with a violet passion, and I admit that I want to be an Alice again, so badly.

Fuck it.

"Yes." My split mind joins its two halves and dives into my heart. A soft moan escapes my slightly parted lips, and Gaige knows I am playing along with his little game.

In perfect response, he says, "Yes, fuck it. Fuck me," a little louder this time while un-clicking his Ink glove, letting it bounce off the floor and roll across the room, trying to catch up with his *please* that now coats the floors, walls, and even the ceiling so it can drip down on me from above.

Before I can truly comprehend what is happening, he violently rips my thigh straps off and turns me over, facedown. Within a few seconds, the table modifies to accommodate my new position. A middle space opens in the headrest to accept my face just as I feel him tug down hard on my braids. The sensation, simultaneously painful and arousing, forces my body into total stillness. The elixir gathering inside me multiplies exponentially.

I cannot see but certainly can hear him click the arm and leg boards back into position. Then he swiftly but tenderly straps my arms and thighs back down, this time with a cold steel board under each foot for a support and a rubbery handle for each of my hands to grip. He places his wanton face into my back and pushes down hard, pressuring and soothing me simultaneously.

Gasping with small, quick breaths, he reaches over to the antique Prime Ink Tray–the one people first used when humans initially surrendered to their undeniable obsession for the pleasures of Ink.

I hear the viewing holster open, able to visualize what it contains from memory without even looking. *Smash.* His hands break the glass protective layer to gain access to the precious artifacts.

Me, a sliver but the whole layer of fragile glass shatters like a million glass fractals all over the ground. I imagine the two-coil electromagnetic tattoo iron whose barred needle grouping will push Ink into my skin as well as the archaic cloth that will wipe away the Ink mixed with my blood.

Now I can understand why the others liked it so much.

Unable to stop myself, I moan softly again, offering up my permission as his actions saturate me like oil drip, drip, dripping off my skin before a Heat. My approval soaks him in return, which pleases me. Oh damn how it pleases me.

With the full weight of his body on my backside, I sense the impressive firm fullness of his finishing stick between his legs and cannot help but notice how similar it is to the shape of the Ink iron. And unable to explain exactly why or how it is possible, I want that fullness inside my every opening.

"Say yes again, please," he buzzes, and that word starts swirling around the room like a two-winged bug destined to teach me something I do not already know about myself.

Please. Yes, please.

I lick my lips.

After all, if I'm going to reel in the whole school of fish with my little performance, I better make this good. So I make it good, real good, so good that even I almost believe it. Or does it believe me? I'm not sure.

Or maybe I am more merciful than I thought, even to lying bastards? Or maybe lying bastards are more merciful than I thought? Or maybe it's something so much more than forgiveness?

Damn, how can anybody be sure of anything in a moment like this–this second that I hope will last forever just like the white rabbit said. Besides, right now, I couldn't care less about anything less than forever in this one brief but eternal second.

"Yes."

He laughs and presses his throbbing stick down harder on my backside.

Chapter Thirty-Two

"YOU WANT IT. I know you do," he says. And I might deny the truth in his accusation, but I hate liars as much as thieves and maybe even more than skag.

"Creep." I gasp, nodding *yes* while my desire to feel Gaige's lips on mine consumes me, taking over what pathetic willpower I have left. It swallows me whole, minus any apology. Me, this Isla, slicked up from the inside.

He reaches around the table and places his right index finger on my lower lip. Unable to deny this smaller shaft either, I draw it in willingly. Slowly at first and then more forcibly, I pull on it with my mouth until I am able to suck and lick it like a sweet square.

Leaning over my back, the fullness of his finishing stick intensifies further, shocking me with its expanded size and unimaginable hardness. It calls my name with an insatiable desire to impress and penetrate every defect within me.

And much to my surprise, another answer offers itself as he whispers my name, allowing clarity to infuse me with purpose. Moisture saturates my womb cloth and drips down my thigh, my piggies wholly certain of my body's proper response in this second. Or is it this forever?

I know exactly what I want from him, exactly what he wants from me–both now and for all time because I always have. So has he, I bet.

My breathing shortens and quickens, escaping all illusion of my ability to control or maintain normal vital signs. Even though I am essentially prone, my thighs strapped down, I can no longer fight the urge to rock my hips front to back with a slight circular motion, gathering speed and pull and time as I press down on the foot bars.

Once he starts the Ink, I will be unable to move, so I better dance now for his pleasure. When I am frozen in that spacetime forever more…I want, no, I need him to feel the moves I can no longer make for him–my delightful Ink dealer–until that eternal second passes and I can move again.

He takes his finger out of my mouth, and I beg for its return, yet he refuses me the pleasure of having it back while he traces my own saliva across my back, saying my name slowly in a light whisper. "Isla, my Jane. My beautiful baby Jane, you are the worthy one. I knew I would find you again. I knew it, baby. I've been waiting so long."

"Yes," I reply.

His oil lubricates my internal chassis uncontrollably as the heat in my center rises even hotter. Is the whole room spinning? Or am I spinning? I just can't be sure as I twirl around the room like his *please* and grunts on the buzzing wings of an insect from earlier. Fuck. Now I'm the one dripping off the ceiling and down onto me.

Is the machine vibrating for us, urging us on? I cannot say. I've never felt like this before–so hot, so famished, so in tune with my entire surroundings while lost in the possibility of what is about to happen in the coming seconds. Or is it forevers? Gods, let me be sure, please. Oh how I had no idea how I'd been starving until I tasted this possibility of pleasure in so much pain.

And even though I cannot see myself, I sense how beautiful I am, glowing like this, through his eyes that peer into, not through me. The same eyes urging, drawing, begging me into his intimate space, so deep, so wide.

His breathing matches mine as he graciously allows me to set the pace even though I can't pace myself. He holds the electric pen in his right hand as he uses his left to rub and pull and pinch my backside. So in gratitude for the allowance, I open my gate to his intensity by welcoming it, willing it to come to me, press into me, mold me, shift me, transform me, own me. *Claim me, please. Make me yours. Only when I am yours can I truly be free.*

Silently, I beg him to make a thousand holes inside me, filling them with his Ink, his unique flavor of colored liquid–the only…or perhaps every…fluid that can perfectly fill the holes that he might make as he penetrates me. My gray insides yearn to be painted with his watercolors too gorgeous to name, so I demand his art paint me the colors only he can create with his brushstrokes on my body.

The faint touch of his left finger traces down my outer thighs, across the inner surface of my knees, and back up my inner thighs. But my annoying womb cloth keeps getting in his way while he marks this outline for my Ink, delaying the inevitable piercing pain…or perhaps pleasure…of his fine, sharp instrument.

Do I recognize the shape he draws as an outline across my full and welcoming buttocks? The same one he now continues down the canvas of my flexing and relaxing inner leg muscles. Or does it recognize me?

Does it matter? Probably not.

In frustration, he moves my womb cloth again, trying to draw around it. Then his impatience gets the better of him. He says, "Fuck it," while he sets the Ink pen down.

He walks to the head of the table, turns my head to the side, and rubs his cheek on my cheek, hard. Then he puts two of his fingers back in my mouth, massaging my tongue as I suck them in response.

"For Gods' sakes, kiss me, Jane," he demands, pulling his fingers out and replacing them with the wings of his fluttery tongue.

A half-formed "yes" is the only response I can manage to mumble as I try to hold on to the insect in my mouth.

Finally, he allows me to catch the bug and presses that wet, muscular beast into the back of my mouth–hard, harder, harder still in the most delightful way.

Before I can possibly get enough, he pulls it away, leaving me begging, dying for one more dose of the liquid skag inside him.

With just this one dose, I am helplessly hooked–a Gaige Ink-freak junkie drowning in my fluids that seep for his muscular tongue and the pressure of it back inside my hungry mouth. He repositions my head and straps it down tightly so that I am totally locked into place without any control over my wiggling body. He slaps my buttocks to still me once more.

Perfectly motionless from the sting of my skin, I gyrate on an imaginary screen that only the two of us can see. Those useless Mozek may record me, but they will not see what I am doing. My caterpillar smoke motions, disguised in my stillness, please him. Or do they please me? Hmmm.

Both, I am sure of it.

As he stretches my skin taut, he makes the first puncture of the outlined image with the needle. *Yes. More.* This, his first entry inside me, underneath my skin and even beyond it, hurts but soothes simultaneously.

He moves slowly at first, but I want more, and this speed will never do. I'm begging now. *Go faster.*

He tries, but my womb cloth gets in the way again. So he rips it off and shoves it in my mouth. I bite down on it and smile, delighted to find something able to replace his bugger of a tongue.

A bell rings somewhere far off in the distance.

He pauses briefly.

"Fuck it," he says one more time and proceeds.

Something tells me that this is not the reprogramming the Mozek are planning for me.

If I wasn't gagged, I might consider asking him to describe the design he intends to Ink, but what's the point? He is a freaking liar like the rest of them, so how can I believe a word he says?

His pictures mean nothing to me.

Who's the liar now?

Even as I think this, to be honest, I already know. I want his instrument, his design, his iron intensity to join with mine.

Why?

Because I want, no, I need to believe every dirty little lie he tells me.

The hoses of his machine roar, and I press firmly against my feet, anticipating his next move; the shading layer will surely come next.

Back and forth, back and forth–black, gray, and every shade in between, his colors so full of pleasure and pain.

He presses into my backside, rolling back and forth, claiming my backside as his private property to mold and modify and color like only he can. *Claim me, please. Make me the only one who belongs to you.*

He wipes.

He pauses to examine his work.

The waiting, the wanting more kills me, so I start sucking on the cloth. The sound pleases him; I am certain that it pleases me too.

"Taste it, Isla," he says. 'Taste the desire you drip for me, baby."

I must have more of his needle–now.

He takes the cloth out of my mouth and replaces it with a sponge soaked in a slightly minty liquid from his tray and begins again. *Thank Gods.*

Shade. Wipe. Press. Wipe.

He gasps and moans. "Yes, Jane. Draw it out, girl. Draw me out, my love."

The vibration, the sound, the experience thrills me. But I want, no, I need more. The needle piecing my buttocks, the arch of my lower back, my hot and undulating thighs as I suck on the sponge isn't enough. I want, no, I need more, damn it.

What, what do I need?

His undeniable firmness inside me, pushing my body to the limit. But that's impossible, isn't it?

I shudder. But it is neither from fear nor cold. It is everything…or perhaps the only thing…else. His flawless burn and peppermint scent sears me outside, inside, and everywhere in between as I draw his liquid farther into me and try, oh how I try, to hold on to it and let it become one with mine.

My buttocks involuntarily spasm, the movement spreading down my leg, across my foot, wrapping around my slippery toes as more of my salt spills onto the floor and across his piggies.

This little piggy wants...

His pace quickens. Then slows.

Wants more.

He wipes and moves faster once more.

Wants so much more.

A drop of blood rolls down my thigh, mixing with my salt, and I love it, love displaying my colorful flavors on the floor for him to see.

No, this little piggy needs more.

He smashes the black Ink against the wall. He will color me now in hues too gorgeous to name. Purple, brown, blue, yellow? These useless words mean nothing to us.

The pressure deepens. Lightens.

He wipes. Presses. Wipes again.

He throws one color aside. Grabs another.

Pushes in. Pulls back.

This little piggy cries out.

A vibration inside me increases. It pulls in and pushes out at the same time. It gathers and withdraws. My face flushes, trying to draw it out further.

"Suck me, Jane. Suck our love like you mean it, baby." He gasps, and I do just like he tells me to because I am a good little girl.

He wipes. Presses.

More blood oozes.

This little piggy bleeds for you, my dealer.

Yet still, I say nothing. Why bother? Words are utterly useless.

He hurts me so good. Soothes me back to okay.

Coats. Uncovers.

Pulls. Pushes.

Undulates. Stills.

Gathers. Releases.

This little piggy...oh,oh,oh.

He wipes. Presses. Wipes again more firmly.

More blood drip, drip, dripping off me and onto his bare skin. My oil mixes with his oils, the colors blending together like a perfect rainbow of love wrapped in a wire so tight, so strong, so hard, so soft, so moist, so dry, so salty, so broken, yet so perfect.

Unable to hold motionless any longer, I shake the handles. Without hesitating, he lessens the grip of his supporting hand and unstraps my left hand, which he places between my slippery thighs.

While still Inking my backside, he shoves my fingers inside me, showing my how exactly to place them into the deep, wet folds, and I vibrate both inside and out from the experience.

This little piggy fingers...

His throbbing digits take over, replacing mine, and I grab his wrist, pushing in and forcing him to do it harder. Like I want it now—harder.

But then faster. Slower.

Deeper. Lighter.

Sharing the glory of the penetrating pain and the pleasure with him.

The needle and fingers, in perfect timing, meet my skin, each time more effectively than the last, bringing the color in.

Caressing it. Trapping it.

Into my space so deep and wide.

The hotness increases.

Overtakes me.

Raises me up so high, higher than any skag ever dared to take me.

This little piggy...yes,yes,yes.

My desire reaches a point, a climax so fulminating that it will not be denied. My buttocks spasm again, and he presses down harder than ever before as I stop sucking the sponge and bite down instead. Then I swallow a drop of my own blood. *Delicious. I've been starving.*

He drops the pen and moans with me as my release consumes everything.

This little piggy explodes within you and you within me.

Nothing else matters but our union, our symphony, our song, our picture. Me—the violin, him—the player. Me—the canvas, him—the painter.

He kicks the priceless archaic Ink needle across the room, and without withdrawing his left hand, makes a motion that I cannot see or feel. Suddenly, the throbbing pressure of his bare finishing stick presses against my shivering back, and with one hot and demanding thrust, he coats me in a warm, minty gel that spews from him onto me.

This little piggy coats me in his elixir.

The ointment, the salve, feels so good–like ice on my fire, warm sun on my skin frozen from hanging like a bag in the Liebhorr for way too many years. Instantly, I want every drop of the ointment he ever has to offer all for myself both in this second and in this forever. *More, please.*

He pulls back the hand from inside me and moves it round in rapid circles on my backside filling every hole anyone has ever made to my exterior with the solution to my every…or perhaps my only…interior problem. Harder and harder, he rubs his mint into my skin until I think I will ignite again. How is that possible? How can this intensity fire again?

Graciously, he pulls the minty sponge from my mouth and replaces it with his dripping fingers, still rubbing the hot goo into my skin, now in my mouth. His flavor, exactly the same as the sponge, joins with my salt, and we are one intertwined flavor.

Oh no. Here I go again.

This little piggy…oh yes, please. More, even more.

A tingling, a vibration coming from inside me instead of the iron or even his fingers, overtakes my mid-section and then escapes in overwhelmingly intense spasms of bliss no words can describe.

Even love is too small to define this.

My insides rupture open for him to see a second time, deep down into the best, the most honest part of me–the part that is already him because it is we.

Gasping, he unstraps my thighs, lays the table flat, and flips me back over to face him, so I open my eyes for him to show his purple back to him, too gorgeous to name.

And he displays my blue, too gorgeous to name.

And like usual, words are still totally worthless to the two of us. So I say nothing. And he says nothing back, which says everything all at once.

He lays his moist chest on mine, and in perfect timing, breathes in and out with me. At first, my breath is more rapid and gasping than his like in the stairwell. But then over time, my respirations and pulse slow down–slow, slower, slower still to match his. Without even trying, I feel his heartbeat directly under his skin come through and finally enter my body so willing to bring him into my space again.

Then I realize that I will never deny him–this purple-eyed master who I cannot refuse, cannot push out of that place in me. Our wires are just too crossed, too raveled, too intertwined.

And for a second that seems to last forever, I am his, and he is mine as we lie together on the Ink table. There is no fear, no goon trying to kill me, no zoo to keep, no lies to tell, no soup to swallow, only salt and mint.

He kisses my mouth as softly as a beetle bug's whispering wings, and my entire body tingles from our joy. And we lie here for nowhere near long enough when the unthinkable happens.

I hear them before I see them. They are coming to kill us; I am sure.

The doors crash open while a band of angry monitors rush in, slinging guns and cuffs. I'm taken immediately back to a memory that is mine but is also not mine. *This is my fault.*

I've been here before.

I have failed them all…in much the same way. I kill them all and fail my test. Cale, Baylor, so few yet so many bairns will die. All of it my fault just like last time. Shame floods me. Regret poisons me. Joy abandons me.

I should fight back and grab the gun while I sling the cuffs on the monitors instead of my dealer. I must kill them, drop them all down the gray pool in R&R to punish them for my guilt, for my failure in this second like so many before it.

"Screw you, assholes," I mutter, still too gasping and breathless to speak clearly.

But just before I grab the closest gun and shoot one of them, Gaige rolls out his arms in submission. They cuff him and slam him up against the wall. *Smack.* His head crashes into the concrete. I expect to see his blood drip down the wall and join my fluids on the floor, but there is none. *No red equals no dead. What?*

Time stops. I shiver, cold like all the countless versions of me hanging in the forever of the Liebhorr–my personal hell.

The entire world disappears, and I accept that I just lost something so precious that I can never hope to name it. But I try to anyway because I need a word to scream or I will die instead of him. "Gaige!"

As my words echo off the unstained wall, I hear the monitor in front curse. "You creepy fucking dealers never get it, do you? You're a prisoner here. You don't own her. You cannot finish with her. She belongs to somebody else. Not you. Never you. You crossed the line, ID named Gaige. You will perish at her doyen's hand."

Gaige shakes his head *yes* and forcibly pulls his gaze from me. He doesn't even argue–like he knows this is supposed to happen, almost like he planned it to begin with. Almost.

He looks at me, his eyes unable to hold mine, and says, "I'm sorry, Jane. I lost control. There was another way. We've lost everything again. I never should have…"

"What?" I ask, confused about what this can possibly mean.

The monitor snarls, "Minister Jaziah, her doyen, witnessed your little Ink session right after he purchased her for his gravaex holocoital chamber. And he will not be pleased with you using that iron to Ink that of all banned Ink designs. Only he can finish with her. You will hang as a traitor."

"Isla Jane? What do you have to say for yourself, you whore?" another spews. Briefly, something flashes into and back out of its eyes.

I am too shocked to question the green…or perhaps anti-green…light.

Instead, I collapse.

Blocking out the sounds around me, I disappear into a string of spacetime so small that no noise from this dimension will ever find me. Lost, like the infamous tenth dimension, I will never let the sounds of this place find me again.

Why?

Because just like all the colors, they are useless to my deaf ears because Gaige is gone and never coming back to call my name again. I will never hear that *please* again, locked out of the harmony of the land of the Gods forever now that I have heard the sweet flavor of his Ink, his nectar, his thrusting flavor and salt mixed with mine as I call out his name and say "yes."

There can only be "no" now. Just like with Cale.

If I don't hear anything, I can still pretend that he's just leaving and will be back, right? What smash? What boom of the fire gun? I don't hear it. It isn't real.

Maybe I'm a possum with plugged ears and that is it, after all. I'm not an Alice, not even a fish out of water. I'm a deaf and dumb possum.

Yet my fucking gills still gargle trying to find the bubbling air in the water that no longer exists to strangle me.

The puffy steps over my body, foaming. "Mutant Ink Jane bitch. Who the fuck do you think you are, slave? Her? You fool."

I also make-believe I never hear this.

Then they are gone…just gone.

I lie here for some indeterminate number of hours, trying not to remember what I do not hear before the doors open again.

A female puff arrives to escort me to my new isolation cell to recover. If she says something to me, I don't hear that either. Besides, why listen to her lies? What's the point? There is nothing she can possibly say that might help me now that I know what songs are possible to harmonize.

I arrive silent and speechless, unable to come up with enough gumption to look into these colorless eyes of mine. But a subtle flash of anti-green catches my eye. Or does my eye catch it? I am too devastated to be sure. Trying to find the source of the light, I look up and stare into a mirror I didn't fully notice when I first came in.

So many things a dumb and blind person cannot notice, I guess. But then I do notice the reflective glass. Or does it notice me? Does it matter which? Definitely not, I am sure.

Why?

Because in a second like this, nothing matters, not even forever because my prison mirror reflects the last thing I ever expect to see. Underneath my navel stamp, peaking from underneath my chafed thighs, draping close my womb…

What? Impossible?

Gasping, I turn around to see…or perhaps hear…a better view over my shoulder and inspect my buttocks. Spilling onto my rear is Ink so gorgeous, so bright, so full of dawn, so full of possibility that I cannot pull my eyes or my ears from it–a beautiful sun to match the one on my foot. Almost. It almost matches. But there is one small but oh-so-huge difference. Not one but two, ah *too,* and this rising sun can never be covered up.

But that is not the difference. This difference matters so much more.

Laughing, I flash back to a memory when I almost asked a question that I wasn't ready to. But now I am.

"Not what, but who is the Rising Sun? Who is the Rising Sun–same as my foot and now backside, same as Gaige's, Skylar's, and Baylor's Ink?"

Staring at my new Ink in total disbelief, I sink into the different that means nothing will ever be the same again. Can this be true?

"Pivotal," I say to myself, and the Augur's voice echoes in confirmation.

"Yes, Isla Jane. Pivotal."

How could I have missed it for so long?

A hundred glances, another hundred conversations scuttle inside, through, behind, and beyond my eyes as the significance sets in.

"Fuck off, Augur," I say.

The voice laughs before it trails away, whispering, "Good girl. My good girl."

Chills coat me head to toe, so I ask again. Only this time, I am screaming, and it is no longer a question but a declaration. "Who is the Rising Sun!"

The possible answers warm and sing to me like a two-winged bird riding the sun. The precious song fills my mind, and for the first time, I truly understand the meaning underneath, behind, and even beyond the words:

In a sea of blinding darkness,
    You are my shining light.
    Without your rays,
    There's only night.
    Will you rescue me,
    And set things right?

My dawn. My only dawn.
    My dawn. My dawn.

So take these eyes,
    And give them sight.
    That search for you,
    On the hope you might.

My dawn. My only dawn.
    My dawn. My dawn.

Your glowing beauty,
    Framed in fight.
    And precious rays…
    I alter the next line, adding,
    Of warm liquid delight.

. . .

My dawn. My only dawn.
  My dawn. My dawn.

In a sea of blinding darkness,
  You are my shining light.
  Can't you see?
  Won't you be?
  The dawn that overcomes,
  So big and bright.

My dawn. My only dawn.
  My dawn. My dawn.

And I translate the confusing term, the lyrics "my dawn", which is not a common noun describing the rising time of the sun but the name beneath the name of a person. "Who is Dawn?" I ask. I'd wait for an answer, but I am pretty sure I already know her. Not dawn, but Dawn.

Is there any possible way for me to deny the obvious any longer?

For sure, she's the only one...or perhaps every one...who can bring out the sun shining again, so I yell at her once more. "Who is the Rising Sun! Who is Dawn!"

Where has she gone? How do I help her save us? I have been here before, looking for her. Actually, we have all been here before; I am sure of it. Well, almost. The difference–this time, I have finally found her.

Trembling, I look at her in the mirror and wink like I usually do to accent the beauty of her, I mean my oddly colored eyes. The same coolant blue brilliance as the eye in the center of the rising sun on my backside. The same. Exactly the same.

And more certain than I have ever been of anything I have ever known before, I answer my own question. "I am the Rising Sun. I am. I am. I am Dawn. I will save us all. And I am the only one who can."

Although it might just be my imagination, I hear a soft and sweet voice enter my mind one more time in response. "You are such a good girl. Bless you, beloved one. As you rise, the City will fall."

About the Author

A. Nicky Hjort is originally from the greater Dallas-Fort Worth area of Texas. She writes stories that cross multiple genre lines, from paranormal romance to Sci-Fi thrillers and back again. And in some subtle way, all of her manuscripts are connected, with their purpose to explore all facets of love and what it has to teach us. Her journey into writing began with her clinical background as a medical doctor when she wrote her first fictional short story about medicine. She hasn't stopped writing since.

Facebook author page: https://www.facebook.com/Author.A.N.Hjort
Twitter: @A_NickyHjort
Website: www.anickyhjortbooks.com
Blog: www.ANickyHjortBooks.com
Instagram: https://www.instagram.com/nickyhjort

Also by A. NICKY HJORT

Other Works By A. Nicky Hjort

https://www.amazon.com/A.-Nicky-Hjort/e/B01M30LVVM/

A Sinister Bouquet: Awakening - Book 1: Devyn Mitchell has a choice… listen to the voice of her unborn baby – or die- again. After a near death experience, Doctor Devyn Mitchell finds herself not only mysteriously pregnant but able to communicate with her fetus. She has two choices: give in to total madness or surrender to her new reality, which just may be the only way she and her family will survive the obsessions of the Homeless Hunter's mind. A true paranormal romantic thriller, A Sinister Bouquet: Awakening, the first of the Sinister Series, will take you right to the edge of what you know to be possible and then drop you in a place so dark, so terrifying, that the only passageway out is through the blinding light of awakening. Wake up. Open your eyes. Finally. We've missed you so. (MA18+ for graphic sexual and violent content)

A Sinister Vision: Know This Much is True – Book 2: Elise Phillips, a doctor in training, has successfully repressed her kidnapping five years prior. The only problem is...she has six and one-half days to remember every terrible detail, or a total stranger will die. But to make matters even worse, in order to save this nameless woman, Elise will have to face something that scares her even more than death–intimacy. Another paranormal romantic thriller, A Sinister Vision: Know This Much is True, the second of the Sinister Series, will take you even further over the edge of what you know to be possible and guide you right back out through the only way left...impossible. Wake up. Open your eyes. Accept your assignment.... The problem is not to find the answer–but to face it. Know this much is true. (MA18+ for graphic sexual and violent content)

Where Tyndra Turns to Ardnyt – The Norn Novellas: In the center of a magical world there grows a beautiful and terrible chasm of climbing plants. On one side of the Ivy Wall we find the hell-of-Tyndra, on the other, the heaven-of-Ardnyt. But legend has it that in the middle…lives a preternatural beast that imprisons and tortures the children from both sides. When the war against time begins, Azza will have to cross over the Ivy Wall, something that has never been done before by a living being. But if she does make it through, she just might discover who she really is and how she became trapped in this alternate reality. A fairytale at heart, this is the first chapter in the epic saga of the youngest and most fickle of the four Norn Sisters. The same feisty immortal creature who must escape her inherent inner darkness to learn the meaning of love. A veritable palindrome from start to finish, the narrative of Where Tyndra Turns to Ardnyt journeys through duality to discover what shocking truths emerge when up becomes down, life becomes death, suffering becomes release, and the most unexpected endings become the most surprising beginnings. Welcome to a place where forwards and backwards are exactly the same direction. Here Where Tyndra Turns to Ardnyt.

Also from the Lavish family

A New Life Series
Samantha Jacobey
https://www.lavishpublishing.com/authors/samantha-jacobey/

An epic adventure, TORI FARRELL's life IS one wild story... escaped from a biker gang and running from drug lords... used by the FBI and hoping to protect her present from her past... IT'S DARK - IT'S BRUTAL, and it's WORTH EVERY MINUTE OF IT!! (Mature Adult, 18+)

Love on the Double Duo
L.A. Remenicky
http://mybook.to/LoveOnTheDoubleDuo

The Monroe brothers fall fast, they fall hard, and they fall forever. But the road to true love isn't always easy.

Loving Jessie's Girl – Book 1: Until AJ Monroe left Indiana after college he had always lived in his identical twin brother's shadow. He had made a life for himself in Denver, Colorado, away from Jessie, away from Indiana. But when AJ feared for his brother's safety, he left everything behind to step back into the shadow he thought he had outgrown. Finding his brother was AJ's only concern...until he met Jessie's girl.

Fiercely independent, Rina Abbot hid her true situation from everyone, including her best friend, Jessie. Out of money and unable to care for her rescue dogs she had no choice but to accept the help of the handsome stranger with a familiar face. Afraid to trust him, she tried to ignore the feelings he stirred within her as they searched for his missing brother.

Finally open about their feelings for each other, Rina's secrets began to wreak havoc on their lives. Would Rina's secrets force AJ to give up his dream of loving Jessie's girl?

Beyond Duty – Book 2: After serving in the Marine Corps, Jessie Monroe has finally found a life beyond war. He's focused on
being an EMT and helping his best friend rescue dogs, until he happens upon a curvy blonde stranded

On the run from her past, Dori Graham is slow to trust any man, and she tries to ignore the spark of
interest she feels for her handsome savior, but a friendship grows between them.

When Dori's past invades her new life, Jessie vows to rescue her. Saving her will take him beyond duty
and into his own personal hell. Calling upon his training as a Marine and the depth of his feelings for
Dori, Jessie will need the mental strength to battle to save her and, ultimately, save himself.

www.ingramcontent.com/pod-product-compliance
Lightning Source LLC
Chambersburg PA
CBHW070903180626

46817CB00003B/891